HELEN MacINNES

"A master of the suspense novel."

The Boston Globe

"A queen of suspense ... Helen MacInnes is, so far as I know, the only woman whose novels fall into the Len Deighton/Ken Follett/Robert Ludlum category of best-sellerdom."

Cosmopolitan

ABOVE SUSPICION

HELEN MacINNES

ABOVE SUSPICION

FAWCETT CREST • NEW YORK

A Fawcett Crest Book
Published by Ballantine Books
Copyright © 1941, 1969 by Helen Highet

ISBN 0-449-20858-3

This edition published by arrangement with Harcourt
Brace Jovanovich, Inc.

Manufactured in the United States of America

First Fawcett Crest Edition: December 1969
First Ballantine Books Edition: October 1985

Contents

The Song Which Frances Sang

Lully, lulla, thou little tiny child,
By by, lully lullay.

O sisters too,
How may we do
For to preserve this day
This poor youngling,
For whom we do sing,
*   By by, lully lullay?*

Herod, the king,
In his raging,
Chargèd he hath this day
His men of might,
In his own sight,
*   All young childrén to slay.*

That woe is me,
Poor child, for thee!
And ever morn and day,
For thy parting
Neither say nor sing
*   By by, lully lullay!*

COVENTRY CAROL: PAGEANT OF THE SHEARMEN AND TAILORS,
FIFTEENTH CENTURY

THIS SONG IS SUNG BY THE WOMEN OF BETHLEHEM IN THE
PLAY, JUST BEFORE HEROD'S SOLDIERS COME IN TO SLAUGHTER
THEIR CHILDREN

CHAPTER I

The Visit

THIS June day seemed, to Frances Myles, very much like any other summer day in Oxford. She walked slowly along Jowett Walk, watching the gentle five-o'clock sun bring out the bronze in the leaves overhead. This was her favorite part of the road leading to her husband's College. On her left, the gray walls which hid the gardens of the Holywell houses were crowned with rambler roses. To her right were the playing fields with their stretches of soft green grass, and beyond them were the straightness of poplar, the roundness of chestnut and elm. Today, there were only a few men practising at the nets: most of them were packing, or going to end-of-term parties. Like herself, she thought, and quickened her pace. She was probably late again. She hoped guiltily that Richard would have enough work to occupy him, while he waited for her at College. He generally had. . . . But it was difficult to hurry on a summer day like this: there were so many things to enjoy, like the twenty shades of green all around her, or the patterns of unevenly cut stones in the high walls, or the way in which a young man would catch a cricket ball and lazily throw it back. Little things, but then the last few months had made the little things important.

She entered Holywell, and hurried along its curve of old houses until she reached the Broad. There her pace slackened again, and she halted at a bookseller's window. Richard's new book on English lyric poetry was well displayed. It was selling, too, which had been a pleasant surprise. (The bookseller had explained that away rather harshly: people were buying strange books now, it sort of soothed their minds.) She smiled to herself in the window at her totally unpoetic thoughts. A selling book would be a help towards another summer among the mountains. Another summer, or a last summer, she wondered, and turned away from the window.

7

Once, all you had to do was to decide what mountains you'd like to climb, and then spend the winter writing reviews and articles to cover the train fares, and there you were. But each year it was becoming more difficult. She thought of past summers in the Tyrol, in the Dolomites. Once you could walk over mountain paths and spend the evenings round a table in the village inn. There had been singing and dancing, and lighthearted talk and friendly laughter. But now there were uniforms and regulations. Self-consciousness and uncertainty controlled even the jokes. Now you might only laugh at certain things. Now conversations with foreigners were apt to end in arguments.

Richard had discussed all this with her last night before they fell asleep. He had voted for one last look at Europe in peacetime, such as it was. There were still countries where one could breathe as one liked. Perhaps the premonition that this day was far from being much like any other summer day for Frances Myles had laid its cold finger on her heart ... Or it could have been the thought of Oxford as it might well be next term. At any rate, the lightness had gone out of her step.

The young college porter was standing at the lodge gate. She tried to make her smile brighter than she felt.

"How is the new baby?" she asked.

He beamed with pride. "Just splendid, ma'am, thank you. Mr. Myles is waiting in his room. He has just phoned down to ask if you had arrived. I'll tell him you're here." He moved back into the lodge. Frances remembered he had joined the Territorial Army in March, just after the seizure of Prague. Nowadays she kept remembering details like that. She hurried through the quadrangle, and began the climb to Richard's room.

The oak was sported. She thumped on its massive panels, and drew back as she heard Richard open the room door first before he could let the heavy oak door swing out. He was smiling, with that guess-what look.

"Hello, darling," she said. "Quite like old times to sport your oak. Why all the precautions?" He wiped her lipstick off his chin as he drew her into the room, fastening the two doors behind them.

"We've a visitor, Fran."

It was Peter, Peter Galt.

He grinned and held out both his hands. "Hello, Frances, you look quite startled."

"Peter! But we thought you were in Bucharest. When did you get back?"

"Two or three weeks ago. I would have written you if I could. I've just been explaining to Richard. I've purposely not written you. And I am not staying with you, either. I am putting up at the Mitre."

Frances turned to her husband in dismay. "Richard, what's the matter with him?"

Richard handed her a glass of sherry. He refilled Peter's glass and then his own, with maddening concentration, before he spoke.

"Peter got into a jam."

"A jam? Peter?" She sat down on the nearest chair. She looked so charmingly anxious under her ridiculous hat that Peter hastened to reassure her.

"Don't worry, Frances. It all turned out rather well in the end. But it did make it necessary for me to be recalled." He grinned, and added, "Ill-health, of course."

"Of course. . . ." Frances was less alarmed, but she was still curious. She waited for an explanation. It was Richard who said in a noncommittal way, as he placed an ashtray beside her, "He got entangled with a spy."

"Well, I only hope she was beautiful," Frances said. "I mean, if you *will* do things like that, you may as well make the most of it." She smiled as she looked up at the correctly dressed young man balancing against the fireplace. She had always hoped that Peter would never get entangled with anyone who wasn't beautiful. She watched his calm face and the shy smile, and wondered. To a stranger, he would seem just another elegant minor secretary to a British Embassy.

"Unfortunately, it was a he," said Peter. "And to be quite truthful, I didn't get entangled with him. He got entangled with me."

"You look such easy meat, really, Peter."

"That was an asset, anyway."

"And so you had to come back to England . . ." Frances was still unable to take Peter quite seriously. "He isn't after your blood, is he?"

"He can't do that. Bucharest dealt with him. But his

friends might think I learned too much before that happened."

"But, Peter, you don't mix that kind of—politics with
diplomacy, do you?"

"He did the mixing. Now I am waiting for all the commo-
tion to die down."

Peter gave a good imitation of his old smile, but Frances,
watching his eyes, was already revising her opinion about this
visit. Something serious was behind it all. When she spoke,
her voice had dropped all hint of teasing.

"Is that all?"

Richard, sitting on the edge of his desk, gave a laugh.

"Out with it, Peter, whatever it is. It's no good being
diplomatic with Frances. She can see through a brick wall as
quickly as anyone."

Peter finished his sherry. As he looked from Frances to
Richard, he seemed to be making up his mind about something. . . . Or perhaps he was deciding how to begin. They
both suddenly realized the change in him. He was an older, a
more businesslike Peter. And he was worried. His fingers
played nervously with the stem of the sherry glass. He was
choosing his next words with care.

"Frances is quite right. I am not in the F.O. any longer:
I've been put onto other work. And that's why I am here."
He glanced at his watch, and his next words were spoken
more quickly. "I'm afraid this visit combines business with
pleasure, and we haven't very much time for everything I
want to tell you. So you'll understand if I begin abruptly. . . .
We haven't the time for any build-up which would enlist your
sympathy, and make things easier for me. I'll just have to
start with the story, and hope for the best.

"First of all, I didn't want to give anyone the idea that I
have been in touch with you. So I didn't let you know I was
coming to Oxford, and I can't stay with you. Even the porter
at the lodge doesn't know I'm with you: he thinks I am
visiting old Meyrick. The reason is—I have a job for you to
do, and I hope you'll agree to do it. It shouldn't be dangerous: tiresome, perhaps, and certainly a blasted nuisance, but
not actually dangerous if you stick to the directions." He shot
a quick glance at Richard, and added with emphasis: "You
are just the people we need for it. You are both above any
suspicion, and you've a good chance of getting through."

Richard looked at Peter speculatively. "What on earth is it?" he asked. "And why?"

"I'd better tell you about the job, first," Peter answered. "The whys and wherefores can wait until the end. I am sorry if it develops into a kind of lecture, but I'd like you to get all the details quite straight. One of the reasons why I thought of you for this job, Richard, is your memory. If you'd take a mental note of things as I explain them, that would save a lot of time."

Richard nodded.

"The job is simply this. I've been hoping that you would go abroad as usual this summer, and that you'd travel by Paris, meet a man there, and then continue the journey as he directs. At the end of it, you should be able to send us some information which we need very badly. That's the general outline. Now here are the particulars. I'll give you no trimmings—just the facts.

"When you get to Paris, just do as you always do. Stay at your usual hotel, eat at your favorite places, visit the usual mixture of museums and night clubs. Keep on doing that, for some days: long enough, anyway, to establish your innocent-tourist reputation. And then, on Saturday night, visit the Café de la Paix. Sit at an outside table towards the left. Order Cointreau with your coffee. Frances will be wearing a red rose. Don't notice anyone or anything in particular. About eleven o'clock, Richard will upset his Cointreau. He will be glad of an excuse not to drink it anyway, if I know Richard. Your waiter will come and mop up. That and the red rose are the signal. A man will approach your table, and that's the moment for one of you to speak. The sentence should begin: 'Mrs. *Rose* told me we must see . . .' and add the name of some place you've decided on. Pretend to talk, keep it all natural, but be on guard for the number which the man will give you, somehow. That's the key of this whole business. For if you go next day, to the place which you mentioned, at exactly *one hour later* than the number which he gives you, you will get into real touch with him. And he has a message for you.

"It's all very much easier than it sounds. He identifies you by the position of the table and the red rose and the upset glass of Cointreau; reaches your table at the time you expect him; hears the name of the place you've chosen along with the right sentence; and gives you a clue to the time for a meeting on the next day. Have you got all that Richard?"

"Yes. But before we go any further, why choose us? I mean, we shall be such amateurs for that job: we'll probably mess it all up. There must be something fairly important at stake, and it seems to me as if you needed someone with quick wits. I don't know if mine have been sharpened well enough—in that way. As for Fran . . ." Richard shrugged his shoulders.

Frances only looked amused. "Darling, I love you," she said. "Do go on, Peter."

Peter took her advice.

"When you get the message, it will probably be in some code. And that's another reason why I want Richard to tackle this job. I can rely on him to get a meaning out of that message. His brain has had just the right training and discipline for that sort of work. Well, the message will direct you to another agent, and he will direct you farther still, and you will find yourself passed on from agent to agent until you reach the chief of them. He's the last one on the line, and he's the chap we are worried about. That is the information we need."

He paused, and watched Richard pour some sherry into his glass. Again Frances had the feeling that he was once more weighing his words very carefully before he spoke. His trouble was to tell them enough in the right order without telling them too much.

"I think you'll find the rest of this travelogue more interesting. We are now reaching the whys and the wherefores." Peter allowed himself the suspicion of a smile. "You've heard of what is called the underground railway in Germany, haven't you? It's a version of the old *Scarlet Pimpernel* technique. It helps anti-Nazis to escape, and covers up their tracks. One of the brains behind it is the chief of this group of agents. On the side, of course, he collects information which has been very useful, indeed. Until about five weeks ago, we had the normal reports from him: accurate and regular. But since then, we have had no really informative messages. Two of them, in fact, were dangerously misleading. Fortunately, we had other sources of information about these facts which made us suspicious, and we didn't act on his advice. These suspicions were increased when two men, es-

caping from Germany by his route, disappeared completely.
They have simply vanished into thin air."

Frances put aside her glass, and leaned forward, cupping
her face in her hands. Richard held a cigarette unlighted. The
eyes of both were fixed on Peter.

"What we want to know is this—before the harvests are
gathered in, to put it quite bluntly—: does the man still exist,
or has he been sending us false messages to warn us that
things aren't just right, or has he been liquidated? So your job
is to follow the route directed by various agents, always
keeping in mind that you are just the simple traveler, until
you find him. The one clue I do know is that he will be an
Englishman, the only Englishman in that chain of agents. I
can't help with his name or appearance, because he has too
many of both. In any case, the less you know, the easier it
will be for you to play your role, and the better it will be for
all of us. He probably won't seem at all English when you
meet him, but if you give him the correct high-signs, which
the previous agent will pass on to you, you will find out that
he's an Englishman all right."

"But why all this agent-to-agent business?" Richard asked.
"Why doesn't the Paris man direct us to him straight away?"

"The plan is his: he invented it to suit his own particular
work. And it has been very successful. It's been foolproof for
a longer time than most systems. It's simple enough. The
Paris agent is the only stationary one, and that's the reason
why he takes so many precautions, just to safeguard himself.
The others move about as their chief directs. It is just as well
to keep moving, for they often work in Nazi-dominated
territory. Each agent knows only the name and address of
the man next to him, and any information they collect can be
posted along the chain of agents until it reaches the chief.
Anyone who wants to get in touch with him must begin at
the Paris end, and no one can begin at Paris unless he knows
how to make the difficult contact with the agent there. There
are only two sources which can direct anyone to manage that
contact. We are one of them; the other is just as careful as
we are. So you see, there is some method in his madness."

"And what about the information which he sends to you?
He must have another line?"

Peter nodded. "Yes, and it's a much more direct way,

naturally. I knew you'd cotton on, Richard. Anything else which strikes you?"

Richard hesitated, and then, as Peter waited for an answer, he said, "The system is obviously pretty safe, except for one drawback. If the chief man himself is caught, then all information traveling out to him will get into the wrong hands. His agents might even be picked off one by one, if he were—persuaded into any confession. *Not* to mention the fate of the poor devils who thought they were escaping from Germany."

"Exactly. That's why the job has got to be done."

"Your man must have been pretty sure of himself to think up that system, I must say."

Peter said, "I suppose it looks that way, but you've got to take risks in his profession. It has been very much worth our while to take a chance on him. And, strangely enough, it is just this kind of system which gets the best results. Until now, he has always been agile enough not to be caught; he has been doing this kind of thing, you know, since we were being pushed round the park in our prams. You may depend on one thing, Richard: he won't talk. Anyway, you see how vital it is to know whether he is still functioning, before the volcano in Europe blows sky-high. We've got to be sure of him, before then."

"Yes, I can quite see that," Richard said gloomily. "But I still think you need a professional man on the job." It was a good sign, anyway, thought Peter, that Richard was still arguing about it. He was clearly not very much in love with the idea, but he was still at the stage of objections rather than that of a downright refusal. Peter wondered if he should tell them anything more. He thought wearily, "I'm devoted to both of them, but can't they see, in God's name, that I was counting on them to accept, or I wouldn't have let them in on all this?" Yet people changed, and being a don at Oxford might very well make you too contented, too unwilling to act against your own security. Richard was waiting for his answer.

"We sent one," Peter said briefly. "We should have heard from him by this time. When we didn't I suggested to my Chief that we should try an amateur; that line served me well enough in Bucharest. A couple of innocents abroad might be able to get through all suspicion. The thing to

remember is that you are *not* agents; don't let yourself get
mixed up in any sideline snooping. All we want to know is
whether an Englishman is there, or not. If things get too hot,
then just pull out, using your own good sense. If there's any
questioning, then stick to your story. You are just two holi-
day-makers having your annual trip abroad. There is one
other point: your job will be finished when either you find
the man, or you've reached the sixth agent without finding
him. He never worked with more in a line. You will have a
margin of safety all through, because the contacting clues
will be vague enough to let you have an out and your
amateur status will be an additional help. That really is your
strongest safeguard."

Richard said nothing, but Galt, watching him closely, was
satisfied. It wasn't a comfortable, peaceful way of life which
had held Richard back: it was the fact that Frances would be
in this too.

"When you've finished, wire to this address in Geneva,"
Peter said. He wrote some words quickly on a piece of
paper, and handed it to Richard, still looking undecided,
worried . . . But Galt knew he had won.

"Better memorize the address, and then destroy it," he
advised. "If you find your man, then wire ARRIVING MONDAY,
or TUESDAY, or whatever day you actually saw him. If you
don't find him, wire CANCEL RESERVATIONS." He drew a deep
breath. "Thank God that's over," he said. "Is it all clear,
Richard?"

"I've got it memorized, if that's what you mean. But look
here, Peter, if you have really decided that I ought to do this
job, don't you think I'd better go alone? I'm not running
Frances into any risks." His tone was grim. Frances looked
at him suddenly. So that was what had made him hesitate.

When she spoke her voice was low, but equally determined. "Richard, I am *not* going to be left behind."

Peter said, "Unfortunately I agree with Frances. Since
you've been married, you've never separated on your holidays. It really would be better if you were just to do what
you always do. And you'll be safer with Frances, because you
won't take risks if she is with you." He looked anxiously at
Richard. "I know it's going to ruin your summer," he began,
and then stopped. He had said enough as it was.

Richard was staring at the red geraniums in the window
box.

"It isn't the ruining of it," he said slowly. "Everyone's
holidays are ruined this year. But I don't think we'd really be
of any use."

Peter was picking up his gloves and umbrella and his black
hat. He was still watching Richard intently. Something
seemed to decide him. He moved over to Frances to say
good-by.

"I would never have asked you if I didn't think you could
pull it off," he said. "And I would never have asked you if
the whole thing wasn't so urgent, Richard. I'd have done it
myself, except that the people we are working against have
got me docketed since Bucharest. I'll be on the files, by this
time. I thought of someone else, but your qualifications for
this job are just what we need. I didn't enjoy asking you, I
may as well say ... Time I was leaving, now. I see I've kept
you late for Frame's party. I met him this morning in front
of the Mitre, and he asked me to come along too." He waved
his hat towards the invitation card propped up on the mantelpiece.

"How long," said Richard, "should this job take?"

"We allowed two weeks to our man, but he knew the
ropes. We'd better say about a month. It will be safer if you
don't hurry things. You will have to spend a few days in each
place to make it look convincing. Remember, I want you to
steer clear of any suspicion, or danger. ... For God's sake,
take care of yourselves."

His voice was normal again by the time he had reached
the door.

"Good-by, Frances; good-by, Richard. See you when you
get back."

The door closed softly, and left a silent room.

Frances was the first to move. She pulled out her compact
and powdered her nose. She readjusted her hat to the correct
angle.

"You'll do," she said to her reflection in the mirror. "Come
on, my love, we are three quarters of an hour later than I
had meant to be late. ... You've got it all memorized?"

Richard nodded. "That's the least of it. Frances, this is the
time to back out. Now."

Frances rose, and looked at the seams of her stockings.

She altered a suspender. "When do we start?" she asked. "As soon as you have finished all your teaching?"

Richard looked at his wife's pretty legs.

"Blast Peter," he said, and took her arm as they left the room.

They talked of other things as they went downstairs.

CHAPTER II

The Party

THE PARTY in Frame's rooms had just reached the right temperature when Frances and Richard Myles arrived. They stood for a moment at the doorway rather like two bathers about to plunge off a springboard. Their host, armed with sherry bottles, pushed his way through to meet them.

"I'm *so* glad," he breathed. "Sorry about this *awful* crowd: such a mob." He turned to welcome some other new arrivals. Actually, thought Frances, he was just delighted that the room was jammed with people talking their heads off. She smiled good-by to Richard. This wasn't one of those ghastly affairs where you knew only the host. They wouldn't have to put on their special act today, when they would meet each other with surprise in the middle of the room, greet each other warmly and start the vivacious conversation of two friends who rarely met. They always found that others, with an ear for preposterous remarks, would drift towards them. As Richard had said, splendid isolation didn't mix with sherry.

But tonight, Richard had already seen two men he wanted to talk to, and Frances waited in the corner she had chosen for herself as three young men gravitated towards her. They had, in their typical manner, only smiled politely when they caught her eye, and had then, without another glance in her direction, started a quiet but determined progress towards where she stood. She noticed Richard was looking round him in that particularly ingenuous way he had when he was most on guard . . . But Peter Galt had not arrived yet.

The three young men arrived from their various directions, and began one of the usual adroit conversations which sherry parties inspire. They all avoided talking present-day politics with an understanding as complete as it was tacit. This was perhaps the last conversation they would have together for a long time, and they wanted to keep it gay. They discussed the Picasso exhibition in London, and his Guernica, and that led to Catalonian art and Dali. Frances wanted to know if the pineapple Cathedral at Barcelona was still more unfinished. (Michael had been there with the International Brigade—it was a bad show about his arm; Frances had heard that the shrapnel still imbedded there might end in amputation.) But Michael steered the conversation to Gaudi and his architectural fantasies. Frances remembered a chapter somewhere by Evelyn Waugh on Gaudi's telephone kiosks. It was an amusing description and they laughed.

"Eternal Oxford: how delightful it is to return and be so far removed from the rigors of life." The voice had a very pronounced, almost too careful Oxford accent. The speaker was tall, and remarkably good-looking. A dueling scar marked his chin, another his cheek; they gave his blondness a certain formidable quality. His smile was very self-possessed. "Mrs. Myles, as lovely as ever." He bowed low over Frances' hand.

Frances collected herself. "Oh, hello. How are you?" She made hasty introductions. "Freiherr Sigurd von Aschenhausen—John Clark, Sir Michael Hampton, George Sanderson. Herr von Aschenhausen was an undergraduate along with Richard."

There was a pause.

"Charming to return and find Evelyn Waugh and Oxford still inseparable." Von Aschenhausen's voice was friendly. The three undergraduates kept a polite smile in place. Frances knew they were placing his date of residence at the University very accurately. She thought of explaining that it wasn't black-satin sheets but Catalonian architecture which they had been discussing, and then gave up the idea as being more trouble than it was probably worth. Even allowing for the foreigner's favorite indoor sport of underestimating the English, surely von Aschenhausen couldn't be serious. After all, he had been to three universities, one in Germany, one in England and one in America. One thing he must know about undergraduates by this time, and that was they were always in revolt. They were never static. The only way they could form their minds was by opposing accepted opinion. Frances herself had seen the swing of the pendulum away from the esthete to the politically conscious young man who Studied

Conditions. The esthete himself had been in rebellion against the realism of the postwar group.

George made some polite remark to cover up their embarrassment. Michael was lighting a cigarette. John was gazing into the middle distance. Frances remembered he was allergic to Germany, since that kick four years ago when he hadn't saluted a procession in Leipzig. The conversation limped along, the undergraduates hoping that von Aschenhausen would go; but he didn't. Frances did her best: she talked about summer holidays. The undergraduates were going to France; von Aschenhausen was returning to Berlin. She explained that Richard and she would like to have their usual view of mountains.

"Where exactly were you thinking of going?" asked von Aschenhausen.

"We were in the South Tyrol last year. I'd like to get back there just once more—" Frances' voice was honey-sweet— "just before the volcano erupts." The Englishmen smiled grimly. The German protested politely.

"What! With this peaceful England? There will be no war, no general war. Just look at everyone in this room. . . ." Unconsciously he straightened his back as he looked around the room. *And there's not a soldier among you* was the implication. He might just as well have said it. Michael flicked a piece of cigarette ash off his wounded arm. He spoke for the first time.

"There's a limit to everything, you know. Good-by, Frances. I must go now. Have a good time this summer."

The others had to go now, too, it seemed.

Von Aschenhausen remained. Frances shook herself free from her embarrassment. After all, he used to be amusing and gay. He had made many friends when he was up at Oxford; he had been invited around a good deal. She wondered how he was getting along in the New Germany; he used to laugh off any political discussions by protesting he wasn't interested in politics. She racked her brains for something tactful to say. It was difficult in this summer of 1939. You were so conscious of nationality now. She was relieved when von Aschenhausen spoke.

"I am afraid that young man did not like me particularly," he said. "Is it because I am a German, or is it his usual manner? I have noticed that a cripple is usually more bitter than the ordinary man."

"Cripple?" Frances' eyes widened; she was at a loss for words.

"Of course, there *is* a change in the attitude here towards me," he continued. "Six years ago I had many friends. Today—well—" he smiled sadly—"it would be better if I came as an exile."

"I wondered at first if you were, and then I thought not."

"How did you know?" He looked at her amusedly.

"By your clothes." She looked pointedly at his Savile Row suit. He hadn't liked that; his smile was still there but it was less amused. Good. Cripple, indeed!

"It is really very sad for a German to find how misjudged and abused his country is. Of course, our enemies control the press in foreign countries, and they have been very busy. They have clever tongues."

"Have they? It is strange, isn't it, how criticism of Germany has grown even in countries which were once really very close to her. I wonder how it could have happened." He looked as if he didn't know quite how he should take that. She gazed at him steadily with wide blue eyes.

He smiled sadly. "You see, even you have changed. It is depressing to return to Oxford, which I loved, and to find myself surrounded by glaciers." Was the man being really sincere, wondered Frances, or was it just another of those poor-mouth stories?

"Perhaps it is the change in you which has changed us."

He looked surprised. "Oh, come now, Mrs. Myles. I haven't changed so very much. I am still interested in literature and music. I haven't become a barbarian, you know. Politically—well, I have progressed. Everyone does, unless he is a cow. I am more realistic than I once was, less sentimental. I've seen the stupidities committed in the name of idealism and abstract thinking. People are made to be led. They need leadership, and with strong leadership they can achieve anything. At first they must take the bad with the good; in the end they will forget the bad, because the ultimate good will be so great for them." He spoke with mounting enthusiasm.

"You believe you have not changed. And yet, under the leadership which you praise so much, you may only read

certain books, listen to certain music, look at certain pic-
tures, make friends with certain people. Isn't that limiting
yourself?"

"Oh, well, limiting oneself to the good, eliminating the
bad—all that is better in the end."

"But *who* is to say what is good for you, or bad for you?
Is it to be your own judgment, educated at Heidelberg,
Oxford and Harvard, or is it to be some self-appointed leader
who can't even speak grammatical German?" Von Aschenhausen didn't like that either. He obviously had no answer
ready for that one.

Frances kept her voice gentle. "You see, you have
changed. Do you remember the Rhodes scholar who preced-
ed you here? Intelligent man, quiet, and very kind. What's his
name? Rotha, wasn't it? You liked him then. But where is
he now? Oranienburg, I heard."

Von Aschenhausen made an impatient gesture. "That is all
very sentimental, Mrs. Myles. It is time that the British really
saw the things which matter. Discipline and strong measures
are needed in today's Europe. It is a more dangerous and
forbidding place than it was six or seven years ago."

"That is just our point," said Frances. "What made Europe
more dangerous and forbidding?"

He laughed, but it didn't sound jovial.

"You are a very prejudiced person, I can see. I suppose
you will now lecture me gravely on the wickedness of Germany's claims to natural *Lebensraum*. It is easy to talk when
you have a large Empire."

"On the contrary, Herr von Aschenhausen, I like to think
of all people having their *Lebensraum,* whether they are
Germans or Jews or Czechs or Poles."

His voice grated. He was really angry. "It is just such
thoughts as these which have weakened Britain. In the last
twenty-five years, she could have established herself as ruler
of the world. Instead, she makes a Commonwealth out of an
Empire, and they won't even fight to help her when she has
to fight. She leaves the riches of India untapped; she urges a
representative government on Indians who were about to
refuse it. She alienates Italy with sanctions. She weakens
herself all the time, and she thinks it is an improvement."

"Hello, you are being very serious in this corner." It was
Richard.

"I've been having lessons in statecraft," said Frances, conscious of Richard's eyes on the two pink spots on her cheeks. I shouldn't let myself get angry, she thought, and listened to von Aschenhausen, once more smiling and plausible. She had the feeling that he was trying to cover up, as if he were annoyed with the impression he had given her. He was very polite as they said good-by. He bowed low, his composure completely regained.

"I hope we meet again," he said. "And don't worry, Mrs. Myles. You will see that England will not be at war. You are all good pacifists, here. Enjoy yourselves abroad."

Richard said, "I hope so," and smiled. He took his wife's arm and piloted her skillfully to the door. Frame waved a sherry bottle from two groups away.

"Lovely party," Frances called over to him, but the noise of voices around her drowned her words. Frame's answer was also unheard. They exchanged smiles of understanding, a wave of the hand, and then Frances and Richard were outside the room into quietness and fresh air.

Richard lowered his voice. "I got to you as quickly as I could when I saw an argument had developed. I thought you had sense enough by this time not to waste your breath arguing with a Nazi. He is, isn't he?"

"Yes. I think he didn't mean to show it, but I made him angry."

"What interests me is what he said to anger *you*."

"Was it obvious?" Frances was dismayed.

"To me, yes. No one else would notice. What was it anyway?"

"Britain."

"Anything else?"

Frances shook her head.

"All right; let's drop it. I hope you weren't too intelligent, though. Peter wants us to be the unworldly don with his dim wife."

Frances stared. "But we needn't start that business until we are on the boat train."

"Probably not: still, you didn't notice Peter taking any chances, did you?"

"I must say I thought he was a little—theatrical. He was very unlike himself."

Richard shook his head slowly. "No to both of these. He

was too worried to be theatrical. By the way, he didn't turn up at the party."

"Perhaps he changed his mind," said Frances.

"Perhaps. Or perhaps he was just being very sure that he wouldn't meet us again. That's probably nearer it." Richard's voice was gloomy.

Frances pressed his arm to her side. "Cheer up, Richard, or you'll have me worried in case I spoil your fun. It's one of the troubles of having a wife, you know. You just can't get rid of her." She was rewarded with almost a smile.

But the sun had gone, and with it the bronze in the leaves overhead. The playing fields were empty. Over the gray walls and the sharply pointed rooftops the sound of bells followed them as they walked slowly home.

CHAPTER III

Farewell to Safety

THE REST of the week passed quickly. Frances was busy with the closing of their house. She also made a hectic dash to London for some clothes she "simply must have." Richard finished the odds and ends of work which face a tutor towards the end of term—but from Peter Galt they heard nothing.

"Which means we are to go ahead," said Richard at breakfast on Wednesday.

That morning, he bought their tickets to Paris and interviewed the bank about a supply of travelers' cheques and some French money. The expense of their unknown journeys had worried him, but his bank manager, who had always been tactful about overdrafts, met him with a discreet smile. The bank had been authorized to give Mr. Myles a letter of credit. Richard did not ask who had authorized it. The bank manager treated it all as something merely routine.

In the evening, Richard hunted through his bookshelves and picked out the Baedekers and maps. He had a fair collection of these, for since his first year at Oxford he had spent part of each summer walking and scrambling his way across mountains into villages. He spread them out around him as he sat on the floor of the study, and lit his pipe. He wondered which he could omit: surely the Pyrenees and Majorca would be unnecessary. Peter had hinted in the direction of Central Europe. Still, it was better to be safe; he knew his way about these maps, and they ought to go along, all of them. He would take less clothes, if his suitcase got too crowded.

Frances came in, her hair brushed loosely to her shoulders.

"Don't overwork, darling," she said with mock concern. "I begin to feel exhausted. I came in to ask you to sharpen my pencil." She held out a miserable stub.

"What on earth do you do with your pencils?" asked Richard. "Gnaw them?"

Frances disregarded this with the adroitness of four years' marriage. She looked at the notebook in her hand, and checked off the items she had written there. Richard watched her as she bit her lip and counted. He felt that wave of emotion which came to him when he looked at Frances in her unguarded moments; and he had the bleak horror which always attacked him then when he thought how easy it might have been never to have met her.

Frances straightened her legs. "That's that," she said. "Just my own things to pack tomorrow after Anni departs. Richard, that is going to be a difficult moment. Other summers, it was different. She always knew she would be coming back in time for October. She seems to feel she will never be back here. I found her packing in floods of tears this evening. I've sent her out now to say good-by to her friends. So there goes the best cook we shall ever have. It was really rather painful this evening. I've got just as much attached to her as she has to us. She wants her father's farm to have the honor of a visit from the *gnädige Frau* and the *Herr Professor,* if they should visit Innsbruck this summer."

Richard finished sharpening the pencil. "Her people were pro-Dolfuss, weren't they?"

"They were. . . . I have a feeling that they have changed. Anni has been very silent about them since she returned last year. One thing she did tell me. Her sister told her that if she came back to England and a war broke out, she would be stoned to death. That is what they said we did in 1914. Isn't it appalling?"

"Well, I suppose if a nation allows concentration camps, it will find it hard to believe that other people don't use similar methods. Cheer up, old girl, who cares what a lot of uncivilized people think anyway? It's only the opinion of the civilized that really matters."

"Yes, but it looks as if a lot of the civilized will be killed because they ignored the thoughts of the uncivilized. Ignoring doesn't abolish them, you know, Richard." She traced a pattern on the carpet with her pencil. "Sorry, darling. I'm tired, and depressed. We've all gone so political these days. I worry and worry inside me, and I think everyone else is doing the same; it is difficult to forget what we all went through last September."

Richard tapped the stem of his pipe against his teeth. "Yes, it's difficult," he said slowly. "I shan't forget helping to dig trenches in the parks, or the paper tape on all the windows, or the towels we were told to keep beside a bucket of water. All the time I was digging I kept wondering whether the trenches would be any good at all, and I knew they wouldn't be. I didn't think much of the towel idea either. But what else was there? And then bastards like von Aschenhausen come along all smiles and bows. And wonder why people are not enthusiastic about them. They blackmail us with bombers one year, and go back on the agreement they had extorted out of us, and then expect to be welcomed as friends. All within nine months. All that, Frances, makes one of the reasons why I listened to Peter. If I could put a spoke of even the most microscopic size in the smallest Nazi wheel, I'd think it a pretty good effort." He had risen, and was pacing up and down the study.

"I think this interruption is due. I see that proposition-look dawning in your eye. Don't try, don't you try to leave me at home. I'm coming."

"I was afraid you were."

"Richard, my dear, you know that whenever you imagine exciting things they always turn out duller than a wet day in Wigan. It's the parties you don't get excited about which turn out to be fun. Now here we are, both thinking of ourselves in terms of Sard Harker. What will happen? We'll go to Paris, and then find that the man does not turn up. I'll wear a red rose for three nights, and you'll spill Cointreau for three nights, until the whole café is gaping at us. And then we'll go on our holiday, wondering if Peter's sense of humor has become overdeveloped since Bucharest."

Richard laughed. "You sound almost convincing, Frances. But I know that you know what I know. This is no bloody picnic."

She rose from the floor, and went over to the window. It was wide open. She leaned forward to breathe in the dewy smell of the earth. The lilac trees at the end of the garden had silver leaves. Richard came to her, and slipped an arm round her waist. They stood there in silence watching a moonlit garden. Frances glanced at him. He was lost in thought.

"If you want to know," he said at last, reading her thoughts in the uncanny way two people living together learn to do, "I am thinking we should photograph this in our memory. We may need to remember it often for the next few years."

Frances nodded. Around them were the other gardens, the mixed perfume of flowers. The walls hung heavy with roses and honeysuckle, their colours whitened in the strong moonlight. The deep shadows of trees, blurring the outline of the other houses, were pierced here and there with the lights from uncurtained windows. The giant elms in the Magdalen deer park stood sentinels of peace.

She said suddenly, "Richard, let's go up the river; just for half an hour."

"The dew is heavy. You had better wrap up well."

"I shall. It won't take five minutes." She kissed him suddenly, and left him. He heard her running upstairs, the banging of the wardrobe door in their bedroom. So Frances had this feeling too, this feeling of wanting to say good-by.

She came downstairs in less than her five minutes, dressed in a sweater and trousers, and with one of his silk handkerchiefs round her neck. They walked the short distance to the boathouse in silence. They got out the canoe in a matter-of-fact way, as if they were defying the moonlight to weaken them. They paddled swiftly up the narrow river. White mists were rising from the fields on either side of them, encircling the roots of the willows which edged the banks.

"When I used to read my Virgil, this is what I thought the Styx might be like," said Frances. Then suddenly, "Richard, what are you planning to do in Paris?"

"Water carries sound," he reminded her. To prove his words, they heard low voices and the laugh of a girl, before they saw two punts drifting to meet them.

"You have your moments, don't you, Richard? By the way, I think you will like the hat I bought yesterday in London. A little white sailor with no crown to speak of, yards of black cloud floating down the back, and a saucy red rose perched over one eye." She heard Richard laugh behind her. "Practical, isn't it?"

"Very," he said, and laughed again. "Good Lord—trust a woman to think up something like that."

Frances was serious again. "Richard, do you think there will really be war this summer?"

"It's anyone's guess. The President was lunching yesterday with Halifax. He said—"

"Halifax?"

"Yes. He said no one in the Cabinet knew. It all depended on one man."

Frances was silent for a space. When she spoke, her voice trembled with its intensity.

"I resent this man. Why should the happiness of the whole civilized world depend on him? Why should I, an English-woman, have to look at my countryside, for instance, and even as I look have to remember that last September I had planned to help to take the Symons children in this canoe up this river, to hide them under the willows until the air raids had passed? I had blankets and towels and tinned food and chocolate all packed in a basket. A Hitler picnic indeed. There is not one of us who hasn't had fear and horror creep into all his associations. As I pass these willows I keep wondering just which one of them might have been sheltering the Symons children, and whether it would have done its job. And all because of one man. Think of it, Richard, there wasn't a farmer who didn't look at his land and the farm-house his great-great-grandfather had built and wonder. There wasn't a townsman who didn't look at his business or his home and everything he had earned for himself and wonder. There wasn't a man or woman who did not look at the children and wonder. Richard, I resent this man and his kind of people."

"You aren't the only one." Richard pointed the nose of the canoe back down the river. "You aren't the only one. We have all had a year of brooding. And we have all come to the same decision. If anything does start, the man who starts it will be sorry he ever thought of himself as a kind of god. But take it easy, Frances. Promise me you will stop worrying while we are on this holiday. It may be the last—" he paused—"for a long time, anyway. There is nothing more that rational beings can do, anyway, except wait and watch. And when it comes, the Symons children will have better protection than the willows this September. And that's something."

"Yes, that's something." Frances' voice was quieter. "But when I meet some of those armchair critics who sit beside their radio in a part of the world which can't be bombed from Germany, and hear them tell me how England should have fought, I am liable to be very very rude. *And* I bet, if war does come, these same people will suddenly start talking about the greatness and glories of peace. Britain will then be just another of those belligerent countries. That is how we will be dismissed, as if neutrality implied a special sanctity. There now, Richard, I've got it all out of my system. I shan't mention it again."

"That's the girl. Remember this part of the river?"

Frances gave a shaky laugh. "Yes, darling. I was a sweet girl undergraduate, and you were in all the importance of your final year. Good bathes we had, too, in just this kind of moonlight. Look, there's some more of us." Some punts were moored under a bank, and the wet figures as they balanced to dive gave a moment's illusion of silver statues.

"I've found the difference between twenty and thirty," said Richard. "At twenty you never think of rheumatics or a chill in the bladder."

They guided the canoe back to the boathouse. They stood together on the landing place in silence, looking at the river and the white mist rising.

They walked slowly home. At the gate, they met Anni.

"Guten Abend, gnädige Frau, Herr Professor." She was a tall girl, with a pleasant open face, and fair hair braided round her head.

"Good evening, Anni. Did you see your friends all right?"

Anni nodded. Her arms were full of small parcels. "We had cake, and tea, and then we sang. It was very *gemütlich.*" She looked down at the parcels. "They gave me these presents," she added. She spoke the careful English which Frances had taught her. "I've had so much pleasure."

"I'm glad, Anni. You should go to bed soon: you have a long journey tomorrow."

Anni nodded again. "I wish you good night, *gnädige Frau, Herr Professor. Angenehme Ruh'.*"

They walked round the garden after she had left them.

"It's funny, Richard. I really am tired, and there is a nice large bed waiting for me upstairs, and yet I keep staying out here looking at the stars."

"I hate to be unromantic, but I do think it is time we got some sleep. Tomorrow's a bad day. It always is: you have a genius for finding last-minute things to do." Frances smiled, and felt Richard's arm round her waist guide her to the house. On the steps, he stopped to kiss her.

"That's to break the enchantment," he said. His lips were smiling, but his eyes were the way Frances loved them most.

CHAPTER IV

Beginning of a Journey

THERE WAS always a feeling of excitement after the unpleasantness of a Channel crossing, while the train waited patiently on the Dieppe siding for the last passengers. They emerged, in straggling groups, from the customs and passport sheds. Frances, already comfortably settled in her corner, watched them with interest. She glanced at Richard opposite her, leaning back with his eyes closed. He was a bad sailor, but he managed things like customs officials very well indeed. Thank heaven for Richard, she thought, watching other wives followed by harassed husbands whose tempers didn't improve under commiserating looks from unhurried bachelors. It was the stage in the journey when most people began to wonder if it all wasn't more trouble than it was worth.

The last nervous lady was helped into the train. The confusion along the corridors was subsiding. They were moving, very slowly, very carefully. Two young men had halted at their compartment.

"This will do," said one, after hardly seeming to glance in their direction. They swung their rucksacks on to the rack, and threw their Burberries after them. Undergraduates, thought Frances, as she looked at a magazine. Like Richard, they wore dark gray pin-stripe flannel suits, brown suède shoes well-worn, collars which pointed carelessly, and the hieroglyphic tie of a college society.

The train traveled gently along the street, like a glorified tramcar. The children with thin legs and cropped hair and faded blue overalls halted in their games to watch the engine. Their older sisters, leaning on their elbows at the tall narrow windows, looked critically at the people traveling to Paris. The women, standing in the doorways or in front of the small shops, hardly bothered to interrupt their gossip. It was only a trainload, and a full one too. All the better for their

32

men, who worked on the piers: the arriving tourist tipped
well. The old men, who sat reading the café newspapers at
the marble-topped tables, looked peacefully bored. One of
them pulled out a watch, looked at it, looked at the train,
and shook his head. Frances smiled to herself. Things had
been different when he worked in the sheds, no doubt.

She discarded her magazines. It was almost impossible to
read on a foreign train. The differences in houses and people,
in fields and gardens, fascinated her. She looked at Richard.
He was staring gloomily at the fields, making up his mind to
move. As he caught her glance, he roused himself.

"Come on Frances, tea or something. You've eaten nothing since breakfast and I haven't even that now." He rose,
and steadied himself. "There's nothing like being back on
solid ground, even if it does lurch at the moment."

They negotiated the two pairs of long legs, with the usual
"Not at all" following them. In the corridor, Richard gave a
grin, and squeezed her arm.

"Excited?" he teased. "I believe you are."

"I have two excitements inside me," said Frances, and
smiled back. It was like being a child again, when a deep
secret (*cross your lips and heart*) churned in your stomach,
and the intoxication of knowing you were important, even if
no one else thought you were, made your eyes shine. Frances
controlled her exhilaration and tried to look bored. She
remembered Richard's words last night. "Keep cool, don't
worry. Don't talk about anything important, even when you
think it's safe. Don't speak on impulse. Don't show any alarm
even when you've just had an attack of woman's intuition. I
can tell from your eyes when you are really worried. We can
talk things over at night when we get to bed. We won't lose
by being careful." *We won't lose!* She had chased away the
exhilaration, and now she knew it had been guarding her
against fear. *We won't lose.* The certainty of the words
panicked her. She heard Richard order tea. *Won't lose, won't
lose, won't lose,* mocked the wheels of the train. She suddenly
knew that Richard and she had never been so alone before,
in all their lives.

"That's better," said Richard as he lit a cigarette. "The
compartment was much too crowded. Now what do you
want to see in Paris?"

It was strange, she thought, how people seemed to change

in a foreign train. More than half in this coach were English, but already they seemed so different. She became aware that Richard was watching her carefully. She smiled to him and calmed her imagination. Nice beginning, indeed, when every stout Swiss commercial traveler seemed to be a member of the Ogpu, or that pinched little governess looked like a German agent. I've seen too much Hitchcock lately, she thought; at this rate I'll be worse than useless.

Richard was talking continuously as if he had sensed her stage fright. She concentrated on listening to him; he had helped her this way before. Like the time she had climbed her first mountain, and had got badly stuck, so badly that she accepted the fact that she was going to be killed, actually accepted it with a peculiar kind of resignation—but Richard had talked so calmly, had compelled her attention so thoroughly, that she forgot she was already dead at the bottom of a precipice, and her feet followed his to safety. He was talking now about the French peasants. A French peasant, he was proving, would not be able to understand *The Grapes of Wrath*.

Frances, watching the farmhouses which seemed to grow from the earth as much as the little orchards which guarded them or the fields so carefully planned to the last inch, was inclined to agree. She thought of the despair of peasants similar to these during the last war, when they saw their fields shell-racked, torn with barbed wire, poisoned with gas, evil-smelling with death. ... And yet, a few years later and these fields were again persuaded back into neat rows of earth, new trees were planted, new houses built.

"It is strange how little credit we give to the courage of quiet people," she said. "We sympathize most with those who find someone to champion their woes. We take all this for granted." She pointed to the farms. "We never think that this could be a wilderness. We look at it and think 'How pleasant to live here,' and yet to live here would mean back-breaking work and a continual struggle, if we wanted it to stay this way."

"There's nothing like self-pity for thoroughly dissipating a man. And when a nation indulges in that luxury it finds itself with a dictator. Wrongs and injustices come in at the door, and reason flies out the window. It's a solution which does not flatter the human race." He paused. "But what on earth brought this up?"

Frances nodded to the fields. "The earth itself."

People were now crowding into the restaurant car, looking reproachfully at their empty plates.

"Feeding time at the Zoo," said Richard. "Let's move." As he concentrated on the problem of francs and centimes, she caught sight of the gray-suited man and girl in a mirror. This was how we look to strangers, she thought. Richard had noticed the direction of her glance. His eyes were laughing.

"Beauty and the beast?" he suggested.

In their compartment, the two young men uncrossed their legs to let Frances and Richard pass. Frances had the feeling that they were interrupting a discussion. The dark-haired undergraduate seemed depressed and worried. She didn't look at the other, because she knew he was observing her in his detached way. She tried to concentrate on her magazines. She resisted the feeling of sleep which the train rhythm invited. . . . She never slept in the afternoon, but four hours' sleep last night could be an excuse. She looked at the field, she looked at the magazines, she looked at three pairs of brown suède shoes. When she awoke, they were in Paris. Richard was handing his rucksack and her hand case with voluble instructions to a blue-overalled porter.

He smiled down at her. "Time to powder your nose, my pet." Frances, in confusion, grabbed her handbag. She hated to arrive so disorganized.

The undergraduates were leaving. Frances' eyes were startled into looking at them over her compact mirror as she heard them say good-by to Richard, and then, more shyly, to her. She hid her surprise enough to smile, and bow, and say good-by to them in turn, before they disappeared.

Richard was still smiling. "Had a good sleep?"

"Marvelous. I've really got to admit I feel better. Did I make any peculiar noises?"

"No, you slept like a child. It quite won all our hearts."

A bulky shadow fell across the doorway. It belonged to a man with a neat black beard and a neat black suit, making his way slowly down the corridor. He was decidedly large, and he carried a suitcase in each hand, so that he had to walk crabwise. He gazed benevolently into their compartment over his pince-nez. Richard didn't seem aware of him.

He chose this moment to ask, "What about dinner at the Café Voltaire tonight?" Frances was enthusiastic. Her clear voice carried well down the corridor.

"Oh, yes; do. And we'll have decent Vouvray."

Their porter waited patiently. The platform was remarkably crowded, thought Richard, for this year of grace. His eyes searched for the two Englishmen. He saw them striding towards the main entrance, their felt hats in their hands. Behind them, at some distance, was a fat black figure, carrying two bags. . . . And then the crowd closed in again. He felt a sudden wave of relief. In the taxi, he avoided discussing anything except the streets and buildings.

Their hotel was one of the small ones on the Left Bank. They had stayed there on their first visit to Paris together, when they had little money to spend, and they always returned to it.

Inside their bedroom, Frances paused and said, as she always did, "It's just the same, even the wallpaper." Unconsciously, she always got the same note of surprise into her voice each year. Richard had come to the conclusion that she was surprised over anyone continuing to endure such wallpaper; she was probably right about that. It was hideously artistic. Frances was already in the bathroom, unpacking toothbrushes. He leaned against the door and watched her disapprovingly.

"Help me, darling," she said, throwing a sponge and talcum-powder tin at him.

"I'm damned if I am going to unpack now. I'm hungry."

"Richard, you know we'll be late tonight before we get back—we always are—and it will be too late to unpack then, and I hate going to sleep without washing or teeth brushing. I'll shake out my Paris clothes now, if you'll run my bath, like a darling." She went back into the bedroom, and he heard her moving about with her light step.

"It's just the thin edge of the wedge, if you ask me," he said. "First it is only a toothbrush, and then it's Paris clothes, and I bet you are starting on the whole suitcase by this time. You've too much damned energy, Frances. After last night, I thought you would never want to look at another piece of tissue paper for days."

"That sleep on the train made me all right." She slipped

off her gray flannel suit. "Talking about the train, who were your young friends? The blond was just too beautiful for words, wasn't he? I felt sorry somehow for the dark ugly one: he was feeling grim about something."

Richard came back into the room, and stretched himself along the chaise longue which stood in front of the tall windows. He propped the rose-embroidered cushion under his head, and watched Frances unfasten her suspenders.

"If you want to know, you can come here. The bath can wait five minutes. It's too hot anyway. You'd only come out a rich lobster color."

Frances looked across the room at him, and smiled as she slipped the smooth silk of her dressing gown round her. She knew Richard, by this time. The bath would have to wait.

From the chaise longue they could watch the green leaves in the small courtyard outside the windows. The fears and uncertainty which had suddenly attacked Frances that afternoon seemed so remote now that they were almost silly. She lay feeling safe and warm and comfortable. Dangers and cruelty didn't exist; nor did lies and treachery, nor hatred and jealousy. It was fine just to lie like this, just to feel safe and warm and comfortable.

Richard watched the smile on her lips. "How do you feel, darling?" So he had been worried too about that attack of nerves this afternoon.

"Wonderful, Richard. Like a contented cow." He laughed. He knew now that everything was all right. When he got round to telling his story, there wasn't much to tell. The men had been undergraduates—Cambridge men. They had been vague about their holiday. The fair-haired man had said something about Czechoslovakia, but the dark one had shut him up rather abruptly, Richard had thought. What had actually started them talking was the man in the black suit. He had passed the compartment door twice, each time looking benevolently at Frances asleep in her corner seat.

"And that," said Richard, "aroused all our protective instincts. The dark-haired undergraduate muttered something about being haunted by black beards since Victoria. The other suggested it might only be a touch of Blackbeard's old bladder trouble again. That sort of broke the ice. I capped that suggestion, and then we just talked. Mostly the fair-haired glamour boy and myself. It turned out he was the brother of Thornley who was up at Oxford in my time. A friend of Peter's. As a matter of fact Peter visited them for a couple of days this week."

At the mention of Peter's name, Frances had stiffened. She didn't like it somehow, and for all Richard's calm voice, she knew he didn't either. She kept her voice low like his. "Complications?" she asked.

"You can't tell. I've been thinking about that. The dark-haired chap was certainly jumpy, but that doesn't prove anything. Probably they really are quite oblivious of anything except their own holiday, and our meeting them was just another of these coincidences. On the other hand, Peter might have roped them in just like us, or used them as decoys, and perhaps Blackbeard was trailing them. If so, then we had downright bad luck meeting them. All we can do is to disinterest anyone who might have become interested in us through them." Richard smiled wryly. "You see, young Thornley didn't mention his brother or Peter until we had reached the station. So there we were, talking for most of the journey, and anyone who passed the door of the compartment might have thought we were all together. The joke was on me."

Frances kissed him. "It probably is only a harmless incident. What about throwing off suspicion with dinner?"

Half an hour later, they left the hotel. The streets were quiet, the restaurants and cafés crowded. A worried Frenchman, hurrying past them, caught sight of a girl's laughing face under a pert white hat with a red rose, and turned to watch. English, he guessed, as he marked the cut of the man's suit and that peculiar stride which goes with such a suit. And without a care in the world, he thought. He hurried on, speculating on that peculiar people.

At that moment he was right. Frances and Richard had abandoned care. Their holiday had begun.

CHAPTER V

Pawn to King's Fourth

JUNE ended with their first week in Paris. They were very
much on holiday. They rose late and breakfasted at their
open window in the warm sunlight which then invaded the
small courtyard. The insignificant little man who had watched
them from the shadows of his room since their first morning
at the hotel still sat far back from his window, but his
interest was waning. He wasn't a romantic, and the appearance each morning of a pretty blonde girl in a dressing gown
pouring coffee for a tall young man who lazily stretched
himself on a couch at the open window was beginning to
bore him. The leisurely manner in which they breakfasted
and dressed annoyed him as much as the sound of their
laughter and their English voices. He was wasting his time,
he thought angrily, as he watched them leave their room
after midday as they always did. The chambermaid could
take care of them.

The second insignificant man who took over at this point
was equally bored. His feet hurt, and he had never been
interested in history anyway. He followed Frances and Richard from one church to another, from exhibition to exhibition, from palaces to slums. Towards the end of the week, he
was beginning to wait for them in a café and let them visit
the inside of the buildings themselves. For he too had become
convinced he was wasting his time.

The third insignificant man, who joined Richard and
Frances while they were having dinner, had slightly better
luck. He liked theaters and night clubs. Even the two
evenings which they spent more soberly, just sitting at a table
in the Café de la Paix, were pleasant, because by that time
he was convinced that the Englishman and his wife weren't
going to complicate life for him. So he relaxed and enjoyed
the thought that his expenses were paid. He was the only one

of the insignificant men who was sorry to receive instructions
at the end of the week to switch over to a newly arrived
American. He had become so accustomed to their obvious
approval of drinking their coffee and liqueur on the pavement in the French manner that he would not have been
surprised to see them approach the Café de la Paix again, on
Saturday night. He would have approved the fair-haired girl's
black dress and the small white hat with its gay red rose
perched over her right eye.

Frances was nervous, so she talked constantly as they
walked up the Avenue de l'Opéra. "I've enjoyed this week,
even if my feet feel two sizes bigger," was how she summed
it up.

Richard nodded. "It hasn't been so bad. Life has been
simpler than I thought it would be. I begin to feel I was
oversuspicious of Blackbeard."

Frances stared. "I haven't seen him again; have you?"

"No, nor any possible relatives, either." Which would have
pleased the insignificant men; no tribute to their ingenuities
could have been handsomer. Richard piloted Frances carefully across the Boulevard des Capucines, and gave her an
encouraging smile. "Cheer up, old girl. The first bathe is
always the coldest."

They had arrived between the dinner and the after-theater
crowds. There were a few vacant tables. Richard led the way
to one on the left-hand side. As they sat down, a waiter
appeared like the traditional white rabbit out of a hat.

"Coffee," said Richard, "and Cointreau for you as usual,
Frances? I think I'll have one too. Yes, coffee and two
Cointreaus."

Frances repressed a wifely smile. He always enjoyed ordering in French, even in moments like these. Poor old Richard,
how he hated Cointreau.

They settled comfortably in their chairs, lit cigarettes, and
looked at the traffic with the right amount of interest. The
people at the other tables were the usual mixture of foreigners and Frenchmen. Two nights ago, the same kind of crowd
had seemed gay and harmless. Tonight they seemed gay.
Frances shook herself out of her imagination to admire the
way in which the waiter poured the Cointreau.

"Penny for them," said Richard.

"I was thinking how people with guilty consciences develop persecution mania."

"Yes, they could, couldn't they? I felt the same." But what worried them most was how long they had to wait. Frances sipped her Cointreau. She noticed with amusement that Richard was restricting himself to coffee. As she listened to him, making conversation with one eye on his watch, she repeated to herself just what she had to say when the time came. She was the amateur actress taking one last look at her script as she waits in the wings. Her cue came sooner than she had expected.

A large, expensively draped woman was making her way with difficulty past their table. It seemed to Frances that it might have been the large lady who had brushed against the table, and sent the coffee swilling into the saucer. Yet Richard's Cointreau glass lay carefully pointed away from them, so that the liqueur trickled slowly over the other side of the table. Richard looked at it with some annoyance and resignation. The large lady continued oblivious on her way, trailing clouds of Matchabelli. The waiter staged his arrival from nowhere. He wiped and apologized with equal vigor.

Frances sat very still. She was conscious of the smile on her lips which had settled there and wouldn't come off, as if she were having her photograph taken. Richard's back was turned towards the man, and he hadn't noticed him yet. She let her eyes travel slowly back to their own table; she sensed, rather than saw, him making his way out of the restaurant. He was walking unhurriedly, and he would pass their table. Now he was almost behind the waiter, whose broad back blocked the narrow passage effectively as he bent to pick up the coffee cups. Richard was watching her. He was waiting.

"I was telling you about Mrs. Rose." As she spoke she flipped her cigarette case open. "Mrs. Rose told me we must see Le Lapin Agile. She said we would like it."

"Why?" Richard seemed more interested in ordering another drink.

That's just my sweet husband, she thought a trifle bitterly, and lighted her cigarette. She noticed the rug vendor with the turban who was silently offering his wares to another table.

"She was born in India," she said. Now let's see what Richard can make of that.

The waiter became aware of the man who was trying to

edge impatiently past him. He stepped aside, but not in time.
He must have knocked the man's elbow, for the cigarette fell
from his hand onto their table. The man caught it as it
rolled, and picked it up. There was just time for them to
notice the peculiar way he wore the watch on his wrist, and
the peculiar time it showed on its clearly marked face.

"India?" Richard was asking with a display of interest.
"Oh, yes, she was a great rope climber in her day, wasn't
she?"

The man had already reached the pavement; he paused for
a moment as he lit his cigarette. He might be making up his
mind how to spend the rest of his evening, and by the time
Frances had replied gently but forcibly he had merged into
the crowd.

"Did I ever tell you about my life among the Eskimos?"
asked Richard, and shook his head in reply to the rug seller.
He sipped the cognac which the waiter had brought, and
added with approval, "Much more like it. Where were we?
Oh, yes, with the Eskimos. . . ." He talked on. Frances was
glad of the opportunity just to relax. She listened to Richard's
inventions with a smile, and waited for him to finish the
liqueur. Then they could get back to the hotel.

The dark-haired, sallow-faced chambermaid had just come
out of their room. The towels over her arm were the obvious
excuse. She smiled in her tired way.

"Good evening, Madame, Monsieur. You are back early
tonight. Perhaps Madame is tired."

Frances agreed to that: she had just caught a glimpse of
herself in the gilt-edged mirror on the wall. Perhaps it was
the very large, very pink flowers on the wallpaper that made
her feel so wilted. Richard said good night rather brusquely,
and opened their door. The woman wasn't usually conversational, he thought, but she must have been surprised to see
them. People generally talked too much when they were
embarrassed. He locked the door behind them, and stood
there, listening. Frances watched his face as she took off her
hat. She liked him when he was worried: she liked the frown
on his brow, the intent look in the thoughtful eyes. It had
been his eyes which she had noticed when they had first met.
She couldn't guess what lay behind their calm grayness; there
was a hint of so many things. If that had been one of the

reasons why she had married him, then she hadn't been disappointed.

Richard seemed satisfied. He had left the door, and started to undress.

"Bed," he said, and his eyes were smiling, now. "And don't, my love, clean each tooth for five minutes, tonight."

Frances laughed, and started to brush her hair, and then stopped with the hairbrush poised in midair. Her eyes were puzzled as they rested on her make-up box lying on the dressing table.

"I could *swear* that . . ." she began.

"I shouldn't," said Richard, his lips smiling, his eyes warning.

Frances bit her top lip. "I shan't be long now," she ended. Richard nodded approvingly. Good girl, he thought; she could take a hint without having it underlined.

Frances always lay on Richard's right side. It was hot and stuffy in the room, but Richard would open the windows before they went to sleep. He held her close to him. They could feel each other's breath coming in little warm waves as they talked, their low voices smothered in the pillow.

"What was wrong, Fran?"

"Someone has been meddling with my things. The cream jars were in the wrong order; you know how I always have them arranged in a certain way. They stand on a little tray, which you've got to lift up to get at the space underneath. Someone probably wanted to know what I kept there."

"What do you keep?"

"Just face tissues and cotton wool and odds and ends."

"Was anything missing?"

"My address book. You know the one, the little one I keep for addresses of hairdressers or hotels or cleaners in any place we have stayed abroad."

"That won't be much help to them."

"But who are they?"

"God knows. It might be friends of Blackbeard, or it might be someone who followed Peter more successfully than he thought. The maid is the obvious agent, anyway. I just couldn't place her when we met her in the corridor. And how did she know what time we usually returned to the hotel? She may have just been interested in how you get that complexion, or she may be yawning in that empty room next door, this very minute." He gripped Frances more tightly, and she let out a sudden squeal. Richard was nearer the truth than he would have cared to be. The dark-haired sallow woman, standing motionless in the empty room, her ear close to the wall, shrugged her shoulders: only murmurs and squeals in bed. A simple-minded race, the English. She moved silently to the door. She could go off duty now and report ... Nothing, as usual.

Frances had asked, "You think we have been watched?"

"Only remotely. Our room has been searched, obviously, but there is nothing incriminating to find. And if they did follow us about Paris, then our movements have been innocent enough. The important thing will be whether anyone realized the meaning of tonight's incident, or whether we shall be watched tomorrow. They can follow us about, otherwise, until they are blue in the face."

"You sound confident." In the darkness, Richard smiled to himself. Confident? He had seldom felt worse in his life.

"The chap we met tonight seemed pretty calm and collected. He made everything look quite simple. Damned clever too. You got it, didn't you? One cigarette, and then, as neat emphasis, the watch which he wore the wrong way round so that we could see that it had stopped at one o'clock. I rather liked that touch."

"To be perfectly frank, I could hardly believe it was the clue. It was so easy."

"Well, it's all we've got to go on. Add one to one ... and what do you get?"

Frances laughed. "It's too simple, really. And if at first you don't succeed ..."

"Darling, why mention that when I'd like to get some sleep?"

"Sorry, Richard." She moved to kiss him and bumped her nose against his chin. "I'll pack tomorrow afternoon, and then we can leave anytime," she added sleepily. She stifled a yawn against his shoulder. "It's all this whispering," she said. "It makes me sleepy."

She was asleep by the time Richard had opened the windows and let the night air surge in with its welcome coolness. He looked at his wife's fair hair on the pillow, the curve of her cheek and the dark lashes. She slept like a child, with her hands resting above her head.

He remembered her voice, blurred with sleep. *We can leave anytime.* Leave, perhaps—but for where, and for what? He cursed Peter and himself. First instincts were often the right ones, when it was a matter of self-preservation. And keeping Frances safe was a matter of self-preservation for him. He should have stuck to his dislike of involving Frances. He ought to have come alone. But it had been easy to be persuaded, for the selfish reason, quite apart from the more practical one that this mission must seem a holiday as usual, that he would have been miserable without her. He lay and thought of the way in which two people, each with their own definite personality, could build up a third personality, a greater and more exciting one, to share between them. When two people succeeded in that, then they were complete. Without Frances, however definite his own personality might be, he was incomplete.

Sleep was impossible. He lay and watched the blackness of the courtyard bleach to gray, and felt the coldness of early morning strike his bare shoulders.

CHAPTER VI

The Agile Rabbit

A SUDDEN coolness had come to the city. Frances shivered as she stepped out of the taxi. Above the roofs of the twisting narrow streets, she could see the illuminated dome of the Sacré Cœur. Behind her, withdrawing modestly into its shadows, was Le Lapin Agile. The doorman, like a nimble gnome in his red cap and tunic, darted down to meet them, and guided them through the narrow gate to the dark doorway.

Nothing had changed since they had last been here. It never did. The old grandfather, who had founded it, had died, but the rest of the family carried on in the way he had established. In the small entrance hall, Madame sat behind the counter with its shaded light gleaming on the trays of cherry brandy. The girl who sang so well to the guitar was leaning on the counter, talking to a young man in his shirt sleeves. She was dressed as usual in a skirt and blouse. There was a sound of a piano and of laughter from the narrow doorway at the end of the counter.

Frances and Richard waited until the applause told them that the Rabelaisian improvisor had finished. The girl nodded approvingly.

"I'll find you a place," she said, and led the way up the few stairs into the room. The long benches on either side of the monastery tables were well-filled, but the girl's eyes, accustomed to the dimness of the lighting, had found a bench where two more could sit. The shirt-sleeved man followed them, carrying two glasses of cherry brandy. You drank either cherry brandy or not at all.

The others at the table made room for Frances and Richard good-naturedly. They joked with the girl.

"Why don't you bring your guitar over here and sing to us?" asked one of the men. "It's only Marius here who is going to do a little recitation next. He is with poem, again.

But we don't need to listen to it, we have been hearing it all evening." His round face creased with laughter. Everyone laughed, including Marius, a little self-consciously.

The girl smiled to Marius. "What is it tonight—a new one? Go on, do it now. I have time to listen, too."

Marius rose and hesitated. His thin, rather hard face relaxed. He might be a student, or an apprentice, thought Frances. He looked apologetically round the table and saw that Frances was watching him.

"I am not sure about the last couplet," he explained shyly to her. They were all looking at her, waiting for her to reply. She gulped, felt her cheeks afire, and decided to risk it.

"Poète, prends ton luth!" she declaimed with her best Alexandrine accent. Everyone laughed again. The fat jovial man was enjoying himself.

"The trouble with women," he said with mock seriousness, "is that they never finish quotations." He looked at his wife. "One of the troubles," he finished. Frances blushed again, and joined in the new chorus of laughter.

Richard was pleased. We couldn't have arranged it better, he thought, and looked sympathetically across the shadows of the room at a table where other foreigners had been grouped together. He leaned back against the stone wall, and filled his pipe. Marius had reached the ancient piano. He cleared his throat, and the conversations and arguments at the other tables politely diminished. He cleared his throat again, and, sweeping back the hair which fell over his eyes, began. Everyone was listening. Richard took the opportunity to look carefully round the room; his seat gave him a good view. He could observe without appearing to.

There was the usual crowd there. At first he couldn't see anyone remotely like their friend of the Café de la Paix. There might be the possibility of disguise of course. He looked at his watch. It was just after one o'clock: time enough. He looked at the large figure of Buddha at one end of the room, and his eye naturally traveled to the large figure of Christ on the Cross on the opposite wall ... And then he saw the man. He couldn't be sure, but something about one of the men at the table at that end of the room seemed familiar. It might be ... He gave all his attention to Marius, who was gathering himself to deliver the uncertain couplet. It was effective, judging by the applause. Marius, flushed with success, was returning.

The girl in the blouse and skirt rose to go.

"I have something new for you tonight," she explained.

"Sing, sing," they chanted.

"She has," explained the fat man, "a most charming voice, and she chooses her songs well. Or perhaps you know?"

"Yes, I know," said Frances.

"Aristide has set some of Villon's songs to music for her voice," the Frenchman continued. He nodded towards the man in shirt sleeves, who was now sitting down at the piano. He played softly to himself, as he waited for the girl to appear.

Marius and Richard had begun a discussion for two about the symbolist poets. Frances turned to the others. They were on to politics, now: one of the women had begun the argument.

"Don't spoil my evening," said the large man, almost savagely. "Politics, politics. There is no living, nowadays." He addressed himself suddenly to Frances. "I am sorry, but you will understand." Frances could think of several reasons. She wondered which of them was responsible. The Frenchman looked at her gloomily; the laugh-lines round his mouth straightened, giving it an unexpected bitterness. His brown eyes had become hard. He leaned over the table on his elbows and his hands marked each point as he spoke.

"Twice within seven months, I have had to look out my old uniform, close my business—I am a contractor—and make my good-bys. Twice. September 1938, April 1939." His wife beside him looked away quickly. His eyes, under the heavy brows, held Frances motionless. She could not even smile in sympathy. "There may be a third time. It will be too much. The third time will be just *two* too much."

Everyone sat silent for a minute, and then all began to talk at once.

"One war is enough for one lifetime," said his wife without lifting her eyes.

The girl in the blouse and skirt had entered again, carrying her guitar. The many voices of the crowded room faded into silence. Even the foreign visitors sat politely curious. The girl raised the guitar, its red ribbons falling over her arm. She smiled to the man at the piano.

"Aristide here has found music for the words of our François Villon. I shall sing two of his ballads."

Frances looked at the silent faces; she wondered how many of them hid the thoughts of uniforms waiting for the third time. It may have been the low sweet voice of the singer, or the simplicity of the music, or the poetry of the words. She felt her heart stifle. In it there were tears for the courage of ordinary people, hot rage against the disturbers of their lives. The Frenchman was right: it was too much. The singer's voice dimmed, sweetly lingering:—

> *Que ce refrain ne vous remaine:*
> *Mais où sont les neiges d'antan!*

Richard's hand lay on her arm. "Steady," he said, "steady." There was something as well as gentleness in his voice. So he had seen the man, or hadn't he? She had no idea of the time. Perhaps they had failed. A moment of panic seized her. But Richard appeared calm. His eyes told her nothing was wrong, only to be prepared.

"I am afraid we must leave soon," he explained to the others. A chorus of genial protests rose.

"Then you must come back often. To this table," said the large Frenchman. "Let us drink to this." They lifted their glasses.

Frances suddenly said, "To all men of good will, who live and let live. And perdition to their enemies, breeders of hate and destruction." She was going to weep after all. Oh hell! ... They drank. The good-bys were over. Richard led the way. The man from the Café de la Paix had just three minutes' start.

Others had begun to go too. A few late-comers were just entering. The little entrance hall was jammed. They made their way through with difficulty. Richard had got his hat, with the help of the man in shirt sleeves. He spoke for a moment to Madame. Still no one came. They left, as slowly as would seem natural, but the man had completely disappeared. They went down the steep steps. It had begun to rain, and the doorkeeper put up his enormous umbrella for them as they waited for a taxi. Richard swore softly. Frances knew then that something had gone wrong. He fished in his pocket for a tip for the doorkeeper, who was showing them his poems which he had printed on single sheets for sale.

And then the door behind them opened, and there was a path of light over the wet pavement. It was the man in shirt sleeves.

"Monsieur has left behind his book." He handed something to Richard.

"Oh, yes," said Richard. He thought quickly. "Careless of me. Where did I drop it?" It was a small book and fitted into his pocket neatly.

"In the hall when you spoke to Madame, and bought some cigarettes. The gentleman behind you saw it fall."

"Well, thank you very much," began Richard, but the man had given an easy wave of his hand and was already back in the shelter of the doorway. Again the street was in darkness; a taxicab had halted on the slope of cobblestones, and the red gnome was shutting the door. Richard leaned forward to give the taxi-driver their address. He noticed that more guests were leaving Le Lapin Agile. They stood grouped round the lighted doorway, and hesitated before the wet pavement. The man from the Café de la Paix was there among them. He might have been with the others, or he might have been alone. But one thing, anyway, thought Richard as the taxi skidded on the greasy streets: no one could say that he had been with the Myles'.

When they reached their room, Richard threw the book on the bed and went into the bathroom. Frances began to undress. She was determined she would wait for her cue. Inwardly, she was annoyed with herself. She had missed everything. She had been so interested in the people at their table that she had almost forgotten about the man, and she hadn't even seen him. She guessed that Richard was satisfied anyway, or he wouldn't be whistling. He undressed quickly, and sat on the edge of the bed as he set the small traveling clock's alarm for half-past six.

"We can always sleep in the train," he said philosophically, and picked up the book curiously. He hadn't even noticed that she had done his packing for him this afternoon when he made a tour of the chief Paris stations. (There were only three ways by which they would probably leave Paris: either by the north or by the south or by the east; and Richard had said it was just as well to know the early-morning express trains which left these stations.) But Frances had been mistaken. . . .

"Did you have a nice afternoon?" He nodded to the suitcases and grinned.

"Thank you, darling. Did you have a nice walk?" There was almost too much sweet solicitude in her voice.

Richard looked up quickly. "Come off it, Frances. You know I told you to leave my stuff."

"Someone had to . . ."

"My poor put-upon wife." He drew her down onto the bed and rolled her between the sheets. Frances began to laugh. It was no good harboring righteous indignation: not with Richard.

He picked up the book again. "Do you mind if I read in bed?"

"Not if you talk first; I'm too sleepy to wait until you've finished reading. I'm almost bursting with curiosity."

Richard was looking at the book in a puzzled way. "Yes, I may take quite a time to get through this." He held it out so that the title was towards her. Frances looked at it with a mixture of amazement and excitement. It was a guide to Southern Germany.

Richard kicked off his slippers and slid in beside Frances. His voice dropped naturally. "You didn't see him? He was there all right. Sorry to hurry you away, but if he didn't mean to get in touch with us inside the room, the only other alternative was for us to follow him out. He left on the dot of two. Then I lost him, or I thought I did. I had been expecting something unusual to happen. This book was the only thing that did. It's it—or nothing."

"And if you don't find any information there?"

"We are completely and beautifully stuck."

Frances adjusted herself comfortably for sleep. "Darling, you had better begin. It looks an all-night job." She yawned heartlessly and closed her eyes.

Richard settled the lamp beside the bed to suit him, and opened the book. It seemed a new edition. He began at the first blank pages, and examined each successive page carefully for any markings. His care was rewarded.

There was a small lightly penciled star opposite one of the sections in the contents list following the large map, title page and two introductions. It was the section on Nürnberg. There were still two other pencil markings on the list of contents; one was a small horizontal stroke, the other a vertical one.

Star first, obviously, thought Richard and turned to the pages
on Nürnberg.

The description of Nürnberg followed the usual thorough
pattern. It led off with stations and hotels and other helps to
tourists. Richard examined the small print carefully. There
were so many helpful hints to tired travelers after each entry,
so many abbreviations of map references and prices enclosed
in neat brackets. It made finicky reading. A careful glance at
a page wasn't enough. Richard groaned and started at the
beginning of the page again. His eye-straining concentration
was rewarded by the time he got to the section on tramways.
Route 2 seemed interesting: from Gustav-Adolf-Strasse *via*
Plärrer, Lorenzkirche, Marientor, Marienstrasse to Dutzendteich. A small horizontal line was neatly penciled before
Marienstrasse. With so many brackets and hyphens and com-
mas and colons mixed into the text, the line was scarcely
noticeable. The marking connected with the pencil line in the
list of contents. Nürnberg, Marienstrasse, horizontal line. He
turned back to the contents' page. The horizontal mark there
lay beside Augsburg.

He studied Augsburg as he had done Nürnberg. Hotels,
restaurants ... He read on carefully, but it wasn't until he
came to the historical details about the city that he made any
further advance. There, among the early benefactors, was the
name of one Anton Fugger (1495–1560). He liked the name
of Anton Fugger, especially with that neat vertical line just in
front of the A.—Nürnberg, Marienstrasse, Anton Fugger,
vertical line. He turned quickly back to the contents' list. It
was difficult to keep his excitement down. He forced himself
not to be too confident. The vertical line marked Heidelberg.

This time, the information began with the air service and
railway station. His eyes might have begun to tire with the
strain, or perhaps he was too excited, or perhaps it was sleep.
He knew he was jumping words. Frances slept comfortably
beside him. He looked at the alarm, and checked it unbelievingly with his watch. It was nearly half-past five. There was no
time to waste. He groaned again, and began to read, with his
fist pressed hard against his chin. The discomfort checked
that seductive idea of sleep.

He read on. Suddenly he sat up. It fitted in. God, it fitted
in. He looked again: *Archæological Institute*, free on—yes,
that was the penciled star all right—*free on Wednesday and*

Saturday, 11 A.M.–1 P.M. So there it was, in its neat circle: Nürnberg, Marienstrasse, Anton Fugger, free on Wednesday and Saturday from eleven until one o'clock. A telephone book in Nürnberg would probably give the number of Fugger's house in Marienstrasse. But how to identify themselves when they met Herr Fugger? There must be some other clue. There had been no writing on the title page. What about a colophon? Failing anything there, he would have to examine the book right through perhaps in Nürnberg itself. But among the last blank pages he found two things. One was a red-rose petal, neatly pressed and pasted onto the paper. On the back of the page there were some music-notes, roughly jotted down in pencil after a treble clef. He whistled the notes to himself. The simple tune was vaguely familiar. All the notes were of the same value; it was this which had made the song seem vague at first. But it now was clearly recognizable. He relaxed back on his pillow and smiled amiably at the ceiling. He had forgotten about sleep. In any case, Frances would have to be wakened in less than fifteen minutes. What he needed now was a tub and a shave.

The sound of the running water drew Frances gradually out of sleep. Slowly and then suddenly she realized she was alone. She awoke fully with a panic of fear.

"Richard," she began, "Richard ..." and then connected the sound of running water with a bath. She was calm again as Richard came out of the bathroom, the towel draped round him with one end slung over his shoulder. He had a crisp, curling beard of shaving soap.

"The elder Cato," he announced, "come to reprimand a slothful wife."

Frances looked at him sadly.

"No response? Is it as bad as that?"

"Go away, darling. I love you, but not at this hour." She settled drowsily on her pillow.

"Not on this morning, you don't, my love." He heartlessly pulled the sheet off the bed. Frances looked resigned. She lowered her voice.

"Where are we going?"

Richard sat down beside her. "Nürnberg."

"You've been there."

"Yes. Wake up, Frances."

"I haven't."

"No."

Frances roused herself. "What else did you find out?"

"You are like a red red rose."

"Oh. . . . I'm *what*?"

"My love. So the notes say."

"Richard, there is something peculiarly horrible about you this morning. God, how I hate men when they are secretly elated." She looked sadly at her husband, and then she began to laugh.

"Good. So you like Cato at last?"

"It's your beard, my sweet." She giggled weakly. "It pops."

"What?"

"The soap bubbles," she began, "listen . . ." She smothered her laughter.

"Anything to cheer a girl up. Are you really awake now? Well, listen, Frances. Get dressed. Get everything collected. Then we pay the bill and depart at once for the station. I got the train information yesterday, so everything is simple."

Frances sobered up. Richard was in earnest now. "All right. What actually did you find out last night?"

Richard was noncommittal. "A name and address in a town and the time we might visit it. Also that your hat will still be worn, and the first seven notes of a song."

"My love is like a red, red rose?"

Richard nodded. "Come on; rise and shine."

He obviously did not want to tell her any more than that, decided Frances as she bathed and dressed quickly, and packed away the final odds and ends. Richard was ready before she had put on her hat. He had finished writing the labels on the suitcases. Frances saw their name followed by the words *Passenger to Nice*. The room, stripped of their belongings, looked colorless in spite of the wallpaper. It was just another hotel bedroom.

The dark-haired, sallow chambermaid came in at half-past twelve. They were generally out by that time. The room looked empty. She had a sudden suspicion. Yes, she was right, they were not only out but gone. The boy who brought up the breakfast trays was whistling in the corridor. She ran to the door.

"Well, I see they have left. It is a bit sudden, isn't it? They must have been early."

"Yes. They didn't have breakfast. Pierre was downstairs on duty when they left."

"They are lucky, wandering about like that with no work to do. Did they go back to England?"

"Pierre said the labels were for Nice, and Michel drove them to the station."

"Nice? Well, some people have all the luck."

She waited for the boy to leave the corridor, and then she went downstairs. She searched for Michel before she slipped into the phone box. It was risky, if Madame saw her—but she couldn't wait until she was off duty. Fortunately this corner of the hall was dark, and she kept her voice low.

"Gone this morning. Gare de Lyon. For Nice. Nothing out of usual last night." Well, that was that nice little fee earned.

When they arrived at the Gare de Lyon, Richard paid the taxi-driver, Michel, as he directed the porter to the train for Nice. They were very early, the porter said. In that case, they would leave their bags at the left-luggage office while they had breakfast. Richard had the satisfaction of seeing the naïvely inquisitive Michel—it was part of his friendly inter-est—drive away. The porter was glad enough to have such a short trip. He departed with his tip, well-pleased. In ten minutes, Frances and Richard returned for their luggage with another porter. This time they drove to the Gare du Nord. Frances looked at Richard in the taxi, as he changed the labels on the suitcases. He was smiling broadly.

"I do believe you enjoy this," she said in amazement.

He laughed. "What about you?"

"I'm hungry."

"Well, we can have breakfast on the train. We'll travel luxuriously and get some sleep before Strasbourg."

As Richard had predicted, they breakfasted well. Frances watched him in the dining car with amusement.

"Every moment you look more and more like a cat before a dish of cream." Richard gave a laugh which degenerated into a yawn.

He said, "Well, I feel something is making sense. I'll tell you all about it as soon as we have finished our visit. Let's go back to the compartment."

"And sleep."

"I'll have a pipe, first."

Frances thought this strange. Richard didn't usually smoke a pipe until after lunch. However, back in the empty compartment she understood. Out of certain pages in the guidebook which he had studied last night he made very efficient lighters. When all that remained of them was curled fragments of charred paper, he threw the expurgated book out the window. It landed satisfactorily in a broad irrigation ditch. Richard watched it disappear, and then relaxed in his corner, stretching his legs. He gave Frances a satisfied smile.

"Everything all right with you?" he asked.

She nodded.

"Good. Everything's all right with me." His eyes closed. "Sorry," he added, his voice fading.

Frances looked at the trees and the fields and the sky. The express devoured the miles. Someone, she thought, ought to stay awake. But the journey was completely uneventful and, apart from an inner excitement at crossing the frontier, it was as dull as the scenery in the last stages of their travels. Once the minor thrills at Strasbourg had passed—when the engine had been changed for a (no doubt) superior German model, when the carriages had the last French dust swept from them efficiently and contemptuously by a squad of German cleaners, when their bags and money and passport had been thoroughly examined—there only remained the sagging feeling of relief. By the time they reached Nürnberg, Frances was cross and tired. She was resigned to a holiday in which the main excitement would merely be a succession of tensions. Richard was resigned to the fact that so far their luck had been almost too good to last.

CHAPTER VII

The Walled Town

IT WAS very late when they did arrive in Nürnberg. Frances waited at the entrance to the Hauptbahnhof and stared across the warm darkness of the enormous square. Richard had told her that the old town lay beyond. Its lights were few. It seemed already asleep within its walls.

The porter had found them a taxi, at last. Richard gave the driver the name of the hotel. The driver looked at them. His face was large and round and expressionless.

"It isn't here, any more," he said.

The porter was listening. "The Königshof is near the same place. It is highly esteemed," he volunteered.

"All right, then," said Richard, "the Königshof."

They sat in silence during the short journey to the hotel.

"You could have walked," said the driver, as they got out of the taxi. He seemed as if he disapproved of their extravagance.

Richard made no reply.

"Did you know the Goldner Hahn well?" the driver asked suddenly.

"I stayed there in '32. What happened to it?"

The man was silent.

"What happened to it?" Richard asked again.

The man hesitated. "Oh—they went away." His voice was as expressionless as his face. Richard noted Frances' speculative interest. He knew what she was thinking.

She was still silent when they reached their room. It was warm inside; the massive furniture made it feel still warmer. She opened a window and looked out into the Königstrasse. The houses had high steep roofs, some of them pitted with attic windows, while others turned their gable ends to the street. This was better, this was more like what she had imagined. She remained standing at the window, watching the moonlight on the roofs. When she moved at last, she found that Richard had unpacked some things for her. She smiled her thanks.

"Cheer up, old girl. You'll feel better in the morning," he said.

I hope, she added to herself.

But when Tuesday morning came and the constant hum of traffic outside their window awoke Frances, she did feel better. Richard was already dressed, and reading his Baedeker. They had breakfast in their room, and discussed their plans as they ate. Richard advocated the minimum of unpacking. No one noticed what you wore here, anyway.

While Frances had slept, he had decided to work in an opposite direction from their Paris experience. Instead of waiting the few days until Saturday came, they would call on Fugger tomorrow, and then they could spend three or four days playing the tourist in Nürnberg. But to Frances, he only remarked that today they could explore the old town, and leave the Castle and the Museum and the churches for the rest of the week.

"Unless I fry to death," Frances said. She looked out at the bright sunlight in the street, promising heat even at this early hour. Resignedly, she chose the thinnest town dress she had. Richard approved of the effect when she was at last ready, but he also looked at his wrist watch just slightly more pointedly than was necessary.

"Brute," said Frances, with her sweetest smile, and led the way out of the room.

There was that feeling of continual coming and going in the entrance hall which characterizes a busy town hotel. Just as well for us, thought Richard. Frances and he were only two more in the constant stream. The other guests were mostly German. They were serious-looking men and women, who walked quickly, as if they had important business to attend to. Perhaps they had. He noted the number of uniforms of one kind or another, and even—astounding thing—quick precise salutes and the violent two-worded greeting. It was astounding because it was so theatrical, so incongruous in a peaceful hotel lobby. He caught Frances' eye, and they both smiled gently. He imagined himself coming into a lecture hall at Oxford, surveying the rows of young faces before him, making a rigid salute and barking out "God save the King" in a parade-ground voice, before turning to his lecture on the metaphysical poets. He knew what his undergraduates would do. They would telephone anxiously for a doctor, two male nurses and a strait-jacket—and they would be right.

As they reached the front door, Frances paused to look at the roughly paved street and then at her shoes.

"I thought the heels were a mistake," said Richard.

Frances looked stubborn. "Well, if I change into my hiking shoes, I'll have to change my whole outfit. I'll manage."

A young man had come out of the hotel door; he halted as he heard Frances' voice, and looked at her, giving what Hollywood has perfected as the "double take." Then the pavement was crowded with the stamp of heavy boots. Frances was separated from Richard by a wall of brown shirts. She stepped backwards to the safety of the doorway, lost her balance and felt her heel sink cruelly into something soft. The young man winced, but stood his ground.

"I'm so sorry," Frances said and removed her heel. "*Verzeihung ...*" That must have been a sore one, she thought.

"Pardon me," the young man said, lifting his hat and trying to walk away without limping.

Frances' handbag seemed to be infected with her embarrassment: it slipped from under her arm, and opened as it reached the pavement. The last uniform had passed, and in the temporary lull Richard bent down for the bag, and jammed the odds and ends back into place. The powder case rolled towards the man, who had turned as Frances had said "Damn." He picked it up, and handed it silently with a twist of a smile to Richard.

"Thank you," said Richard, and he meant it.

"You're welcome." He raised his hat again and walked quickly away, as if afraid of what Frances would do next. Richard looked down at her and shook his head.

"You surpassed yourself there, my sweet Dora. Now if you would really like to go somewhere, we can start on the old town. This way." He caught her arm as she moved off in the wrong direction.

"He was rather nice-looking. American, wasn't he? I liked his voice."

"Yes; yes; and rich baritone," Richard answered absent-mindedly. He was looking for a place to cross the street.

The exploration of the old town took care of the morning. Two o'clock found them exhausted in a beer restaurant, Richard having decided that the heat of the day called for a liquid lunch. Frances, atoning for the slow progress caused by her shoes—she *had* managed, but at a price—sat in sweet martyrdom as she talked and laughed. It was strange how the smell of beer clung to the room. The coffee did not taste very much like coffee, but she sipped it and kept her eyes off the beer mugs. She had never liked the stuff; from now on she would hate it. Even the table smelled of beer. Richard was asking her a question. How would she like a tram ride? Heavens, there was nothing she wanted less.

"Must we?" she asked as pathetically as possible.

Richard nodded. "I'm afraid so."

She lowered her voice. "Telephone book?"

"No good. I had a look at it when you were powdering your nose."

"Nothing there at all?"

"Nothing."

Frances resigned herself to the inevitable. "Well, let's go now, and get it over."

Richard finished his beer slowly. It was a good thing that one of them was having fun, thought Frances. Then she began to wonder. She had been in such a constant depression ever since they had arrived in Nürnberg. It was as if Gibbon's idea of the Middle Ages had interpreted itself here in the tortuous streets, the thick walls, the narrow crowding houses. A triumph of religion and barbarism.

"Well?" said Richard.

"I thought I liked Gothic."

"You like it spiritual and aspiring, my sweet."

"Perhaps it is that. Tell me, Richard, was Gibbon ever in Nürnberg?"

Richard laughed suddenly. Curious faces turned to look at them. They waited until the interest had subsided, and then they left.

"We must take a No. 2 tram, but God knows in which direction," said Richard.

"Going east or west?"

"Roughly east."

"Then it's this side."

A tramcar was approaching; there was no time for any argument. He followed Frances aboard with some misgivings, and then watched her trying to appear oblivious as the conductor agreed that they would be driven along the Marienstrasse.

"On a moor, or a hill or some place like that," said Richard, "but in a strange muddled-up town ... It's quite beyond me how you know these things."

Frances relented. "I cannot tell a lie, darling. You saw the Lorenz Church?"

"Well, yes. We were just beside it."

"Well what way does a church point?"

"East, of course. . . . Upon my Sam." He grinned. "You know, Frances, just at the stage when a man thinks women have no brains, they confound him by some low cunning like that. Go on, have your laugh. You deserve it."

As they approached the Marientor, he pressed her hand.

"Keep your eyes open," was all he said. Frances remembered the name he had told her last night. They sat in silence, watching the shops and business houses, as the lumbering tramcar clanked its slow way along the Marienstrasse. They were now in the newer part of the town—the street was broader, and the names on the shops were less easy to see. Frances guessed that Richard had the idea that Fugger might be the name of some business; it was the one chance. For if there had been no Fugger of Marienstrasse in the telephone directory, then the only other way to find Mr. Fugger was either to make enquiries at the post office, which would be dangerously stupid, or to explore the Marienstrasse themselves. There must be a name to see, somewhere, or else no one could possibly get in touch with the retiring Mr. Fugger.

The tram had come to the end of the Marienstrasse. They had seen nothing which could help them.

"We'll have to walk. Sorry, Fran; you must be tired." They got off the car at the next stop, and started back towards their street.

"We'll try this side again," said Richard, and took Frances' arm. They walked slowly along, and covered two thirds of the street. Then Frances suddenly felt Richard's hand tighten. They stopped, as they had done at half a dozen other points

in the street. It was a small book-seller's shop with a narrow
window space and doorway, completely overshadowed by the
larger, more prosperous buildings on either side. They looked
at the books displayed in the window. They were mostly
curiosities, with the title pages open to show the brown spots
of age. There were also some music books. One, a collection
of songs, was lying open.

"Very interesting," Richard said, and they walked on. He
hoped Frances wouldn't look at the sign above the window.
She didn't. It was of no help, anyway. It merely said BUCH-
HANDLUNG in faded letters; but above the door had been small,
neat, white lettering: A. FUGGER.

CHAPTER VIII

A. Fugger

NEXT morning they left their hotel at half-past nine, and began their search through the bookshops of Nürnberg. Richard wanted a certain collection of early German lyrics. The two bookshops which they first tried were very modern; they specialized in books with streamlined printing and magnificent photographs, or in imposing editions of carefully selected authors. In the second shop, the assistant shook his head decisively. The only place they would be likely to find such a book might be in the smaller, secondhand dealers'. They thanked him, and walked towards the Marienstrasse. It was just eleven o'clock as they reached the small bookshop with the brown-spotted title pages displayed in the window. Richard noted that the books had been changed since yesterday, except for the collection of old songs, and that it had been moved to another corner of the window.

Inside the shop, there was the sleepy, dusty feeling which its outside had promised. The bookshelves ran ceiling height around the walls, and there were books overflowing onto the two large tables which crowded the narrow room.

At a corner of one table, a girl with glasses was working with scissors and paste. She had a white face, and dull blue eyes, and her hair was tightened back so ruthlessly that it hurt Frances to look at it. She looked up expectantly as the door creaked shut behind them. Frances had the feeling that the girl was disappointed. She left her work reluctantly, and came forward with no smile on her pale lips. No, she didn't think they had any such edition. She had never heard of it. As she made out that they were foreigners, she asserted her knowledge still more: she was sure, absolutely sure that such an edition did not exist. She neither offered to verify it from any catalogue, nor moved over to the poetry section to find anything else which might interest Richard. He exchanged glances with Frances, and then he searched in one of his pockets and brought out a small clipping. He handed it to the girl.

"The edition does exist," he said, as politely as he could. "Teubner printed it in Leipzig in 1836."

The girl took the sheet of paper, and held it without looking at it. The truth is, thought Frances, she doesn't want us here at all.

Richard raised his voice. "Is there anyone here, then, who *does* know about German lyric poetry?" The girl's face was still expressionless, but her eyes shifted for one moment to a door in the back wall of the shop.

"We haven't got it," she said.

"I'm sorry," said Richard. Frances knew by the cold edge in his voice that he was angry. She moved over to the pile of books on the nearest table, and lifted a volume. If it came to a test of endurance, she was determined to outlast the girl.

"Music, here," she said with charming surprise. She kept her voice as lighthearted as she could, and gave the silent girl a dazzling smile.

"You don't mind if I look through these? Thank you so much." Without waiting for an answer, Frances proceeded to blacken her white gloves on the dusty covers.

The door at the back of the shop opened. A short, stout man entered. He was in his shirt sleeves, and mopped his brow with a handkerchief. He had shut the door behind him, but not before Richard had smelled something singeing, something burning. Paper, could it be?

The small man looked at the girl in some irritation as he said, "I thought I heard customers." He turned his back on her abruptly and listened to Richard's questions. The girl picked up her scissors again, and went on with her work, but Frances noticed that she made only a pretense of being busy.

The bookseller was interested. "That was a very fine collection," he said. "I had a copy at one time, but I believe it was bought. Over here I have some of the older editions of lyrics; I've so many books I sometimes forget what I have." He pointed to the farthest bookshelves. His eyes were fixed for a few moments on the red rose of Frances' hat.

She said, "I am very interested in some of these old song collections." She waved her hand towards the music table. The bookseller looked at her gloves in dismay.

"But the books are filthy," he cried. "Ottilie, where is the duster?" Ottilie mumbled something about the next room.

"Get it then," he said sharply. Ottilie went reluctantly towards the back door.

"Helpful creature," said Richard, more to himself than to the others. Frances had already picked up a large green volume, which she had noted particularly. Songs of All Nations read the fading gold letters. She turned quickly to the page which the index had numbered. She smiled to the bookseller.

"You are very kind," she said, and smoothed down the page with the back of her hand. She held the book flat on the table so that both men could see the song title clearly. The bookseller's eyes flickered as they read "My love is like a red, red rose" (*translated from the English*). And then he smiled gently, his round fat face creasing with genial puckers. He mopped his brow again, and Frances closed the book carefully. She had just replaced it exactly when Ottilie was with them again. She had come back very quickly indeed, for such a slow-moving person. She shook her head disapprovingly over the soiled gloves.

She actually spoke. "It would have been better to take off your gloves," she said.

"But my hands would have become dirty."

"It is easier to wash hands than gloves."

"But I couldn't put my gloves on again, over dirty hands," explained Frances gently. Ottilie shrugged her shoulders, and then suddenly became aware of the fact that the two men had gone to the far corner of the room. Frances hardheartedly pointed out a book to dust. It was a curiosity on early Church music.

"Do you like to sing?"

The girl said, "Sometimes." She looked as if she were going to follow the men.

"Do you like Mozart or do you prefer Wagner?" Frances continued relentlessly.

"Wagner." If eyes could poison, I am already writhing on the ground, thought Frances.

At that moment, the bookseller was shaking his head sadly. His voice was clearer. "No, I am afraid it's gone. Ottilie, do you remember a small book bound in red calf which I bought from Professor Wirt?" Ottilie shook her head too; she made a movement as if to go over to where the men stood.

"Have you got any editions of *Lieder* for a soprano voice?" cut in Frances with her disarming smile. Ottilie threw one last glance at the bookseller. The words "edition," "Leipzig," "difficulty" reached them. It sounded the usual business talk. Ottilie searched for the songs. Despite the foreigner's smile, there was a certain firmness in her tone of voice. Ottilie knew that type of customer. The quickest way to get rid of them was to find what they asked for; they knew what they wanted. If only she had recognized the type when they entered the shop, they would have been away by this time. But they had seemed easy to deal with, judging from their appearances. She found two editions, and watched Frances look through the contents with interest. Her last suspicion melted as the men came back to the table.

Richard addressed Frances. He spoke in English, carefully, noting the sudden gleam of concentration in Ottilie's eyes. He chose simple words, which would be understood by anyone who had had English at school.

"He cannot find the book. He must order it from Leipzig. Perhaps it may not be there. It may take time to find it elsewhere. It is a pity."

Frances recovered herself, and said gravely and just as clearly, "I am sorry. Perhaps we should go to another bookshop." She was enjoying herself immensely.

Richard returned to German. "My wife suggests another shop. Would you be so good as to advise us?" The bookseller smiled benignly. He dictated two addresses to Ottilie, who wrote them down, and Richard put the slip of paper in his pocket.

"If you cannot find it," the bookseller said, "then come and see us again. If I am not here, then Ottilie will take the order." He was looking speculatively over Frances' shoulder, out into the street. "Good day," he added suddenly, and walked with quick short steps to the back room.

The abrupt ending startled Richard. He saw a look of warning in his wife's eyes. She had either noticed or felt something. As Ottilie wrapped one of the songbooks for Frances, they made their way to a bookcase near the door. Richard observed that the girl was glancing at her wrist watch, that she was taking little interest in tying up the parcel. As Richard handed her the money, she seemed as if she were not even counting it. . . . And then the front door swung open. It opened with such terrific violence that the hinges shrieked a protest which made Frances jump.

Three large men strode in, nearly upsetting Ottilie. Richard could have sworn that there was almost an approach to a smile on her face. She gestured quietly towards the back door. The three men strode on. Their boots hypnotized Frances. They moved as if they belonged to the same body. They drew their revolvers. The leader turned the handle of the door, and then kicked it open. But there were no shots, no voices. Frances found herself breathing again.

She looked with just sufficient amazement at the girl. "What's wrong?" she asked. "Burglars?" The girl gave her first real smile. Frances watched its contempt and was satisfied.

The men filed out of the back room. Their self-assurance was replaced by bad temper.

"Where is he?" the leader snapped. The girl's smile faded. Contempt gave way to fear.

"He went in there." She pointed to the back room. "There is no way out."

"There is a window, fool. Who are these?" He nodded towards Frances and Richard.

"Customers." The girl was sullen in her disappointment.

"What is your name? What do you want here?" He fired questions at Richard.

Richard looked surprised, and then let the right tone of slight annoyance creep into his voice as he answered. Frances registered appropriate amazement but she left everything to Richard. This was his show, and he was doing remarkably well as the innocent bystander. He was explaining at some length that they had tried two other bookshops and had failed in their search for this book; that they had been directed to the smaller secondhand dealers; that the book was still unfound; that the assistant in this shop had been good enough to write down the names of two other shops where . . . He at last found the slip of paper with Ottilie's sharply pointed script, and handed it to the leader of the men. Ottilie, on the verge of tears, verified the statement. It suddenly dawned on Frances that A. Fugger was gaining some very valuable minutes. It seemed to dawn on the leader

too, or perhaps his first suspicions were fading. He impatiently interrupted Richard's description of the book.

"I shall leave this man with you to get further particulars.
I have work to do." He stepped back, brought his heels
sharply together, and raised his arm. He barked out his war
cry. Now we're sunk, thought Frances. She saw Richard
stiffen slightly, and then relax again as he gave an inclination
of his head and said, "Good day."

The German trooper raised his voice. "I gave you our
German greeting!"

"And I gave you our English one." Richard's voice was
very quiet. "That is only politeness."

At the word *politeness*, the German looked searchingly at
Richard, and then at Frances. They held their expressions,
and returned look for look. There was a moment's tension,
and then the two uniforms had marched away, leaving the
third to produce a notebook and pencil. It was a good sign
that they hadn't been taken to some kind of police station,
thought Frances, and touched the wooden table.

It was all over in ten minutes. The Nazi snapped his book
shut. They all made such businesslike gestures, thought Richard irritably. Did it really prove greater efficiency to walk
with a resounding tread, to open doors by practically
throwing them off their hinges, to shut an insignificant notebook with an imitation thunder clap? Probably not at all,
but—and here was the value of it—it made you look, and
therefore feel, more efficient. The appearance of efficiency
could terrify others into thinking you were dynamic and
powerful. But strip you of all the melodrama of uniforms and
gestures, of detailed régime worked out to the nth degree, of
supervison and parrot phrases and party clichés, and then
real efficiency could be properly judged. It would be judged
by your self-discipline, your individual intelligence, your mental and emotional balance, your grasp of the true essentials
based on your breadth of mind and depth of thought. Richard studied the young man opposite him. Viewed dispas-
sionately, he was tall and thin; he was already going bald; his
chin was weak despite the posed pout of the lips; but whatever strength his chin lacked, his eyes with their intense stare
sought to gain. It was a pity the effect was so like that of a
goldfish.

"That is all," the Nazi said. "We shall find you at the hotel if there is anything else we need to know."

Frances leaned over the table and fixed him with wide-open, innocent eyes. "Why?" she asked gently.

"Why?"

"Yes. Why? We are English visitors, we visit your book-shops, we buy a book, and then you ask us questions and questions because the man who owned this shop was a burglar."

"A burglar?"

"Well, don't tell me he was a *murderer!*" Frances was shocked. The trooper looked perplexed.

"I mean," explained Frances as if to a child, "in England the police come to arrest a man if he is suspected of a crime like theft or murder."

The man exchanged a look of amusement with Ottilie. Then he said stiffly, "This is not England, thank God."

"Quite," said Richard.

Frances was keeping her jaw clenched; keep me from laughing out loud, she prayed, especially when it comes. It came. The arm shot out, the heels clicked, the magic words were invoked. The Myles' bowed and said "Good day," gravely.

When they left A. Fugger's bookshop, Ottilie had again picked up her sicissors and was bending over the table.

"Charming wench," said Richard. "One of the higher types, I suppose, of Nordic womanhood."

Frances had her own private joke. "No one told her to stop her work, and so she goes on. How long will it take before she realizes that she is already out of a job? Richard, if ever a sailor needed grog, that sailor's me."

They walked back to the old town at a medium pace. They didn't see anyone following them, but probably someone would. Richard, continuing his role of the wandering scholar, discovered another small bookshop with much secondhand material. The assistant, a pleasant young man with really gentle manners—Frances sat on a chair and watched him with a mixture of pleasure and relief—promised to make enquiries for the book, after Richard had spent half an hour in the poetry section. He bade them good morning like a human being. In fact, thought Frances, he is the first really obviously human being I've met since I arrived here.

When they got to their hotel, Frances went upstairs to change her gloves. Richard sat in the entrance hall and looked through a Nürnberg paper. It seemed as if the inhuman Poles and the wicked Jews were behaving with abominable, not-to-be-tolerated cruelty to the Germans who were living in Poland. The editorial worked itself up into a fine lather. It made crude reading. By the time Frances came downstairs, he was very bored. It was not only crude, it was an insult to intelligence.

He looked at Frances, and was instantly aware that something had happened. The look she gave him was too intense. She surprised him by suddenly standing on her toes and kissing him; but it brought her close enough to him so that he could hear the word "Searched," spoken with motionless lips. So they had taken advantage of their slow return to the hotel, as he had hoped they might. He returned her kiss and said, "Good."

Frances saw the American, whose foot she had mutilated yesterday morning, halt in amazement. On an impulse, she smiled to him. He reddened as he raised his hat and turned hastily away. Perhaps he didn't like to be found looking quite so amazed.

"Let's eat," she suggested. "I'm ravenous. Only, not a sausage place." She shuddered. Last night's dinner had been at one of the sausage showplaces, small and amusing, except that the whole menu was devoted to sausage. It was strange how her mind, as well as her stomach, rebelled when the choice was sausage or sausage or sausage.

"I'd like an omelet, and not one with apricot jam in it either, and fruit, and some hock, and coffee such as it is," she decided.

"I must say that for someone who comes from England you are pretty snooty about coffee."

"Well, it is even worse than ours, and that's something."

They found a restaurant near at hand, where they had their late lunch. They ate it leisurely, and sat smoking their cigarettes long after Richard had paid the bill. The room had emptied, much to the annoyance of two uniformed men who were seated in one corner. As Richard said, it made things look a bit too obvious. The men may have come to the same conclusion. At any rate, they rose at last with bad grace, and on their way out clumped past the table where Frances and

Richard sat. Richard had a Baedeker opened in front of him—lying between his elbows as he leaned forward to light his fifth cigarette. As the men passed, he looked up and spoke. Would they be so good as to help him? He and his wife were strangers, and wondered if it were possible to explore the charms of Dutzendteich this afternoon, or would it be better to make a day's excursion? The men were obviously at a loss for words. One said yes, the other said no, and then they both left the table.

"Well, it might be better to see the Burg this afternoon, after all," said Richard. Even if the men couldn't understand any English, at least the clearly spoken *Burg* would stick.

Frances watched their progress to the door. "They are phoning," she reported.

"Time to leave," said Richard, and tucked the Baedeker prominently under his arm. They walked quickly to the door, past the man at the public telephone and his worried companion. Frances gave him a sweet smile. She felt suddenly generous.

They entered a tramcar, at the Königstor, which carried them westwards and then northwards round the whole town. The heat was intense. Frances was glad of the open windows of the tram, which, as it moved, gave at least the impression of a breeze. They skirted the thick walls and their broad dry moat, and at last reached the Castle. There were a number of visitors to the Burg. Frances and Richard mixed casually with them and made a leisurely tour of the grounds. They didn't look back once. Richard said it would make whoever was following them in whatever uniform happier. It would have been discouraging for them really if Frances had insisted on carrying out her idea of looking back every hundred yards, smiling broadly and waving a cheery hand. . . . And Richard didn't really mind being followed in this way. They had nothing to hide . . . now. He added to himself, if A. Fugger made it, that is.

Richard had left the Five-Cornered tower to the last. He had a feeling that Frances might discover another allergy there. It was full of frightfulness, he remembered.

"Are you sure you really want to see this— It is rather monotonous, you know—" he asked as they reached the doorway. "There's no law compelling us to go in."

Frances looked surprised. "Why not? It's only an old

prison tower with a torture chamber. I've been to the Tower
of London, and the Conciergerie ..."

Richard shook his head doubtfully. "This one could teach
those places a thing or two." But he had only piqued her
interest. Frances had already entered. Richard bought the
tickets, and followed, with a shrug of his shoulders.

He had been right, after all, but Frances wouldn't admit it
at first. Halfway through the tour of the long rooms, she
began to move more quickly as the exhibits became more
diabolic. Her eyes viewed unbelievingly the directions for
extracting the greatest amount of pain which were hung on
the wall above each instrument of torture. They were printed
in black-letter for the most part, and were complete with
diagrams, in case the minute detail of text wasn't sufficiently
clear to ensure the fullest effects.

She suddenly spoke. "The cold-blooded beasts." Her voice
was a mixture of incredulity and disgust. A tall young man,
standing morosely before an intricate object of spiked iron,
whose function had been to pierce and tear and burn all at
the same time, turned as he heard her voice. There was an
expression of fellow-feeling on his face, followed by a look of
recognition. Frances, whose remarks had been for home
consumption, stopped in embarrassment. The man looked as
if he would speak, and then didn't. Frances felt he was
leaving it to her.

"How's your foot?" she asked. "I'm really sorry, and I
assure you it isn't a habit of mine."

"That's all right." His face relaxed, but he still didn't smile
with any enthusiasm. "Enjoying this?" he added, with just the
right note in his voice.

Richard grinned; he liked this man. "They made it quite an
art, didn't they? The pages from the *Torturer's Handbook*
are peculiarly thorough," he said, and won a smile from the
American. Something caught the man's eye at the other end
of the room, and a slight frown appeared; but it was gone so
suddenly that Frances wondered if she was beginning to
imagine things. She looked carelessly in the same direction.
There were two uniformed men, who seemed to be interested
in them rather than in the exhibits. She let her eyes pass
through them, then over them, and then on to a German
family who were arguing over one of the printed directions
with naïve interest.

"Is there much more of this?" she asked.

The man said, "Piles of the stuff. I've just taken a look into the tower place and gotten a cold welcome from the Iron Maiden. There are several models of her."

"She would seem mild after these. At least she would kill you, and not turn you into a piece of gibbering flesh," said Frances. She turned to Richard. "You win. I thought I could manage historical objectivity. After all, I was brought up on Foxe's *Book of Martyrs* . . . But where's the way out?"

The American smiled. "It's past the tower dungeons. You can't escape them."

Frances looked at him. "You are in league with my husband. Our name is Myles, by the way. Would you come and have something to drink? I'm parched."

The American gravely acknowledged that he was parched too, and he knew of a good beer place just down the hill. They left the Five-Cornered Tower, to the amazement of the man on duty at the exit door, who pointed out to them that they had only seen half of the display. Outside, it was pleasant to feel the warm sunshine, and see the green trees and ordinary people looking neither efficient nor thorough. And then a detachment of troopers marched past them; actually, they were only a group of men going to some meeting, but they had chosen to march in military formation. Their faces were expressionless under their uniform caps. Frances felt her depression return. Men who marched like that, who dressed like that, whose faces held the blankness of concentration and dedication, were a menace, a menace all the more desperate because of the hidden threat.

"You are looking very solemn," said the American.

"I was thinking of icebergs. You know, one tenth above to impress you, and the rest beneath to terrify you."

"*If* you know the peculiarity of icebergs," said the American, with a quick glance at Frances. "There are still plenty of people who think there's very little of them under the water. But why did you come to Germany this year? I haven't met any English here so far. At first I thought you might be here to worship at the shrine, but you seem to have the wrong reactions for that."

Richard answered that. "Oh, the usual inquisitiveness. We wanted to see for ourselves. We haven't been in Germany proper since the new era got well under way. We thought this might be our last chance."

They had reached the Rathaus-Keller, and the American hadn't any opportunity for further questions until they were settled at a table, and beer was ordered for the men— Frances insisted on tea. She noted that her order gave the American some delight, although he really was very polite about trying to hide his amusement. I suppose I ought to play true to form, she thought, to keep up the national character. She had begun well with the big-footed note when she had trampled on him yesterday, and tea in the afternoon was another authentic touch; tonight, she really ought to ask him to dine with them, and wear a dinner dress. Only, Richard and she never traveled with dinner clothes; it would be such a pity to disappoint him. However, the American seemed less amused, and more convinced, when two hot cups of tea had produced more visible coolness than his two steins of beer. Frances caught his eye.

"There's method in our madness," she suggested, and noticed he looked a little disturbed, as if he had been found impolite. It was difficult talking to someone who didn't know you, especially when you both had a common language and thought that that made everything easy. There was always the chance that your words would be taken to mean too little, or too much. That was what made all the English-speaking peoples so damned touchy with each other. Someone who spoke a foreign language had more allowances made for him.

"By the way, we don't know your name, yet," Frances said. "We can't go on just calling you 'the American.' " The man smiled. Thank goodness, thought Frances, he gave up the idea that I was trying to reprimand him. He was searching in his pocketbook for a card.

"This makes it easier," he said. He was, they read, HENRY M. VAN CORTLANDT from High Tor, New York. He was, he said, a newspaperman, originally working in New York City, but now on an assignment in Europe looking for symptoms.

"War?" asked Richard.

"Well, perhaps that. What do you think?"

Frances looked at the well-cut features opposite her, and the well-brushed fair hair. The jaw was determined; the slightly drawn eyebrows gave a certain intensity. You would hardly notice the color of his eyes; it was as if the other features of his face overshadowed them. His skin was tanned—if it hadn't been tanned it might have seemed pale, even sallow. He had gone on talking without waiting for Richard's reply, and he talked well, with a fluency which showed he had either thought about his subject a lot or had already argued it into a neat pattern. As he talked, he smiled a good deal, showing very white, even teeth; but in repose, his mouth looked firm, even tight-lipped. Frances watched him as she listened to the well-tailored phrases. A very direct, a very controlled and a very impulsive young man.

"But surely you never took Munich seriously?" he was asking Richard.

And a rather disbelieving one, too, it seemed.

Frances spoke. "We were still at the stage of taking anything seriously or at the least hoping we could take it seriously, as long as the magic word of peace could be spoken. Until this spring. The march into Prague ended that coma."

Van Cortlandt shook his head. "Well, we never thought that in America."

"You mean you think we have been playing a kind of game? That we shall go on playing it, as long as we can keep ourselves out of war?"

"Well, if you put it so frankly, yes."

Frances leaned forward on her elbows. "Your President doesn't think so. I hear you've been calling him a warmonger because he really knows what's going on in Europe."

"Nice weather we've been having," suggested Richard. "Warm, though."

The American went on: "But Britian's policy for the last years ..."

"I know," said Frances. "In America it is called isolationism, freedom from foreign entanglements, unwillingness to die on foreign fields. We've been trying all that. It hasn't worked. We admit it ... we've come out of the ether ..."

"And you're telling me that Britain is going to take off its nice clean coat and get its nose all bloodied up in defending Poland? What would you get out of it anyway?"

"A country fights for two main things, either for loot or for survival. We'll fight along with our friends for survival. The Axis is after loot. If Poland, or any other country, is attacked, then it is the signal for any nation who doesn't want to become a part of Germany to rouse itself. It may be the last chance."

Van Cortlandt smiled comfortingly. "Don't worry. I don't think you'll find your country at war. Your politicians will always see plenty of other chances."

"That's my main point. The politicians won't dare. The people are aroused now."

Van Cortlandt still looked unconvinced. "Well, that's a new one to me. We have some pretty swell news-hounds, and they nearly all scent out more appeasement."

"Their sense of smell has led them to the wrong lamp post this time. They will look very funny there, when the trouble starts."

"I tried the weather," said Richard, "and that wasn't much good. I think we'd be better talking about something else, for neither of you is convincing the other in the slightest, and we'll know soon enough which of you was nearer the truth. As Count Smorltork said to Mr. Pickwick, 'The word poltic surprises by himself.' Anyway, I have the unpleasant but increasing conviction that all of us who argue so much would be wiser if we learned to make aeroplanes or shoot a machine gun. That's only my academic point of view, of course. But that seems the only answer for certain people."

He nodded to a group of men in brown shirts at another table. "Now what about dinner?" he added.

Van Cortlandt rose. "Sorry, I've got to see a man."

Richard rose too. "We are sorry too. We shall see you again soon, sometime, I hope."

"Yes." The American's voice didn't seem overjoyed at the prospect. "Thanks for the beer. Good-by."

Frances looked after him sadly. "He really was so nice, you know, before he got caught up in his theories. I suppose if your country is three thousand or whatever it is miles away you can afford the luxury of pros and cons. I think you punctured him, someplace, Richard. He's probably saying we are one of the 'bloody English' at this moment."

"Nonsense. He handed criticism out. If you do that, you have also got to expect to take it. Anyway, hairsplittings are really becoming so very out of date. The time for theories is really past. But keep off politics, after this, Frances, even if you feel you have got something approaching an answer.

What do you say about something to eat, and then a movie, and then bed?"

Frances nodded her approval. There was much she wanted to know about A. Fugger. She stopped worrying about van Cortlandt and began thinking of the little man who had walked with quick short steps into that back room. Had he got away? Could it be that the Nazis were already picking out each agent in the chain, or was A. Fugger wanted on another charge? They would find out, one way or another, but it would be unpleasant waiting.

Richard had looked round the large room. At a discreet distance, the two men who had visited the Five-Cornered Tower that afternoon were sitting at a table. They had become hungry, it seemed, and had just ordered food. Richard waited until the steaming plates were put in front of them, until they had taken their first mouthful.

"Now's the time, Frances." She abandoned A. Fugger, and followed her husband quickly to the door. He seemed amused about something. As they left the room, he turned back to see the two men rising angrily to their feet.

"Would you mind, Frances, if we went to the flicks first of all, and then ate when we came out? I think that would be an idea." Frances saw the gleam in his eye. There was a joke somewhere.

So they went to a picture house. After fifteen minutes, Richard decided he couldn't see through the large woman in front of them, so they moved quietly to different seats, behind their original places. Richard's joke seemed to be getting better and better.

As he explained to Frances in bed that night, "They were hungry and when we landed in the cinema, they might have gone out in relays for their dinner. Then we moved our seats, and they didn't notice it at first. It was pretty dark, you know. We were just sitting down behind them when they noticed we were no longer in our first seats. That was really funny. It was easy for them to find us again, as the place was almost empty, but for five minutes they had quite a bad time of it. That probably decided them to stay together, standing at the back of the theater in case we changed our minds again. I could feel them getting hungrier."

"Why didn't we lose them when we had the chance?"

"And make them realize that we disliked being followed?

They'd interpret that as a guilty conscience. Better pretend that it seems very harmless and amusing, the kind of silly adventure which you like to tell your friends about when you get home."

But about A. Fugger he wouldn't say anything.

"The less you know from now on, the better for you, my sweet." And that was that.

It was Frances who lay awake tonight. She thought of the bookseller; of the tall American who had either been offended, or bored; of the constant rhythm of marching boots. When she fell asleep her thoughts were still with her, and chased her through the Five-Cornered Tower. Richard was beside her, for she spoke to him and heard him answer, but she couldn't see him. A. Fugger was there trying to show her the way out, but he spoke in a strange language and she kept straining to understand it. The American was there too, observing everything, but contenting himself with a sad smile when she took the wrong turning. It must have been the wrong turning although it had seemed the only right one, because then there was no way out, and she was looking at the Iron Maiden, and the face was that of the girl Ottilie, and the hands were real. The fingernails were long and pointed, and they were colored blood-red.

CHAPTER IX

Nürnberg Incident

RICHARD watched Frances closely, next morning. She had drunk several cups of tea and smoked three cigarettes. He kept silent about last night. Whatever had disturbed her sleep would gradually lose its detail and, if he didn't emphasize it by referring to it, it might lose its importance and merge into the vagueness of dreams that are past. He thought of something to do which would be interesting without being exciting. They would have to spend at least one more day in this place, perhaps even two or three if it seemed a good thing to do.

He made his voice as normal as possible. "What about the Germanic Museum today? It should be innocuous, and you'll like the costume section. If you ever do more designing in Oxford, you may find some good ideas there. Better take your notebook and pencil."

Frances nodded absently; she was wondering when they might leave Nürnberg and where they would have to go. . . . And there was always the thought whether A. Fugger had escaped. If he had been caught, there would be, no doubt, some ingenious way of trying to make him talk. And yet, did any trusted agent, such as he must have been, ever talk? Weren't they chosen for their capacity to keep silent even under the greatest persuasion? But then, they were human beings too. Somehow, her notebook and designs for Oxford dramatics seemed very remote this morning. Richard's voice had been light, but the slight emphasis with which he clipped his words proved that he was not as carefree as he would have her believe. She decided wisely not to pester him with questions about their plans. He was probably completing them now.

The silence in which they traveled to the Museum bolstered up this idea in Frances' mind. Their two watchdogs

attached themselves at a reasonable distance. It seemed as if
it it didn't matter if they were noticeable. Frances thought
this over. They had been so very obviously under watchful
eyes, and their room had been so very obviously searched.
She came to the conclusion that this might be especially
subtle technique. Perhaps Richard and she were to feel perse-
cuted, intimidated, very much in the power of a mighty
secret police. The very cold-bloodedness of this cat-and-
mouse game was to make them leave Germany if they really
were only harmless tourists. If they were less innocent than
they seemed, then they might be trapped into making a
mistake. As for the mistake which they might make . . .
Frances couldn't think of any agent trying to get in touch
with one of his men at this stage. He would be liable to lie
low, and he would most certainly try to lose the men who
were trailing him. That might be it: if they were guilty, they
might make clever efforts to free themselves from their two
shadows. It was the natural reaction of any secret agent to
outwit the other fellow. That indeed could be their mistake.
She began to understand just how intelligent Richard had
been last night, when he hadn't left the picture house.

But one thing still needed explaining. If the Nazis thought
they were worth terrifying or trapping, they would surely not
let them wander about for the next few days without some
real shadow trailing them—someone, Frances began to believe, who would do his job very efficiently and secretly,
someone who would keep on the job after the two men had
been eluded. The more she thought of this, the more convincing she found it. It never paid to underestimate your op-
ponents. Better credit them with too much than too little.

She looked at Richard. She became surer that he had
guessed this too: yesterday he had taken such care not to
lose the uniformed men. As they crossed the broad Sterntor,
and found themselves momentarily isolated from people,
Frances spoke for the first time.

She said, "They aren't the only ones." It was half a
question.

Richard squeezed her arm affectionately. "Right you are.
Too obvious." That confirmed her guess why they hadn't
slipped out of the cinema last night, instead of innocently
changing seats. One thing gave her some amusement: it
looked as if the two stooges didn't know of a third man

themselves. Otherwise they wouldn't have swollen their ankles, standing hungrily at the back of the picture house. They could have relaxed, depending on their accomplice, if they had known about him.

They were in the Museum until it closed at four o'clock. After that, all Frances asked was to be allowed to sit somewhere for a long long time, with something cool and liquid on the table before her—in the open air, if it could be managed. Richard arranged it, by taking her to a near-by restaurant where there was both a garden for Frances and beer for himself.

He looked thoughtfully at her as they sat in the coolness of the trees.

"I think the city heat is too much for you, Frances," he said at last. "It might be better for us to leave Nürnberg and go nearer the mountains. There's a nice little resort south of Munich on the Starnberger See. There's good bathing there. Or if you wanted some climbing, we could go farther south into the Bavarian Alps." He hadn't taken the trouble to lower his voice. Frances wondered which person at the surrounding tables would be interested in all this. No doubt their bodyguard were draping themselves behind some concealing tree, but she had ceased to worry about them.

"I've quite enjoyed it here." *Like hell I have,* she added under her breath. "But I should like to see some real country views for a change. I find the pavements very hot. And yet, you have simply got to walk if you want to see any of these too too lovely buildings." The saccharine dripped over her words. Richard was leaning back in his chair, smiling pleasantly at his wife. His eyes were applauding her; his mind was keenly aware that the handsome woman, who sat two tables away from them, was watching the foam in her beer glass with great intentness. Or perhaps she always studied beer in that way. If the woman had been interested in their conversation, he had at least this comfort: she could have heard every word of it.

They both thought it a good idea to return to the hotel and rest before dinner. Frances thought she would lie down for half an hour, and read. Richard thought he'd like a bath. He left the bathroom door open and, as he cooled off in the tepid water, he could hear a page being turned. Once she laughed. He was happier about Frances. The Museum had been a good idea; there was nothing like a Museum for calming one's emotions. This game was simple enough, he thought, and cursed the latherless soap. This game was simple enough if you could convince yourself that you really were on holiday; that as long as you carried no unexplainable documents and neither received nor sent any, as long as you were an apparently harmless tourist, nothing could really touch you. You could give yourself away, of course. If you became flustered or lost your nerve because of the continual feeling of threat which hung over you, you might do something which was either stupid or too clever. Either of these actions would be a dangerous weakness. It was no good trying to pretend that a threat didn't exist. It did, all the time. What you must do was to ignore it: acknowledge it and ignore it. The only real danger points were those of the actual contact with an agent. If you were discovered at that moment, nothing on earth could help you. Well, the danger point in Nürnberg was past. It had passed when Fugger had spoken so softly that he had had to strain to hear him. He had been looking down at the title page of a book, and the bookseller was searching through some other volumes.

"It is better in Innsbruck at this time of year. The Gasthof Bozen, Herzog-Friedrich-Strasse 37, is recommended. The owner is called Hans, and will help you. He likes music and red roses as we all do."

That had been neatly sandwiched in between their discussion on editions and editors. He had the satisfactory feeling that A. Fugger had escaped. He was too wily a bird not to have had all his preparations made for just such a day as yesterday. It wouldn't have taken him long to get through a window and lose himself in the labyrinth of passages and small streets which lay behind the shop. There were plenty of rooms there to have rented as a hide-out, or as a place to change your identity. Or perhaps A. Fugger already had another neatly established identity practically next door to his bookshop. There was no limit to the ingenuity of a foresighted man with sufficient time to arrange things.

Suddenly, there was a firm, businesslike knock on the bedroom door. He heard Frances say "Come in."

It *might* be a maid: some excuse, any old excuse. From the bathroom, he could only see the windows of the bedroom and the heavy green brocade curtains. But in his mind's eye he could see Frances, dressed in that pink frilly thing of hers and lying on their bed, raise an enquiring eyebrow from the novel she had been reading.

He heard her say, "Yes, it is warm, isn't it? Please leave the towels on that chair. My husband is having a bath. Thank you. Good day." It was only when he heard the bedroom door close sharply that he realized he was sitting bolt upright in the bath, his muscles tensed. Frances had remained where she was on the bed; nor did she call through to him. Thank heavens for that. She must have had a fright when that knock came; it hadn't sounded like a maid. He got out of the bath quickly and made some pretense of whistling as he dried himself.

When he entered the bedroom, Frances was lying on the bed with her eyes fixed on the bathroom door, waiting for him. The novel lay as it must have dropped when the maid had left the room. He felt her force her voice to say naturally, "Hello, darling. Cooler now?"

He lay down beside her, and with his head close to hers on the pillow, she whispered, "The knock ... I thought he had been caught."

"Don't worry, Frances. I don't think he was. Please don't worry."

She was laughing softly, but it was a poor imitation of her laugh. It was becoming louder; her hands were cold.

"Snap out of it, Fran," he whispered. He slapped her jaw sharply. That helped. At least the laughing had stopped. He lay with his arm round her shoulders, quietening her with his firm grip.

"We'll leave here tomorrow," he said at last. "I'll get you to the mountains for some days."

Frances had recovered, and was looking rather ashamed of herself.

"Yes," she said, "I can always push someone over a precipice if there's any monkey business there."

Richard grinned. He was so unworried, so confident, thought Frances. It made her feel better just to look at him.

"That's the idea," he said.

After they had dressed, they went downstairs for dinner in the hotel. Frances had recovered completely. She had worn her smartest dress as a tonic, and the results were good. She

was amusing and gay, even over a not particularly good
dinner—German cooking was not at its best this summer.
Many of the people in the restaurant turned their heads to
watch the slender, fair-haired girl. She was easily the loveliest
woman in the place, thought Richard with justifiable pride.

"That rest did you good, Frances," was what he said.

Frances only referred once to that afternoon. "You
mustn't worry about me, Richard," she said. "I'll be all right
now. I am like that, you know. At college I used to get quite
panicky three weeks before the examinations were due. But
once I had got my worry over, I was always perfectly cool
when the examinations came. In fact, I used to enjoy them.
Sort of legitimate showing-off, you know, with no one to
reprimand you for being an exhibitionist. Well, I think it will
be the same when whatever is going to happen happens. I
was thinking about the war, particularly, Richard. The more
I see of Germany, the more I know that a showdown *must*
come, some day; and perhaps the sooner the better, before
they are all turned into robots. When I think of the children
leaving school each year, all of them carefully educated in
the Nazi way, I honestly shudder to think what the rest of
the world faces in ten years' time, if it waits. So don't worry
about me, or start regretting that you brought me. I'm just in
the process of adjusting myself between two very different
ways of life, between peace and war. Coming here was a
good idea after all: it reconciles you to the adjustment."

Richard knew Frances was right in her self-analysis—she
was like that—but his job right now was to see that her nerve
didn't crack before she had reached the cool, calm and
collected stage. That would probably come before the end of
this journey; at least, he hoped so. Her handicap was imagination. It was more difficult to face unpleasantness when you
had imagination. But, as she had said, coming here helped to
reconcile the adjustment. It also hastened it, thank heaven.

"I know," he said, and began some amusing suggestions
about what they could possibly be drinking.

"It's really only habit which makes me order coffee. A few
more days and I'll probably lose it," Frances said.

"It's extraordinary what people can swallow for the sake
of their beliefs. I heard of a practising surrealist who spent
many months eating his wardrobe."

"That sounds a good story," said a man's voice. Both Richard and Frances looked up in surprise.

"Hello, van Cortlandt. Glad to see you."

"May I come over here, for a while? I wanted to tell your wife . . ."

"I know," said Frances quickly. "I'm sorry I got so hot and bothered yesterday in that discussion. You know, it isn't easy for us to look at these things disinterestedly."

"And I came over here because I began to feel I might have seemed too darned callous. You see, I'm trying to look at things disinterestedly, and I'm finding that isn't easy, either."

"Well," said Richard, "now that we have all kissed and made friends, what will you have?" They all laughed, and van Cortlandt said he would have beer. Frances had a feeling that he disapproved of them somehow because they were English, and yet was surprised into liking them when they caught him off his guard.

"As a matter of fact," he was explaining, "I watched you being the only real human beings in a roomful of stuffed dummies, and I thought we were fools if we didn't get together. We may be a lot different, but we aren't just like—" He nodded over his shoulder in the direction of those concentrating on the mastication of specially chosen vitamins to build a specially chosen race.

"Zombies is, I believe, the technical term," suggested Richard. "Now would you really like to hear the story about the wardrobe?"

They talked for an hour, and then decided to have a moonlight walk. The bodyguard joined them outside the hotel, Richard noted. As Frances explained that they were probably leaving tomorrow for the mountains, he wondered just who had been watching them inside the hotel dining room. Not that it mattered, not now.

They didn't choose any particular way, but just followed any twisting street which would lead them to the banks of the Pegnitz. Away from the bigger streets, the lights were economically dim, but it seemed safe enough—even with the two men marching behind them at a discreet distance. In the narrower streets where there were so few people, the men were ludicrously obvious. Richard wondered if they never felt the ridiculousness of the whole thing. The American, after his first glance back at them, had ignored the two pairs of feet keeping time with such perfect precision. Later, Richard wondered why he never then questioned the American's lack of interest. Perhaps he was relieved that van Cortlandt appeared to think that this was only normal; it would have been difficult to pretend that they hadn't noticed a thing. At the time, he only felt grateful for van Cortlandt's tact. It was a little surprising in such a forthright, I'm-just-a-plain-man type of individual. Perhaps the American found that frankness could be a very useful front, just as many a Britisher found understatement a safe enough refuge.

Both van Cortlandt and Richard were in good form. They talked with a good deal of the fervour and conversational abandon which have an unexplained way of suddenly appearing between two strangers, as much to their own surprise and enjoyment as to that of their audience. Frances was very well content to be the audience. They had just cruelly dissected Gothic art, and were proceeding to rhapsodize over Baroque, when Frances clutched their arms, and they moved closer to her.

From the quiet blackness of the little alley to the left of them came a bitter cry, the high, self-strangling cry of fear or pain, or both. They looked at each other.

"And just what is that?" asked Richard quietly. He made as if to move into the alley. There was another cry. Frances felt her stomach turn, sickeningly. Van Cortlandt and Richard looked grimly at each other.

"You stay here with your wife. I'll investigate." The American had taken a step along with Richard into the alley.

"Halt!"

The abrupt command came from behind them. The two men had increased their pace to a run, as they had seen the foreigners become curious.

"Halt!"

Van Cortlandt and Richard stopped; they looked belligerently at the men. Frances came to the rescue.

"Something's wrong—a murder or something—down there."

The brown-shirted men exchanged looks.

"We advise you to take a walk," the older one said.

"But something is wrong," the American protested.

The trooper who was doing the speaking said, "We advise you to take a walk. It is only a Jews' Alley."

So that was it. Frances thought for one moment that van Cortlandt was going to jab his large, clenched fist right in the middle of that mock-pleasant smile. There was a minute's silence, broken only by a faint moaning. Frances turned abruptly and walked quickly away. The others followed, and they heard the Germans laugh at something one of them said. They were silent until they were almost at the hotel, and then van Cortlandt spoke.

"That's it," he said savagely. "Just as you are enjoying yourself and are thinking that life isn't so bad after all, you meet that. Blast them to hell."

"It's our last night here, thank heavens," Frances said.

"I've got to stay for two or three days more, and then I'll get the hell out of here. Austria's next. I'm working towards Vienna. I have enough material as it is, already, but I can't print half of it. The nice kind people in the other world would think I was a liar, or another sensationalist; and my boss would say I was sent out to report and not to do propaganda which would harm his organization."

"Is that considered at this date?" asked Frances.

"From the strictly business point of view, yes." Frances began to understand why newspapermen were cynics.

They were silent again. All the charm of the night had been broken. Hans Sachs had given way to the Iron Maiden. As they said good-by in the hotel lounge, van Cortlandt gave them his card, and wrote his New York business address on the back of it.

"That will always be able to tell you where I am supposed to be, anyway," he added, with the attractive smile which had quite won Frances yesterday. Yesterday, or was it weeks ago? They gave him their address in Oxford, and watched him write it down in his diary. Oxford, thought Frances, where the only scream in the dark came from the little Athenian screech owls. Firm handclasps—*they* were something friendly and honest, anyway.

"Tomorrow," Richard said firmly, as they went upstairs to their room, "tomorrow we leave."

CHAPTER X

Frau Köppler Recommends

EARLY next morning they left for Munich. It was a town they had both known well in the old days. Richard expected that they might be still under some kind of supervision, although their uniformed bodyguard had been left behind the walls of Nürnberg. So he chose the simplest things to do. In the afternoon they walked through the central streets, and for once he had no objections to window-shopping. In the evening they visited the Hofbräuhaus.

Frances was pathetically eager to watch the people, the same people she had seen each day when she had been an art student here in 1932. She seemed as if she were trying to read a riddle. Eventually, she gave it up.

She shook her head sadly. "I don't understand it, quite truthfully. There is something in the German soul or mind which baffles other races; there must be. On the surface, all they have got out of it is a new grandiose building here or there where they can listen to more speeches, and I can't think of anything more boring. And they have also got a lot of uniforms, and high-signs, and a firm military tread. But to all appearances, the shops aren't any better, the restaurants aren't any better, the food is worse, so are the theaters and the books. The clothes of the people do not look any more prosperous; and the trains always ran on time here, anyway."

"They have also got Austria and Czechoslovakia and lots of promises," suggested Richard.

"And concentration camps, and universities which are travesties, not to mention the hatred of three quarters of the world at least."

Richard began to wish it had not been necessary to enter Germany. He thought of the pleasant holiday they might have been having in Switzerland or in the French Alps, or in Ragusa. Some place where the things you saw didn't immediately start grim speculations . . . anywhere except this doomed country. That was what had depressed Frances so much, this feeling of doom which was apparent to the outside observer when he saw how blindly these people accepted their grand illusion. Richard felt as if he were watching passengers in a train whose engine crew were increasing speed, disregarding brakes, while the tracks in front were steep and twisting. Either the train would make the journey in record time, or they would end in horrible disaster. The strange thing, the terrifying thing, was to see the passengers accept the ominous swaying of the train along with the conductor's glib assurances; to watch them disregard the fate of the passengers who did raise some objections, even although they had once praised the intelligence of those they now abandoned so heartlessly. And the strangest thing about it all was the fact that all of these passengers—except the children, who were encouraged to stand at the window and cheer violently—all of them had been in a previous train wreck. No wonder Frances was depressed. She had always believed that men were intelligent animals.

If only the methods of hate and force had been resisted at the very beginning: not by other countries (for *that* would have been called the unwarranted interference of those who wanted to keep Germany weak), but by the people of Germany, themselves. But, of course, it had been more comfortable to concentrate on their own private lives instead of dying on barricades, if in the last extreme they had had to pit force against force. It was easier to turn a deaf ear to the cries from the concentration camps, to harden their hearts to the despair of the exiles, to soothe their conscience with praise of the Fatherland. And now, it had come to the stage where other peoples would have to do the dying, on barricades of shattered cities, to stop what should have been stopped seven years ago.

Frances spoke again. "I wonder where it will all end . . ."

"In the hall of the Gibichungs," Richard said bitterly, and with that he discarded the problem of the German mind.

On Sunday, the ninth of July, they arrived in Mittenwald. If Richard had been alone, he would have risked going straight on to Innsbruck, but with Frances beside him it was quite another matter. It was probably just as well that there was Frances, to keep him from taking chances which might lead to disaster. Some days in Mittenwald would help to smooth out any complications which might have begun in Nürnberg—and Frances needed the mountains. That was important to remember, with Innsbruck and whatever else lay ahead of them.

At first, Richard would only take her for a short ten-mile walk. "Your legs are out of training, and your feet need hardening," he insisted. The following day, they did fifteen miles. On the next, they included some climbing. By Thursday Frances could manage the Karwendel Peak without any trouble. It was on that day that Richard had begun to feel at ease again. The sense of being shadowed had gone, and Frances seemed as if she had successfully reached her past-worrying stage.

They had climbed steadily since eight o'clock, resting almost on top of the mountain to eat the sandwiches the hotel had provided that morning. They sat on the path, their legs hanging down over its edge as it dropped steeply away. Richard watched Frances open the thick hunks of bread, and extract the little grains of caraway from the slaps of soaplike cheese. She dropped them gravely one by one over the cliff, on whose edge she swung her tanned bare legs. Above the heavy-wool socks and the flat-heeled shoes, they looked like a schoolgirl's, thought Richard, with that attractive mixture of slenderness and strength. The light breeze ruffled her hair, which had curled round her brow with perspiration, and flapped her loose silk shirt. She had tied her cardigan round her neck by its sleeves. Her excavations for caraway over, she slapped the sandwich together, and took a lusty bite. Richard found himself smiling. There was something touchingly intent in her face as she looked at the Isar rolling rapidly far below them.

"It is lovely," she said quietly, "quite lovely. Look!" She pointed up the valley, with its green fields and winding ice-blue river. " 'God made the country, man made the town.' Pity man couldn't learn better."

"He is a messy imitator. He thinks complexity is a proof of progress."

They were silent, with their own reactions to the simplicity of the scene.

At last, when they had finished their lunch, Richard rose.

"Time to move," he said, and helped Frances to stand up on the narrow path. "Fifteen minutes to the top and then we shall see Austria."

"We have plenty of time," Frances said, looking at the sun. "It won't take long to come down."

Richard shook his head reproachfully. That was one thing he couldn't teach Frances; she couldn't resist coming down a mountain quickly. She would never make a real mountain climber. She was plucky enough, though. She was following him up the last difficult stretch to the top with no outward trouble, although inwardly she was probably cursing in despair. She hated going up a mountain just as much as she loved coming down.

As they regained their breath on the top of the peak, they faced the Austrian Alps, rising in rugged waves of gray stone, snow-streaked.

Richard pointed. "Over there lies Innsbruck. We'll go there tomorrow. We have been recommended by one of your school friends—Mary What-d'you-call-her—to stay at the Gasthof Bozen in Herzog-Friedrich-Strasse."

Frances nodded. "Mary Easton will do. She's now married to a man in Central Africa."

"That's remote enough," said Richard, and then changed the subject. Frances took her cue from him, and they began the descent in high spirits which lasted until they came into the little hotel in Mittenwald.

They had put up at the hotel where Richard had once stayed as an undergraduate on a reading party. In those peaceful days, there had been crowds of foreigners, mostly American or English. Tonight, as they sat in the half-empty restaurant, it was all so very different. The owner of the hotel, Frau Köppler, still sat in earnest conversation over a little table with her special friends. She still wore the long-skirted black day-dress which seemed to be part of her. On Richard's first visit there, that table had always been the subject of jokes by the people of Mittenwald who came in for their beer, or their game of *Skat*, or to dance and sing if there were an accordion or fiddle to accompany them. Richard looked towards the part of the restaurant which had been partitioned off for the local people. He remembered how shocked Frau Köppler had been when the undergraduates had preferred to drink their beer there, instead of in the

room she had arranged for her guests. Then one of the jokes
had been that she was pro-Nazi, and that she was plotting
with her special friends at her exclusive table. The joke was
increased for the laughing Bavarians because Frau Köppler
was a Northerner and they said she was going to Prussianize
them; and the word *verpreussen* had also come to have a
coarser meaning in the South. Now it seemed as if the joke
had become fact.

Richard wondered, as he watched Frances arrange the
pieces on the chessboard, whether Frau Köppler was as
happy as she thought she would be. The hotel certainly was
less flourishing: the only other foreigners in the room were
an Italian family who talked volubly and excitedly and tightened Frau Köppler's disapproving mouth. The prices for
German guests were much lower, and those tourists who
arrived in the middle of the day brought their own food with
them. It was an extraordinary sight to watch them open their
parcels of bread and sausages at the restaurant tables, ordering one glass of beer, clean plates and knives. Frances was
particularly shocked when she found that not even a tip was
left for the overworked waitresses.

Richard saw Frau Köppler look over to their table. He
pretended to be absorbed in the game of chess. They were no
longer shadowed, he felt, but it was noticeable that Frau
Köppler had taken quite a lot of interest in their movements.
It could very well be possible that such a strong Nazi as
herself might be asked to mark anything suspicious about
them. It was the kind of little job which she might enjoy
doing; it would add to her feeling of authority. As he waited
for Frances to attack with her knight, he wondered whether
that look predicted anything, protected his bishop with a
pawn, and waited. The music from the wireless set ceased. It
was a pity, thought Richard, that the sounds of frying could
not be eliminated instead of music with foreign or non-Aryan
influences. A man's voice began to speak, peremptory as on a
parade ground. As Frances ignored the pawn, and daringly
took his bishop, Frau Köppler rose to her feet, and walked
over to them.

Richard had risen to his feet too, taking the opportunity of
offering Frau Köppler a chair to warn Frances with his
eyes—and then the unseen voice ended its exhortations and
the music of a very rich band filled the room. Even as the

preliminary cymbals clashed they all knew what was coming.
Frances remained as she had been, and lit a cigarette. Frau
Köppler stood rigid beside the chair, looking straight ahead
of her into the wall of the room. Poor old Richard, thought
Frances, and watched him redden slightly. He couldn't sit
down as long as Frau Pushface was standing, and she knew
he wouldn't stand for that song. A hymn in glorification of a
well-known pimp, he had called it. Frances smoked uncon-
cernedly and watched the chessman fall from Richard's hand.
It rolled under another table, and by the time he had re-
trieved it, the chorus of the Horst Wessel song had ended and
the Munich time-signal tune was being played. Frau Köppler
sat down, bowing as she did so. Richard sat down too,
looking very polite and innocent.

"I hope I am not interrupting you," Frau Köppler began.
"Are you enjoying your holiday?"

They said yes, they were, Mittenwald was a most delightful place. Frances let Richard handle the greater part of the
conversation. She wasn't quite sure, to begin with, why they
were being honored with a visit. It wasn't very much like
Frau Köppler to unbend to any of her guests, particularly
foreigners. She was a tall woman, but she held herself so
erectly that she seemed taller than she was. Once she must
have had some beauty. Her features were still excellent, but
the yellow hair and blue eyes had faded, not in the soft and
kindly way which gives a certain charm to age, but bleakly.
Perhaps Frau Köppler would have thought such charm only
a sign of weakness; she probably preferred the appearance of
strength even to the point of hardness. She was, thought
Frances, a grim-looking creature. She had the foundation for
beauty, but the spirit was lacking. Even as she talked, she did
not relax. She gave a funny twist to the phrase *Behave
naturally*. Because Frau Pushface was behaving naturally,
although she could never be natural.

She turned to Frances. "I am glad you are enjoying yourself. It is good for people to travel in the new Germany.
There are many things we want to show them."

Frances looked quickly at Richard, and then back at Frau
Köppler. She couldn't think of an answer that wasn't impolite. She smiled, which was always a solution, even if a weak
one.

Frau Köppler hadn't expected an answer, for she went on,

"You speak German very well, very well indeed. No doubt you have visited our country before? Did you come to Mittenwald by chance, or were you recommended to come here? I am always interested in what brings people here."

The question was out. What a bore it must have been for her to bother to make conversation in the hope of disguising her curiosity, thought Frances. It was a pity, after all her trouble, that she did not know Richard, and so couldn't interpret his smile. He always looked like that when the game was being played his way. He was ready with his answer.

"The mountains," he said. "I enjoyed them so much when I stayed here some years ago that I wanted my wife to see them."

"You stayed here before?"

"Yes; at this hotel. It must have been almost eight years ago. It was in the off-season, at the very end of September. We stayed until we returned to England to our University."

"Ah, yes. I remember now. There were nine students and two very young professors." She must have known all the time and verified his name from the visitors' record. It would have been better if she hadn't mentioned it at all. It only angered Richard. He had given her the benefit of the doubt, and had thought she was a simple-minded woman doing what she thought was her duty. Now she was a simple-minded woman who enjoyed setting traps and catching people in them. It shed a new light on her position as uncrowned queen of the village. She would wield her political power in rather a mean way.

"Yes," he said. "It was what we call a reading party."

Frau Köppler's voice was just slightly less assured.

"Well," she said, her tone on the defensive, "you see for yourselves that we are just the same, only so much happier." Her voice was polite; it would have been friendly if the smile on the lips had been less fixed. Richard looked straight into the faded blue eyes which didn't smile at all. He said nothing. She looked at the large picture of the unhappy-looking man with the ridiculous mustache, which hung prominently on the wall.

She tried again. "Thanks be to our Leader. Do you not admire all he has done for us?"

There was a difficult moment.

"The military roads are the best I've seen, and the buildings for speeches and political gatherings are very handsome," said Frances quietly.

Frau Köppler turned to her with some annoyance. "And a hundred other things. Look at our unemployment. We haven't any. Look at yours in England. It is so large."

"Yes, unfortunately it is," broke in Richard. He was damned if he was going to let this pass. "But we are very frank about our unemployment figures."

"What do you mean?"

"We count people as unemployed if they are being trained under Government schemes for new trades, or if they are casual or seasonal workers and just don't happen to be working on the day when the census is taken. So when you talk about England you ought to remember that."

"But that's madness ... People trained by the Government unemployed?"

"Or facing facts. They can't plan to become settled members of the State unless they have a steady job, can they? Turning them into an army is not a solution, unless waging war is one of their country's plans."

Frau Köppler dismissed the point as negligible. ... Her patience was wearing thin.

"How long will you stay here?" The directness of her question interested Frances. The velvet glove was off.

Richard was unperturbed. "I think we'll leave quite soon, now. We've done most of the walks and climbs which we intended to do ... Actually, we have been just discussing tonight where we should go next. Perhaps you could advise us. We had thought of the Dolomites, but I believe it is difficult to visit there, this year."

Frau Köppler was silent; she didn't want to discuss the South Tyrol.

"I think it would be too tragic to go there this year," said Frances. "Last time we were there, only two years ago, in fact, the people were so sure that the end of Italian domination was in sight. They had a second Andreas Hofer, working secretly in Bozen, and they really believed that the heart of the Tyrol would bleed no more. And now they have been forced to leave their land or to remain and become Italians. I often wonder what they think about it all."

A faint pink color surged under Frau Köppler's pale skin.

"Then there's Bohemia," said Richard. "But I think it would be equally difficult to visit there, today."

"And of course there's Salzburg. But then the singers and conductors whom I used to admire so much aren't there any longer." Frances' voice had just the proper note of regret.

Frau Köppler looked first at her, and then at Richard. They were watching her politely, waiting for her to suggest something.

"You are very near Austria, here," she said.

"Yes, Austria is lovely," said Frances. "I remember the wonderful time I had in Vienna, three years ago. Everyone was so gay and charming. You think we should go to Vienna?" Richard watched Frau Köppler's rising embarrassment. Her theory that nothing was changed, unless for the better, was not standing up very well. She shrugged her shoulders.

"Vienna has no mountains, of course. I forgot you liked them. Perhaps the Austrian Tyrol ... it always was popular with the English."

"Do you know of any particularly good place?"

Frau Köppler gave the advice they had wanted.

"The train from here goes direct to Innsbruck. It is the center of hundreds of excursions."

"That sounds a very good idea," said Richard. "We can go there tomorrow and then make our choice from that point. Thank you, Frau Köppler, you have been the greatest help." He rose as Frau Köppler stood up.

"You seem to travel a good deal." It was almost a question.

Frances smiled. "It is a necessary part of one's education, we think."

Frau Köppler stood with her lips and arms folded. "Perhaps. But it is strange that so many English travel about, as if they were rushing away from their own country."

Frances looked at her for a moment. "But the explanation is simple. It is only when the English travel in foreign lands that they learn to appreciate many things about their own country. Good night, Frau Köppler."

They turned again to the chessboard. Frances lit a cigarette with some enjoyment. When she came to think of it, the conversation had been rather like a game of chess, itself. From their point of view, it had been really quite satisfactory.

As Richard took her Queen, she thought of A. Fugger, and his neat, businesslike exit. It was just possible that the police or Gestapo or whatever they called themselves—there seemed to be so many organizations in this country, all with uniforms and high-sounding titles—it was just possible that they wanted to capture him for another matter altogether. He might have sold banned literature, or helped people to escape, or he could have distributed secret pamphlets. She remembered his first belated appearance, and the smell of burning paper which had come from the back room in the shop.

She felt a sudden rise in confidence; it seemed as if these few days of wind and sun had benefited her mind as well as her body. The mental paralysis which had gripped her last week was gone. She knew now that no matter what happened, she must keep hold of this courage and hope. If she lost these, then all was lost. Tonight she could face a hundred Köpplers, even Nürnberg itself. It was such a relief to be nearing the last stages of this strange journey that even danger seemed welcome.

"Check," said Richard, "*and* mate, I think." He grinned self-consciously as he saw Frances smile. He could conceal his disappointment at losing a game better than his delight at winning. He bent down to pick up her handkerchief where it had fallen under the table. He tickled her under the knee.

"Sorry," he apologized with mock seriousness. Frances saw that Frau Köppler was looking at them.

As they rose, all conversation at Frau Köppler's table ended. The four men there were watching them intently, while Frau Köppler gave a queenly bow. There was the little white-bearded astrologer who was Herr Köppler, who typed all day in his room and came downstairs in the evening to sit by his wife. There was a fat, genial man; another fat man, not at all genial, who always wore a uniform and his hair cut so short that it bristled; and the young schoolteacher, very conscious of his discipline and learning, acquired at a Party college. Baldur, the Almost Human, Richard had named him when he had first seen him. The group of men stared openly at Frances as she crossed the room. Richard returned Frau Köppler's bow, and Frances said good night, looking serenely oblivious of the gazes in her direction. She felt suddenly glad that she didn't live in this village. There were other reasons, apart from the fact that she was English and obviously stupid, why Frau Köppler disliked her. I'm too effeminate, she thought, and giggled as she took Richard's arm to go upstairs.

CHAPTER XI

At the Gasthof Bozen

ON FRIDAY they arrived in Innsbruck, and succumbed, as they always did, to its outward charm. They left their luggage at the station, and walked towards the Maria-Theresien-Strasse through busy streets bathed in the soft yellow light of the late afternoon sun. As Frances said to Richard, it was always difficult to tell who was on holiday or who was at work in Innsbruck. There were as many short leather trousers, green-feathered hats, and peasant-pinafored dresses among the young men and women at work as there were among the groups of holiday makers; but two changes became more and more evident. The holiday makers had the hard German accent of the North, and there was the Uniform.

The cafés were busy at this hour. The tourist shops, with their colorful peasant clothes, little wood carvings, flower charms and vermilion-tinted postcards looked gay to the passing glance. Frances knew from experience not to stop and look at them. Most of the articles were less imposing, were even crude, close at hand. They had a sort of Present-from-Brighton touch. It was pathetic, she thought, that "Tyrolean" clothes, bought in the smart shops of large cities far away from the Tyrol, should be better-looking than the originals they copied. It was the tragedy of city hands being more skillful in cutting better material, of colors more carefully blended with the sophisticated designer's eye.

And now they were approaching the Herzog-Friedrich-Strasse. Frances was looking at the people, at the way in which the towers and steeples around them were superimposed on the background of jagged mountains. One of the chief attractions of this country was its White-Horse-Inn quality. It could be felt even in a town with tramcars and tourist buses. If this region were to lose that, it would lose

99

much. Frances wondered whether the people prized the asset of charm which lay in their countryside, or would they ever be persuaded into thinking it was effete or sentimental or valueless, persuaded into an ill-fitting imitation of the hard Northerner?

Richard's thoughts were already at the Gasthof Bozen. The best thing to do on this job, he decided, was to have a general idea of what he was going to do while he still kept his eyes open for any possible short-cuts. A girl, carrying a basket filled with flowers, had paused before them to rest for a moment. She was almost a child, and the flowers were simple garden flowers, arranged in rough bunches. Richard stopped Frances. He returned the girl's smile.

"From our garden," she said, holding out a bunch.

"They are lovely," said Richard. "But I think I like this bunch better. How much?" He lifted a bunch with some roses in it: two were red. They paid the girl, and crossed over into the narrow Herzog-Friedrich-Strasse with its arcades and balconies. As they approached No. 37, Richard took Frances' arm. They entered the insignificant doorway with its worn sign. On either side of the doorway were busy little shops with overcrowded windows, as if everything they had for sale must be displayed. Still, they had been comforting, thought Frances, as the heavy door swung behind them shutting them off from the cheery babel of the busy arcade, and left her gripping Richard with one hand and the bunch of flowers with the other.

For it was dark in the entrance hall, dark and silent. It was narrow and unfurnished; it contained only the staircase which lay in front of them. The faint light which broke the darkness came from above, possibly from a landing. It reminded Frances of some of the older houses in Oxford, except for the stuffy, sickly smell of stale beer and tobacco. She noticed that Richard brightened. His dislike was the cafés with creamcakes. As he moved towards the stairs, she broke off a red rose, and fastened it through the lapel buttonhole of her flannel suit.

She wished she felt as confident as her heels sounded on the wooden staircase. It twisted in an uneven curve to the left and they had reached the landing, fairly broad and square in shape. This was where the light came from. It hung over a desk which faced the staircase. There was a man at the desk, watching them through his small half-closed eyes. Or it might have been the largeness of his face which gave his eyes the appearance of smallness. Like two bullet holes in a lump of dough, thought Frances. He was middle-aged, his figure had spread with his years, his square-shaped head bristled with cropped gray hair.

At either end of the landing, which seemed to be the real entrance hall to the hotel, were swing doors. They led to two rooms, one which must be at the back, the other at the front, of the house. From the front room came the surge of men's voices, whenever a waitress pushed open the swing door. The back room seemed to be the kitchen or the taproom, or perhaps both. The two waitresses hurried towards it with empty beer mugs, and returned to the restaurant with them filled again. The two women were so busy that they hardly glanced at Frances, as she waited for Richard to finish his arrangements with the square-headed man. As the swing doors were pushed open, she could see some of the nearest tables. The men round them were middle-aged, bulky, with faces red from arguing or laughing or drinking beer or all three. Blue tobacco haze coiled over bald heads. There were uniforms everywhere. Once a waitress swung the door wide open, and held it that way with her shoulder and hip, so that another woman could pass through with carefully held tankards of beer. Then Frances saw the flags and the outsize photograph. She looked at the desk where Richard was signing all the usual papers. It had a photograph, too, scowling benevolently down on a row of keys hanging on numbered hooks. They seemed to have landed in one of the Party's own particular haunts.

Richard had finished writing. He beckoned to Frances. Perhaps the man had looked for a moment at her buttonhole, but Frances couldn't be sure of that. His eyes had a way of wandering vaguely, as if he were ill or very tired . . . And then a green-aproned boy appeared, and she concentrated on filling in the details in the printed form. Now the signing was all finished, the man handed Richard a key, and abandoned them to the boy in his slow-moving, disinterested way. As they were led up the wooden stairs, irregular and creaking, he sank heavily back into his seat, and resumed his occupation of staring into the middle distance.

Frances glanced at Richard. He gave no sign of disappointment. He was talking to the boy, and was giving him the checks for their luggage at the station. The boy would collect it, Innsbruck fashion. Clever of Richard, she thought, to remember that. An arrival by taxi in this narrow street, with its mixture of medieval houses and small shops, would have been pretentious and stupidly conspicuous.

The way to their room led them up two flights of wooden stairs. Frances had the sudden alarming feeling of being suspended in midair. The only support of the stairs seemed to be the wall on her left. On her right was a large well sinking into the hall landing below. There were banisters of course, but they were thinly spaced and quivered to her touch. After that, she climbed the rest of the stairs well towards the wall side, and tried to ignore the way in which the steps sagged gently towards the well of the staircase. She wished she wouldn't imagine at such moments what a fire would be like. Probably one could make a spectacular, if undignified, exit by scrambling down the front of the house from balcony to oriel window . . . Probably.

The boy replied eagerly to Richard's questions. He seemed a friendly kind of person. Frances suddenly realized this was the first really friendly smile and voice they had met in two weeks. Except, of course, for the American. She thought of a London bus conductor or policeman, and felt a wave of homesickness strike her. This was the first time she had ever felt like this, abroad. Perhaps she was noticing too much this year, but then this year you couldn't be blamed for being coldly analytical. It would have been more comfortable to have visited Germany as a guest, to have been taken out and around by friends. Then you might not have the time to notice or compare policemen and bus conductors. Then you wouldn't take a late evening stroll past a Jews' Alley. But somehow, in spite of the grimness, Frances preferred this way; there was less chloroform, this way.

Their room faced the street and was pleasant in its simplicity. No massive furniture here, thank heavens, to smother you in bad taste. Clean poverty had its virtues. Frances went over to one of the windows. Along the street, the varied house fronts rose tall and narrow over the arcades where the shops hid. At the open windows, she could see women in their dirndl dresses looking down on the street. It was as if she were in a theater, one of those little opera theaters where white patches of faces look out of the boxes rising in tiers like those of a wedding cake. Guardi would have enjoyed detailing this scene.

Someone was standing behind her. She turned quickly. Richard was gone. It was the thin dark boy in the green apron. He held out a vase of water to her, and pointed to the flowers which she still carried in her arms.

"Thank you. That is very thoughtful."

He relaxed with a smile as he heard she could speak German.

"The gentleman has gone to the lavatory," he explained carefully.

"Oh . . ." said Frances, suddenly stymied.

"Where would the lady like the flowers?"

"Could we move that small table near that mirror and place them there?" He approved of the decision, and watched her arrange the flowers.

"I think that is pretty," she said, to break the silence.

"Very pretty, gracious lady." His brown eyes were friendly. "I shall go for the luggage now, and I shall come back with it as quickly as possible." His smile was infectious. He might have been going to play a game of tennis instead of pushing a cart with luggage through busy streets.

"Thank you." Frances paused. "What is your name?"

"Johann, gracious lady."

"Thank you, Johann."

He paused at the door. "Is there anything the lady needs? The maid is having her supper. She will be here soon." Frances shook her head, but he still stood at the door, his eyes watching the corridor. Suddenly he turned with a smile.

"Here is the gentleman," he said. "Good evening, *gnädige Frau.*"

"Good evening, Johann." So he had been staying with her until Richard came back, as a sort of watchdog. Was the hotel as peculiar as all that? She heard Richard's voice, and there was a smile on his face as he entered the room.

"Thank God for a friendly face and a kind word," he said.

"Yes, I like Johann."

"His name is Johann?" Richard's voice had changed: it was tighter, quicker. Frances raised her eyebrows, and watched Richard sit down on the bed, his eyes fixed on the scrap of rug at his feet. Johann—Hans—Johann. No; it probably wasn't ... probably. He looked up to see Frances standing beside him, looking puzzled. He caught her arm, and pulled her down beside him.

"Anything wrong?"

"I don't think so." He lowered his voice, although the walls in this old house must have been thick enough for safety. "I was just thinking . . . What was Johann like? Chatty? I noticed he hovered about here, until I got back."

"Politeness, and really good manners. That's all. What people used to call a well-brought-up boy. You know, I had the funniest feeling that he didn't approve of this hotel, and wanted to ... oh, it's silly. I am going all romantic."

Richard remained serious. He was still half-lost in his own thoughts.

"Frances, it's the rummiest place. I went to see where the bathroom was, and I took the chance of having a look round, in general. Most of the rooms on this floor seem empty, but I was almost run over by three expansive uniforms on their way downstairs to join the party. You noticed it, by the way?"

"Yes; it looked like an old boys' club."

"It probably is. All I've seen so far are middle-aged men, looking rather pleased with themselves. It may be one of those pubs where Nazi meetings were held secretly when Austria was still banning them. Either we've arrived in the middle of a reunion of some kind or they always are reuniting."

"That's cheery, I must say."

"I don't know if it is as bad as it looks for us. Our friends wouldn't quite expect us to come here if we had a guilty conscience, right into the spider's parlor, as it were. And then Johann told me that they used to have a lot of English and American tourists here, students who were having an inexpensive holiday; that some Americans turned up earlier this summer, but that so far we are the first Britishers. He noticed I had written Oxford University on that form at the desk downstairs, so we fit in, in a kind of a way. University people are generally thought to be odd."

Frances noted that he looked strained and tired.

"What about a spot of food, and some beer?" She smiled as she saw him brighten at the idea. She stood up and smoothed her skirt. "I'll wash first. Where's the bathroom?"

Richard grinned. "It's absolutely unique, Frances. You'll love it." She knew from his tone that she wouldn't.

"Where?" she asked philosophically.

"Straight along the corridor, past the staircase, to the back of the building. You'll find it on the balcony there. It's a square box to one side. You can wave to all the people sitting out on their balconies round the back courtyard. It's really very matey."

Frances said very slowly, "Richard, you are pulling my leg. I'll see for myself."

She walked quickly along the corridor. Apart from the additional local color of two pairs of large black boots outside one quiet room—Richard had been surprisingly discreet about that—everything was exactly as he had described it.

As they went downstairs, Richard was whistling softly to himself in a preoccupied way. Frances paid little attention; he often did that—but as they reached the desk, she suddenly realized that the last few bars had taken shape into something she knew. *My love indeed my love is like a red red red red rose.* Richard was laying their key on the desk, in front of the large, shapeless man. Without rising from his chair, he nodded his square head with its bristling hair, and grunted in reply to their good evening. He only looked for a moment at Frances' hat.

When they came in, he was still sitting there. He rose slowly and grudgingly to hand them their key. All his movements were those of a lethargic and not particularly amiable man.

This was all that happened for two days as they left or entered the hotel. The room which served as the restaurant was empty in the morning. The swing doors were propped open to air the place, the chairs were piled on the tables, and the two waitresses in old dresses were washing the floors. The tobacco smoke was gone, but the smell of beer still hung in the air. In the evening, the swing doors were closed, shutting in the dull hum of voices, except when the hurrying waitresses, now dressed in their bright dirndls, elbowed them open. Then the wave of voices rose and fell. They were always men's voices, thick and heavy. Frances wondered about the grass widows, deserted for the excitements of politics.

On Sunday morning, the silent man startled them by asking if they were comfortable in their room. They said they were, and waited. But he only hooked their key onto the board behind him, moving so slowly, with his back turned to them, that they knew the conversation was over. They didn't need to look back at the desk, as they took the first steps down-stairs. He would be lowering himself slowly into his chair, folding his hands across his massive paunch, and settling his eyes on his favorite spot on the wall above their heads.

As they returned that evening, climbing slowly up the stairs to the rhythm of Frances' high heels, they braced themselves to face the desk, but no one was there. Just as Richard was wondering if he should risk getting their room key without arousing the owner's displeasure, Johann appeared. Herr Kronsteiner had just gone to have his supper, he explained, and moved round behind the desk. He had taken off his apron, and had become a very dignified Johann. Well, anyway, thought Frances, that disposed of Richard's theory that Herr Bristleneck did all his eating and sleeping at the desk. But Richard seemed in no way dismayed at having his theories confounded: on the contrary, he was in remark-ably good humor as they climbed the rest of the stairs. He was whistling to himself again, softly, and absent-mindedly it seemed. But the wink he gave Frances as they walked down the corridor to their room was not at all absent-minded. Just as they reached the door, the whistling had slid into a recognizable tune. Richard opened the door quickly. He was not disappointed. Inside, standing at the window, looking at the street, was Herr Kronsteiner.

He stood just far enough behind the white curtain to see without being seen. He turned slowly round to face them as the door closed. Richard's whistling only stopped then.

Richard said quietly, "Good evening." Frances noticed that Herr Kronsteiner also kept his voice low as he answered. He was smiling politely, his eyes fixed vaguely on the wall behind them.

"I came to leave your account in your room, and then I thought I heard you coming upstairs. So I took the opportu-nity of waiting, so that I could explain any details which might seem doubtful. Many of our foreign visitors find German figures puzzling. I shall be away tomorrow on a short journey, and I may not return before you leave." For a man of Herr Kronsteiner's loquacity, it was quite a speech.

Richard's expression was unchanged. "Of course. It is just as well to be quite sure and to have all the details perfectly clear."

Frances glanced at him. There was just a shade of emphasis, a slowness in the phrasing of the words, which gave them a double meaning to anyone who looked for it; but if Herr Kronsteiner perceived it, he gave no sign. He held two envelopes in his hand; he chose one of them carefully and handed it to Richard. He waited. Richard ripped the envelope open, and extracted a sheet of paper. Frances, still watching him, saw a shade of disappointment pass over his face. The envelope had contained a bill, just an ordinary hotel bill. The name of the hotel headed the piece of paper, followed by the name of the proprietor. It was RUDOLF KRONSTEINER. He saw Fugger's head against the row of dusty books, saw the scarcely moving lips ... "The owner is called Hans ... He will help you ..."

"Thank you. I think everything is quite clear." Richard spoke abstractedly. Would he risk it? It was now or never, he felt. On what he said or did depended everything, everything, including Frances' safety. At least the man had come to their room, with a very elaborate excuse. That had been the first step, either for or against them. The next step was his. He was amazed at the calmness of his own voice. "Except, of course, one silly idea I had. I thought you were the proprietor."

"I am," the man answered gravely, but his interest seemed aroused for the first time.

"Really? Then it's my mistake completely. I thought the owner's name was Hans, not Rudolf."

Herr Kronsteiner smiled. "Everyone knows that it is Rudolf." He looked at the envelope which he still held in his hand.

"God in heaven, how could I have made such a mistake? I gave you the wrong bill. My apologies, Herr Professor." His calm smile belied the amazement of his words.

To Frances, sitting on the edge of the bed, her hat with its red rose lying beside her, it seemed as if here were not only a maddening man, but also one who either enjoyed his own mystery, or—and that was a disturbing thought—believed in precaution even within those thick walls. Thank heavens, Richard and she had made only general conversation here, except when they had lain close together in bed. Could their low voices, deadened by the soft feather pillow, have possibly been heard, even if this room was wired for sound? Richard's precaution, which from the very beginning she had been inclined to deplore secretly, now lost all its theatrical appearance and began to look like wisdom.

Richard was smiling too, as he read the second bill very carefully. He was memorizing something.

"Everything is quite clear now," he said. "Would you like the bill paid this evening, or will tomorrow do?"

"That does not matter very much, but we have a rule in this hotel that all accounts must be paid each Monday. Tonight or tomorrow, it does not matter. One more thing I must trouble you about. All the rooms in the hotel have been reserved for a political conference this week. It begins on Wednesday."

"Oh, we intended in any case to leave Innsbruck either tomorrow or Tuesday." Did we indeed? thought Frances. The reply had pleased Kronsteiner. He had given his warning, and Richard had taken it. He positively beamed, although his voice was as impersonal as ever.

"In that case, I am glad I saw you this evening, for I may be away when you leave. I hope you have enjoyed your visit here."

"Very much indeed." It was Frances now who spoke. It seemed to her that it was time she said something. Herr Kronsteiner bowed, and moved with unexpected quickness to the door. He paused before he opened it, slowly, cautiously. Without looking back, he suddenly slipped out. They couldn't hear his footsteps in the corridor. For a large, heavy man he could walk with surprising lightness.

Frances felt that someone ought to say something. "Was the bill high?"

"No, it was rather reasonable. Now what shoes did you want to wear?"

Frances looked at the bed ... But if Richard wanted to go out again, there would be a reason. Any suggestion he made had its purpose. She knew that by this time. She changed her shoes and washed her hands and face in cold water. She felt the better for fresh powder and lipstick. She

wound a white chiffon scarf as a turban round her head; she
was beginning to hate the sight of the red rose, anyway. As
she finished tucking the ends of the scarf in place, she saw
Richard watching her in the mirror. He was smoking his
pipe, and in the ashtray beside him were the crumbled ashes
of the paper which he had used as a lighter. His Baedeker
was open on his knees.

"Ready?"

Frances nodded. She picked up a clean pair of white
gloves and a fresh handkerchief. Richard had risen and
replaced the guidebook in its drawer. He emptied his pipe
into the ashtray, and stirred the ashes with his penknife until
he was satisfied that no piece of charred gray paper could be
seen. The bill which had been handed to him first by Kronsteiner he left lying on the little table beside the flowers.

Downstairs, Johann was still at the desk. He interrupted
his conversation with two men, whom Richard recognized as
belonging to the uniforms which had practically marched
over him on the evening of their arrival, to wish them much
enjoyment. He could recommend the film at the cinema in
the Maria-Theresien-Strasse. His friendly brown eyes followed Frances downstairs, along with the open, noncommittal stare of his companions. One of them said something, the
other laughed. Frances took Richard's arm, and pressed it.
Her quietening touch, she called it. They heard Johann's
voice raised in their defense.

"But the English are a truly German race."

"Which is probably the highest praise one could have from
a German," said Richard bitterly, as they closed the heavy
front door. "I wish," he added, "that we could afford the
luxury of a scene. Just once."

Perhaps Richard had been infected by Herr Kronsteiner's
supercaution. Anyway, he had varied his technique tonight.
As they crossed the square towards the Maria-Theresien-
Strasse, he chose the moments of isolation to tell Frances
they would leave tomorrow for Pertisau am Achensee.

"It looks a decent sort of place on the map," he said with
some pleasure.

"Are we near the end?"

"We'll know when we meet him."

"Then what?"

"We'll go to Ragusa, and post back the letter of credit."

"And if we don't find him this time? We haven't many days left, have we?"

"We'll have to try again, and perhaps again. After that, if there are no results, I'll wire Geneva, and we'll get back to London. We were given a month. It's now the sixteenth of July. I think we'll manage it in time."

"Then you have a suspicion this may be the last stop?"

Richard only smiled as an answer. They had reached the pavement and, surrounded once more by Sunday-evening crowds, they walked in silence towards the cinema. Outside its doors, Frances paused to look at the stills.

"I think I'd rather have a drink," she said.

"You've got sense," an American voice said behind them. They both turned in amazement. Yes it was, it was Henry van Cortlandt, sardonic grin and all. He shook their hands as if he really were pleased to see them.

"It was your wife's hat sort of thing which caught my eye. It's pretty smooth; not the kind of headgear a good *Hausfrau* wears. I've just been in there, and I came out halfway through. I've been wondering what to do until it's time to go to bed. And now you are here in answer to my prayers. The drinks are on me. We'll catch up on local color. I know a place where we'll get plenty."

As they walked towards the restaurant, there were explanations. Van Cortlandt had finished his assignment in Germany, and was now heading through the Tyrol to Vienna. He tactfully did not ask them where they had been, or where they were going. Frances filled in the gaps with what she always called girlish gossip. Tonight it served its purpose well enough.

As they sat at a table in the beerhouse, they all relaxed and prepared to enjoy themselves. Both Richard and van Cortlandt had stories to tell, and there was no need to worry about the conversation. It was pleasant, thought Frances, to lean on a table, to watch the curling cigarette smoke, to listen to laughter and voices raised in friendly argument. There was one thing about living under this kind of government—every moment of enjoyment was treasured. You appreciated any moments without fear or restrictions, and when they came your way, you made the most of them. There was a pathetic kind of determination to have a good time in the faces around her. It had touched even her. When they had sat down at this table tonight, she had made up her mind that she was going to enjoy herself. She was going to forget everything except that they were on holiday.

The men ordered their second large steins of beer. Frances left the conversation to watch the people around them. She noticed a young man, sitting alone at a small table, making the best of his splendid isolation. He was vaguely familiar. He looked suddenly towards them, and his eyes met hers. He hesitated. Frances felt that he knew her, that he was waiting for her to smile. When she didn't, he looked away quickly, and became absorbed in a large family party in front of him. Richard became aware of her look of concentration. He stopped what he was saying to van Cortlandt to ask, "Anything wrong, Frances?"

"I'm just thinking, darling."

"It looks rather painful." Both men regarded her with some amusement.

"I've got it . . . the young man in the train."

Richard didn't look any the wiser.

"The *beautiful* young man in the train to Paris. Your friend's brother, Richard, you know the one. He's here."

"Young Thornley. Good Lord. Where?"

"Over there."

Richard looked. "You're quite right, Frances. It is."

"He looks rather lonely."

"Well, we're not nursemaids." Richard was annoyed.

Van Cortlandt laughed at Richard's expression.

"Why do the English abroad avoid the English abroad?" he asked.

"Well, you know what we call a holiday . . . a change. But actually, he may not want to join us, and might only do it out of politeness."

Van Cortlandt looked surprised. He wasn't convinced. "Now who would think up that reason?" They all laughed.

"He might be waiting for someone, but I think he looks too bored for that. He is not annoyed; he is just bored." It was Frances again.

The young man decided everything by looking towards their table, and smiling wholeheartedly in his embarrassment at finding three pairs of eyes focused on him. Richard gave a wave of his hand, and the young man rose and came towards them.

"I hope you don't mind my butting in," he said, "but I have got very tired of laughing by myself." The American looked at Thornley just the same way he had looked at Richard and Frances when he had met them in the Five-Cornered Tower. It was a quiet summing-up, disconcerting in its frankness, but Thornley, like the Myles', pretended to be unaware of it. He sat down beside them, and started to talk. He was amusing, and seemingly lighthearted. Frances watched van Cortlandt make up his mind; after he had had half an hour of Thornley, she felt the judgment was mainly favorable. She sighed with relief; she felt responsible for Thornley. Van Cortlandt had decided, she could guess, that Thornley was a nice, amusing individual with a lot of charm—and not much else. It would depend on how much he got to know Thornley before he could revise that estimate. Frances guessed also that van Cortlandt hadn't thought any revision would be necessary.

"Where's your friend?" asked Richard, when the rush of conversation offered its first pause.

"Tony? Oh, he should be here any day, I hope. That's why I'm hanging about Innsbruck. We went to Prague, you know, and didn't find ourselves made welcome by the—authorities. Things were a little difficult, really. It seemed easier if we split up, and if I came here to let him get his job done."

The mention of Prague had interested van Cortlandt.

"Did you run into trouble?" he asked.

Thornley nodded. "A little." He saw that they were all waiting for him to explain. He could hardly ignore the interest in all their eyes.

"Is Tony in danger?" asked Frances. At least, that would give him the chance to say no, and to turn the conversation.

"Actually, he is looking for a girl."

Van Cortlandt and Richard exchanged glances.

"What's wrong with that?" asked the American with a smile.

"Nice healthy pursuit," agreed Richard.

"Usually," said Thornley. "But in this case she is the daughter of a professor who wasn't exactly popular with the new régime."

"Don't tell us, unless you want to," said Frances suddenly.

"Probably I'd be better confiding in someone. You've no idea how miserable you begin to feel inside when you can't talk to anyone. I've been waiting here just like that for two weeks. . . . The story is simple and innocent enough, Heaven knows. Tony began worrying about this girl when he heard her father had been removed. He had met her in England last summer, and since May he has become determined to get to Prague to see if she were all right. He had the idea of marrying her and getting her out of the country as a British citizen. Well, we got to Prague. It wasn't particularly pleasant for us, being English." He paused reflectively. "It became obvious that I was inclined to get involved in things, and there was no sign of Tony's girl. In the end, he thought it was better for him to do the job alone. He can control his temper better than I can. So I came on here, and I'm waiting for Tony and his girl to arrive. I said I would wait until the end of July."

"What happens if he doesn't turn up before the end of the month?" asked van Cortlandt.

"That would be a nuisance. I'd have to go back to Prague."

"I'd like to join you."

"Would you?" Thornley was pleased. "It's mostly strain, I warn you. Not very pleasant, really. The Czechs are suspicious, the Germans are intolerable. I can't say I blame the Czechs, at all. It is just like that all the time, you see, and then you start to be haunted by the girl, too. Tony's infected me."

"Did you know her?"

"I've seen photographs. And Tony would say something, now and again. She seemed a winner."

"Perhaps she is in hiding with her father," suggested Frances.

Thornley looked at her. His gray eyes were colder, brighter. "He is definitely dead," he said gently. It was the kind of gentleness which shocked them all into silence. Frances noted, as she lit another cigarette, that van Cortlandt was looking at Thornley in a different way. The revision process had no doubt begun.

Richard ordered more beer, and coffee for Frances.

"We are leaving tomorrow," he intimated, "for Pertisau."

Frances blinked her eyes, and tried to look unconcerned. It was hardly the change in conversation which she had expected.

"I envy you," said Thornley. "Good place. Mountains and lake, and plenty of atmosphere. At least, it was, four years ago. I suppose it is still: the small villages keep to their own ways longer than the towns, and mountains and forests don't change."

"I envy you, too," agreed van Cortlandt. "Sidewalks in summer become just one café table after another for me. Climbing isn't up my alley, though. I've never understood why people go up, when all they can do is come down again. But I'd like some real swimming. I haven't had much chance of it, this summer."

"Then why don't you both take a few days off, and come along?"

Both van Cortlandt and Thornley looked surprised.

"You both look as if you could do with some time off," said Richard, and left it at that.

Thornley and van Cortlandt eyed each other speculatively. Each was probably wondering if the idea would be as attractive tomorrow as it seemed tonight.

"It sounds all right to me," said the American.

"It certainly seems a good idea," said Thornley.

"I've some business to do here. It depends on that," qualified van Cortlandt.

"And I'd hate to butt in," finished Thornley.

They both looked at Frances. She sipped her coffee, and regained her composure.

"Richard never makes a suggestion out of mere politeness," she said. "If he actually invited anyone, then that means he really would like them to accept." She smiled to the two men, and added, "I think it would be fun."

"Yes," agreed Thornley.

"Well, I've had a grand evening," said van Cortlandt. "It would be a pity to miss any others we could have. If I can arrange the business on hand, I'll take you up on that suggestion."

Richard finished the debate. "We'll be there for about a week, and if we leave before you arrive, we shall phone you and let you know. If you can make it, then turn up anytime you feel like it. We'll leave it at that. I don't know where we shall stay, yet. Let's say the Hotel Post; there's always a Post in Austria. If you can't manage it, then we'll see you in London, we hope."

They rose, and straggled to the door. The restaurant was nearly empty; it must have been later than any of them had imagined. They parted with a good deal of warmth. Frances, who had been drinking coffee, wondered how much the beer had to do with it all. She watched the American and the Englishman walk away together, still talking their heads off.

"I'd like to see them again," she said and took Richard's arm. "I wonder if they'll come. You know, Richard, you did give me a shock when you suggested it. Won't it complicate matters?"

Richard shook his head. "Beer or no beer, I liked them. It's strange, how you can meet some people, and you might as well have been spending the evening looking at a fishmonger's window. And then again, you meet others, and a small flag waves, and you are a fool if you ignore it."

"Especially nowadays," said Frances. "I'm all for gathering the rosebuds while we may."

The street was almost empty. The light tap of Frances' heels alone broke the silence. She waited until they had reached a part of it where they were sure of being quite safe. She lowered her voice.

"Did the second bill tell you whom we are to see?"

"He's a chess collector, this one. Welcomes any fellow-enthusiast to view his collection. It should be easy getting in touch with him."

That was all Richard would tell, then. When Frances spoke again, it was about van Cortlandt and Thornley; she was still worrying about endangering them.

"They can take very good care of themselves, these two. If they come. What's more, we were told to behave completely normally. So I did."

Frances added nothing to that. For one thing, they were approaching the hotel. For another, she had the dawning suspicion that Richard was going to leave her under the young men's protection while he was being a fellow-enthusiast. She would see about that.

CHAPTER XII

Background for Terror

JOHANN was charmingly regretful in his mild way, next morning, when he found them completing their packing. He advised Richard about the trains, and arranged to take their suitcases to the station. As he spoke, he watched Frances pack bottle and hairbrushes into her fitted hand case.

"How beautiful," he said involuntarily, and then reddened as Frances looked up in surprise. "That leather, how is it made? I have admired your shoes each day. The material is so good." He looked at their flannel suits. "I don't quite understand it," he went on. "Are English sheep and cattle and horses so very much better than other countries'?"

Frances kept her face serious. "No, Johann, I don't think they are. Perhaps it is because the English are a slow and careful sort of people. Sometimes slowness has results." She would like to have added that even if his country hadn't got materials like these, they had always plenty of tanks and aeroplanes, but she didn't. Johann's sense of humor didn't stretch to the irony of that.

"Yes, they are a slow people, I have heard. Their thoroughness is different from ours; sometimes it seems strange that they should ever get results." He hesitated. "May I ask the *Herr Professor* a question? Do you think there will be war?"

Richard paused in locking his suitcase. He chose his words carefully.

"Well, that depends, Johann. It depends on Germany. If she makes war against Poland, then there will be war."

"But why should England go to war for Poland? The Poles are not worth it."

"They do not deserve to be obliterated."

"But you did not go to war for the Czechs."

"You agreed that the British are slow. It has taken time to change them from hopes of peace to a determination to

116

fight, if it is necessary. If Poland is attacked, the British will see *that* as a sign that fighting is necessary. It is quite simple, Johann. If Germany does not want war, then she must not attack Poland."

"Another war would be a dreadful thing," said Johann.

"Do many of your friends feel that way?" asked Frances.

"Of course, *gnädige Frau*. We are human beings."

"It seems so strange then that Germany should have twice built up the most powerful army in the world, within thirty years. Armies cost a lot of money, Johann. And the money is wasted unless the armies are used, and pay for themselves by winning. It is a very dangerous thing to build up a huge army when the rest of the world is at peace."

Johann was searching for a reply; what was it he had heard so often?

"But," he said at last, "we have to prepare against attack."

"From whom?" asked Frances gently.

"From all our enemies. France for instance."

"Johann, do you really think that if France was prepared for attack she would ever have had to sign at Munich? Tell me, when you lived in what was called Austria, were you all afraid of being attacked by France? Did you feel then that you must have the biggest air force in the world?"

Richard signed to Frances to ease up. As he explained afterwards, it would only land the boy in trouble if he really started to think for himself.

Johann was indeed looking worried. "If only you could live in our country for some years, you would understand, *gnädige Frau*." Frances, in obedience to Richard's signal, contented herself with smiling.

Richard spoke. "The cases are ready, Johann; you can take them away whenever you like. Leave the checks for them downstairs at the desk, and we shall get them there."

"Yes, *Herr Professor*." Johann looked unhappy about something. Perhaps it was that he hadn't made any converts to his cause. Or perhaps, thought Frances, he had found a question which the answers he had learned did not fit.

"You have made our stay very comfortable," said Frances, and was glad to see him cheer up. "And when you have that hotel of your own in the Tyrol, you must let us know, and we shall come and stay there one summer." Johann flushed with pleasure; he saw that she meant what she said.

"It would give me the greatest pleasure to have you at my hotel, *gnädige Frau*," Johann said with unexpected dignity.

"Good-by, Johann," said Richard. It was always he, it seemed, who had to close Frances' conversations. Johann bowed deeply, smiled for Frances again, and left them at last.

Frances walked over to a window, and looked silently down on the street.

"You would have made a good father confessor," said Richard, and lit the cigarette which she held between her lips. It was really extraordinary how people would talk to Frances; more extraordinary how she would listen.

"Don't let the tragedy of the human race get you down at this time of the morning. Come and have some breakfast, first." He drew her gently from the window. "An empty stomach only turns thought into worry."

Frances smiled and kissed him. "You keep worrying about me, Richard."

"Well, whenever you start a train of thought these days, it runs non-stop to the sorrows of the world."

"I'm sorry, Richard. I'll give up the habit."

"Do. It would be frightful if you ever began to enjoy it."

Frances laughed. "A kind of mental pervert, working herself into depths of depression to enjoy her secret thrills of pity? No, thank you, Richard. Instead, I'll become accustomed to the idea that man is born in pain, lives in struggle, dies in suffering."

"Well, that's a better defense against the new Middle Ages than the nice ideas you got from your liberal education."

Over a café table, they made their plans. Frances was suddenly demanding action. She wanted to get to Pertisau as soon as possible. By the time they had finished their late breakfast and had walked back to the hotel, the baggage checks awaited them, along with a final bill. Herr Kronsteiner had already left, it seemed, and Richard paid the grim woman who sat behind the desk. He left more than the usual tip for Johann, placing it inside an envelope along with his card on which he had written *Good luck with your hotel*, and a tip for their invisible chambermaid. Perhaps she had been this grim-faced, silent woman.

At the station, their luck still held. The train for Jenbach would leave in less than half an hour. From Jenbach they could hire a car to take them to Pertisau. ... But it wasn't until they were in the train, with their suitcases settled safely above their heads in their compartment, and they were watching the pleasant valley of the Inn spreading out before them, that Richard really relaxed. He admitted to himself for the first time that he was surprised that they had got away so simply, that his distrust of Herr Kronsteiner had been unfounded. He had looked like a man who would sell his own sister to the highest bidder. He must be a pretty useful kind of agent to have; crooked men would trust him, because they thought they could use him. Richard was still speculating about Herr Kronsteiner when their short journey ended, and the train stopped briefly at Jenbach to leave them and some other tourists on the sunlit platform. Richard lifted the two suitcases and joined the largest group which had jammed round the exit. Frances kept very close to him, slightly behind and slightly to one side, so that the man who was taking the tickets would only notice her, and no more. And then they were out into a broad roadway of hot white dust. There were two decrepit buses and some cars. The tourists, once the first burst of activity of leaving the station was over, had begun to straggle as they made up their minds. That gave them the chance to hire one of the cars. They had already left the station road, and were turning into outskirts of the little town, before the others had found seats which suited them and places for their luggage.

Their car finished the steep twisting climb from Jenbach, and regained its speed on the road leading round the western side of the long narrow Achensee. Halfway up the lake, the road ended. And there was Pertisau, smiling with the sun on its green meadows to welcome them.

It wasn't the usual village. It gave the appearance, as the road curved into the bay in which it lay and they could see it for the first time, of being a landscape architect's dream. At the edge of the shore, divided from it by the last of the road, were the hotels and chalets. Behind these, in the large sweep of meadows stretching back to the wooded mountains, lay the peasant houses like a scattered flock of sheep. A very small, neat pleasure boat was taking on passengers at the small neat pier. Everything was neat, even the arrangement of flags fluttering from the bathing houses on their own part of the shore, or the pattern of striped umbrellas shadowing the tables in front of the hotels. It was, self-admittedly, an artificial tourist center, but its smallness and neatness gave it much charm, and some dignity. The forests and mountains were very real, anyway. The valleys between the mountains converged on Pertisau like the lines of a sundial. There would be good walking and pleasant climbing, thought Richard with some satisfaction.

Frances was frankly delighted. She had watched some of the dull collections of houses as they had skirted the south end of the lake, and had wondered dejectedly if any of them could be Pertisau. In her relief, she was enthusiastic. Even the fact that the Hotel Post had no accommodation to suit them could not dampen her high spirits. The manager of the hotel was sorry, but there were no double rooms vacant. If the lady and gentleman would consider separate single rooms, or a room in one of the villas ... There were some which catered to visitors when the hotels were full ... Most comfortable ... Highly recommended. And of course they would have their meals at the hotel.

So they left their luggage at the hotel, and followed the manager's assistant across the road and over a field to a house. It was called "Waldesruhe," although the woods were at least half a mile away. But it seemed both clean and comfortable. Frances liked the petunias in the window boxes and the balcony in front of their bedroom with its magnificent view of the lake. Richard liked the impersonal owner, who took everything for granted in her calm, disinterested way. This sad-faced woman would not add to their complications. But he hadn't counted on Frances.

When he returned from the hotel again, after making "arrangements" as the manager euphemistically said, and leaving notes for van Cortlandt and Thornley, he found the quiet landlady talking to Frances on their balcony.

"It really wasn't my fault," said Frances. "It was simply that she was delighted to see someone who didn't come from Germany. They are having a rather bad year, here. Most of the visitors are Germans. With special rates, of course; and they spend next to nothing. They crowd into the hotels, and all the other visitors are chased away. I expect it's the way they eat their soup. Remember?"

"I believe you, darling."

"Really, Richard, all I said was, as she stood and looked at me on the balcony, 'How lovely it all is.' It was said to myself. And then she began to talk."

"Darling, don't explain. You're too kind; you just won't hurt people's feelings. You'll let yourself in for a lot of boredom, some day."

"I rather liked her, Richard. And she kept looking at me, not rudely, not inquisitively, but just as if she wanted to. All the time she talked, she was looking at me, and the strange thing was that I didn't feel embarrassed. There was a sort of pathetic expression in her eyes. I just couldn't ignore it."

Richard laughed, and kissed his wife. "Darling," he said for the third time, "I love you. Now come and see Pertisau."

They went down the light-pine staircase into the square-shaped room with its small windows and fluttering starched curtains. Like their bedroom, the furniture was simple in comfortable peasant style. Frances noted the number of hand-embroidered or crocheted mats on every available surface in the room. Frau Schichtl must have a lot of spare time, she thought, and followed Richard through the doorway onto the coarse green grass which surrounded the house. They chose a narrow road which led them through flowering meadows away from the lakeside and its holiday loungers. Richard was thinking about something.

At last he said, "Where does Frau What's-her-name sleep? Do you know?"

"Not near us, my pet, if that is what has been worrying you. There is an empty room next us. It separates us from a Leipzig honeymoon couple, and these are all the rooms upstairs. And a bathroom of course. The name is Schichtl, anyway."

Richard looked admiringly at her. "Now don't tell me that you found all that information popping out of Frau Schichtl's cash register. . . . I must say, my Frances, you have a knack."

"Now," said Frances, "it's your turn to tell me something."
"What?"

"Don't be a brute, Richard. No one can possibly hear us." She looked at the houses across the fields, their wide over-hanging roofs anchored with roped stones, their window boxes gay with rich-colored petunias. Under the broad eaves sheltered neat piles of logs.

"You take a long time to think up an answer, Richard."

"Well, darling, there's no need, is there, for you to know more than you do already?"

"Richard, will you stop doing a Pimpernel? I don't talk in my sleep and, anyway, I sleep only with you."

Richard watched two distant figures cutting the grass. Their scythes flashed rhythmically. "All right," he said. "This is all I know. We were to come to Pertisau. There is a Dr. Mespelbrunn who has a house here. He collects chessmen. We have to see him, and tell him we heard about his collection in Innsbruck. That is what makes me think that he may be the man we are looking for. None of the others knew where we came from. But here we have Dr. Mespelbrunn who knows about Innsbruck. He is also a musician, it seems, and likes to talk music as well as chess. His love is again a red rose. If he doesn't think we stink, he will unburden himself. And then we can have our holiday, and send old Peter his Geneva telegram ARRIVING FRIDAY. That's all."

"So that's all. ... Now, Richard, just tell me what was written in Herr Kronsteiner's second bill."

"More or less as I've said."

"Well, what was that?"

"You're an exasperating creature, aren't you?"

Frances only smiled and waited.

Richard looked at her, and then recited: *"Innsbruck recommends you to Pertisau am Achensee. Dr. Mespelbrunn. Collector of chessmen, songs, flowers."*

"Thank you, my sweet. I just wanted to be quite sure you weren't trying to do me out of some fun."

Richard was all injured innocence. "Now, really, Frances—"

"I mean, could you have possibly thought of Henry van Cortlandt and Robert Thornley as such nice bathing companions for Frances while you went—mountain climbing, for instance?"

Richard began to laugh. "Some day," he said, "I'll have to believe in woman's intuition, or is it just woman's suspicion?"

"Now that's all settled," said Frances, "let's look at the view."

Their road had led them clear of all the houses. The fields now lay behind them; in front lay scattered twisted trees on a stretch of green grass. It was here that the paths into the converging valleys began. They found a rough wooden seat under one of the small twisted trees beside a small stream. Only the gentle murmur of the running water broke the silence of the valleys. The mountains circled round the meadows, and the sky had arranged its high summer clouds in appropriate clusters to balance the juttings of the peaks into its clear blue.

"It's a neat job," said Richard, at last, "almost too neat to be natural."

"Yes, as if a stage designer had advised nature how to make a really Tyrolean set. I expect a chorus of villagers to enter at any moment."

"I've been wondering at that. It's not exactly a hive of activity, is it? There were a few men over there working with the hay, or long grass, or whatever it is. We've seen one woman scrubbing a table at her door, and another woman gathering in some washing. Now and again I heard the sound of trees being felled in the forest. Perhaps they find tourists more profitable than the land."

"Found," emended Frances. "Here are some children anyway."

Three large-haunched cows ambled slowly towards them, the bells at their throat sounding a gentle melancholy with each lazy step. Behind them were the children, four of them, their straight hair sun-bleached and their bare feet and legs stained nut-brown. The cows wandered past them, flicking the flies from their dun hides carelessly. Frances, looking at them, thought of some people she knew.

"Bored is the word, not contented. They have been bored so long that they don't know what to do about it. Numbed into contentment."

The children had halted. They were staring at Frances, at her suit and her silk stockings and her high-heeled shoes. When she spoke, they retreated, still staring stolidly, and then when they were at a safe distance they turned and ran, whooping with laughter, after the cows.

Richard was grinning with amusement.

"Nice to be young," said Frances. "Then you can laugh at the other fellow, and leave it at that. You never think that the things which make you laugh can also strike you cold with horror."

"Stop thinking about goose steps and a property mustache," advised Richard.

"Don't worry. I'm out of the dangerous stage of being mesmerized with fear. If I'm cold now, it's with anger."

"That's safer, anyway, when you are dealing with those birds," Richard said, and rose. He took her arm affectionately. "Nice little avenging fury you'd make."

They chose another road back to the shore of the lake. It led them towards a group of trees, sheltering houses more closely grouped together. As they approached this small center, they noticed two or three little shops, and even some women and children, in the road which had almost become a village street. There was an inn and a beer garden, which looked as if the inhabitants of Pertisau might be able to enjoy themselves after all without any help from tourists in imitation dress.

"Signs of civilization," said Richard, but he surprised Frances by not entering the beer garden. A small shop which was part of a house seemed to attract him. They crossed the narrow street, and looked at its window filled with wood carvings. Most of them were of the Present-from-the-lovely-Tyrol variety, but on the back shelf were a few carvings of really good design and careful workmanship. The finest of these were two chessmen. Frances knew Richard was pleased.

"This may be as good a way as any," he said, and led Frances into the shop.

It had been the living room of the house. Now there was a table facing the door, on which more carvings were displayed. Behind this, under a window at the side of the room, was another table covered indiscriminately with shavings, chips, blocks of wood and instruments to cut and mold them. On the bench beside the table was a man. He rose slowly, coming towards them with a half-carved piece of wood still in his hand. He looked at them keenly, and then smiled.

"*Grüss Gott!*" he said.

"*Grüss Gott!* May we look at your carvings?"

"Of course. The lady and gentleman are welcome." He went back to his bench and started his work again. Now and again, he would look up to see what held their interest. He nodded as Frances admired some figures of the Three Kings. His best, most careful work was given to Biblical themes; to them and to the chessmen which Richard was now examining with interest.

"How much are these?" asked Richard. The man watched his face as he told the price. It was reasonable for the amount of work in the carvings.

"It takes much time," the man said, as if trying to excuse the charge. Frances wondered how often it had been rudely beaten down by people who had ignored the time, the skill and the love which had gone into such work.

"The price is not high for such craftsmanship," said Richard. "I'd like a set of these to take back to England."

"The gentleman collects chessmen?" The woodcarver was delighted. "Then you will see something. I have still better ones; some which I do not sell." He rose, quickly this time, and went to a heavy chest at the back of the room. He opened a drawer and took out a large box which he carried carefully to his work table.

"If the lady and gentleman would come over here . . ."

They went, and as they looked at the contents of the box, they found it not difficult to express their admiration.

"I do not sell these; they gave me too much pleasure when I made them," the man explained. Frances noted the large clumsy hands, knotted and gnarled with age, and wondered at their expertness, at the delicacy of their creations.

"Do you ever make copies of them, for anyone who wants to buy them?"

"Sometimes. But it takes a long time. A gentleman who lives here in the summer months has asked me to copy them for him during the winters. I have made him one set, and here is another which I am now carving for him."

They were suitably impressed.

"He must know a lot about chessmen," said Richard, hoping for the best. It came.

"Herr Doktor Mespelbrunn? Yes, indeed. He has a large collection. He lived in the South Tyrol before he came here, and he has some Grödnertal pieces."

"Really?" Richard hoped his admiration of the Grödnertal woodcarvers was emphatic enough.

"But why do the lady and gentleman not go to see Herr Doktor Mespelbrunn's collection? He shows them to people who really admire and understand."

Richard looked doubtful. "I should like to see them very much, but after all we are complete strangers to Dr. Mespelbrunn. I shouldn't like to disturb him, especially as I am only an amateur ..." Richard's words were cut short by the old man's laughter.

"The lady and gentleman would not disturb the Herr Doktor. He doesn't work; he writes music." The woodcarver's joke lasted him quite a long time.

"Perhaps," said Richard, when he could, "perhaps I may have the honor of being introduced to the Doctor some day when I visit you again."

The woodcarver pursed his lips and shook his head.

"He doesn't come down into Pertisau much during July and August. He doesn't like tourists. But if you pass his house—it is the large house with the red shutters on the Pletzach—you should visit him. You can say that Anton advised you to go. It is a very beautiful collection."

"Perhaps we shall," said Richard, and dismissed Mespelbrunn from the conversation by placing an order. He insisted on paying Anton half the price in advance, the rest to be paid when the pieces arrived in Oxford.

"That seems fair enough," Richard said to Frances as they walked back to the lakeside. "By the time he can start work on them, summer will be over, and then he will know whether it is any use starting them at all. I've no doubt that he will be worried about the deposit, but he earned it."

They met groups of men returning from the woods, with their axes slung over their shoulders. They were lean, weather-tanned men, slow-moving and silent. They might have been a group of Scots shepherds, with the same strong bones and rugged faces. There was even the same upward lilt in their voices, as they gravely answered *"Grüss Gott."* Some of the older men smiled in surprise as if they hadn't expected the old greeting from a present-day visitor. Children had finished their task of herding cows, and were playing outside the open doors of the houses. Their clothes made them look like miniature adults. Smoke was beginning to curl up from the stone-anchored roofs. There was the smell of cooking food in the air, and the high tight voices of women when they are hurried and tired.

Down at the lakeside, there were also preparations for supper. Here the women were changing one undistinguished dress for another, and no doubt fixing their hair as unbecomingly as possible. Those of them who had already succeeded in looking grim enough to satisfy the requirements of a superior race sat at the tables in front of the hotels, contemplating their husbands with housewifely virtue. The men talked and looked at each other. The women looked at the men. Behind them, the shadows of the mountains were mirrored in the still waters.

A gramophone played in the little café where the younger men were. There were not so many young men, Frances noticed, nor were there many young girls. Perhaps the new Germany had other plans for the holidays of its youth.

"A few more years of this, supposing that there was no war," said Frances, "and no one, who wasn't a German, could bear to come to the Tyrol."

"I always know you mean what you say when your sentences run away with themselves," teased Richard. And then he was serious again. "We had better not rush things at this stage. The ice gets thinner as we get farther out, you know, and the shore is less easy to reach. I've a feeling we ought to play doubly safe. Peter's man, the one he sent out before us, must have managed Nürnberg and Innsbruck; although to tell you the truth, I had begun to think when we were in Innsbruck that we had reached the snag. So we are going to be very innocent for a couple of days. We'll relax. What about climbing that blighter tomorrow? It's an easy one to begin with." He nodded to the Bärenjoch, black with the sun behind it.

Frances smothered a smile over her husband's idea of relaxation.

"All right, darling," she said.

They left the quiet road, and turned towards the Villa Waldesruhe. It was as peaceful as its name. There was no sign of the honeymoon couple or of Frau Schichtl. As Frances unpacked, she sang. Richard dropped his book on the balcony, and listened as he looked at the steep drop of the mountains on the other side of the darkening lake. He didn't know when Frances had stopped singing, or how long she had been watching him from the door. He rose hurriedly.

"One of those adequate five minutes," he said awkwardly. He looked at Frances' hair and lips. "Darling, you are going to be thought most awfully decadent. The master race will disapprove."

"Too busy eating soup," said Frances. "Nothing, not even their principles, could ruin their appetites." She was right.

CHAPTER XIII

Reinforcements

THEY did climb the Bärenjoch next day. As Richard had said, it was easy, and it was also useful. Richard spent a lot of time on the peak, studying with his map and pencil the lie of the valleys which met in the green plain of Pertisau. They could see the Pletzach, flowing at the base of the mountain opposite them like a very narrow, very loosely-tied white ribbon. If they were to follow the stream up round that jut of mountain into the valley which it sheltered, they should find Dr. Mespelbrunn with his chessmen and music books. Frances watched Richard. He was interested in the mountains, unsuspected from the lakeside, which stretched into the distance in rough-tongued waves. Two of the valleys led to paths which would take them over that sea of jagged stone.

"Looking for a quick way out?" asked Frances.

"It wouldn't do us much good in that direction," said Richard. "That's Germany. I wish to heaven that Pertisau had tucked itself near the border of a nice healthy place like Switzerland. Still, even if we have to make a dash for it, it is just as well to have a choice of directions. Yesterday I was worried because Pertisau was such a bottleneck."

"You seem to expect fireworks. It's difficult to think of any danger or evil lurking in this kind of place." Frances settled down on Richard's Burberry, and fished for a cigarette in one of its pockets. She lit it, and lay back to look at the sky.

"How are we going to do it?" she added.

Richard folded up his map carefully and put it into his pocket. He stretched down beside her and watched the clouds.

"I think Anton is our best bet. We'll just walk in, one of these days, and ask if we dare have the great honor and pleasure of seeing the chess collection. Anton's name will get us past any servant who's about the place. All other excuses are pretty obvious."

"Such as?"

"Well, you could need a drink of water, but unfortunately there's a nice mountain stream running down that valley. Or you could sprain your weak ankle, and need help to get back to the village. But that's rather a poor effort."

"I'm glad it is."

"So we shall just blow in, probably on Thursday or Friday, when Pertisau has looked us over and accepted us. There's no use risking everything by an enthusiastic dash. For if this Mespelbrunn is Peter's man, then an explanation for his silence would be the fact that he was under observation. And if he is under observation, then his visitors had better be very natural indeed."

"He must be able to speak German pretty well, if Anton and the others in the village accepted him."

"It's his job. The accent hereabouts, anyway, is so peculiar that he could easily pass himself off as a real Berliner. When he is in Berlin, he has a Viennese accent, no doubt."

"Well, I am looking forward to meeting him."

"Are you definite about that?"

"Quite. You aren't going to leave me out at this stage. You know, Richard, the man in Paris was very efficient. So were the others, but they seemed simpler, somehow."

"I should think the Paris man is second in importance to Mr. Smith himself. The beginning and the end, as it were. Fugger and Kronsteiner are just moveable pawns in the game."

"I keep worrying about poor old Fugger," said Frances. "I wonder if he did get away."

"If he hadn't, we wouldn't be here. Or, we would have been continuously followed until they could catch us with another agent. Don't worry about A. Fugger. He's a wily bird." Richard suddenly sat up and watched the mountain-side.

"I thought I heard voices," he explained. He was right. Below them were two men.

Frances rose to her feet. The two figures paused and then waved their arms and shouted.

"It's Henry M. and Robert Thornley," Frances announced.

"You know," she added in amazement, "I never thought they'd come."

Richard got up. He waved and halloed back. Van Cortlandt yelled something which they couldn't make out; but Thornley was laughing, and they laughed too. The American seemed to be in good spirits. He kept calling remarks to them which sounded funny although they couldn't hear them.

At last the two men came over the last piece of rock, and dropped on the ground beside Frances. The American regained his breath, and pointed to his face. It was crimson.

"Well," said Frances, "if you will climb at twice the normal pace and make wisecracks to go with it—"

"This," said van Cortlandt with as much pride as if he had been fishing for marlin, "is my first mountain."

"We are overcome," said Frances gravely, and handed him some sliced orange. "It was a most spectacular appearance."

Robert Thornley explained. "We motored from Innsbruck this morning, at the most ghastly speed you ever saw. We found the hotel, and then your house. A nice old thing—"

"Frau Schichtl," suggested Frances.

"—told us you were up here. It looked easy, so we came."

"All lies. Perfidious British lies," said van Cortlandt. "I drove Bob as gently as if he were in a wheelchair on the Boardwalk at Atlantic City. When we found you weren't there with flags of welcome, he dragged me away from a very nice little table beside a lot of water. And then he told me it was no climb at all. Just kid's play." He looked sadly at his shoes. "They'll never be the same again."

Frances laughed. "Remember to borrow some of our first-aid kit tonight."

"Do you mean to tell me I'll feel worse tonight than when I climbed this mountain?"

"Your feet will, in these shoes. Cheer up; it wasn't a bad climb for your first."

"Wasn't bad? It's darned fine if you ask me."

"Well, have a sandwich," said Richard. "We're glad to see you."

As they ate, they explained further. The pavements of Innsbruck had become hotter and harder after the idea of Pertisau had been put before them. Last night they had met and celebrated together, and had suddenly decided to get away from cafés and conducted tours for three days. Van

Cortlandt felt he was due a vacation, anyway, and Thornley was becoming bored with being bored.

"It's the first real holiday I've had in two years," said van Cortlandt. "I'm always either going someplace or coming away from it, and I've always got an eye open and an ear listening. I'm going to forget all that for three days. I'll have to be back on Friday. Until then I am going to have some peace for a change."

Frances caught Richard's eye. "How do you like the view we arranged for you?" she said quickly.

Richard pointed out the different peaks. Over there was Germany. Down there were the Dolomites, and then Italy. Here the Danube would be flowing to Vienna. Back there would be the Alps of Switzerland.

"So this is what makes some people want to rush up to the top of every mountain they see," said van Cortlandt. He looked at Thornley pointedly, so that they all laughed, but in the end he was the last to leave the summit.

That night the promise of Innsbruck was kept. They enjoyed themselves. By the time they had finished dinner, and had gone into the hotel lounge for coffee, most of the other guests had disappeared.

"They must get their beauty sleep," suggested Frances, and giggled. She was in rather good form tonight. She had been worrying during the last two days that if the two of them did come to Pertisau, perhaps the party would be a failure. But everything was going well. She looked at van Cortlandt, leaning forward to catch Thornley's words with a smile on his lips, a smile ready to break into a laugh when the point of the long story was reached. Richard was lighting his pipe contentedly, his eyes on Thornley who had now risen to his feet to give full justice to the climax. It was when they were all laughing that Frances noticed the man. He was watching them. He sat alone at a small table, a dark-haired man with bold black eyes, heavy eyebrows and a prominent jaw. He was probably about thirty, guessed Frances; and already his muscles were running to fat, but he was powerful enough. She noticed the tightness of his shirt over the expanse of his chest, and the collar which, already tight from the thickness of his neck, seemed all the tighter because of a black tie firmly knotted. It was a strange way of dressing for a summer evening. The jacket slung over a chair was a drab green, his only concession to the Tyrol, for he wore black breeches and boots. Just as a retired Navy man can be spotted by his taste in neat navy blue, so it was easy to guess how this man had spent much of his time. Take away the Tyrolese jacket, and add a black one, and a heavy black cap, and a holster at his belt, and a rubber club, and he was typed as accurately as in a Hollywood casting office.

His eyes had been fixed on Thornley. They suddenly swung round to Frances and became aware of her scrutiny. Frances let her eyes pass through and over him, fixing them on the deer's horns just above his head. She held them there until he had stopped looking at her, and had risen from his table. He threw some coins down with a careless gesture, ignoring two which fell on the floor. She was very busy lighting a cigarette, as he walked loudly out of the room. Van Cortlandt had noticed the last few moments, and was watching Frances with a smile of approval.

"You got out of that nicely," he said. "That's one of the boys in the back room. I'll lay you five to one."

"Big odds," said Thornley. "Don't tell me that the Gestapo finds its way to a place like this."

"They'll find their way to any place, even into countries which aren't under Germany—yet," van Cortlandt replied sourly. "They give me a bad taste in my mouth," he added. He began a story about them. Frances listened, but she watched Richard. Apart from a tightening of his lips, he did not seem disturbed by anything.

"Not one of the pleasanter types of humanity," summed up Thornley. They all agreed on that, and rose. An evening walk before they went to bed seemed a good idea. Van Cortlandt looked at his wrist watch, and raised his eyebrows.

"It's only a quarter of ten," he protested. "I haven't been to bed at this hour since I was in kindergarten."

"Don't you feel you'd like to be a dog, and just risk it once?" Frances asked gravely. He looked at her quickly, and then laughed.

"I'm learning something by living among the English. I now know when to risk a laugh."

Richard and Thornley had gone ahead. Frances slowed her pace. Van Cortlandt was trying to disguise a limp.

"Let's sit here, until the others come back," suggested

Frances, as they passed some chairs tilted drunkenly against a table.

"Thanks . . . this foot is a nuisance."

"I'll give you some stuff to doctor it, tonight. Everyone has foot trouble on their first day in the hills."

He looked at her, and hesitated. He said suddenly, "You know, you're all right. I have to admit that I didn't think so much of you when we first met. Apart from being easy on the eyes, of course. I thought you were a hidebound Tory."

"You must have thought me rather suppurating." She smiled, and added, "Perhaps I am. But I'm no Tory."

"So I found out this afternoon. That was quite a talk we had, coming down that hill. I've been thinking it over since, and although I still stick to my own opinion, I begin to see why my remarks in Nürnberg made you so mad. You must have thought me—" he paused for the word.

"Smug?" suggested Frances gently.

"Now, that's pretty steep. Or did you?"

"Well, I must say I thought you inclined that way."

Van Cortlandt looked glum. "Well, that's a fine impression to hand out."

"I didn't do so well myself, did I?"

They both laughed, and then Frances was serious again. There was a sadness in her voice which she no longer tried to disguise.

"You see, if it comes to a showdown, it's the much criticized Britisher who'll have to foot a good part of a pretty bloody bill. We'll need words of encouragement from the sidelines, not jeers. And I wish you could believe me about appeasement. After all, you wouldn't call America a prohibition country today, although you lived with it for years."

"I see your viewpoint," said van Cortlandt. "It's another angle, certainly. But . . ." He shrugged his shoulders.

Frances was silent. The moon was on the water of the lake, and she could see van Cortlandt's face, white in the blue light. He looked even less convinced than his words. A thwarted idealist he had said, this afternoon. Cynic would have been the same thing. She shrugged her shoulders too and tried to smile. Van Cortlandt was watching her.

"Do you know you were being followed in Nürnberg?" he asked suddenly.

"Yes."

"In a jam?"

"Not so far."

"Sorry if I seem inquisitive, but I just wondered when I saw that bird circling us tonight."

"I don't think that meant much. Sort of incidental music."

The American looked embarrassed. "Look, I know you would have told me about it, if you had wanted to. But all I'm trying to get at is this: if you are in a jam, you can always let me know."

"I can't tell you about it, Henry. Not because I don't want you to know, but because there's no use complicating things for you. I'll tell you all about everything later—in England, if you'll come and visit us there."

"You needn't worry about me. Mrs. van Cortlandt's little boy can take care of himself."

"But you are not so sure about us?"

"Oh well. I mean, you're not the kind of people to handle trouble; you're not tough enough. I wish I could put it better. I mean—"

Frances nodded and laid her hand on his arm.

"You're all right, too," she said.

There were footsteps on the road, and they could hear Thornley's voice, and then Richard's in a fluting falsetto.

"What the . . ." began van Cortlandt.

" 'Merchant of Venice.' Last act, I think, at the beginning." She began to laugh. "We can manage the midday sun but not moonlight. Meet it is you set it down in your tables, Henry. You know, that chapter on the peculiarities of the British."

"Now when did I tell you I was doing that?"

"All books on European travel or politics have one. Why, no foreigner would believe he was looking at an Englishman unless he was funny-peculiar or funny-ha-ha."

"And what does the Englishman think about that?"

"He doesn't really care what people think about him, as long as he knows himself."

Richard and Thornley had timed their duet well. Richard managed to get the last line in, just as they reached Frances and van Cortlandt. He grasped Thornley's arm in a fair imitation of maidenly flurry.

"But, hark, I hear the footing of a man," he ended, and looked wildly round.

"You'd be safe enough if you looked like that," said Frances.

"Limping, anyway," added van Cortlandt, "so you're safe twice over."

"That role doesn't really do my powers justice," said Richard. "You should see me as the second witch in 'Macbeth.' Now that's something."

"Not tonight," said Frances hastily. "Let's all limp home to bed."

The four of them linked arms, and limped in unison towards the hotel. As Frances and Richard said good night, van Cortlandt looked as if he wanted to say something, but he didn't. He seemed worried again.

They crossed the road to the Villa Waldesruhe. Frances was silent as they went upstairs, and silent as she removed her earrings and brushed her hair. And then she remembered about van Cortlandt's limp. She searched quickly for the methylated spirits and boracic and lint. Richard made a good-humored grimace, and started putting on his shoes again. She heard his footsteps echo on the empty road outside, and began to undress. When he returned, she was already in bed.

"That fellow was back again, talking to the manager."

She blinked sleepily. That fellow—"Oh, Beetlebrows?"

"Yes. He must think we are lunatics, chasing about at this hour with first-aid."

"All the better," said Frances, "or isn't it?"

"Does no harm. Only next time, my sweet wife, do remember such things before I get my shoes off."

"Yes, darling." She yawned prodigiously. "... doing to-morrow?"

Richard folded his trousers before replying. When he did, Frances gave no answer; she was, like the rest of Pertisau, asleep.

CHAPTER XIV

The Singing of a Song

FRIDAY came quickly for Thornley and van Cortlandt, slowly for Frances and Richard. They had enjoyed the bathing and climbing, the strange conversations which had a habit of cropping up, as much as the other two, but, as Frances said, Friday was like taking medicine; she wanted to get it over as quickly as possible.

On Friday, the mists were on the mountains, and the waters of the lake looked gray and uninviting. It takes salt water to make a bathe, when the sun isn't shining. Van Cortlandt was disappointed, for this was his last day. On Saturday he had to meet a radio man in Innsbruck, who wanted some impressions from him for a broadcast to America next week. Thornley thought it would be better if he motored into Innsbruck with van Cortlandt. He had begun to worry again about Tony and his Czechoslovakian girl. He wanted to make sure that his Innsbruck hotel hadn't mixed up his Pertisau address.

Over their eleven-o'clock beer, the arrangements were made. And then came the suggestion from Thornley that once the Innsbruck business was finished, he and van Cortlandt should return to Pertisau for a couple of days. At this, Richard looked slightly taken aback. By Sunday, God knows what would have happened. The two men noticed his slight hesitation, the vagueness of his reply. There was what Frances called a pregnant pause. She felt miserable, trying to explain to them with her eyes and her smile that it was no lack of enthusiasm for them which had caused Richard's embarrassment. Van Cortlandt suddenly saw daylight.

"Of course, your movements are indefinite, we know," he said and looked hard at Thornley. Frances had the feeling that he had told Thornley about their being followed in

Nürnberg. The feeling was confirmed when she heard Thornley make a good follow-up.

"We can phone from Innsbruck, and find if you are still here. That is, if you don't mind."

"That would be fine," said Richard, obviously sincere, and the difficult moment had passed.

"It's a pity you must leave today," said Frances. "There's a dance this evening." The men looked bored at the idea.

"No, not in one of the hotels," she went on, reading their thoughts. "It's the real thing, held in one of the inns back near the woods. They build a platform outside the inn, and everyone comes from miles around to dance in their best clothes. Some of the costumes are really perfect, and it's fun to see people really enjoying themselves."

"When does it begin?" asked van Cortlandt.

"Nineish."

He shook his head. "Too late for me; we'll have to leave about six. But say, if you go, tell me about it, will you?"

"How on earth did you find out about the dance? There's no notice up anywhere that I could see," Thornley said in amazement.

"Oh, I have my agents," said Frances, and then blushed as Richard looked amused. "Actually, it was Frau Schichtl. She told me about it this morning, and said very pointedly that we would be welcomed."

"That's rather strange, don't you think, considering their German cousins are all over the place? You would think that they would be the ones who were welcome, and that we outsiders would be avoided like the plague."

"Lower voice," suggested Richard quietly.

Frances followed the suggestion. "No, it was quite the opposite. Frau Schichtl was eager for us to go and meet the real Austrians. She offered me the Sunday dirndl dress her daughter used to wear. Very lovely it was too."

"She really is awfully decent, you know," Thornley said. "She waylaid us yesterday when we came round to beat you up."

Van Cortlandt stared. "Bob, what the—"

"To beat you up or to hound you out or to collect you," Thornley explained as an aside. "Anyway, while we waited in that downstairs room, Frau Schichtl was baking in the kitchen. It was a damned good smell, too. So we looked in and made some jokes in terrible German, and we had to taste the cake just out of the oven. Haven't done that for years."

"I seem rather left out of all this," said Richard.

Frances laughed. "No, you aren't. Frau Schichtl said you were very well brought up and *so* polite. And she loves your imitations of the Bavarian accent."

Richard reddened. "Oh, come!" he said, and the others laughed.

But van Cortlandt had sensed a story.

"Where's the daughter?" he asked Frances. She studied her hands and said nothing.

"I won't use it for copy, if that is what you are thinking," he added with a wry smile.

Frances hesitated, but the others' curiosity had been wakened.

"She is dead. Some years ago, she went to Vienna to study singing. Frau Schichtl had saved a little money, and the girl was eager. She must have had some talent to get her way like that. But instead of becoming a great singer, she fell in love and got married. He was an active Social Democrat. They were planning to come here to visit Frau Schichtl; they hadn't much money, so they had to plan it carefully. And then the Nazis arrived. The husband's name must have been on their blacklist. They said he committed suicide. Nothing more has been heard of the girl." She paused. "Frau Schichtl says that I look very much like her, when she left for Vienna."

Van Cortlandt said, "She may not be dead."

"Frau Schichtl hopes she is."

There was a silence.

Then van Cortlandt said again, "Just another. That's what gets me down. It isn't just an isolated case. Wherever you go beneath the surface in this damned Nazi setup, there's tragedy, or something twisted. Nothing but complications, and fears, and threats. Even those who think they've jumped on the bandwagon are still standing on one leg. Only the dumbest of them can forget they are on the edge of a volcano. A nice crop of neurotics they'll be after whatever is going to happen has happened."

"Or corpses," said Thornley unexpectedly. "They'd make a fine row of corpses." He looked speculatively at the froth rims in his beer glass. The story of Frau Schichtl's daughter had started him thinking again about Czechoslovakia, thought Frances. She watched them finish their beer, each man with his own thoughts. The truth was that there was no peace of mind left for anyone—for anyone with a heart.

Richard had risen, and changed the subject. "Now about this afternoon. Frances and I thought we'd take a walk, and let you pack and make your arrangements. We'll be back to give you a send-off about six. That's the time you thought of, isn't it?" It was more of an intimation than a suggestion. Thornley caught van Cortlandt's eye, and the two men exchanged smiles.

"That suits us," the American said, and then added almost too casually, "and if you can't be good, you know what."

Frances and Richard left Waldesruhe at three o'clock. Richard had calculated that the distance from Pertisau to the red-shuttered house was about two miles. Yesterday, as they had climbed a hill with a view of the Pletzach, Thornley had pointed the house out to them—standing isolated in a high meadow above the little river. It was a good sort of place to have for the summer, he had observed. He was one of those who got a simple kind of pleasure in choosing sites for houses which he would never be able to own. There were already three places on the surrounding hillsides which he had selected as admirable for a summer chalet.

As they passed the Hotel Post, Thornley waved to them from the doorway, but he made no move to talk to them. As they entered the road which would lead them up the Pletzach, Frances glanced involuntarily over her shoulder. He was still standing at the hotel door, his hands in his pockets, and she had the feeling that he was making a very good pretense of not watching them. So his appearance at the door had been no accident. That gave her a comforting feeling. At least someone who knew them could vouch that they had left Pertisau quite normally. The deceased when last seen appeared to be in good health and normal spirits.

"He's a good person to have around in a crisis."

"Who is?" asked Richard.

"Bob Thornley. He tries to avoid discussing anything he feels very deeply about. It's as if he were afraid to let himself get emotional. He covers up with a funny story or one of

these jokes against himself. And yet he notices quite a lot
that is going on around him."

"He's no fool. Neither is Henry, but in another way. Did
you know that Bob was an amateur golf champion of Bel-
gium and Germany? Henry unearthed that. He would, of
course. Now there's another who is afraid of his emotions,
but he takes refuge in being so damned critical that he
becomes a sort of perpetual Doubting Thomas. Yet underneath, he has plenty of the right reactions. His heart is in the
right place even if he has trained his mind to respond with a
firstly, secondly, thirdly. When he forgets about that, then
you feel he's made of very real flesh and blood. I bet his life
is a conflict between what he thinks is the clever thing to do,
and what he wants to do."

"And which wins?"

"I said he had the right reactions."

"He certainly had them this morning. I liked him when he
lost his temper. He summed up everything I feel very neatly.
It's strange how well Bob and Henry seem to hit it off; they
have so many differences. I suppose it is a case of accepting
them, and resisting the urge to reform the other fellow."

"They've both got sense," said Richard, and taking advantage of the fact that they had passed the houses at this side of
the village, and that they were the only people on the quiet,
narrow road, began to discuss their plans for the last time.
He had chosen to approach the house quite openly and
directly, so that if it were being watched, their reason for the
visit would be believed. If they were to approach it in any
roundabout way, it would be difficult to explain such caution.
Frances could see the sense in that, although it seemed
almost too simple to her just to walk up to the house and ask
for Dr. Mespelbrunn. In spite of her determination to keep
cool, there was already a feeling of excitement prickling her
spine.

It was just half-past three when the road, now scarcely
broader or more definite than a cart track, curved round the
foot of the hill which buttressed the mountain range on their
right. Only then could anyone from the road see the house. It
was planted neatly in the middle of a broad green meadow
on the sheltered side of the hill, the side which had been
hidden from them as they approached from Pertisau. It lay
peacefully isolated. There was no sign of any life in the

wooded valley which it commanded, or on the mountains which walled in the valley.

Behind them, the jutting arm of the hill had so completely cut off the road by which they had come that Pertisau seemed blotted from the map. The mists had risen from the mountains, and the wind had dropped; the branches of the trees were motionless, the leaves were still. There wasn't even the sound of a woodman's ax. Even the Pletzach had subdued its chatter; it slipped, smooth and shallow, over its gravel bed.

"This is where we branch off," said Richard, as they reached a low wooden bridge over the stream. Across it was a path leading up to the fringe of trees which grouped themselves round the meadow. Behind the house, they thickened into a small forest which covered the slope of the hill like a neatly clipped beard, and spread onto the mountainside, which lay behind. When they reached the first of the trees, they saw that a track separated from the path to take them across to the front entrance of the house.

Richard looked at Frances. "Smile for the dicky bird," he said, and forced one out of her. They left the shelter of the trees to climb up the gently sloping grass. Frances wished she felt as cool as Richard looked. His small talk on the beauties of nature was faultless. For once, she could not think of a thing to say.

It was a small house, sturdily built, with the usual overhanging eaves, a balcony encircling the upper story, and shutters with the conventional heart-shaped decorations. The large window boxes at the edge of the balcony were filled with petunias. Perhaps there were more windows than a peasant would have thought necessary, but otherwise it was the kind of house which someone who had lived in, and loved, the Tyrol might build as a summer escape from his town life. Someone who had indulged his taste for an additional romantic touch in the red of the shutters. They made a convincing and yet inconspicuous landmark.

The heavy front door was closed. Richard knocked, and as they waited, they looked at the stretching valley below them. Thornley had been right; it was a perfect place to build a house. The rain clouds of the morning had disappeared, and the sun warmed the stillness all around them. They heard the door open behind them, and they turned to face a woman.

She was past middle age, large-boned, with the impassive face of a peasant. Her graying hair was tightly knotted at the back of her head; her large-knuckled hands kept smoothing her apron.

"Good day," Richard said.

The woman nodded, but did not speak.

"Is Dr. Mespelbrunn at home?" At the name Mespelbrunn her eyes moved quickly from Richard to Frances, and then back again.

Richard tried again. "I am interested in chess collections, and I have been advised by Anton in the village to visit Dr. Mespelbrunn, who has some very fine pieces, I believe. If Dr. Mespelbrunn were at home, perhaps he would have the great kindness to let me see his collection."

The woman was still silent. She was not altogether stupid, thought Richard, remembering the quickness of her glance. Could it be that she was afraid? Then the woman suddenly looked behind her, and drew quickly away from the door. Yes, it was fear, all right. A man came out of the shadows. He must have been listening quite quietly all this time.

"Dr. Mespelbrunn?" he asked. His voice had a hoarseness which coarsened his accent. He had pushed the gray-haired woman to one side, and stood in the sunlight with a smile on his dark face. It was the man who had watched them in the Hotel Post three nights ago.

He was as swaggering as ever as he held the door wide open and bowed them politely into the house. Frances felt her legs prepare to run back down the hill as she looked at that welcoming smile; but Richard was waiting for her to enter. They found themselves in the large room, a mixture of a sitting room, a lounge, and a study.

"She's just a dumb peasant," said the man with a still broader smile. Richard ignored the remark. He repeated the sentences he had addressed to the woman.

"But of course." The hoarse voice was being genial, but the effect was far from pleasant. "If you wait here, I'll get Dr. Mespelbrunn. He is reading in the summer house."

The man left them abruptly, his heavy heels sounding on the hardwood floor with a precision which grated on Frances' nerves. She exchanged looks with Richard, but neither spoke. She had hated this man at first sight. Still, they must see Mespelbrunn before they passed any judgments. The man might be only a very clever touch of realistic color. She remembered the grim Kronsteiner and his hotel. There was no doubt that Peter's friend had a peculiar sense of humor. This might only be another example.

She drew her cardigan more closely round her shoulders, and lit a cigarette. She walked slowly round the room, feeling it like a cat. It was a pleasant room, a man's room, smelling of pine logs and tobacco. She noted the walls of natural wood, the leather armchairs, more comfortable than elegant, the functional disorder of books on every table and music on the piano. A low table stood in front of the deep couch before the open fireplace. An open fireplace—perhaps an Englishman lived here after all. Yes, in the interior of the room there was a certain touch. An Englishman lived here. She turned to Richard. He was standing before the piano, his hands deep in his pockets, his lips pursed. He nodded silently to a piece of music displayed prominently on the stand. It was their old friend. He shook his head disapprovingly. Rather obvious, was what he thought. He moved away from the piano towards the fireplace and lit another cigarette. They heard footsteps outside; a man's voice spoke as if to a dog. It was only a short command, but the words were English. She sat down in the nearest chair and tried to look as calm as she didn't feel. Richard's calm gray eyes held her own for a moment, and then she started to count the steps in the staircase at the end of the room. She had reached the ninth stair when the front door opened.

They both stared in amazement. The tall man who had entered was equally taken aback. He recovered himself before they did.

"Well, really," he said in perfect English, "this is a pleasure."

Richard smiled; his eyes were calm again. "How extraordinary to meet you here," was all he said.

The Freiherr Sigurd von Aschenhausen moved quickly over to Frances and bowed low over her hand. She smiled, but inside she was angry. An Englishman, indeed, with that acute Oxford accent so carefully cultivated in his years of free scholarship. Would Mr. Rhodes have enjoyed this joke as little as she did? Probably less . . .

"We came to see a Dr. Mespelbrunn, or rather his chess

collection. We were told in the village that it was the thing to do." Richard looked at von Aschenhausen blandly.

The German smiled. "Well, you've found him, you know."

"Are you— But why on earth—" began Frances, and hoped that the laugh she gave was sufficiently amused. "How really very funny. But why take such a wretched name as that and give up your own perfectly good one?" Help me to talk gaily, dear Heaven, she prayed, to talk nonsense like a sweet little fool.

"It's perfectly simple," said von Aschenhausen. "When I live here I have to be very careful; it would be impossible to use my own name." He paused but the Myles' only looked at him with polite surprise.

"It would be too dangerous for me," he added, lowering his voice. But they still looked at him politely, as if they expected him to go on.

"Cigarette?" he asked Frances, and flicked open his gold cigarette case. As he lit her cigarette, she noticed the bracelet on his left wrist. The bracelet was of fine gold, too.

She pretended she thought he had meant to change the subject. "You are looking very well," she said. One up, she thought, as she noticed the flicker of disappointment in his eyes. "You have a charming place here," she rushed on, before he could reply. "I think all of Pertisau is delightful."

"Yes; it is beautiful," von Aschenhausen said, emphasizing the stronger adjective. Someone ought to tell him, thought Frances, that he ought to have said "Do you think so? I'm so glad" and left it to his guests to do the praising, if he really wanted to perfect his imitation.

"You look very thoughtful," he remarked.

Frances came back to the room with a jolt. "Oh, I was thinking about forms of politeness."

"Now you have made me feel I must be very careful. I wasn't very polite according to your standards, I am afraid, when we met at that Oxford party. Why didn't you tell me then that you were coming here?"

Richard entered the conversation. "Well, first of all, we thought you were in Berlin. And, secondly, it was pure chance that we did come here. We were at Mittenwald, you know, and then one evening someone or other started to talk about the beauties of the Tyrol. You know the sort of thing:

you discuss some place, and then you feel you'd like to go there, and then you go."

"Charmingly quixotic," said von Aschenhausen.

"And the most quixotic thing of all is that you should be Dr. Mespelbrunn," Frances said. She felt his interest quicken. "I had imagined someone quite different, you know." The tension was growing. "You see, I once read a book about Pertisau. It was called *The Constant Nymph*. So when we were buying some things in Anton's shop, and he said that *the* chess connoisseur of the district was a Dr. Mespelbrunn, who just adored visiting chessmen, as it were, I suddenly thought 'Another Pertisau eccentric; how amusing.' He gave you a terrific build-up, you know, until I became quite intrigued. It was really I who am responsible for the visit, because Richard went all sort of diffident. Didn't want to trouble you, and all that sort of thing. But I expected to find a house filled with a remarkable family of chess experts and unrecognized geniuses, and here you are, a very comfortable bachelor. You've really let me down, rather. I shan't be able to romanticize again without Richard ... well, just look at him. He is enjoying his joke, isn't he?"

Richard was indeed looking amused.

"I'd still like to see the collection, if I may," he said.

"I'm afraid it isn't here at the moment. It's being exhibited at Innsbruck." Von Aschenhausen looked as if he really were disappointed too. Or perhaps it was genuine: at the beginning of Frances' little speech, he had hoped for something, something more than he had got by the end of it. He tried again.

"I think you have been mistaken about me. I've already apologized for our Oxford conversation. Can't you see there's no other course for me? Some types of work—" he paused effectively on that word—"need strong aliases."

His meaning, accompanied by that shrug of the shoulder, that pained eyebrow, that so straight, so direct look into Frances' eyes, couldn't have been plainer. In another minute, thought Frances, he will start telling us anti-Nazi jokes, just to show us how mistaken we have been about him. She looked as if she believed him; Richard nodded sympathetically; but neither of them spoke.

Von Aschenhausen waited. And then he began to ask about Oxford. His visit this summer had lasted only for a day; he had had little time to find out all about his old

friends. Frances could see where this line would lead him. So
he was interested in Peter Galt, was he? She left it to
Richard to handle the conversation this time. She suddenly
wanted to leave, but they couldn't do that until von Aschenhausen was satisfied. She looked out of the window. Her
thoughts turned to Mespelbrunn. Where was he? Probably
dead. Perhaps dead and buried on the mountainside opposite
her. She watched the sunlight strike on the dark rich green of
the fir trees, and the shadows lengthening on the hill. The
afternoon was ending. She turned impatiently to the two
men.

Richard, by some feat, had switched the conversation over
to the women's colleges in Oxford, and there it had stuck,
imbedded in the higher education of women. He refused to
abandon his advantage; he had got the conversation to a nice
impersonal subject, and he was going to keep it there. He
was politely defending the new freedom of women. Women
had learned to compromise successfully between developing
their mental powers and retaining their charm. The aggres-
sive unfemininity of the original blue-stocking was already
disappearing. It was only a matter of time and adjustment to
a freer aspect of life.

Von Aschenhausen smiled his disbelief. "They are too
emotional. They are limited in reasoning power. They are
weaker, both physically and mentally. They can never be
equal to men. Compromise, adjustment, matter of time. . . .
You couldn't be more English, Richard." The use of Richard's first name carried all three of them back, back to a
time when suspicion and hatred had only brooded in the
hearts of a few vengeful men. In the silence that followed,
they looked at each other. There was no need to translate
their thoughts into words; they were clear in their eyes.

The German spoke first. "You need not reproach me.
What Mrs. Myles said at that sherry party was true. Our
countries have gone different ways. And I have my work to
do. But I think, as I said already, that you have been
mistaken about me. It is a compliment, I suppose, to my
powers of acting. I never knew they were so good as that."
He shrugged his shoulders again and gave a rueful smile. You
are not making a bad job of it, right now, thought Richard.
Von Aschenhausen had been well cast for the part he had to
play. To anyone who did not know that he was German, he

would appear to be the authentic Mespelbrunn. Now, he was making the best of a very bad piece of luck: here were two people who could know that he was no Englishman. His hints at anti-Nazi feeling were just enough to win their sympathy, disarm their suspicions. He didn't protest too much, either; he had to pretend that their visit was innocent, in case it really was. He couldn't make any declarations; he had to give them confidence, and perhaps they would show their hand once that was established. His difficulty was that they might very well be only interested in chessmen. Considering everything which was at stake, he was not making a bad job of it at all, thought Richard again.

Von Aschenhausen suddenly rose, and walked over to the small table which was used as a bar. His voice was charmingly ingenuous.

"You used to play well. Why don't you now, while I mix some drinks?" As he measured out the whisky, Frances was aware that he was watching Richard move to the piano with more than friendly interest.

"Hello," Richard said casually, "what's this you've got? Do you sing?"

"Only for myself. You go ahead."

Richard noted the soprano setting of the song, and smiled gently.

"It's a good song, but not my cup of tea. What about 'The Two Grenadiers' or something with hair on its chest? I'll need the music, though. I'm very bad at playing things by ear." He turned to a pile of music and started to look through it.

Frances rose and went over to the piano.

"You are both so modest. I'll sing for you instead." She saw Richard stiffen slightly, and give her a blank look. Von Aschenhausen was watching her now. She returned his smile sweetly and sat down on the piano stool. Richard cursed silently to himself; surely Frances had not been duped by an earnest pair of blue eyes. Surely she couldn't . . . He cursed to himself. If he could only reach that little table and upset it by accident before she started to sing . . . But as he moved, the first notes sounded through the room, and the words of the song gathered strength as her voice grew more confident. Richard looked at von Aschenhausen. His politeness had vanished. The dueling scars on his face were very noticeable.

Frances finished the last melancholy chords. She stood up and faced von Aschenhausen. She spoke directly to him.

"It is called 'The Slaughter of the Innocents'—one of the old Coventry Carols. Do you know it?" Her voice still held the sadness of the song, but there was a challenge in her eyes.

"Sentimentalizing history, isn't it?" His accent was less English.

"Maybe. But it's only when you think of history as blood and tears that you can ever learn from it." She saw he understood the meaning underlying her words just as he had understood the application of the song. The cap fitted. Let it, she thought savagely.

There was a sudden crash upstairs, and then the thuds of hollow blows. The noises ceased as startlingly as they had begun. Von Aschenhausen saw the surprise on their faces. He was suddenly casual and polite again; he smiled easily.

"Don't worry," he said. "That's the dog. We keep him out of the way when we have visitors. He's very savage with strangers. He is just about due for his exercise, and he always lets me know very forcibly when it's time to take him out for a walk."

"Oh, we mustn't keep you, then," Frances said. "I am sure we have stayed too long, in any case."

"I am sorry I had to disappoint you about the chessmen. They may be back by Sunday. Come and see them, then."

Richard, still listening for further sounds, said they would be delighted to come, perhaps at the beginning of next week. He was thinking about the dog. It was strange to keep an animal locked up inside a room upstairs; that would hardly improve its temper. But of one thing he was certain: von Aschenhausen was determined to get them out of the house, as quickly as possible.

Frances had already reached the door. As von Aschenhausen opened it for them, they heard two other sounds from upstairs. Weaker sounds, much weaker. But they ignored them, and said their good-bys as if nothing had happened. And they equally ignored the dark man with the hoarse voice, who stood astride outside the front door, his thumbs tucked inside his belt. At a nod directed upstairs from von Aschenhausen, he sprang quickly past them, mounting the steps three at a time. Von Aschenhausen had regained his usual composure, but his smile was too fixed. He stood at the door and watched them until they had reached the trees. Frances hated the feeling of his eyes on her back; she forced herself to walk naturally, as if she were strolling down Holywell. Only now would she admit to herself what she had first known at a sherry party in Oxford. The man who had once been numbered among their friends had long since become an enemy. It was a painful admission.

When they gained the road, Frances took a deep breath.

"Well, I've made another step in my education," she said. Richard did not answer. He was lost in thought.

"What's wrong? You haven't forgotten the Geneva address, have you? Or what?"

Richard shook his head. He seemed to be paying little attention; rather, he was watching the road as if he were trying to remember something.

"It's just about here, I think," he said as if to himself. He saw Frances looking at him curiously. "Just about here, that the shoulder of the hill stopped hiding the house. We'll give it another twenty yards."

The road twisted farther behind the jutting hill; and as it passed through a fringe of trees, Richard suddenly pulled Frances up the short steep bank into the shelter of the branches. It was all so quick that Frances did not have time to say anything; her surprise held her silent. Richard looked back over his shoulder, and then relaxed his grip on her arm.

"The shoulder hid us, and they couldn't follow us yet. Not with the road so open as it is."

"What's wrong?" Frances asked again.

"Something. Haven't quite made up my mind."

He advanced into the small wood, and Frances followed; the feeling of confidence which had come to her as they left the path and reached the road quickly evaporated. Von Aschenhausen had discovered nothing, except that they didn't like the politics of his country—and that couldn't have surprised him, even if it angered him. What worried Richard? He had reached a large tree, which had sheltered the ground from the morning rain. There they regained their breath. It had only taken them two minutes to reach here from the road.

The wood had grown over a large mound, and from this

elevation they had a clear view of one part of the road, neatly focused for them by the way in which the trees grew. They could see without being seen. Richard moved slightly to the left to get a better sight of the one visible patch of road. From this point, it could be seen even if they sat down. He seemed satisfied—but not with Frances' dress. He pulled off the red silk handkerchief which she wore tucked into the neckline of her white shirt.

"Put on your cardigan properly," he advised, "and button it right up to cover that white collar. I don't like the red socks: they shine up miles away. Here—" He reached for a handful of earth mold, and covered the red wool with an efficient layer of clinging brown earth.

"Here yourself," said Frances with a good touch of annoyance.

"My pet, you aren't in this for the benefit of your color schemes." He kept his voice low, but there was enough sharpness in it to tell her he was worried.

"Well, I'm glad that the cardigan is green, or I'd be rolling in the mud at this moment, I suppose . . . What's *wrong?*"

Richard put one arm round her shoulders, and kept his eyes fixed on the road.

"Frances, what did you think when you heard the noises upstairs?"

So that was the trouble. She looked at him in surprise.

"Well, it could have been a dog," she said.

"Forget about that dog. What were the noises like? As you heard them, and not as they were explained away?"

Frances studied her muddied socks for some moments. She had been standing beside the piano; the drinks they hadn't touched had gleamed amber in a ray of sunlight.

"Well, candidly, the first sound seemed a crash, as if something heavy, like a piece of furniture, something solid, had fallen. And then came some thumps."

"Well?"

"They might have been a fist, but I don't think any fist could have hammered loudly enough for us to hear, even allowing for wooden floors and ceilings. No, I don't think those thumping sounds came from a fist. They were too powerful for that. I thought afterwards that it *could* have been a dog leaping against a heavy door. A big dog."

"But those thuds were clear-cut. They were sharply

defined. There were no scrabbling noises, which generally end a dog's jump against a door. Even when we were leaving, and we were standing at the foot of the staircase, there were no whines, no pawing sounds. Peculiar kind of dog it must have been."

Frances looked at Richard, who kept his eyes fixed on the road. She was beginning to see the reason for his worry.

"Yes," she agreed. "There were only clear-cut thuds. Sort of staccato thuds."

"And the last two, which we heard at the bottom of the stairs, and which should have sounded clearer to us if anything, were actually weaker."

"Yes." Something haunted her memory. "Wait," she added. If only she could think what it was that had that kind of sound. Something she had heard that afternoon . . . in that room.

"Richard—" her voice was excited now, and Richard laid a finger on his lips warningly—"Richard, if a dog jumped at the door as we are supposed to believe, the thud on the door would have a different sound from a thud on the floor, wouldn't it? Well, do you remember when that bull-necked man left us to go and tell Mespelbrunn that we had arrived? He swaggered across the floor and his heels made that same flat sound. The thumping was not against a door, it was on the ground. And I don't believe it was made by anything so soft as a hand or a dog's paw. You were perfectly right, Richard."

"You are more right, still. Good for you, Fran. Now for a spot of reconstruction. We heard a crash, as if a piece of furniture or something solid had hit the ground. What about a chair? And what about someone tied to the chair? That would make the crash quite as heavy as we heard it. Then there were the thumpings, harder and stronger than the blows from a fist. What about two legs tied together? Then they would have to be brought slowly up and allowed to fall on the floor. That would give the kind of noise we heard, all right; for with the legs or ankles tied the heels would strike the ground together. It also accounts for the fact that the blows got weaker. It's pretty difficult and tiring to attract anyone's attention that way."

"But everything was so quiet in that house until those last five minutes."

"Yes, until after you had finished your song."

"Whoever it was recognized it?"

Richard nodded. "Yes. . . . He couldn't have made out our voices when we were talking. And there would have been no hope for him if he had heard a German song sung by a German voice. But there was hope enough to try to attract our attention when he heard an English voice and a song which practically only an Englishman would recognize."

"So he may be our man? What on earth can we do, Richard? We've found him and we haven't found him." This was something which Peter Galt had not thought of; they should have either met an Englishman, or found he was dead. Something nice and straightforward, and not a hopeless complication like this.

"What's our next step?" she asked dismally.

Richard drew a slab of chocolate from his pocket. "Eat some of this," he suggested. He looked at his watch. "It's well after five now. We had better wait a bit. If any chance comes, we'll seize it. If no chance comes, I'll take you back to Frau Schichtl's, and come back here myself tonight. I'd like to look around."

"You've no gun," said Frances in a very low voice; her fears stifled her. "Perhaps he isn't our man after all," she added persuadingly.

"It's some man, anyway. I'd still like to look around. Henry may carry a gun. If so, I'll borrow it. If not, then I've always got my stick." He patted the *makhila* which lay beside them. Frances looked at the Basque stick of rough wood, with its round leather handle and its sharply pointed ferrule. It didn't look much protection; the iron point on the end was only good for helping you up a steep hill. Richard noticed her expression. He unscrewed the handle with a suspicion of a smile.

"I never showed you this. It's rather gruesome." The head of the stick and part of the top of it slipped off, and a wicked eight inches of pointed steel emerged. It was firmly fixed to the rest of the stick, and transformed it into an ominous weapon.

"I'm not bloodthirsty," he added. "I bought it on that Pyrenees trip, when I was an undergraduate, because I liked the way the Basques swung these sticks with the leather thong of the handle fixed round their wrists, when they were returning from market. Going to the town, they kept the cattle in order with the steel point. Coming from the town, they screwed the handle back in place and slipped the thong over their wrist, and swung it jauntily—with their jacket over one shoulder, and money in their pocket, and a smile for all the girls. I liked the contrast."

Frances looked at him incredulously. "And I've looked at that stick for years, and I never ... When you told me it was used for goading cattle, I thought it was the ferrule at the end of the stick which you meant." She began to giggle; any joke seemed doubly good at this moment.

Richard's smile broadened. "Really, Frances, you're wonderful. Have you ever seen Basque oxen?" He laughed quietly, and then kissed her. "I wouldn't part with you for all the gold in America," he said.

Frances recovered her seriousness. "Now that I've supplied the comic relief, how long are we going to stay here, and what shall we do, if and when and where?"

"First of all, I was curious to see if we would be followed. We weren't, it seems. Von Aschenhausen perhaps was quite convinced that we were harmless fools. I shouldn't be surprised, though, if he checks up on our travels. You know the Teutonic thoroughness. That may have been the reason why he had that afterthought of inviting us to come back and see the chess collection: just so that he can know more about our movements when he meets us again. Probably, too, someone will be sent to keep a watchful eye on us until we leave Pertisau. That's very probable. That leads to my second idea. I've been hoping that Beetlebrows might make one of his evening calls on Pertisau. If he does, then we'll improvise."

"And I'll be quite useless," said Frances bitterly. "What you need is another man with you. And then we might be able to do something."

Richard didn't answer that.

"If we could get to the house in a roundabout way, or something—" Frances went on—"but then we'd have to face two men, armed, as well as the dog—if there is one. It would be madness. What you need is darkness, and someone like Henry or Bob, or both. And at least one gun. It's hopeless."

"Let me do the worrying, Frances. I'll try nothing unless one of them leaves. I can manage one of them alone, easily, if I can get to the house unseen. There is no telephone, and that will be useful for us: I'm depending on Beetlebrows, and his visits to Pertisau." He looked at his watch again. "It's getting near his usual time."

Frances wondered why Richard was so confident that there were only two men to worry about . . . But his eyes were fixed on the road. She sat beside him and waited in silence. She felt she had made enough wifely objections to last for the next few hours. After all, she had insisted on coming. Richard had been against it. Wifely objections would only be doubly irritating. So she sat and finished the job of converting her red socks into a rich chestnut-brown.

CHAPTER XV

The Mountain

IT COULD only have been about ten minutes later when Richard's arm tightened round Frances, and pushed her quickly flat on the ground. She felt a stone dig into the small of her back, but Richard's grasp was firm. She lay still and watched him. He was lying flat on his stomach, his head only raised enough to let him see that free patch of road. It was the black-haired man, cycling towards Pertisau, with a wolf-hound at his heels ... And then he was out of sight: the other trees hid him from Richard's straining eye.

Richard relaxed his grip, and Frances sat up and rubbed her back. The stone had become a boulder.

"So that leaves only von Aschenhausen," said Richard with some satisfaction.

Frances forgot her good resolutions. "How are you so sure?" she asked.

"If there were others, then the noises upstairs would have been silenced more quickly. And von Aschenhausen had to signal to that man to stop guarding the front door. It was only then that he was free to go upstairs and attend to the noises. If there had been others to stop us from getting away—supposing it had come to that—then he would not have stuck outside until he got the signal."

"But why only two of them?"

"It's a small house, and if a group of men had arrived to live there, the villagers would have started to talk. Then any prospective visitors might have had suspicions aroused. I expect that black-haired fellow poses as Mespelbrunn's new servant." Richard looked at his watch, and then added, "We had better let him get halfway to Pertisau, and then he can look round as much as he likes and it won't trouble us."

"They haven't anything definite against us, have they?" asked Frances.

"Nothing except the fact that we were found in a suspected shop in Nürnberg, and that we presented ourselves to an obviously suspected Dr. Mespelbrunn with a highly suspect form of introduction. They may dislike the coincidence. Perhaps von Aschenhausen has started to check up on us already. There isn't any phone, but he has some kind of radio transmitter and receiver, I'm sure. Perhaps Beetlebrows is going down to Pertisau to keep an eye on us. Perhaps all that. And again, von Aschenhausen may be congratulating himself on getting rid of a pair of unwelcome visitors, and Beetlebrows is cycling down to Pertisau to see a girl, or have his beer, or to keep his figure. I think myself that it's safer to overestimate your enemies than underestimate them, so I'm prepared to believe that they don't like us one bit."

"Von Aschenhausen certainly didn't like me," Frances said, and laughed gently.

"I could have strangled you, myself, when you played that trick at the piano. You had me as jittery as he was. For a moment I thought you were going to play that damned music."

"Was it as good as that? Darling, you've made me very happy."

"It was too dangerous, Frances. Never give in to your impulse for the artistic, not in a situation like that."

"Oh, it was safe enough. He thinks women have no brains. Even at the very end, he only thought I was parroting some phrases I had heard you say."

Richard smiled in spite of himself. . . . And then he looked at his watch impatiently, and then he looked at the warm glow of the evening sun.

"I wish it were darker, but we can't wait. Come on, Frances."

They made their way back to the road, and paused at the edge of the trees. There was no one in sight. They crossed quickly into the rough field which stretched towards the stream, skirting the foot of the hill. They covered the uneven ground quickly but carefully.

"No twisted ankles at this point," said Richard. Frances nodded. She was concentrating on the varying firmness of the treacherous clumps underneath her feet. The stream was shallow, fortunately. They crossed by choosing stones either jutting up or only lightly covered by the racing water.

Frances congratulated herself on having her shoes only wet, and not swamped entirely. And now they began to climb the hill itself, aiming for a point in its shoulder which would bring them just above and behind the house. This side of the hill was dangerously open; there were no trees, only grass and shrubs which ultimately gave way to the rocky spine. Again Frances had the feeling that the hill which they were climbing was the buttress, and the mountain behind it was the cathedral. It was like a finger pointing out of the mountain's clenched hand. The climb was more difficult than it looked from the road, for there was no path to lead them over the easiest ground.

Two thirds of the climb found the undergrowth thinning out quickly. They paused for breath, while Richard scanned the ground above them. He shook his head as he noticed the increasing number of small screes. It was madness to try to scramble over their treacherous surface; the stones now under their feet were as knife-sharp as when they had been splintered from smashing boulders. The ridge of the hill was of rock, and, at this distance, there was a dangerous look to the last fifty feet. It would be slow work getting over that. He looked along its side to the place where the hill joined the mountain. Just at that point there seemed to be a slight hollow. It was the bed of a mountain stream, now dry, but no doubt forming a gleaming cascade of water in the spring.

"Our best bet is to strike for the stream," he said. "It will take us farther away from the house, but the dry bed of a torrent is easier than a miniature precipice." He pointed to the crest of the hill. Frances needed no convincing. They began to climb obliquely up towards the bed of the stream, avoiding any falls of loose gravel, and choosing ground where some persistent green still showed. That at least gave them some guarantee of safety.

It was slow work, until they suddenly met, to Frances' joy, a small track which had the same idea as Richard. It must have begun at the road, near the place where the shoulder of the hill had formed a jutting curve, and had traced its modest way parallel to the shoulder's crest.

"We could have followed this all the way," said Frances, with some exasperation, following their own course up the hill with a bitter eye.

"No, it began too close to the house. The road at that

point might have been watched by Herr Von-und-zu strolling in his nice soft meadow."

Frances was standing very still. "Well, we only postponed it," she said so quietly that Richard stopped and turned to see her face.

"Down there," she added. Richard followed the direction of her eyes. The valley beneath them was no longer empty. Along the road which led from Pertisau a man was riding a bicycle.

"Like the hammers of hell," Richard said, and swore gently but wholeheartedly. "Don't move. Keep just the way you are."

"He looks like an ant," said Frances.

"Louse, you mean." Richard was worried. "I wonder now ... what did he learn at Pertisau to send him back at this rate? No one there knew when we were returning, except Henry or Bob; and he can't have been talking to them."

"I wonder if he saw us. Do you think he would take me for another piece of greenery! There are at least two pieces of scrub near me." She looked fearfully at her socks, but the loam had been reinforced by some mud which she had blundered into on the soft bank of the stream. Richard watched the cyclist as he reached the curve in the road.

"He hasn't slackened pace yet; it looks as if he might not have noticed us. If he had, I should think he would have slowed up just to make sure. God, that dog can keep up a terrific clip."

"What shall we do?"

"There's still daylight for some time," Richard said thoughtfully. "Once we are up there, we ought to have a wonderful view of the back of the house. Damn it all, if only I had left you in Pertisau, and come by myself."

"Then you wouldn't have had either an old English song, or these noises. Let's go on, Richard. I don't like the idea of going down the way we came up. And once we get up—we are very nearly there anyway—we might find a decent path on the mountain itself to lead us back to Pertisau. There's no law against us trying to climb our way back towards the village and if anyone wants to know why we took so long, well then, we got lost. That's all." But the truth was, she added to herself, that Richard would have gone on if he had been alone or with another man—and that settled it.

Richard still looked doubtful, but he was wavering.

"Well, we can watch from the top for half an hour, and if it all seems hopeless, then I'll get you back to the road before it's dark."

"All right. Let's move, Richard."

They started to climb the last stretch of hill.

The path was apologetic. At best, it was little more than a foot broad; at its worst, it effaced itself altogether under slides of stones. As they crossed these slowly, Frances held her breath. One slip here, and she would go rumplin' tumplin' down the Tankersha' brae. She kept her eyes fixed on the next step ahead, and avoided looking down to her right. For there the hill now fell steeply away, carved out by erosion into an adequate quarry. If this path had lain across a field, you could run along it, she argued. So there was no reason why she couldn't walk along it here, provided she didn't know how far she had to fall. And then the green scrub was again growing thickly, and they had reached the bushes and dwarf trees which edged the bed of the stream. The sides of the dry torrent, and even the bed itself, were piled with large rocks. They formed a staircase. A giant's staircase, thought Frances, but at least if she slipped here she would always have a boulder behind her, to block her fall.

They were both breathing heavily with the effort of hoisting themselves over the rocks which would form the bank of the torrent when the snows melted in the spring. But the worst of the climb was already past. The boulders in the bleached bed of the stream were thinning out, and the ground was leveling. They were approaching the saddle between the hill and the mountain. As it opened out before them they saw that it was broad and gently sloping. They left the stream which was turning towards the mountain itself, and walked quickly over the grass towards some scattered rocks on the saddle's crest. From there they could see the valley with the red-shuttered house. When they reached the rocks only half of their expectations was realized. All they could see of the house was some blue smoke which curled up lazily over the tops of the farthest trees.

Richard smiled wryly. "Anticlimax department, I'm afraid. It seems I dragged you up here to admire the view, Frances. I'm sorry."

Frances let her muscles relax. She pushed her damp hair

away from her brow to feel the full coolness of the evening breeze.

"You can always study the paths," she said.

Richard was already doing that. The saddle seemed the meeting place of the paths on the hill and the mountain. If he could get Frances back to Pertisau as quickly as possible, and if the moon was as clear as it had been last night, then he could use the mountain paths to bring him right up behind the house. He could see both of them clearly from here; neither was difficult. Eastwards towards Pertisau stretched the first path he would use, which would bring him easily onto this saddle; and then, from here, there was a westward path, cutting across the mountain where it formed a background for the house. He could see at least one track descending from it into the trees which encircled the back of the house. Then he might try some stalking right up to the outskirts of the house itself. Thornley would be a good man to have along; he knew his way about a mountain. It was just as well that he had come up here after all. He looked at the mountain paths, and photographed what he saw in his memory.

Frances, lying beside him, her chin cupped in her hands, had been staring at the forest beneath them. Her eyes followed the well-marked path, which led from the saddle down through the trees towards the house. This was probably the path which began at the bridge in the valley. She looked at the trees, as if by sheer will-power she might see through them, through the walls of the house itself into that room upstairs. She was comparing her reactions as she had left that house to those of Richard, and the result did not flatter her. She had taken it for granted that their job was over, that there was nothing left to do except send a telegram and then go away and enjoy themselves. She had believed the story about the dog because she had wanted to believe it; it was a subconscious desire to be rid of complications, to avoid any further trouble. Now she knew that she wouldn't have been able to enjoy any holiday. She would have had to face the fact ultimately that it hadn't been a dog, and she would have remembered it just as long as she would remember the cry in a Jews' Alley in Nürnberg.

She suddenly stiffened.

"What was that? Richard, I saw something down there."

"Where?" He turned to look down the hill towards the house. The path, beginning near where they lay, twisted its way towards the forest. Beyond the last trees, the smoke curled from the chimney.

"Down there. Look. The twist in the path hid it ... near the trees. Richard, it's a dog."

Richard grasped her wrist and the strength of his hand calmed her.

"So he did see us," he said.

The dog, bounding up the path towards them, had stopped and was looking backwards. When the two men came in sight, he again bounded on.

It was von Aschenhausen and the black-haired man. The path was broad enough to let them walk abreast. They carried no sticks, but their hands were deep in their jacket pockets. Their eyes searched the hill around them. Once they stopped, while the man looked towards the westward path on the mountain, but it had only been some animal which had attracted his attention. He had quick eyes all right, thought Richard.

"Keep cool, Frances. They haven't seen us yet."

Again the men stopped, and this time they separated. Von Aschenhausen left the path, and began to climb directly up the shoulder. His pace had slowed down, but even from that distance it was evident that he could climb. When von Aschenhausen reached the top, he would be just about the place which they first attempted to reach. Richard reflected with some pleasure that the east side of the shoulder, which the German would then have to descend, would cramp his style a little. His plan was to encircle them, obviously. The black-haired man was plodding steadily up the path to the saddle where they lay; the dog bounded ahead.

As they backed cautiously from the sheltering rocks, and raced back over the gently sloping ground, Richard was thinking quickly but nonetheless clearly. Von Aschenhausen had taken the much more difficult way because his companion was probably a less expert climber. So much the better for Frances and himself. He would rather face brawn than brain, any day. You could outwit the former. They must make for the bed of the stream; that was their only hope for cover. Once they were hidden by the boulders and the bushes which twisted round them on the torrent's banks, they could

follow the bed until they had reached the fields and the
woods round the Pletzach—and then they would be safe
enough. The incriminating thing for them would be to stay
on the shoulder overlooking the house. If von Aschenhausen
didn't find them on the hill, they could find an explanation
for their late return to Pertisau. And he would have to
accept it, because he wouldn't be able to disprove it. But it
all made tonight's plans almost impossible. They would be
closely watched from now on.

If Frances had been thankful for grass under her feet
when she had first reached the saddle on the way up, she now
almost wept with relief. She could run swiftly on this surface
and, what was just as important, run silently. She had the
feeling of desperate effort which she used to have as a child
when she played Cowboys-and-Indians and she was one of
the chased. It was no longer a game, but the old terrifying
feeling of strained muscles bogging her down, of feet sticking
to the ground, was still there. She must go faster and faster,
but her body refused even as her mind urged her on. She
sagged, her heart pounding and a strange thundering in her
ears so that she couldn't swallow. But Richard's hand, which
had not loosened its grasp on her wrist from the moment
when they had first seen the dog, pulled her up and on. They
had reached the stream.

Their run had slowed down to a scramble, but the first
large rocks were near them. Richard had let go of her wrist
now; they needed the use of their hands to steady themselves
through the boulders. It would have been quicker work if
they hadn't had to avoid any clatter of stones. Richard was
thankful for what he had been cursing only half an hour ago,
for the fact that they had worn rubber-soled shoes today to
go visiting, rather than their nail-studded climbing boots.

The man could not have reached the top of the path yet;
nor could von Aschenhausen have reached the crest of the
shoulder. As the stream bed plunged deeply in between the
crags, Richard looked over his shoulder. They were hidden
now, thank God, from both the shoulder and the saddle of
the hill. There was no man in sight. But there was the dog. It
had marked them from the saddle, and instead of waiting
there for the dark-haired man, had followed them. It hadn't
barked. There was something uncanny in the silent way it
calculated its powerful leaps over the rough stones, to alight

on smooth rock. Its speed was checked by its twists and turns, by the way in which its thick haunches would brake suddenly on the steep side of a boulder. But its direction was unerring.

Richard hurried Frances on. They had passed the point where the track on the side of the hill had met the stream, and they were on strange ground now. The bed plunged still deeper, the banks were rockier, and more thickly screened by small wiry mountain trees. Their speed increased again, for the bed was less cluttered with boulders. The stones under their feet were sharp and uneven; those stones would hold up the dog, anyway. And then the stream curved round a mass of rock, and they saw that the narrow gorge before them suddenly ended. In front of them was nothing but space, and the precipice over which the torrents would pour in the spring, falling in a series of cataracts to the valley beneath.

They looked at each other, trying to hide the dismay in their hearts. To their left was the open mountain rising steeply; to their right, over the high bank with its crags and bushes, lay the landslide which Frances had called a quarry. They were neatly trapped.

Frances backed away from the edge of the precipice instinctively. Richard stood, his eyes turned towards the mountain, looking for some short-cut up to that eastward-bound path which would lead them to Pertisau. The ground was open, and there was little cover, but if the man had followed the dog into the bed of the stream, his view of the mountainside would be blocked by the height of the banks long enough to let them reach that point in the path where there were some trees and scrub. Anyway, there was no other choice.

And then, behind them, they heard the panting of the dog. It had followed the boulders on the banks of the stream, and now it was poised above them, eyes gleaming, teeth showing wickedly. Even as they had turned, it gathered its muscles to spring. Frances was the nearer. She heard Richard's voice behind her, low, urgent.

"Down! On your face!"

She was hypnotized as the animal, now more wolf than dog, hurled its huge weight down at her. She heard the snarl, saw the teeth ready to tear. Her eyes closed involuntarily as the slavering jaws aimed at the level of her throat, and she dropped on the ground. She felt it pass above her body, striking something beyond. Richard . . . Richard . . . That sound, what was that sound? She raised herself on an elbow, afraid to turn her head, afraid to see. Just behind her, so that she could have touched it with her foot, lay the dog. Its throat was spitted on the steel goad of Richard's stick. Richard rose, his face white, his hands still braced on the stick's shaft. The force of the dog's leap had knocked him backwards. He tried to shake the animal's body free from the stick, but the eight inches of steel were firmly embedded. With a grimace of disgust, he put his foot on the dog's chest, and pulled the stick as if it were a bayonet. It came out slowly.

From farther up the bed of the stream had come the rattle of stones, as if a heavy man had slipped badly. Richard pointed to the bank on the mountain side of the gorge. Frances rose, and moved with difficulty towards the protection of its rocks. The man would not see them until he had got well round the bend, and then he would see the dog first. There was no time to hide it, even if they could have brought themselves to touch its dead body. Richard followed her, the stick still blood-covered. He should have wiped it on the dog's coat, he knew; but he couldn't. He felt sicker than he liked to admit.

"Through there," he whispered, pointing between two boulders. Frances obeyed, keeping her head and shoulders low. By using the uneven rocks and the thick bushes for cover, they managed to clear the stream's high bank. The man in the stream bed would not see them, because of the twist in its course. Von Aschenhausen, now probably over the shoulder, might be on the difficult track which had led them to the stream. It had taken them a good fifteen minutes. It would take him as long; there was no easy way.

They paused for a moment. Behind them lay the bank; in front of them was the mountainside, its slope covered with scrub which would hardly reach their knees. They heard the man's steps now, in the bed of the stream. He would just be coming round the bend now. The footsteps paused, and then quickened. So he had seen the dog. They heard his oaths. Richard still hesitated, wondering if they should stay quietly where they were, hidden by the boulders. . . . And then he remembered. The bloodstains. They had laid a pretty track.

"Go on," he whispered to Frances.

She looked at him despairingly. "I can't lead. You must. I'll go over the side." She pointed to the steep drop down to her right. The landslide which had created the quarry and the cataract behind them had done its work here too. The shoulder met the mountain with a spectacular precipice. Their only hope was to keep away from the treacherous edge and work up towards the mountain path as quickly as possible.

Richard had already moved ahead. There were no more blood drops from the stick. If they reached the shelter of that boulder ahead before the man could follow their trail through the rocks on the bank, they could take cover there. If he didn't see them, it was possible that he wouldn't start to search this nasty piece of mountainside by himself. He might even think this way impassable and that they had doubled on their tracks upstream again. Judging from the noise the man had made as he had come down the bed, he was not much accustomed to climbing. That was something to be thankful for.

Richard moved quickly and carefully, conscious that the ground sloped on his right towards the precipice. The boulder he had picked out as a refuge lay farther up the hill, farther away from the edge. That would cheer up Frances. And then it was that he became aware that her footsteps were not following; or was it possible that anyone could walk so quietly as that? He turned slowly, carefully balancing his weight. Frances stood almost where he had left her. She had moved up the hill slightly, back towards the rocks. She was standing quite still, her body pressed against one of them. That damned precipice, he thought, and started despairingly back towards her. But she shook her head and waved him towards the shelter of the boulder. She had heard the man climbing laboriously, the leather soles of his boots slipping on the stony surface. She moved slowly up behind the rock to which she had been clinging, avoiding the large stones which were loose to her touch. The fear, which had paralyzed her legs so that she couldn't follow Richard, suddenly left her. All she felt now was anxiety for him. She pointed frantically towards the boulder; but he didn't or wouldn't understand. He was coming back to her.

The man was almost over the bank. Like them, he had chosen to keep in cover. Perhaps he thought they were armed, and was taking no chance of silhouetting himself against the sky. He would come out down there, just where they had emerged from the bank, for it was the easiest way through, but although she had followed his progress with her ears, it was a shock suddenly to see him there, only ten feet away. He hadn't looked up towards where she remained motionless behind the rock. If he had seen her, he ignored her; his eyes fixed on Richard. He pulled out his revolver. It was a large, efficient-looking black one. Then, as he saw clearly that Richard was unarmed, he stepped forward out of cover. If he had expected Richard to throw himself on the ground, or to turn and run, he was disappointed. The two men stood scarcely twenty yards apart, looking at each other. There was a smile on the man's face. He was like a cat playing with a mouse. He lifted the revolver slowly, slowly. Frances raised the heavy stone which she had gathered in her two hands and threw it with all her strength from above her head.

It caught him between the shoulder blades, and sent him staggering forward. Frances saw him make a frenzied effort to regain his balance, half-turning towards her as he fell. Even then, he would have been safe if he had braked with his elbows and dug in his feet. But he had only one idea; he twisted quickly round to shoot. The sudden movement cost him his one chance. She saw the rock splinter beside her, and then heard the crash of the revolver. It was then that he realized his own danger. Frances, crouching at the side of the rock, saw the expression of hate on the man's face give way to fear. She saw him drop the Lüger, his hands claw the ground, too late. There was nothing on the sloping edge to grasp except loose stones. He was clutching one in each hand as he slipped over the precipice. His scream fell with his body.

It was Richard who stood beside her, trying to loosen her grip on the rock. He put his arm round her waist and helped her up the sloping ground, back towards the stream. They had followed the sheltering bank almost to the flat ground of the saddle before Frances realized they had retraced their path.

"Richard," she said, "I'm going to be awfully sick."

"Darling, try not to. Not now. There's von Aschenhausen

still. He should be almost at the stream by this time. He must have heard the shot and the scream."

She passed a hand wearily over her white face. Her voice was flat. "I forgot about him. Do you think he has seen us?"

"I hope not. We've kept under the shelter of the bank all the way up, and we are on the mountain side of the stream, while he is, or was, on the shoulder side. Anyway, he will have plenty to occupy his attention down there. It will be quite a job looking for his boy friend. He will probably think we headed for the path on the mountain. It isn't likely that he would guess we are going to use his own path down to his house."

"Richard!"

"Yes, we are. It's quite the safest way down. I don't like the idea of the mountain path now that the sun is almost gone." It was true: the mountain was hazier, and the light had turned a cold-gray. Ahead of them was the only glow in the sky, where the setting sun colored the clouds.

"Keep low," Richard warned, "as we go across the saddle. And watch the sky line." They broke into a crouching run as they crossed the grass, and when they approached the top of the saddle, they used the boulders to black-out their outlines to any watcher beneath them. They crossed the top by lying flat on the ground and edging their bodies carefully over. When they had reached the western side of the rocks, behind which they had lain this afternoon and looked down into the valley, Richard stood up and helped Frances to her feet. Normally, he thought, she would have giggled at the ludicrous figures they must have made in the last ten minutes. She would have had some joke to make about the rips on her clothes, the bruises and scratches on her legs. But she said nothing, only faced him with her large eyes still larger. He felt her hands; they were cold, like marble. He pulled out his flask of brandy.

"It's safe enough on this path," he said. "Take a good swig, Frances."

She took it obediently, and handed the flask back in surprise.

"Not even a cough or a sputter," she said in amazement. Richard's anxiety lessened. It was a good thing if she had started noticing her reactions.

"Got your wind?"

She nodded. "I'm all right." The brandy had warmed her, and the sickness was gone.

"Well, I'll let you do what you've always wanted to do. I'll let you run down a hill."

She was almost smiling. He caught her in his arms and hugged her.

And then they were running, carefully but steadily, down the broad path. Richard kept to the outside, holding her right hand as they ran. Their speed increased when they reached the darkening wood, for the path had broadened and was softened with pine needles. It twisted through the trees in zigzag curves, and these they shortened by slipping and sliding down the dry earth of the banks. The wood was already asleep. There were no sounds except the muffled pad of their feet, the occasional snap of a dry twig, the heaviness of their breathing. The trees were thinning, there was a little more light, and they were passing the edge of the meadow and the track which led to the house. Down there, in front of them, were the bridge and the road itself.

Then Richard caught Frances tightly. Through the quickly falling dusk they could see a car on the roadway, and the men talking beside it.

"O God," said Richard.

Frances looked at him in surprise.

"What's wrong, Richard? Don't you see who they are? It's an American car."

She was right. They started forward again. The two men looked as if they were getting into the car.

"Hoy!" Richard called softly. The men halted, and turned in amazement. And then they ran over the bridge to meet them.

"Well, I'll be—" began van Cortlandt, and then stopped as he looked at them. Richard pushed Frances into his arms.

"Get her into the car, and look after her. Park off the road, and not where it can be seen from the house. Keep the lights off. Be ready to start at a moment's notice. Need your help, Bob. Are you game?"

Thornley took his eyes off Frances' face and the cut on her shoulder where her ripped cardigan and blouse showed blood.

He nodded. "I'm ready," he said, and moved off after Richard.

Van Cortlandt watched them go towards the dark house.

"Now just what's this all about?" he said. Frances tried to smile.

"I sang and we heard noises and they said it was a dog." Her voice was low and tired. He caught her as she stumbled forward, and carried her to the car.

He moved the car as Richard had said, and then turned to look at the girl beside him. She hadn't fainted; she had just collapsed ... Pretty thoroughly, too. There were tears running down her cheeks.

"I haven't got a hankie. I lost it," she said in a muffled voice.

He looked at her torn clothes. "I'm not surprised," he said, and handed her the neatly folded one he kept in his breast pocket. "Try this."

Frances saw his concern. "I'm all right, really. All I need is a good cry."

"Well, go ahead," he said. "I've another handkerchief in my hip pocket. They are all yours." He was rewarded with a weak smile.

"I can talk, now," she said at last. "I don't suppose you have anything I could eat? I'm sort of empty inside."

"Only candy. I could give you a drink, though."

"I've had one. Candy will do, beautifully."

He watched her curiously as she ate the bar of chocolate.

"You can tell me as much or as little as you like," van Cortlandt said. "I'll not use it."

Frances looked at his firm mouth and worried eyebrows.

"I know, Henry. I suppose it's only fair to let you know what's happening, seeing that you are partly mixed up with it now, anyway. Do you mind if I eat while I talk?" Van Cortlandt restrained his grin. These people, really ... There, he was catching it from them. *Lost it*, she had said apologetically, when she looked as if she had almost lost everything else, including her life. *Eat while I talk, do you mind?*

"Remember, not a word of this to anyone. Not until we are all safely out of this country. It's—" She hesitated for the right word.

"Dynamite?"

She gave her first real smile. "Yes, dynamite."

She tried to get the things she would say into the right order. Her story was slow and halting. She began with the

visit that afternoon to the Englishman who was no Englishman. Van Cortlandt listened attentively and patiently, his
eyes trying to see her face in the darkness. He didn't miss the
pauses, when she would struggle for words and the story
would take a leap forward. She was near the end of it now.
There was a note in her voice which held him silent through
the long hesitations between the phrases.

"... and missed ... and fell ... over a precipice. We
climbed back on our tracks and crawled and ran and then we
saw you."

"And what about the German whom you knew?"

"I suppose he would try to trace the other. He must have
heard the shot, and the scream." She stopped suddenly, and
there was another pause. "There were signs of the fall, you
know, where the stones slipped."

Van Cortlandt whistled. "Well," he said, "that was quite an
afternoon you had yourselves."

Frances said nothing to that. She tried to see out of the
car, but it was almost dark. "I wonder why they are so
long?" she said.

"Don't worry; they can take care of themselves," but his
face was less confident than his words.

"I could kick myself," he added. "I'm the big mouth who
gave you away."

Frances looked at him in amazement. "You know, I
haven't asked you how on earth you got here. You should be
in Innsbruck, and Bob, too. I was so glad to see you, I forgot
to ask."

"Well, it was like this. Bob saw you start off, and when
you didn't get back before six as you had promised, he got
worried. My guess was that you had forgotten: you were sort
of vague about it. But he just shook his head gloomily and
said he was going to wait. So we hung about, and then that
black-haired guy arrived on his bicycle. I was standing at
the hotel door—Bob was somewhere inside—and he had a
look at our suitcases and the car. Just then the hotel man
came out, and stopped to speak to me. He said we were late.
I said yes. He said was there anything wrong? And *I* said you
hadn't got back yet. At that, the black-haired chap got onto
his bicycle and went over to Frau Schichtl's. I didn't like
that. And I liked it less when he must have found out you
weren't there, because he shot past us and went right back in

the direction he had come from, with the dog just behind him.

"I had the sense to ask who he was. The hotel man shrugged his shoulders and said something about the house with the red shutters. And then Bob came out, and he and I had some beer, and we talked it over. And the later it became, the worse we liked it. We went to see Frau Schichtl, and we worried her too. But anyway she could tell us the quickest way to get to the house. That worried Bob still more, because it was the road you had taken that afternoon. Then we thought we would go see for ourselves. Bob said you hadn't been prepared for a long walk or climb when you left the village; he had noticed you weren't wearing your boots, and that clinched the argument. We thought we would ask at the house and find out if anyone had seen you; we were both hoping that perhaps you had tried a short-cut home and had sprained an ankle or something.

"Well, we got to the house, and we knocked loudly enough, but we got no answer. Silent as the tomb. We were talking about what we should do next, and we were just about to leave, when we heard Richard."

"Thank Heaven for that," said Frances quietly.

They were both silent.

"I'm tired," said Frances suddenly, and he saw her eyes close. He reached for the rug and wrapped it round her, and pillowed her head more comfortably against the back of the seat. She was already asleep.

He strained his eyes through the darkness, but he could only see the outlines of the bushes and trees. He could hear nothing, except the gentle breathing of the girl beside him. Poor kid, he thought. What was that Gilbert and Sullivan thing? "Here's a how d'you do . . ." It was all that, and more. Expect the worst, and you won't be disappointed, he told himself. He slipped some gum into his mouth, and settled down to wait, with his gloomy speculations for company. What interested him most in Frances' story was the omissions.

CHAPTER XVI

Frau Schichtl Intervenes

AS RICHARD and Bob Thornley moved towards the house, Richard gave a concise and abbreviated version of what had happened. Like Frances, he was careful to be vague about Mespelbrunn, but his account of the way she had saved him on the mountainside was included.

Thornley listened in silence, and then as Richard finished speaking in the low voice which was almost a whisper, said, "Pity you didn't get the other blighter, too."

The house was just as van Cortlandt had described it to Frances. Silent as the tomb. They tried the front door and windows. As they expected, they were locked. The back door was locked too.

"Goes to bed early," whispered Richard.

"Who?"

"The maid. Or else she was packed off home."

"Can't risk breaking a window, then?"

"No, she may be asleep in her room," Richard said. He pointed to a window. "That may be our room. Can you climb?"

Thornley looked at the balcony at the side of the house. He grinned.

"Easy meat," he said softly. He swung himself up easily from a windowsill. He had a professional way of feeling for a hold and using his feet. Richard wondered if he were one of the Cambridge roof climbers. In that case, it *was* easy meat. Thornley had hold of the balcony now; he pulled the rest of his body up slowly until he could swing a leg over the railing. The whole thing looked so simple that one would hardly have guessed the strain on his arms and shoulders. He disappeared silently over the edge of the balcony.

Richard kept close to the shadow of the house. Above him, he heard a shutter being tried. Then there was a shadow

172

on the balcony, and a whisper. "Barred and bolted. Hopeless.
I'll try another room." The shadow vanished.

Richard waited. The minutes seemed like hours. He
thought he had heard a shutter being forced open. . . . And
that sound might be a window. He began to blame himself
for not having tried to climb up himself, even with his stiff
shoulder and torn knees. What the devil was keeping Bob?
Just as he was trying to think of the easiest way to get up, he
heard Thornley's voice in a whisper above him.

"Here. Lend us a hand." He was supporting another man.
Richard watched Thornley help the man over the railing, and
then lower him, holding on to the man's wrists. Richard
braced himself to take the man's weight as he dropped.

"Right," he whispered. Thornley, half over the railing,
grunted, and let go of the man's wrists. Richard caught him
by the thighs as he fell, and they rolled over together on the
grass. Thornley swung himself lightly down beside them, and
helped them to their feet.

"Winded?" he asked the man.

"All right, thanks. Neat job." He stood up shakily, and
looked from Thornley to Richard.

"Who was here this afternoon?" he asked.

"I was," Richard said.

The man turned to Thornley. "There's a summerhouse at
the edge of the wood, beside two tall trees hiding a mast."
Thornley looked towards where the man pointed, and
nodded. The man went on, "There's a wireless set there, and
a motor bicycle. Can you put them out of action?"

"We'll start for the car," said Richard, as Thornley grinned
and turned to sprint for the summerhouse. He put the man's
arm round his shoulder, and held him at the waist; together
they walked slowly towards the path. The man might have
been thirty or fifty; he was one of those bird-faced Englishmen whose age it was difficult to guess. He was of medium
height and thin. His hair was mouse-colored; his eyes were
nondescript. His voice had no marked accent.

"Why were you here this afternoon?"

"We were directed to Mespelbrunn from Innsbruck."

"And you found him?"

"Not the one we were looking for."

"Who are 'we'?"

"My wife and myself."

"You look as if you had met trouble."

"Complications. I left my wife in the car."

"You've a car? Good."

"And an American: a reporter."

"Not so good."

"He's a decent sort. We can trust him."

The man shook his head and cracked a smile. "Trust no newspaperman; they've an itch for a story. If he asks question, I'm Smith, who helped escapes from concentration camps. That's true, anyway. Who's the other, our blond Tarzan?"

"I know his brother."

"I'll be Smith for him too."

They had reached the fringe of trees. There was no sound of running footsteps from the wood above them. There was still some safety, yet, thought Richard. He wished Thornley would come. The man's weight was tiring him.

"How are you feeling?" he asked.

"Shaky and stiff. But better every moment. Good to be free again."

"How did they get you?"

"The man who posed as Mespelbrunn was supposed to be in sympathy with the underground movement. He even helped some escapes. Got at me through them. How were Nürnberg and Innsbruck, by the way?"

"Nürnberg had to make a run for it. Innsbruck was getting suspicious about something."

They paused while Richard changed his hold on the man; the steepness of the path was a strain.

"And just what happened to my two bodyguards?"

"They chased us on the hills. Von Aschenhausen is probably coming back now. The other fell over a cliff."

"Too bad," Smith said, and looked at some burns on the palms of his hands. "And the dog?"

"Very dead."

Smith's face relaxed slightly. "You've been busy."

When they had reached the bridge, Thornley overtook them.

"There was also the bicycle, itself," he reported. "I buckled its wheels. Strangely enough, it took the longest time."

Richard looked up towards the darkness which was the

forest and the hill; they were both now indistinguishable.
They were probably safe—probably.

"Could you run, if we both helped?" he asked Smith.

"I can try."

They linked arms round him, and half ran, half swept him
along the road.

Van Cortlandt had heard them. He had the engine running, and the back door of the car open for them, by the
time they reached him. They thrust Smith into the car, and
stumbled after him. Richard heard the man draw his breath
in sharply when his body was thrown into the corner of the
car as it jerked onto the road, and began the rough journey
back to Pertisau. But even if he was hurt, he was safe.

Richard leaned over to look at Frances. She was still
asleep.

"How was she?" he asked. The American answered without turning his head.

"Surprising. She'll be all right when she wakens. Best thing
for her."

Richard relaxed, and leaned back against the seat, taking
care not to jolt against Smith.

Thornley suddenly gave a laugh. "I haven't had so much
fun for a long time," he said.

"I'm glad someone enjoyed himself," Richard said. "What
happened upstairs, by the way?"

"The window you pointed out was barred and bolted like
nothing I ever saw in a private house. So I tried the next
room, and the shutter there was only latched in the usual
way. I used my knife, and got it, and then the window, open.
The light was pretty bad; I just could see dimly. A sort of
man's bedroom it was, with a desk at the window. There was
a lot of stuff on top of it. I was hoping I might find some
keys, but there weren't any. But I found this."

He held up something in the darkness of the car.

"Electric torch. Damned useful, too. It was black as pitch
in the corridor outside, and in the room where I found your
friend. They had tied him up again."

"And very welcome you were," said Smith. He was rubbing his wrists and ankles with his knuckles. He didn't use the
palms of his hands.

"Were you always tied up?" asked Richard.

"Always when any visitor was seen approaching the house.

And then, I was gagged too, like this afternoon. During the nights, I was handcuffed to the bed. In the daytime there was always one of them on guard. They also had fixed bars onto the window. On the door they had put safety chains. They used to leave it just a chink open that way through the day, so that I'd feel someone was always watching me."

"It made things quicker for us," Thornley explained. "The lock on the door was the usual type; after that there were just a couple of those chains and a heavy bolt. They didn't expect you to be reached from the outside."

"I'm glad you were still alive," Richard said.

"They just didn't want me alone. There was a lot of information they thought I could give them. I couldn't give it if I were dead."

"Judging from the time they kept you, they didn't get very much."

Smith gave a bitter smile. "Nothing of any use. Every now and again I'd pretend I was weakening; that encouraged them to keep me alive for just another few days. And then, they'd like to confront me with anyone who had come looking for me, and had been trapped. They like drama, these chaps, you know. Faked confessions and all that. They got a man from London, and two poor devils from Germany. Von Aschenhausen did the talking, and his man did the persuasion. He's good riddance."

"What about the maid?"

"Oh, old Trudi . . . She was terrified. When they took over, she just had to go on serving them as if nothing had happened. Threats against her family. You know. They locked her up in her room at night, which was quite needless of them. She was much too frightened to have done a thing for me. It is extraordinary the amount of power you can get over certain types of people if you just terrify them enough."

They were coming to the village. Smith leaned forward.

"Keep to the dark roads, and away from that inn where they are dancing. Keep well over to your left. Just grass, anyway."

They saw the lights round the platform outside the inn. Through the trees came the sound of a polkalike tune. They bumped over grass, as Smith had said, and then they were on a narrow graveled road which led towards the scattered lights at the shore. Smith directed van Cortlandt again, and the car swung south, running silently and smoothly along a track which would take them behind the string of hotels on the lakeside.

Smith had taken charge; his voice was still as cool and impersonal as when Richard had first met him.

"What were your last actions when you left here?"

"Van Cortlandt and Thornley were leaving by car; my wife and I were going for a walk."

Smith spoke to the American. "You've paid your bill, got your luggage, and actually left?"

"All here, Captain," van Cortlandt said.

"Good. You can stay out of the picture, then."

He turned to Richard. "You and your wife had better leave the car at a safe distance from your hotel. Or perhaps it would be better if *you* went alone. Can you remember the things she'll need? Don't forget her make-up box, especially the mascara. Bring something for me, too. And money. Is there more than one entrance to the hotel, so that you could slip out without being seen?"

"We are staying in a house. I think we could both go. Quicker if there were two of us."

Smith nodded. "Much. If you think you could slip away without being spotted. With ordinary luck, we have got about an hour's start. We'll take the car to the south end of the shore road. There are some trees and a good stretch of grass just off the road near the last hotel. We'll wait there. The moon won't be up for a while."

Richard had been shaking Frances gently. She sat up and looked round her in a bewildered way.

"So am I," said van Cortlandt good-humoredly. "You go with Richard. We'll wait for you. Good luck to both of you."

"Thanks," said Richard. "We'll need it." The car was slowing down. Henry was no fool, thought Richard. He had halted the car behind that chalet which hadn't been rented, standing dark and silent with its shutters tightly fastened.

He slipped out of the car into the blackness. Van Cortlandt helped Frances into his hands. He put his arms around her, and walked her over the grass. Behind them, they heard the car move smoothly away.

Waldesruhe lay just ahead. There was a light at the back of it. That would be the kitchen. The hotels around it were silent. There were lights in the bedrooms, as if most of the visitors were going to bed. Those who were going to the dance must have already set out, for the road was empty.

There was the usual weak light in the downstairs sitting room of the house. It lighted the bottom steps of the staircase. Farther up, Frances stumbled in the half darkness, and they halted, but they heard no movement from either above or below them, and they went on to their room.

It was Richard who shut the windows, drew the curtains, and lit the two candles. He didn't risk a brighter light. From the outside, this room would still seem to be in darkness. Frances looked wearily towards the bed; she had never appreciated how soft and white it was. On its counterpane was spread a very charming dirndl. Richard had seen it too, and paused at the wash basin as he poured the drinking water into a glass.

"Take a long one," he advised, when he brought the glass over to Frances. "What's that for?" He nodded to the bed.

"Frau Schichtl wanted me to wear it to the dance." Frances peeled off the mud-caked socks with a grimace. Richard brought over a damp sponge smelling of pink geranium.

"Do your face and shoulder," he commanded. He poured water into a basin and carried it over to where she was sitting. He helped her pull off the tattered cardigan and blouse. As she cleaned the cut on her shoulder, he bathed her feet and legs gently.

There was a knock at the door. Frau Schichtl's voice said, "May I come in?" They looked at each other in dismay. Again there was the same timid knock.

Richard was about to say Get to hell out of here, but he checked himself in time. That would only add to their troubles. If they kept silent, perhaps the woman would think she was mistaken and go away. Instead, the door opened. He rose to his feet.

Frau Schichtl paused in dismay. "Oh, excuse me. I am so sorry." She was just about to turn in embarrassment, when she noticed Richard's leg . . . And then she looked back again at Frances, holding the towel over her shoulder, and she saw the basin lying at her feet. Richard still held a dripping sponge.

Frau Schichtl came in, closing the door quickly and quietly behind her. Her kindly face was clouded with worry and fear. She came over to Richard and took the sponge gently out of his hand, and knelt down beside the basin.

"You must bathe your own leg, Herr Myles. It is cut very badly. I should get you some hot water."

"Please don't; there isn't any time," said Frances, and then bit her lip as she looked at Richard. It was so easy to make a slip when you were tired and miserable.

Frau Schichtl looked quickly up at her face. She compressed her lips, but she said nothing. She dried Frances' legs very gently.

"Have you iodine?" she asked.

Richard handed it to her, and she put it onto Frances' knees very lightly.

"Now some talcum powder on top of these scratches and they won't show."

Frances smiled gratefully, and then grimaced as she covered the cut on her shoulder with iodine.

"We got lost on the hills," she explained.

Frau Schichtl cleared away the towels and the basin of water, keeping her back carefully turned to Richard, who had started calmly to undress.

"I knew something must have happened," Frau Schichtl said. "Your friends were worried. They left hours ago. And now you can't go to the dance. You would have looked so pretty in that dress. It would have made me very happy to see you in it."

"I should like to wear it, all the same," said Frances, looking at Richard. That dirndl would be just what she needed. "We may go to the dance."

"But you must go to bed."

Frances shook her head. Frau Schichtl looked quickly from Richard, dressed in clean shirt and shorts, to Frances, fumbling in the chest of drawers for some underclothes.

"I think you are in trouble," she said slowly, at last.

Richard said nothing. He was distributing his money and Baedeker, letter of credit, passport, into the pockets of his tweed jacket. He was trying to think how they could leave the house ... Unless they were to tie and gag Frau Schichtl and lock her in this room, and the idea sickened him. Still, what else?

"I thought that when I came in here, first. You were so quiet going up the stairs. So quiet in the room."

Frances had slipped into the dress; she combed her hair, and creamed and powdered the bruise on her forehead, before she turned to face Frau Schichtl. She smoothed the apron.

"It is so very pretty, Frau Schichtl. Perhaps I may spoil it ... perhaps I shouldn't wear it?"

Frau Schichtl shook her head slowly. "It is your dress now. I have no more use for it." Her voice had a quiet sadness; she was lost in thought.

Richard smiled to himself as he watched the transparent relief in Frances' eyes. A man wouldn't have had any scruples, not at a moment like this. He folded a suit to take to Smith, along with socks and shirt and tie.

"You are going?" said Frau Schichtl.

"We are going," Frances said. Frau Schichtl moved to the door before she spoke. Richard watched her tensely. But the sad smile on her face was honest and friendly.

"You will need food for the journey," she said. "Is it these Nazis?"

Frances nodded.

"I knew it. Ever since that rough fellow came here so rudely this evening. ... Will there never be an end to all this hunting of people? They must not catch you ... not as they caught my daughter. Where can you go?"

"If we hurry, we shall be safe," said Richard quietly. He hadn't rested since he had reached the room. He was now helping Frances to get her make-up things into her bag. Mascara and all. They were ready, almost.

Frau Schichtl spoke again. "When you leave, go out through the kitchen and the back door. I shall hand you bread and cheese. I wish you a good journey to a safer land."

"We cannot thank you enough," Richard said.

"It is a small thing. Perhaps I am repaying my daughter's debt to someone who helped her."

"For your own safety, Frau Schichtl, remember that you haven't seen us. You heard us come in and go out again. You thought we had gone to the dance. Can this dress be traced to you?"

"No. There are many like it, and it is a long time since my daughter was here. I have forgotten I ever had these clothes. I shall see you in two minutes, at the back door."

The bedroom door closed gently.

Frances looked as if she might cry. She tied the scarf which lay on the bed beside the hand-knitted jacket round her head, and knotted it under her chin. She buttoned on the white-wool jacket. By the time she stared at herself in the glass, she had recovered control of herself. She looked at herself critically in the mirror.

"I'll do," she said.

Richard nodded, and tucked the bundled clothes under his arm. He picked up his one decent hat. They looked round the room; Frances' eyes flickered for a moment as they rested on the fitted suitcase which Johann had admired so much in Innsbruck. Richard had given her that when they were married. As they went downstairs she wished that she did not get so much attached to certain things. She hoped Frau Schichtl would be allowed to keep it—not some little tart of a local *Gauleiter*.

The light was still on in the sitting room, but the curtains had been drawn, so that they could cross the room safely to the kitchen. It was in darkness, and the back door was open so that they could see the stars in the sky beyond. In the shadow of the opened door, Frau Schichtl handed them a large package silently. They didn't speak, but their hands caught hers and held them tightly for a long moment ... And then they were gone.

They walked quickly over the grass, keeping as much in the shadow of trees, even houses, as was possible. The moon had risen, and the meadows of Pertisau were silvered and treacherous. From the distance came the music of a fiddle and a concertina, and an echoing "*Juchhe.*"

They had reached the last hotel. It stood far back from the road, with large gardens carefully cultivated. They skirted these, thankful for the shrubs and bushes which would make it difficult for them to be seen clearly. . . . And now they were on the road, walking as softly as they could. Smith had said something about trees, Richard remembered. There were some just beyond that patch of grass. It meant that they would have no cover at all until they reached the trees, and they might be the wrong ones. He had a strange empty feeling inside him as they covered the white stretch of road, with the silvered grass on one side of them, and the lake rippling with maddening calmness on the other. Probably

hunger, he thought. He resisted the impulse to run, to cover
the open ground as quickly as possible. And then he heard
the car warming up. It backed out onto the road from the
shadow of the trees, just as they reached them. The doors
were open, and they were pulled in by eager hands. The car
shot forward, and they heard Thornley say, "Good work!"

It was lighter in the car now, because of the moonlight.
Smith nodded his approval to Frances.

"You've made good use of your time," he said, and began
to examine the clothes they had brought him. "Mascara?" he
added.

"And food," Frances said. She opened the parcel of food
and shared it out.

The atmosphere in the car had changed. Van Cortlandt,
without taking his eyes off the road in front of him, joked
with Frances as they ate. Thornley had produced the torch
again at Smith's request. He held it ready to shade it, when
Smith needed it. Richard helped Smith rip off his clothes. He
exchanged looks with Thornley as the shirt came away and
they saw the cruel weals on Smith's back. But Smith took no
notice of their stare. He was whistling to himself as he drew
on the new clothes. With Richard's help he managed not at
all badly, although there was a difficult moment as he tried
to pull on Richard's shirt. It was only by the stiffness of one
arm that they noticed it was bruised at the shoulder into a
purple jelly. The clothes were loose for him, but the effect
was passable.

He began on his face, now. Thornley held the shaded
torch, and Richard tried to steady the small mirror from
Frances' bag. Smith creamed and powdered the ugly bruises
which showed. He darkened his eyebrows skillfully, altering
their shape, and with the same pencil shaded in the lines of
his face. Then he found the small pair of scissors in the bag,
and looked at them thoughtfully.

"We'll have to stop to get rid of these anyway," he said,
kicking the rags on the floor which had been his clothes.
"Better draw up for a moment; this is as good a place as
any." It was the beginning of the hill down into Jenbach. On
their right was a steep ravine, thickly wooded. They could
only hear the water of the stream. It was impossible to see it,
at this point, for the undergrowth. Thornley slipped out of
the car with the old clothes, and disappeared down the steep

bank. When he came back, he reported that he had found a nice thick bush, not very far down. It had been too risky to go any farther.

"Not a place for picnicking, or a roll in the hay," he said. "They should rot there peacefully."

Smith had finished emphasizing a widow's peak with the scissors.

"All right," he said, and van Cortlandt drove on.

Smith took the mascara cream and rubbed it on the back of his hands. Then he tried to smooth it on his hair like brilliantine, but it was too difficult.

"Let me try this," suggested Richard. He remembered what he had seen of Smith's palms. "I tucked a pair of chamois gloves into that jacket pocket," he said as casually as he could. "I find them useful for traveling."

Smith shot a quick glance at him. "Thanks. I'll need them." He looked at his hair in the mirror. "That's about enough; don't need much of that stuff. Thanks. I'll comb it through now."

As Richard wiped his hands, he watched Smith carefully combing the black cream through his hair, finishing by making a neat center parting. The finishing touch was a slight dab of face powder onto the hair above the ears. The transformation was complete.

"Not bad," said Thornley with a grin. "They'll never recognize you, unless they see your back."

Smith gave his first real smile. He had cleaned the back of his hands of the mascara, and was rubbing some cream into the burns on his palms and wrists. Frances had looked round, and remained staring, so that van Cortlandt took his eyes off the road for a moment to look too. He grinned widely.

"All you need is a monocle and you'd be a natural for a Budapest café," he suggested. Smith looked pleased, but he didn't volunteer any information.

Richard suddenly remembered the label on the inside pocket of the jacket. Smith ripped it out and read it with interest.

"Nice to know your name," he said. "But it would have taken some explaining. Thanks. What about the hat?"

"It's all right. You'd better take my stick, too. But don't unscrew it until you are in a safe place and can wash it. It's rather messy. What about a passport?"

"That can be got. By the way, I think you should go right away to this address in Innsbruck. They'll see about a passport for you." He scribbled some words on a page from Thornley's diary, and handed it to Richard.

"What about some cash?" asked van Cortlandt.

Smith patted the jacket pocket. "It's already here. That's about everything I think." He looked at Richard, and there was a kindly look in his eye.

"Richard." Frances' voice was urgent. "I've just remembered . . . what about our bill?"

The men all laughed, even Smith.

"It's all right, Fran. I've left enough to cover it inside my suitcase. It will be searched, you know."

Van Cortlandt seemed to be enjoying a rich joke.

The car was entering the village of Jenbach, running down through the steep street with its motor silent. There were few people out at this time. Jenbach was mostly asleep, it seemed. Smith was watching the street carefully.

"Just at that corner," he said to van Cortlandt, "beside the road with the trees. The station is just to the left." He turned to Richard. "I seem to have caused you a lot of trouble. But perhaps you'll find some consolation in the fact that I really happen to have discovered something which will be extremely valuable. Quite apart from my own comfort, you really have been most useful!" He leaned over to Frances. "And thank you for your song. Good-by."

The car slowed down. It paused for a moment, and they saw his shadow mix with that of the trees. He was walking, leaning heavily on Richard's stick, Richard's hat tilted over his eyes, towards the station, as the car swung to the right for the Innsbruck road.

CHAPTER XVII

Innsbruck Revisited

THEY would reach Innsbruck in half an hour, or even less. Richard leaned back into the corner, and closed his eyes. It was little enough time to decide on their own plans; but at least they had done the most they could for Smith.

The road was smooth and made driving easy. On their right were continuous mountains; on their left was the broad Inn valley and the railway line. Van Cortlandt pointed out the lights of a train moving towards Jenbach.

"That takes care of your friend. We've only you to worry about now," he said. Richard nodded. He wondered if Smith would really take that train, or whether there had been some little house near the station where he might have a friend. He had better stop thinking about Smith. He roused himself to reply to the American, who had looked round at him curiously.

"I've been thinking about that, Henry. I think we should follow his example and rid you of ourselves as soon as we get to the outskirts of Innsbruck. Then you can arrive as if nothing had happened, with the excuse if it's necessary of motor trouble and slow driving. You know the sort of thing. I think that's the only way."

Thornley said, "It's not a very good way for you."

"We'll manage, somehow—if we get that passport."

"And some money," said van Cortlandt. "You'll not go far without plenty of loose dough. Your travelers' cheques or your letter of credit will raise hell at any bank in Greater Germany. That chap just about cleaned you out, didn't he? He was a cool customer, all right."

"He has to be. I expect he has done more than that for others when they were in a jam." What was it Frau Schichtl had said in that sad slow voice of hers? Repaying a debt to someone who had helped her daugher ... only the way she had said it was better than that.

"Help each other, or God help you?" asked van Cortlandt, half-seriously. "Have you any cash, Bob?" He threw his wallet into the back seat. Thornley caught it, and added his share. He counted it carefully.

"It will just about pay for the passport. I expect it will cost quite a lot. You'll need more than this. I can cash a cheque at the bank tomorrow, but how can I get the money to you?"

"Look," said Richard, "you dump us somewhere just outside Innsbruck. We can walk to that address Smith gave us. I think it's this side of the town. Have you that light, Bob? I'll just make sure." He studied his Baedeker. "Yes, we can reach it all right. In this costume, we'll look like any other couple returning from a moonlight walk. Your story is that we left you this afternoon to walk over the mountain towards Hinterriss. When we didn't return, you thought we must have gone right on to Hinterriss and stayed the night there. So when it reached eight o'clock, you left. You had a business appointment to keep. You were delayed in getting to Innsbruck by motor trouble. Henry, try to see your man tonight when you arrive; have a couple of drinks with him in some well-known restaurant."

"I'll need them," van Cortlandt said with a grin.

"Remember you never saw a house with red shutters. You never saw us after we set out for our walk. That's your story and stick to it."

"That's our story and we're stuck with it." Van Cortlandt was still grinning. "But what's your angle?"

"We'll get to that house, and arrange about a passport. They may take us in for the night, or send us to a safe place. And Bob will get the money, as he suggested. Tomorrow one of us will meet you some place about eleven o'clock. It may be Frances; she is better disguised than I am. The station is no good; it will be watched. A restaurant is dangerous ... too many waitresses with an eye for their customers." He paused for a moment or two. "Try the Franciscan Church. It will have plenty of sightseers on a Saturday morning. You can potter about the Emperor Maximilian's monument; carry a catalogue, or a newspaper, and have the money in an envelope. Slip the envelope inside the catalogue. When you

see Frances, go and sit down in the church itself. Choose a
nice dark side. When you finish your meditations, leave the
catalogue behind you. Frances will then slip into the seat
you've just left. Would you mind doing that for us?"

Thornley repeated the directions rapidly. "I think I've got
it all," he said

Van Cortlandt said, "I must say for a couple of amateurs
you two are showing high form."

"We go to the movies," said Frances gravely. He looked at
her serious face, and then decided to risk a laugh.

"It's that dead-pan look you English have when you have
your little joke which makes us think you've no sense of
humor. You don't look as if you expected anyone to laugh."

Frances was smiling now. "Well, that doubles the joke for
us. Our pleasures are really very simple."

"You mean that if I hadn't laughed just now, you would
have been laughing because I didn't laugh because you didn't
laugh."

"I would have had my giggle inside," admitted Frances.
"Don't you think it's funny, too?"

Van Cortlandt just shook his head sadly. "About as funny
as *Punch*. And much more dangerous. It makes people underestimate you."

"But that can be funny, too."

"It's dangerous."

"What's dangerous?" Thornley asked. He was shading the
torch again to let Richard study a map.

"Being underestimated," said Frances.

"Oh, *that!*" he said, and went back to the map.

Richard explained. "After we have the cash, and the passport, we'll make for the border. The nearest one is the
Brenner."

"That's guarded heavily," warned van Cortlandt. "The Italians are keeping an eye on the South Tyrol."

"Well, it will depend on our disguise whether we risk the
train to try the mountains. If it's guarded heavily, then the
Swiss frontier will be thought to be likelier. And the Brenner
is probably more strongly guarded on the Italian side than on
the Austrian. That suits us."

"And after that?"

"We'll make for Paris."

"When do you think you'll be there?"

"With luck, we'll leave Innsbruck by Sunday at latest. Say next week end in Paris. We'll leave word for you there with the Consul. We'll celebrate together. The evening's on us."

"I wish I could," said van Cortlandt, "but I'm a working man. I'll see you later in England on my way home. I have your address. There's one reward I would like, and that's the whole story."

"I promise you it," Frances said. "And please come to see us. Any time." She said it so warmly and earnestly that van Cortlandt reddened, but he looked pleased.

"I hate to be the skeleton at the feast," he said, "but what if you run into difficulties in Innsbruck?"

"We'll let you know; we can phone you. If we can't phone then it's too dangerous for you to help us. You've been dragged into quite enough trouble, as it is."

"I'll have finished my business there by midday tomorrow. I can be free for the next two days, if you need me. Leave a message at the hotel for me, if I'm not there. Say that the *Times* has an assignment for me. That will pass all right, and it's phoney enough for me to know it comes from you. I'll let Bob know, unless he's mixed up with his Czechs."

"There is one very important thing, Henry. Send this message to Geneva early tomorrow. Please don't forget. RESERVATIONS UNCANCELLED. ARRIVING FRIDAY. And memorize this address." He repeated it carefully. "Got it? Good. It's really important."

The lights of the town gleamed in front of them across the Inn. Frances turned to Richard, and smiled.

Van Cortlandt said quietly, "I have to spoil the party, but there's a couple of cars on our tail. I've seen their headlights for some time now, but they are still far enough away, if it should be your friends. I'll slow up round the first bend. Get ready."

Frances and Richard looked at each other. Frances remembered how van Cortlandt had increased his speed just when he had asked about difficulties in Innsbruck.

"We'll say our thank-yous in Paris or Oxford," said Richard. "Good-by, meanwhile. And don't forget to turn up. And remember the telegram." He was holding the door open in readiness. They were reaching a bend in the road.

The car slowed up. They slipped quickly out.

"We'll see you," Frances said quietly, and then without

looking back, she raced with Richard for the cover of some bushes. Safely hidden from the road, they watched the tail-lights of van Cortlandt's car streak along towards the town. They waited for some minutes, and then they heard the roar of a powerful engine. A large black car, followed closely by another, flashed past them. Richard watched them disappear after van Cortlandt.

"Henry was right, I think. Two cars together look as if they had urgent business. I hope they stick to that story."

"They will," said Frances. "I can see Bob looking rather sleepy and bored, and Henry looking very righteously indignant, calling on his rights as an American citizen. They'll play it up beautifully between them. I wish I could see it."

"You're better here. How are the legs?"

"Not so bad. My arm is stiff, though." She shivered.

Richard put his arm round her shoulders, and drew her beside him. They waited in silence. One other car passed along the road; its moderate pace reassured them.

Richard watched the clouds in the sky. He chose the time when one of them, thick and white, began to cross over the face of the moon; and they were back on the road. They reached the first houses without any trouble. It seemed they were in an open residential quarter, with scattered houses and gardens, or what might be called parks, surrounding them. Richard remembered they were either in or near the district for the large garden restaurants and family excursions ... All the better.

It was also a district for late-evening strollers, making their way slowly back to the town. Ahead of them were a young man and his girl, with their arms linked round each other. The man talked, and the girl would laugh as she looked up at him.

"Watch the technique," said Richard, and measured his step so that they kept a short distance between them and the couple. He clipped his arm round Frances' waist, and she giggled in spite of herself.

"Perfect," he said, and won another laugh.

Perfect, he repeated to himself, as they followed the man and girl towards the bridge over the River Inn. In front of the bridge was a broad, open stretch of ground, where other roads met the one they were on. From the other roads came some more men and girls, forming a slow and scattered trail back to Innsbruck. And there were some cars. These were being stopped by two efficient-looking men in uniform, as they approached the bridge.

Richard looked down at Frances, and said some words to her in German. Just in front of them were the couple they had followed. The two uniformed men gave the group of four a brief look, and then turned back to the driver they were questioning.

Once they were over the bridge, they left the man and girl. He was still talking; she still looked up into his face and laughed. They would never have noticed who had walked behind them or who had passed them. Richard had taken a street which turned away from the river. After the bright lights at the bridge, it seemed dark and safe. But the journey to the house was like a nightmare for Frances. Richard had kept their pace unhurried, so that they appeared just two more walkers going home with the usual reluctance. The slowness of their steps increased her fatigue. She was painfully conscious of each muscle she had to use, of the hardness of the pavement which hurt her back with each step, of the cracks in the stones which caught her dragging feet. The ill-lighted streets heightened the dark houses; their silence sharpened every sound. It was less than a mile to the address which Smith had given them, but to Frances it seemed more like five.

Richard had knocked as Smith had marked it down on the piece of paper: a spondee followed by a dactyl. In his pocket, he fingered the part of the instructions which he had kept, the part with the curious little design marked on it. The rest of the paper had been torn up and dropped piece by piece from the car. As they stood in the darkness of the doorway and looked anxiously up and down the dingy, badly-lighted street with its empty pavements and sleeping houses, he had begun to wonder if he had got mixed up with the address. They were taking a hell of a long time to answer. He visualized the piece of paper as he had seen it in the car. The name, the address, and then *Knock* — —, —ᵛᵛ. Then the words *Destroy at once*; and then *Keep*, and a lightly drawn arrow to the foot of the page where the design had been sketched. He remembered everything, even to the jagged line at the top where the page had been torn from

Thornley's diary. He felt Frances sag against him. He knocked again.

The door opened so quickly that he knew someone had stood behind it waiting for the knock to sound again. It was only slightly open, and in any case it was too dark to see anything; but the someone waited.

Richard's voice was hardly above a whisper. "Herr Schulz?"

The door opened wider and a woman's voice answered "In!" They heard the door close behind them gently; a heavy lock was quietly turned. The hall was unlit, but light came from a room at the back of the house. The woman who had let them inside led the way towards the lighted doorway. She turned to them as she reached it, and motioned them to enter. Frances saw that she was quite young. Her face was what Richard would call just medium: it was neither pretty nor plain. It was quite expressionless.

Richard had looked past the woman into the bare, poorly furnished room. A man laid his newspaper aside, and watched them keenly from where he sat. He said nothing, just sat and looked. Richard spoke, slurring his words as he had heard the Bavarians do. The man still sat; his eyes were impassive. He picked up his newspaper again.

"But my name is not Schulz," he said, as Richard paused.

Richard's eyes met those staring down at him from the large flag-draped photograph on the wall. For a moment, doubt halted the beat of his heart. He felt the sweat break in his palms. . . . And then he was aware that he was still clutching onto the piece of paper in his jacket pocket. He pulled it out, and handed it to the man, still watching inscrutably.

The man glanced at it and threw it on the table.

"Who gave you this?"

"A man from Pertisau."

"Was his name Gerold?"

"No. Mespelbrunn."

"Where do you come from?"

So that explained Smith's aside as he had handed him the paper in the car.

"From over the mountains," Richard said.

The man looked at him again, and then at Frances who

had slumped into a chair. He nodded to the woman. She closed the door, and stood there, leaning against it.

"Sit down," the man said to Richard. His voice was warm, almost friendly. His eyes were now alive, kindly. "Relax. Relax. No need to look so cold. Are you hungry?"

Richard nodded. The woman moved from the door where she had been standing and went into another room. It was probably the kitchen. Richard heard the sound of a pot being placed on a stove.

"Relax," the man said again. "And how is our friend from Pertisau?"

"He is now well."

"So, he was—ill? We thought so ... we have not heard from him for a long time. Well, that's good news. Good news. What about you? You said you wanted a room. Is there anything else?"

"The usual."

"You are leaving our happy Fatherland?" The man's voice was filled with heavy sarcasm as he looked up at the picture on the wall. "Well, it can be arranged. How are you traveling?"

"To Italy. Probably by train. And as quickly as we can."

"Of course; that is understood," Schulz said, and smiled. "You might go as Americans or English. You look very like them. Do you know the language at all?"

Richard shook his head.

"You'll have to go as Germans, then. How would an engineer do? Or a schoolteacher? I'll get you the right clothes. That will cost you extra, of course, but you'll find it worth every pfennig. Every pfennig."

"How much will it cost?"

"How much have you?"

Richard restrained a smile. After all, Schulz had been right that his help would be worth every pfennig.

"Only three hundred marks," said Richard. "We can get extra tomorrow to cover the railway fares."

Schulz seemed pleased with the directness of the answer. "Good," he said. "Good. Three hundred marks will do."

He rose from his chair and went over to Frances. He walked with a marked limp, but he held himself erect. Richard placed his age as about forty. He was almost bald. His face and body had thickened with middle age. Frances, white and silent, looked up and saw the shrewd eyes behind the thick glasses, the kindly smile on the broad mouth.

His voice was gentler. "You look afraid of me. You must lose that afraid look. Sometimes people stay here for almost a week, until they lose it. You must look very happy and proud when you cross the frontier. You are the wife of an engineer, who is taking you for a holiday to Florence. But we must change your hair; it is too pretty. Lisa!"

The woman came back from the kitchen. She carried two bowls of steaming soup.

"Lisa, what color would you make this hair? Black?"

"Not with these blue eyes. Brown is less noticeable."

"Good. Make it brown, mouse-brown. We can begin tonight. That and the photographs. Then tomorrow we can get the clothes, and the papers. And you will be all ready to leave tomorrow night. Is that quick enough for you? Now, eat up. Eat up."

The warm bowl of soup brought life back to Frances' hands. She held her fingers round it, and felt the warmth steal into them. It was almost as good as eating. She felt warm, warm and safe. She looked at the clock on the table. It was almost midnight. She felt warm and safe, safe for the first time in six hours.

The man was watching her curiously. "Eat up," he said gently. "That's good, isn't it?" It was the most wonderful soup she had ever tasted.

The man was speaking to Richard. "You've had a difficult time; you've come far, today?"

"Yes, we've come far."

"You will be able to travel tomorrow?" Schulz was looking doubtful.

Richard, remembering Frances' resilience, smiled. "Oh yes, we shall be all right. We recover quickly. We can keep going until we reach Italy. And then ... well, it won't matter then anyway."

"When you first spoke of Italy, I thought I might advise you to try the mountains. They would be safer. But—" he looked at Frances doubtfully—"I think you will have to stick to your plan about the train. We shall do our best to make the train safe for you. Ready, Lisa? Good. Good."

Richard had finished eating, and the man began to cut his hair. On the table, the woman had arranged basins and some bottles and a saucer. Frances felt her eyes begin to close. Schulz waved his scissors towards her.

"If we can get her into that chair at the table before she falls asleep, Lisa can manage," he said. "We'll soon have her upstairs in bed."

Frances was helped into the other chair. I'm being very silly, she thought, but the trouble is that my eyelids are too heavy. She stretched her head back against the neck rest on the chair. It was hideously uncomfortable, but the eyelids won the struggle. She had dim sensations of the woman's fingers working with her hair, of water trickling across her face.

When she was awakened, she saw Lisa looking at her with almost a smile. It was enough to warn Frances of what she might see in the hand mirror which was held out to her. That look which only one woman can give another, that look of pity and amusement combined, roused Frances as no dash of cold water could have done. She took the mirror. Her hair was as bad as she had suspected; dull brown, lifeless, with the thickness at the back pinned tightly into a mean little knot. Frances stared in a kind of horrid fascination. Of course it would have had to be her hair, she thought, just because it had been her secret pride.

Richard was grinning at her. Then she saw that he was including himself in that grin. His hair had been clipped until it bristled. There was a funny look at the back of his neck. She began to laugh. She had the pleasure of seeing the half smile on Lisa's face give way to a look of surprise.

The man looked up from arranging a large box camera on some books on the table. He smiled encouragingly.

"That's better," he said. "Pretty ones find it harder to escape. Now, if you'll sit over here, we'll soon be finished, and you can go to a real bed."

The woman was clearing the table of its litter of basins and towels and hand dryer. She seemed to accept all this madness as a natural way of spending one's night.

Richard was being photographed now. He bulged his eyes, tilted his chin truculently, and looked on the point of uttering a loud "*Heil!*"

"Good," said Schultz, "good."

It was Frances' turn. She remembered to stare stolidly in front of her and part her lips slightly. We are all quite mad, she thought, or perhaps I am really asleep and dreaming. Sleep . . . sleep . . . it had a pleasant sound.

Schulz nodded approvingly. "That's what we want," he said. "That's what we want."

They followed the woman up a dark staircase to a room which was cold and shadowy in the meager candlelight. Frances felt Richard draw off her clothes: she awakened slightly as she heard him swear when his fingers stuck with some fastening on the strange dress. Then the cool rough sheets slid round her.

She could not have risen if six storm-troopers had come thundering up the stairs.

CHAPTER XVIII

Frances Is Frances

FRANCES awoke with a feeling of compulsion. She had something to do. She lay in the strange bed and looked round the room for the first time. Slowly she began to remember what had happened last night. Her hand went to her hair; it felt dry and coarse. So it hadn't been a dream . . . And there was Richard, with his hair cropped like that of a child who has had fever. He was still asleep; his arms were thrown above his head; his face was relaxed. She looked at the cracked ceiling, at the limp curtains drawn over the window. Why had she awakened, what was it that had to be done?

Frances felt herself slipping into sleep again, and caught herself just in time. There was something she had to do. Her eyes fell on her handbag which Richard must have brought upstairs last night and thrown onto the rickety little table under the fly-spotted mirror. That was it, of course. The money. A sudden fear that she was already too late to meet Bob Thornley urged her quickly from the warmth of her bed. After the first dizziness—she had probably moved too suddenly—she felt all right. Her body had recovered surprisingly from yesterday's punishment; even the shoulder was healing nicely.

Richard's watch told her she had ample time. She washed and dressed quietly. She searched in her handbag, and powdered her face and lips so that her natural color was hidden. Then she removed all traces of powder with her handkerchief. With the dull-brown hair and the subdued face there was quite a difference. She could do nothing about her eyes, though. They were larger and bluer than ever. However, unless she met someone who really knew her, there was little chance of her being identified with the fair-headed English girl whose description was no doubt being circulated. She combed her hair with a center parting, pinning the ends tightly into a knot at the back as the woman had done last night. Before she left the room, she found Richard's Baedeker in his jacket pocket, and verified from its Innsbruck map the best way to reach the Franciscan Church. At the door of the room, she stopped. Some small change might be useful. With a suspicion of a smile she searched Richard's pockets, and took half of what was left. It would be just enough to pay for a ride in a tramcar and the admission to the Church, if there was one. She kissed Richard lightly again. He didn't even stir. She closed the door gently and went quietly downstairs.

Lisa was in the sitting room. She seemed surprised.

"I thought you would sleep all morning."

"I must go out."

The woman shook her head disapprovingly.

"I must get money for the journey."

The woman accepted that. "You had better have some coffee, first," she said. "I've just had a cup. I'll get one for you." She went into the kitchen.

Frances waited, and looked at the little room, and the corner of the badly-kept garden at the back of the house, which she could just see from her seat at the table. Lisa was not unkind, but there was a certain businesslike attitude which paralyzed any conversation. Frances was glad of that; she was somewhat self-conscious about her Bavarian accent. She drank the coffee, and looked at the patch of garden. She felt a kind of excitement inside her. She would have liked to have given a war whoop—but Lisa was there. Her matter-of-fact kind of sanity smothered Frances' impulse, and she contented herself with looking at the garden and having another cup of coffee. She rose to leave.

"Not that way," said the woman. "Go out by this door: across the yard. Keep near the wall, under the trellis, and it will shelter you. Enter the door at the other end of the path. Walk through that house, and you'll find yourself in a shoemaker's shop. Just say as you pass that Lisa sent you. You'll be all right."

"Would you tell my husband that I'll be back about twelve?"

The woman nodded, and threw a *loden* cape lightly round Frances' shoulders. "Leave this in the shop," she said. She didn't wait for Frances to thank her. She was already carry-

ing the coffee cups into the kitchen. As she turned to push
the door open with her hip bone, she smiled—a friendly,
encouraging smile. And then the kitchen door closed behind
her. Frances turned toward the door in the living room which
she had thought was a cupboard door. It led on to a narrow
paved path beside a high wall, from which a coarse green
climbing plant stretched greedily over the trellis above her
head. In front of her were the backs of the houses on the
next street.

Everything happened as Lisa had said it would. The cobbler in the front shop scarcely paused in his work as Frances
slid the cape onto the counter. He didn't seem to hear her
words. Outside in the street, there was the usual activity of a
respectable working-class neighborhood. Housewives carried
shopping bags made of knotted string. Children were grouped
round doorways. Boys cycled wildly. Some of them wore a
kind of uniform, others the usual short leather breeches and
white stockings. She walked with increasing confidence to the
end of the street. If she followed the tramlines from there,
she would reach Museumstrasse, and then it would be easy to
find the Church. It was the long, but the safe, way and she
had plenty of time.

The walk was not unpleasant. In the busier streets, she felt
still safer. She was just another girl dressed in another dirndl.
At the corner of the narrow street which led to the square on
which the Church stood, the traffic was heavy. Frances
tried to avoid two women whose breadth filled the narrow
pavement. She was swept against the window of a shop.
Climbing boots, sports things, she noticed, and then, with her
eyes still fixed on the window, she collided with a girl coming
out of the shop's doorway. She was a tall, blonde girl, her
arms filled with parcels.

Frances halted in amazement, and then stepped aside with
an apology. The girl remained standing, her eyes on Frances'
face, but Frances hurried on. It was Anni, looking just as she
had looked in their garden at Oxford on her last night there.

"I looked at her too directly. She half-recognized my eyes,
or perhaps she saw that I knew her," Frances thought. She
glanced at her reflection in another window. She couldn't see
much resemblance to herself, but she would have to watch
her eyes, and her way of walking too. It was much too
smooth. She would have to set her heels more firmly on the
ground, in a kind of jaunty march. As she turned the corner

to enter the Church, she looked back over her shoulder. Anni was still there, and, as Frances looked, she made up her mind and started towards the Church. Frances already regretted that afterlook. What a fool she was. She quickened her pace and hurried up the steps of the building.

Inside, there was the usual crowd of Saturday-morning visitors. She paid the admission to a man with heavily pouched eyes and a drooping mustache. At least that would prevent Anni from following her inside the Church: she had never spent a penny more than she could help in Oxford. Perhaps Anni was already thinking she had been mistaken.

In the nave where the Maximilian monument was she saw Thornley. He was standing, appropriately enough, in front of King Arthur's statue, with a catalogue in his hands. It was good to see him again, looking so untroubled, so completely unconscious of everything. She wandered round the statues as the other visitors did. She didn't look at him as she rudely passed in front of him to reach Theodoric the Terrific, King of the Ostrogoths. When she had admired sufficiently, she walked slowly towards the little chapel. Thornley was seated in the shadows. As she moved slowly towards him, he rose, and they passed each other without a glance.

The catalogue had been left on a chair. She sat down beside it, her wide skirt spreading over it. She waited while the other visitors came and went. Some sat down, some tiptoed about talking in penetrating whispers, others knelt. After long minutes she dared to move her fingers under cover of her skirt and feel for the small flat envelope inside the catalogue. Slowly, without any visible movement, her hand pulled it out and folded it into her palm. It was done. It was over.

She reached the street, and slipped the scarf off her head. As she tied it round her shoulders, she slipped the envelope into the bodice of her dress. Under the fringe of scarf, it wouldn't be noticed—and it felt safe. There was no sign of Bob. But there was Anni. She had got rid of her parcels, and had been sitting in the little square of trees opposite the Church. She had seen Frances; she was almost running across the street. Frances bit her lip. There were two storm-troopers standing in front of the Church steps. If she avoided Anni, their attention would be attracted. There wasn't any time, anyway. The men had already noticed Anni's haste and were watching her with casual interest.

Frances made her voice enthusiastic. "Anni! I haven't seen you for weeks! How are you?"

Anni looked at her in amazement; she was speechless. It was the accent which had dumbfounded her. It was no longer the carefully spoken German which she had heard in Oxford. Frances was glad of the silence. She began to walk along the pavement, her hand on Anni's arm warning her with some pressure. They were passing the two troopers, whose interest had become more anatomical.

"How are your Mother and Father?"

"Quite well, *gnä*—" The pressure on Anni's arm stopped her politeness.

"And your brothers?"

"Also well."

"And your sister?"

"The same."

They had passed the two men safely. Frances relaxed.

"Cheer up, Anni. You look so worried."

Anni suddenly led her across the street towards the garden in the square. In the quietness there, she faced Frances.

"*O gnädige Frau!*" She looked as if she were going to cry.

"Cheer up, Anni. It's all right. But don't call me that."

Anni said, "I knew something was wrong. I have been so worried about you."

"How?"

They were both talking in undertones, pacing slowly under the trees. Anni blinked back her tears.

"I knew you were here in Innsbruck, about a week ago. One of my brothers has a friend. He is the houseman in the hotel where you stayed. He knew I had lived in Oxford, of course, and he told me about the two English guests who came from there. That was how I found out that you were here."

"That was Johann, wasn't it?"

Anni's cheeks colored. "Yes. When he learned I had lived with you, I made him promise not to tell my family that you were here."

Frances was surprised. "Why, Anni?"

Anni looked confused.

"My sister always disbelieved me about England. When I told them about your house and clothes, she would only laugh. If she had learned you were staying in that place, she would have made fun of me to everyone."

"We stayed in *that* place because we like the old town, Anni," Frances said gently. That was true. They had chosen to live in the old town when they had last visited Innsbruck, although the hotel then had been an innocent place compared with their choice this time.

Anni looked relieved that Frau Myles was still smiling.

"Yes," she said, "that's what Johann told the police to-day."

Frances almost stopped walking.

"Anni, tell me all you know."

"I saw Johann this morning. We usually meet when I cycle into the town." Anni blushed again, and hesitated, but Frances waited in silence. "Early this morning, the Gestapo came to the hotel, and searched and questioned. They asked very particularly about you and the *Herr Professor*. Johann only knew that you came from Oxford and that you were on holiday."

"What about the owner of the hotel?"

"He left the hotel just after a telephone call came for him very late last night. No one has seen him since. So Johann was in charge when the police came. They seemed very angry."

Frances said nothing. Mr. Smith seemed to think of everything, she thought, even of the fact that their travels in Germany and Austria would be retraced. She would have liked to know how he had got that telephone call through to Kronsteiner without giving himself away. Possibly it had come through another agent . . . But if there had been a ghost of a chance left for their simple-traveler story, it had vanished along with Kronsteiner. His disappearance would confirm all the suspicions against them. Anni's face grew more worried as she watched Frances walk so silently beside her.

At last Frances asked, "Do the police know that you were with us in Oxford?"

Anni shook her head. "Johann never said anything about that. He didn't want to mention my name."

"I am sorry that we met today, Anni. I had better leave you now; it is too dangerous for you."

"But, *gnädige Frau*, I must help. What is wrong?"

"We must leave Austria at once."

Anni was silent. Then at last she said, "Johann could lead you over the mountains."

"Into Germany? That's worse still."

"He also knows the South Tyrol. He was born there. He escaped over the mountains when the Italians were conscripting the Austrians for the war in Abyssinia."

"That border is now heavily guarded." What was it that Schulz had said last night when she was half-asleep? . . . something about advising the mountains rather than the train, if she hadn't been so exhausted . . . But she was all right now; Herr Schulz wouldn't hesitate to advise them to go by the mountains if he saw her today. She disliked the idea of the train, for in a train you were trapped in a box.

Anni was speaking again. "But there is a way, if you know the mountains. Johann knows."

Frances was tempted. But she said, "No, Anni. Besides, Johann must not risk anything for us."

"He would do it if I asked him."

"No, Anni. Better not. Don't tell anyone that you have seen me; not even Johann."

Anni was still searching for some plan. "I can't ask you to come to our house. My sister hates the English, although she has never known any. My brothers would not help. They are afraid like my parents."

"Thank you a thousand times, Anni. But you must not help."

Anni began to cry. Frances watched her tears with distress.

"Please don't, Anni . . . we shall be all right."

"Where is the *Herr Professor?*"

"He is waiting for me. I must go now, or he will be worried."

"Please tell me the address. Then when I have thought out some plan I can come to you this afternoon and tell you about it."

Frances had an idea. "You said Johann knew a way over the mountains? If he could draw a map of it would you—" no good saying *post it*; perhaps Schulz was known by another name altogether. Frances paused. How on earth were they to get hold of the map?

"I'll bring it to you," Anni said eagerly.

"Then you must come when it's dark. Can you get away this evening without making anyone suspicious?"

"On Saturday, yes. I look after my brother's shop then, and I am often late before I reach home."

"And don't tell Johann that the map is for us. Please, Anni. It would be safer for everyone. Can you think of some excuse for him?"

Anni said she could manage Johann. She repeated the address which Frances told her. Tonight she would slip the map under the door of that house; and then she would forget the address forever. She promised. She was smiling again, as Frances said good-by. She seemed happier now that she could be of some use after all.

Frances recrossed the street. She felt she had every right to be pleased with herself. Such a map would be most useful, if, for instance, the train seemed too risky. There was no doubt that the search was on. She thought of Kronsteiner. Trains would be watched, perhaps searched. As for giving Anni the address—well, Anni would keep her promise. The secret would be safe. Anni was under no suspicion. She would not be followed, as Henry or Bob would be ... And Anni did not know the importance of the house. It would seem just a rooming house to her. There were plenty of such houses in that district.

Everything began to look easy; and that was probably her undoing. If Henry could drive them almost to the frontier, they could follow the path over the mountains, and then meet Henry somewhere on the other side. He could take along their Schulz clothes, pack them somewhere in his suitcase, and they could change in his car once they had finished the climb. It was all so simple. She imagined Richard's look of surprise and amusement when she would present him with the idea. It wasn't at all bad, she admitted with some pleasure to herself. In her excitement, it was understandable that she forgot. She forgot that if you are playing a part you must live it, and forget your own identity. She should have been Mitzi Schmidt going to meet Fritzi Müller; but at the moment she was very much enjoying being Frances Myles.

She walked quickly with her light smooth step. If she hurried she would not be late for Richard. The man in the restaurant, who had chosen a window table next to where a young American and Englishman had sat, saw the Austrian girl who walked in that familiar way. He was suddenly alert. The color of her hair and of her face were different, but there was something equally familiar in that hint of a smile and the tilt of the nose, the shape of the eyes. She passed. He recognized the set of the shoulders, the shape of her legs. Yesterday he had watched them in a green meadow, from a doorway. He didn't need to verify his guess from the table next him, where the restless Englishman and the talkative American had suddenly become still and silent.

Van Cortlandt and Thornley looked at each other.

"He's gone," said Thornley needlessly. "God, he's recognized her."

"Are you sure it's that man?"

"Richard described him. Fits in. Cheek slashes, fair hair, gold-chain bracelet."

"He thinks it important enough to leave us alone, anyway," van Cortlandt said gloomily.

Thornley rose abruptly. "I'll follow and phone you at the hotel, if I can find where he has taken her. I'll phone you anyway. You had better stick to the hotel and wait for a call from Richard. He's bound to give you a ring when Frances doesn't turn up."

Van Cortlandt began to object, but Thornley had already left. The American paid the bill gloomily. He was just to go back to the hotel and wait. He was just to wait for phone calls. That was fine; that was just fine. There were times when playing the neutral tried even a neutral's temper.

Thornley saw the tall German and the girl in the Austrian dress ahead of him. The German had made no attempt to catch up with her. He was walking at some distance behind her. That way she would lead him to Richard.

Thornley crossed the street as a precaution, but either the German had not expected to be followed, or he didn't care. Nothing these English could do at this stage would prevent the drama from drawing to its close. ... But he had not reckoned with the inspiration of the amateur.

Thornley saw several bicycles parked outside a café. He

calmly swung himself onto one of them, and raced after
Frances. His improvising was more successful than he had
hoped. Three angry young men rushed out of the café
and mounted bicycles too. Their yells were enough to make
everyone in the street look round. And Frances had looked.
And she had seen, too, for her step slackened and then she
turned abruptly into an alley. The German broke into a
run, and a slow-moving motor car suddenly ignored all rules
of traffic to cross over to him. Thornley cursed himself for
ever imagining that the German would be alone. A short
command had been given, and the car speeded into the next
street. Thornley guessed that it probably led round to the
other entrance of the alley. He hesitated, wondering desperately what his next move should be. And then the three angry
young men caught up with him. They were in uniform.

"I am very sorry," he said. "I was going to bring the
bicycle back. I thought I saw a girl I must speak to, and she
was far away. There was no time to ask your permission."
One of the boys looked amused, but the owner of the bicycle
was less amenable, until he noticed the money in Thornley's
hand.

"To pay for the wear on the tires," said Thornley tactfully.

"Where is she now?" asked the one who had smiled.

"She went up that small alley."

"But it has another entrance! There's a short-cut! Come
on. There's still time if we hurry."

Thornley found himself cycling furiously with the three
young men grouped round him. The romantic one was enjoying himself. The other two were obviously intending to find
out if the story about the girl was true. They followed a very
narrow side street, which brought them suddenly onto the
road which the car had taken . . . And there it was just ahead
of them, standing at the end of the alley, ready to drive off.
The back of the car was towards them, and the only one
whose face they could see was the German with the scars. He
was just getting into the front seat beside the driver. Behind
was Frances wedged in between two uniforms.

Thornley screened himself behind the young men as they
dismounted. They had stopped as soon as they had seen the
open Mercedes. They were looking at him strangely.

"Was that your girl?" the romantic one demanded. His
tone had changed completely. Thornley, his eyes fixed on the

disappearing number plate of the car, shook his head. He was all disappointment.

"No. But from the distance their figures and legs were the same, though."

This proved a mild joke. The kindliest of the three relaxed again.

"Just as well she wasn't your girl," he said comfortingly. "She won't enjoy herself at Dreikir—"

"You talk too much, Fritz," interrupted the one who had taken the money. The third young man had stopped laughing. There was an uncomfortable pause.

"What about some beer?" Thornley suggested. They were stiffly sorry. There were meetings this afternoon, and processions. There was much to arrange before it began. They had all suddenly become very important. They straightened their shoulders and gave him a co-ordinated farewell. Thornley gave them a careless wave of his hand and thanked them again, solemnly. They swung onto their bicycles, but he noticed that the one he disliked looked carefully over his shoulder to watch him enter the restaurant which he had suggested. He stayed there for a few minutes, long enough to let the cyclists leave the street, long enough to write down the curious number of the black car and to find the telephone with its directory. But there was nothing under Dreikir—

He left the restaurant. Perhaps he might try the post office. He could have a letter to send, and he had forgotten the address. . . . And then he remembered Prague. No, the post office wouldn't do. It might be dangerous; too risky. It was obviously quite useless trying to trace the car. That would rouse instant suspicion. He remembered the guarded look on the young men's faces when they had first seen the car, the way in which they had dismounted so quickly at a safe distance. One thing he did know: the young man who had talked almost too much had recognized von Aschenhausen. That had been obvious.

He left the street as quickly as he could, in case the suspicious young man had changed his mind and returned, and walked quickly towards van Cortlandt's hotel. The shops were crowding round him once more. He noticed a tourist office and halted. Inside, he found a number of people booking their seats for that afternoon's excursions. They crowded round the various tables, each with its clearly-

marked notice of a special tour. Beside the one labeled
BRENNER, a quiet man stood. He was watching: watching and
listening. It was the only advertised excusion for anywhere
near a frontier. Thornley noted the size of the group round
that table—the Brenner was popular, it seemed—and decided
to risk it.

He approached the desk marked INFORMATION at the
other end of the large room. Behind it, a girl was handing
out timetables and a few kind words to two men. Thornley,
with his fair hair, his shorts and light gray tweed jacket, his
almost white stockings and nail-studded shoes, felt safe
enough beside them. The men were satisfied, at last, and left.
He purposely chose the same place they had been asking
about. That would take less time for the girl; and it might
muddle her, later, if she were questioned.

The girl smiled at his request. "Kitzbühl? It is very
popular today. You will find all information in this." She
handed him one of the brightly illustrated folders which she
still held in her hand. He opened it as the others had done,
and studied its pages.

He looked up with a smile. "This is excellent." The girl
seemed pleased. "Now, would you be good enough to tell me
where the post office is? I have just arrived in Innsbruck."

"In the Maximilianstrasse."

"Is that far from here? I am late for an engagement already."

"It is quite a little way."

"It concerns a letter I want to post at once, and I have
mislaid the address. I remember it began with Drei. Dreikir—
like that."

"Ah—Dreikirchen. We used to have buses which visited it.
But not now." She was looking at him curiously. "Do you
know someone there?"

Thornley took his cue. "I was given the address two years
ago. But my friend will still be there. I never heard that he
had gone."

"Did he belong to the Church?" The girl had lowered her
voice.

"He was studying." That seemed to be the correct answer.

"It's all changed now."

"Well, they will redirect the letter ... I'll post it at once.
Now would you advise today or Monday for Kitzbühl?"

A man and a woman had come up behind him.

"Today will be more crowded."

"And the bus will leave outside this office?"

"Just across the street. I hope you will enjoy yourself at Kitzbühl. Everyone does." She was a nice girl, the kind who really liked to please the customers.

Thornley thanked her, and studied the folder as he made his way out of the office. The queue at the Brenner table was still large. The man beside it was listening intently to each excursionist's request.

On the pavement, Thornley drew a deep breath. He stuffed the folder into his pocket. It would make a nice little souvenir along with the electric torch. The policeman's helmet hanging above his mantelpiece at Cambridge began to seem a poor effort.

All he could do now was to go to van Cortlandt's hotel. He hoped to high heaven that Richard was already worried about Frances, and that he had phoned. At least they knew the name of the place. . . . That was something.

CHAPTER XIX

Double Check

RICHARD woke about eleven o'clock, and his worries began with the empty bed beside him. He ought to have wakened in time to see Frances and talk to her. In fact, he ought to have gone himself, even if Frances had been more adequately disguised. He dressed quickly, cursing at his slight stiffness, his lateness, his difficulty in shaving with cold water.

When he got downstairs, the woman had reheated the coffee. It was black and bitter, but it cleared his head. Twelve o'clock, the woman had said. He drank more coffee in spite of its taste, and read the newspaper. There was no mention of the Pertisau incident. So they were keeping it quiet, meanwhile. Von Aschenhausen might be making desperate efforts to turn his failure into success, before anything was made public. If he had kept Smith on his own responsibility, in the hope of presenting his chiefs with a large and very complete haul, then he would be in a dangerous position himself, if he had failed. He had tried for too much; he had been too ambitious. That would make their own escape twice as difficult. Von Aschenhausen would have to catch them or face very unpleasant consequences. . . . And then, there was the matter of his pride, and revenge. Vindictiveness was one of the strongest German traits. Richard sat and looked at the patch of garden as Frances had done. But his feelings were very different.

Twelve o'clock had long passed. The woman was sympathetic, but calm: there was no need to worry. Innsbruck's streets were very difficult for strangers, and she assured him for the second time that his wife's appearance was safe enough.

But by one o'clock, the woman was anxious too. She was obviously afraid for Schulz and herself. Richard did not blame her.

"Can I phone safely from some place near here?" he asked. She nodded, and pointed across the back yard to a house in the next street. And then the doorbell rang. They looked at each other, with hope and fear allied in their eyes. Richard moved behind the sitting-room door, where he could see through the chink into the hall. He saw her open the front door slightly. Someone handed her an envelope, and he heard a familiar voice.

"May I see the *Herr Professor?*"

Richard was startled. It couldn't be, it couldn't ... But the door had opened farther, and there was no doubt.

"Anni!" he almost shouted. "Come in!"

The woman was so taken aback that Anni and her broad smile were already inside the house. Richard seized her arm and pulled her into the sitting room.

"Anni," he said again. "How on earth did you get here?"

Anni was delighted with his amazement, just in the same way as when she used to produce a triumph of a cake for a birthday surprise in Oxford. For her answer, she took the envelope back from the woman and handed it proudly to him. Frances, he thought; it must be a message from Frances. What had happened? Was she waiting somewhere for him? He ripped the envelope roughly open. All it contained was a small diagram, a sheet of paper with a map and no names.

"There's the Brenner," said Anni, pointing to a small penciled circle. "I thought it was better not to write in the names; instead, you will memorize them. That is why I had to see you."

Richard looked quickly from the map to Anni. "How did you know we needed this? How did you know you would find me here?"

"The *gnädige Frau* ... didn't she tell you?"

"When did you see her?"

"After she came out of the Church."

"At what hour was that?"

Anni looked worried. "About a quarter to twelve. I reached my brother's shop just after twelve, and that was the time Johann comes to see me on Saturdays. You see, that is the afternoon my brother goes to the mountains—he's a guide on Saturdays and Sundays—and I look after the shop for him, then. So when Johann came, I got him to draw this, and I brought it to you at once. The *gnädige Frau* said tonight, but that was only because she was afraid for me. I thought you might want it now, so that you could leave at once. I didn't tell Johann about you. I promised I would tell him later, and it will be all right because he liked both you and the *gnädige Frau*."

Richard sat down for a moment. Anni saw the look in his face.

"The *gnädige Frau* told you nothing of our plans? What is wrong, *Herr Professor*? Is she not here?"

"No," said the woman gravely, "she has not come back yet."

"But she said she must hurry. She said you would be worried if she didn't . . . Oh, *Herr Professor!*" Anni was so upset that Richard rose and took her hand. So his fears had been real. While he had waited and worried, something had happened to Frances. Something must have happened. If he could only stop feeling so damned sick with worry. This was no damned good, standing here patting Anni's hand like a blasted idiot. Something had to be thought of, something had to be planned. They had lost an hour already.

"Tell me, Anni, how did you recognize Mrs. Myles?"

"I looked right into her eyes, and they recognized me. And then there was something in the way she walked, the shape of her legs. It was because I know her so well that I could recognize her."

"Then someone else who knew her well might have recog—" He couldn't finish. He left Anni, and walked to the window. He stood with his back to them, looking out into the garden. He thought of van Cortlandt and Thornley. He must get in touch with them, and at once . . . But what then? What then? He must stop this. He had to keep calm, had even to forget that Frances was his; he had to think of all this mess in the way he had thought of Smith, as a kind of problem. And he needed all his wits about him to find a solution. Emotion would only hinder; worry might lose her forever.

He turned back to the room. "Anni, could you go back to the shop and wait there until an American and an Englishman come to buy climbing boots?"

Anni heard his calm voice with amazement, but it lessened her fears. If the *Herr Professor* saw some hope, then there was hope. She listened to his descriptions of the two men who would come to buy climbing boots. She memorized their names carefully, and the message she had to give them. The Hungerburg at four o'clock. Anni was not enthusiastic about that message. The Hungerburg was so big that they might miss each other. It was safe enough for them there, she agreed, but they might be late before they met each other. She didn't like to take the responsibility of the message. If anything went wrong, then she would blame herself.

"It would be better to meet them in the shop, and see them yourself. It would save time," she suggested. "There is a storeroom at the back of the shop with its own entrance. You could wait there until your friends arrived. My brother has left already, and Johann must go back to the hotel as soon as I get back to the shop—I left him in charge so that I could come here. There will be no one there except me." She laughed at any danger to herself. If the worst came, he would be an unknown customer; and there was the back entrance losing itself in courtyards and alleys, so that even if everything went wrong there was at least a chance to escape. Richard agreed with her in his heart. It would be the simplest solution, and the quickest one. That was the chief thing. Now that the suggestion had come from Anni herself, he accepted it gladly.

Anni had left by the back door, with a *loden* cape thrown round her shoulders. He waited for two or three minutes until she would be safely out of the other house, hoping against hope that Frances might suddenly appear. The woman was obviously worried, but she was unexpectedly sympathetic. Herr Schulz would be home any minute now; she had the dinner table ready for him. And he would be able to advise them. Meanwhile, she offered him a bowl of thin brown soup with dumplings submerged in it. He must eat. Richard declined as politely as his revolving stomach would permit; worry churned him up inside like a Channel crossing. He had his eyes on his watch. Three minutes, he had thought, would be time enough for Anni. In any case, he couldn't wait any longer. He suddenly left the room.

"Say Lisa sent you," the woman called after him.

The formula worked. The cobbler obligingly made the call for him, and then left him alone with the telephone. He heard van Cortlandt's voice, and such a wave of relief swept over him that he realized he had been afraid of getting no answer.

"Hello!" said van Cortlandt, and waited. "Hello, there!"

"Van Cortlandt?"

"Speaking."

It was easier to talk now; the words which had deserted him came rushing out.

Van Cortlandt said, "Oh, yes, the *Times*. I'm sorry I'm late with that article. Glad you called. I thought you would because of this delay."

"Serious?" So van Cortlandt knew already; that saved explanations.

"At the moment, yes."

"Well, there's another article to write. Beauties of the Tyrol. Have you any climbing equipment?"

"Just my own two feet."

"Well, better add something to that. If you haven't boots, get them this afternoon. This is a rush assignment. Go to any good sports dealer, and he will advise you. There's Schmidt, or Spiegelberger, or Rudi Wachter. He is particularly good. You'll find him on the Burggraben near the Museumstrasse."

"Good. I'll go there at once. Hope to see you soon."

"I'll see you soon. Get a move on with the article, won't you? No delay for this one."

"Sure; you can depend on me. Love and kisses to Geoffrey Dawson."

"And mine to Luce." Richard heard a sudden laugh at the end of the phone, and then silence.

In the sitting room, Richard found Schulz sitting at the table, his head well down to his bowl of soup. Of Lisa, there was no sign. Schulz, busy with a dumpling, motioned him to a chair and pointed to the soup pot. Richard poured himself some coffee, and gulped it down. He thought of the brandy in his flask, but they might need that later on.

"I must go at once," he said. "My wife—"

"I know." Schulz wiped his lips, and swallowed some water. "I know. Lisa told me. There are all your papers and clothes." He nodded to a large envelope and a neat brown-paper parcel on a side table. Richard rose, and brought the envelope over to the dinner table. The document looked convincing; the photographs had just the right moronic look.

"Were we quick enough for you? That's everything I think; everything. You've paid me. Have you any money left?"

"I'll meet some friends," Richard said.

"Well, good luck."

Richard's words came haltingly. "My wife may have been arrested. They may trace her movements to this house."

Schulz swallowed some more soup noisily. "Don't worry about that. I had already decided to change my address. I saw your friend Kronsteiner early this morning, at my place of—business. He had a message last night from our friend who used to be at Pertisau. So we are on the move again. Lisa is packing now." He smiled as he saw the relief on Richard's face. Richard prepared to go. They shook hands silently.

Then Schulz suddenly spoke. "Courage!" he said. "Courage! It's the only real weapon we've got. A man can win when he still has his courage."

Richard nodded. "I'm sorry if we have upset your plans."

"They are always being upset, but we go on. And don't worry about Kronsteiner. He's all right. He's much changed since his visit to me this morning." Schulz threw back his head and laughed. Kronsteiner's change seemed to amuse him ... And then he went back to his soup. "It would be a pity to leave it," he explained, his voice once more matter-of-fact.

Lisa met Richard at the doorway. "This was all left upstairs," she said, and held out his small razor case, and Frances' bag. He nodded his thanks, and watched her slip them safely into the brown-paper parcel.

"We'll give you five minutes, and then we leave," called Schulz, in the middle of the last dumpling. "Good-by, young man, and courage."

Lisa gave him her first and last smile.

He closed the door softly, and walked unhurriedly down the street. The brown-paper parcel attracted no attention. It was almost two o'clock.

CHAPTER XX

Rallying Ground

ALL INNSBRUCK seemed to be marching that Saturday. There had been two parades already, complete with bands, banners and uniforms. The onlookers crowded into the principal streets, through which the processions passed, and even after they had gone the people waited. Perhaps there were still other processions to come. By avoiding the main thoroughfares, Richard walked quickly through the deserted little side streets, and he arrived at the back entrance of the Wachter shop in record time. There was no one in sight, as he opened the back door and walked quietly into the small room which Anni had described as a storeroom. This was it, all right. He moved carefully and slowly between the neat stacks of boxes to a crate under the small, high window. No one would be able to look in through that window, unless he brought a stepladder along with him. He sat down on the edge of the crate, and waited. He could hear a murmur of voices, and once Anni laughed. The sounds were distant enough to assure him that a room lay between the storeroom and the front shop itself, where Anni was serving a customer. No one had seen him, no one had heard him enter; so far, so good. If anyone were to look into the room, the rows of boxes would hide him. He began to feel better.

The two doors worried him, all the same. He rose suddenly, and examined the lock of the door by which he had entered. It worked easily, so he locked it. Better that, than to risk some unknown visitor using this street door at an awkward moment. It would be a simple matter to unlock the door and escape by the alley, if any complication arrived. There was that other door, the one which must lead into that middle room; but he couldn't do anything about it until Anni appeared.

The voices were silent now. The customer must be going,

for he heard the accustomed formula, and Anni's dutiful echo. There was a sound of a bell. Of course, that would be the door closing. Anni must have brought back one of those doorbells as a present for her brother after all. She had said she would. He smiled in spite of himself. It was rather odd to hear the familiar Oxford sound right here in Innsbruck. It made him think of a dark little shop, with the smell of rich tobaccos in the air, and neat white jars on its shelves; and the polished brass scales, on which the light and dark tobaccos were weighed before they were mixed and then carefully emptied into your pouch; and the darkened oak counter, with its rubber mat for your coins, and the change which came to you from the old wooden till; and then the gentle note of the bell as you opened and shut the door.

The bell was silent again, and he heard Anni's footsteps approaching. The door into the middle room opened, and she stood straining her eyes into the dim light. He stepped out from behind the boxes.

"God be thanked," she said.

"Did you hear me at all?"

She shook her head. "No. I've been coming through here between visits from customers, just to make sure. Have you locked that door? Good. I'll lock this one too. The room next you is a dressing room, where customers try on sports clothes if they want to. If anyone should go in there, just keep quite still. But if anyone with a loud voice tries the door, and rattles it, and asks me angrily for the key, then leave at once."

The front doorbell rang.

"It has been very useful, that bell," said Anni in a whisper. She turned to go, but Richard caught her arm as he heard a cheery voice call: "Anyone here?" from the front shop. That must be Thornley. It was.

"That was a darned lucky break, if you ask me," said van Cortlandt in English. Their voices sounded as if they brought good news.

Anni looked at Richard inquiringly. He nodded, and she went through to meet them.

He heard the men ask about climbing boots, but Anni's voice was too low for him to know what she had answered. He heard them suddenly quieten, and follow her quickly towards the storeroom.

She locked the door behind them, and they were left alone in the room, standing there looking at each other.

"God, and aren't we glad to see you," said van Cortlandt.

"Frances?" Richard asked.

Thornley spoke. "They got her. Just the rottenest luck. It was the fair-haired blighter with the bracelet who saw her, and recognized something. They've taken her to Dreikirchen. That's all I could find out. That and the number and identification marks of the car." He groped in his pocket for the sheet from his diary where he had scribbled the signs down in that restaurant, just after the boys had left him.

The door was unlocked, and Anni entered the room with Tyrolese jackets over her arm. She handed them to van Cortlandt and Thornley.

"Where is Dreikirchen, Anni? Is it a village or a house? Have you ever heard of it?"

"If the doorbell rings, get back into the dressing room, and try these on, in front of the mirror," she said to the American. "Lock this door behind you, and put the key up on that high shelf, there." She turned to Richard. "Now that we've made things safe, *Herr Professor*, there is only one Dreikirchen near here. It's just two hours' walk from here—to the south of Innsbruck. If you follow the Brennerstrasse, you will reach the Berg Isel, and Dreikirchen is to the right of that. I will show you on the map; you have one?"

Richard had already taken his Baedeker out of his pocket, and was searching for the Berg Isel. Anni looked over his arm, and pointed with her finger.

"There's the road. You see that small line on its right? That is the side road which takes you to Dreikirchen. There it is—these black squares grouped together."

"Is it a village, and why isn't it named?"

"It isn't a village. It is too small—just a few small houses and the monastery and three little chapels. Monks used to live there."

"Who lives there now?"

Anni seemed embarrassed. She wasn't sure. She had heard her brothers talk, of course, but they had never explained. One of their friends had been sent there.

"Is it a concentration camp?" asked van Cortlandt.

Anni was shocked. Oh, no. Nothing like that. There were boys at Dreikirchen, who were being educated. Specially

chosen boys and young men. She admitted there were
rumors. Of course, there always were rumors, but people
didn't try to find out about rumors, not if they were wise.

"Has it any connection with the Gestapo?" asked van
Cortlandt again.

Anni looked frightened. There were rumors, she said ...
And once Johann had made a joke about that in front of one
of her brothers, and that was the only time they had quar-
reled. Richard thanked her; that was all she knew or wanted
to know.

As she left them, Thornley stopped her. "If you were to
see a large black car with these numbers on it, what would
you think?" He held out the page from his diary.

"Special car," she said.

"Secret police?"

Anni nodded. "I must go back into the shop," she said, and
left them.

"Were you followed?"

"We were at first," said van Cortlandt. "And then we had
a break. The whole place is jammed with people. So we got
mixed up with two processions, and here we are without our
tail. We are probably safe for another ten minutes, until he
reports to headquarters and they give him a list of our
shopping places. They no doubt listened in to our talk on the
phone today. So now let's get busy."

Richard said, "Thanks for all you've done. It would have
been hopeless without you."

"Say, we're in on this too," said van Cortlandt. He turned
to Thornley. "Imagine that ... he thought he was going to
get rid of us at this stage. It will take three of us to find
Frances. And she's got to be found."

"We'll find her," Thornley said quietly.

Richard didn't waste any more time. He spread the map
before them.

"We'll meet here," he said, pointing to a part of the road
as it touched the Berg Isel. "Bring a car, and all your things
packed. And take this parcel and pack the things in it into
your case. It's our stuff for Italy."

"I've arranged about the car," said van Cortlandt. "That
radio man agreed to an exchange. He'll keep his mouth shut.
He's going to Vienna this afternoon, and is traveling the
Jenbach road. I've already told the hotel I'm going back to

Pertisau to look for my friends. It all fits in nicely."

Richard looked at the American with respect. "That's a pretty good effort, Henry. Well, that's about all. Meet me at that place any time after four o'clock. That will let me get out there safely. And bring some chocolate and cigarettes."

"Say half-past four," said van Cortlandt. They shook hands.

"We'll be seeing you," he added, and followed Thornley back into the shop.

Richard waited for Anni. She hurried into the storeroom, and unlocked the back door.

"Good-by, *Herr Professor*, and give the *gnädige Frau* my . . ." She bit her lip. "Please let me know when she is safe. Please."

"Yes, Anni."

"Please hurry, *Herr professor*."

"Yes, Anni." What could he say to thank her enough for what she had done? Anni seemed to sense his difficulty. She smiled sadly.

"I am only repaying your kindness in Oxford. The *gnädige Frau* was always so good to me." She opened the door and motioned him out.

"*Auf Wiedersehen*, Anni." He gripped her hand and held it.

"*Auf Wiedersehen*." Her smile was quivering. And then the door closed behind him, and already his steps had taken him far enough away to keep Anni safe.

Here was the street corner, and the crowds. He loitered with them until he saw Thornley and van Cortlandt leave the shop. They were carrying two or three parcels. He watched them until they were lost in the crowd.

He felt suddenly hungry, but he had just enough money to take him to the Berg Isel by tramcar. That would save his legs for tonight's climb. He and Thornley could get Frances over the frontier, and van Cortlandt could take their clothes by car, and meet them in Italy. On the Berg Isel, as he waited for the others, he would memorize that map which Anni had given him, and compare it with his own. He felt safe enough, partly because of the number of people on the streets, partly because von Aschenhausen would be the only person in Innsbruck who could recognize him—and von Aschenhausen was with Frances. The German was playing a

Above Suspicion

deep and subtle game. If he had taken Frances to Dreikirchen, it was because her arrest must be unofficial until he had got the information from her which would help him to retrieve his failure. Frances knew enough to compensate him for the escape of Smith, and even that might be made temporary, if Frances could be persuaded. If Frances could be persuaded.

The journey to the Berg Isel, although dull and safe enough, was one which Richard would never forget.

CHAPTER XXI

Approach to Dreikirchen

VAN CORTLANDT and Thornley made their way as quickly as they could through the crowd. They stopped twice: once to buy some biscuits and chocolate, and once to buy oranges. Van Cortlandt already had some brandy. In this matter-of-fact way, they quietly dicussed their plans as they walked along to van Cortlandt's hotel. Thornley, with unexpected pessimism, had not unpacked his bag and in any case he always traveled lightly. Van Cortlandt, although most of his belongings always remained in his trunk or suitcases, had a lot of odds and ends to clear up in his room. So it was Thornley who would have the job of phoning van Cortlandt's broadcasting friend and of telling him the time they would meet him. He already knew the place where they were to exchange cars. Van Cortlandt had thought that out, this morning. Thornley was also to telephone Cook's agent, and have him collect van Cortlandt's heavier luggage, with the directions that it was to be sent on to Geneva.

Van Cortlandt was quite philosophic about it all.

"It was coming," he said. "I've got to the stage when I can't write at all. I've developed a sort of censorphobia. Every word I get down begins to look as if it won't get through anyway. And it's about time I changed my beat. If there are any surprises coming in the world's history, it won't be from this direction. They are all set for Poland. I'd do better to go there, myself. See it from the other angle."

"I had a letter this morning," Thornley said unexpectedly, and his tone made van Cortlandt look at him. "I'll tell you about it later. It was from Tony, on his way home."

"The girl?"

Thornley shook his head. "Alone."

Van Cortlandt was startled. He had never imagined that Thornley's face could have such an ugly look.

"Pretty bad?" he asked.

Thornley only nodded.

They finished the journey in silence. When he left van Cortlandt, Thornley's voice was normal again.

"I'll see you at four," he said.

It was four o'clock exactly when Thornley arrived at the garage. Van Cortlandt was already there, examining his car. The mechanic had lost interest, and was busy with some other work. He had overhauled the car this morning and had found nothing seriously wrong although they seemed to have had a lot of trouble last night. These Americans, if only they'd take the trouble to learn about the insides of a machine, they would save themselves a lot of money ... But then they were all millionaires, and that ruined them. Now, it was said, they were all starving in the streets. What people had to suffer in other countries! Anyway, the car was perfect now; and he had been paid; and he had other work to do, plenty of it what with all the others at the parade. He had advised the American not to miss the processions: that was something to see. That was something to impress anyone. But the American had only smiled and nodded. Perhaps he couldn't understand German. And now the American was pottering around his car, pretending he knew all about the engine, looking for anything that had been left undone. Let him: there was plenty of more important work to be done. The money had been paid. The job was over.

Van Cortlandt motioned Thornley into the automobile, but he himself didn't enter. He kept his eyes fixed on the entrance of the garage. When the boy appeared, carrying two suitcases, van Cortlandt had the money ready in his hand. The boy was gone as suddenly as he had arrived, the suitcases were in the car, and they were driving smoothly out of the door.

"Quick work," said Thornley approvingly. "That was rather a brain wave of yours."

Van Cortlandt grinned as he guided the car expertly through the traffic.

"How did you manage?"

"It was easy enough," Thornley said. "You know what a rabbit warren my hotel was—no lift, just staircases and passages. Well, I paid the bill, said I was leaving for Pertisau roundabout five, and apparently went back to my room. I came down another staircase and took one of the back exits. I wasn't even followed."

"If I was, I lost him in the crowds. Processions have their uses. Helluva lot of uniforms today. They seem to crawl out from under every stone. Wonder what's it all about?"

"Just any old excuse. It depresses me."

"That was the Myles' reaction."

"Aren't you? It looks as if we shall all just have to learn to march too. No one can stop that spirit with arguments or good deeds."

"Well, I must say I think it *needs* stopping. But I don't think there's a democracy left with the guts to do it. We are all tied to our mothers' apronstrings—and big business keeps bleating about peace and prosperity. Between the apronstrings and the bleating, we'll all hesitate until it's too late. That is what depresses me."

Thornley said nothing to that. There were things stronger than apronstrings and bleatings, he felt. But it was no good talking about courage; you could not prove it by talking about it. It was like a pudding: the proof was in the eating. He contented himself with watching the way in which van Cortlandt drove. The timing at the corners of the streets was perfect. If any car were following them, it would be jammed by the traffic from the cross streets. Van Cortlandt had forgotten his depression, and was enjoying himself. He seemed particularly pleased when they crossed the bridge and turned west towards the Jenbach road. The two uniformed men on the bridgehead had noticed the car; this amused van Cortlandt particularly. By the time they had reached the beer garden, the traffic had thinned out and they could see clearly that no car was following them.

Van Cortlandt's eyes searched the few cars parked beyond the entrance to the garden. They widened suddenly.

"Good man," he said with some satisfaction. "Space for us, and all." He drove neatly in beside a dark-blue car. Its subdued color made it almost invisible beside van Cortlandt's. Its doors were unlocked, and Thornley slipped into the back seat. He found himself calmly handing out the suitcase he found there to van Cortlandt, who gave him their cases in exchange. The easiness of the whole business took his breath away.

A thin man in an American suit and hat was walking leisurely towards them. He threw his cigarette away as he reached his new car, and gave van Cortlandt a sardonic grin as he opened its door.

Van Cortlandt got into the blue car. "Drive like hell," he said to the steering wheel.

"Sure," the man said to himself. He backed the car smoothly in a half circle, so that it faced in the direction of Jenbach. Thornley looked after the speeding car, and watched it disappearing round the trees. Anyone who might have been watching would have difficulty in knowing just what had happened. The only way in which he could see what man had got into what car would have been to walk past them. And no one had.

Van Cortlandt watched his car until it was out of sight, and then he swung back on the road by which they had just come.

"He's all right," he said, reading Thornley's mind. "We are just two Americans who traded cars. So what? If there is anything phoney about that, then we just act dumb. He doesn't know much about our game. He was a newspaperman himself, once, and he guessed I was on to a story. And he hates the Nazis' guts. What's more, he got a bargain in cars. We're all happy."

Thornley guessed that van Cortlandt was putting a very good face on the whole business. He had been proud of that car. He was a strange mixture, thought Thornley: just as strange and unpredictable as he himself found the British. That would surprise him. Thornley smiled. Van Cortlandt saw it in the mirror.

"What's the joke?" he asked. "I could do with one myself."

"The Nazis' guts. It is funny that it should be one thing on which most Americans and Britishers can agree wholeheartedly, without any reservations. The average Frenchman hates the Nazi, too; but half, or at least part, of it is due to the fact he is a dangerous neighbor. Now you and I don't hate the Nazis because they are German. We hate the Germans because they are Nazi. And if you didn't, you wouldn't be driving a strange car to God-knows-where into God-knows-what, this afternoon. You'd be standing at a street corner shouting "*Heil!*" with the rest, and feeling all uplifted and mystic. You like the Myles', I know, but if the Nazis didn't curdle you up inside, you wouldn't be doing all this. In fact, we've got to the stage where anyone who opposes the Nazis is worth helping. Isn't that it?"

Van Cortlandt grinned. "About. I didn't tell you how I felt when I arrived here? I was going to be the complete neutral observer. My stories were going to be a model of detachment. Can you imagine that? My angle was that the Germans had had a tough time of it. If they only had gotten a square deal ... All that hash. It only took me a few weeks to find out that every deal was square if it benefited Germany, and to hell with the rest. Now I don't mind them looking out for their own rights; we all do. But what got me down is the way no one else has any rights, unless they say so. That's the rub. They are always in the right, and the rest of us just misunderstand them. Criticism is just another stab in the back from Jews and Communists. They've kidded other people so long now that they've started kidding themselves."

"Perhaps it is because they've developed two standards," suggested Thornley, "one for Germany, one for the others. They really believe that anything which is good for them can't be evil. That is how they can lie and commit all kinds of treachery. If it is for the benefit of the Fatherland, then it doesn't seem a lie or a piece of treachery to them: it makes everything moral."

"But then, there are the exceptions."

"Yes, and they should be thanking God for the exceptions instead of driving them into exile or putting them into concentration camps. If it weren't for them, after the next war Germany might be blotted from the map."

Van Cortlandt shook his head. "You can't destroy a whole nation."

"Can't you? Just wait to see how Germany will try it with some of her neighbors. She will give the rest of us a few tips. And it worked with Carthage, too. Don't look so worried, Henry, the exceptions will get Germany her second chance. Or is it a third?"

Van Cortlandt shook his head. "God knows," he said wearily.

They had circled round Innsbruck to the west. That avoided the main streets, which were crowding up once more. They passed several formations of uniformed young men. It seemed as if they were all marching their way to some meeting place. Neither the American nor the Englishman said anything but as they passed one set of exhibitionists in goose-stepping precision their eyes met in the mirror above van Cortlandt's head.

On the road which led to the Berg Isel (the road which led to the Brenner Pass eventually, as van Cortlandt carefully pointed out) three large black cars passed them in quick succession. They were filled with young men sitting uncomfortably erect, their faces white blurs under the uniform caps. Van Cortlandt heard a quick movement behind him, and turned to see Thornley looking through the back window of the car. He was repeating something to himself.

"Yes?" asked van Cortlandt. Thornley was clearly excited.

"One of these cars, that's it, one of them."

Van Cortlandt smiled. "Your grammar does your feelings proud," he said. 'What about it, anyway?"

"One of these cars is the same one I saw this afternoon with Frances in it. Don't you see, Henry, if they have left Dreikirchen, it will be all the better for us?"

Van Cortlandt thought over this for some moments. "*If* they left Dreikirchen," he said. He was probably right, thought Thornley gloomily. And yet, pieces of luck, both good and bad, had the oddest way of turning up. Whichever way you added up your plans, you should always leave a margin on either side for luck.

"Any time now," said van Cortlandt. He had slackened the speed of the car as they approached the small railway halt; there were few passengers waiting on the toy platform. Richard had said he would be near here. Their eyes anxiously watched the road ahead and the paths which led into the surrounding woods, but it wasn't until they were round a bend in the road which hid them from the halt and its inn, and the car had stopped completely to let Thornley get out, that Richard stepped from behind some trees.

"I was beginning to think that we had missed you," van Cortlandt said, worry sharpening his voice, as the car moved on.

"Sorry," said Richard. "I forgot to ask you the color of the car, and I wasn't sure. Couldn't risk anything. Sorry. How did everything go?"

"According to plan."

"Good. Now, we've about five minutes more on this road, and then ten minutes more to the right. I did some map studying while I waited, and there seems to be a small road or track of some kind, just before we get to the Dreikirchen road. If we follow that track, then we can approach the place from the back. If it had been dark, we could have risked the Dreikirchen road itself. But we'd better not wait for darkness. We haven't time."

Thornley looked at Richard's white, set face. There was a gauntness about it which worried him.

"Had anything to eat?" he inquired casually. Richard shook his head, and then took the slab of chocolate which Thornley handed him. He ate it with his eyes fixed on his watch. He doesn't know or care what he's eating, thought Thornley; it might be linoleum for all he knows; he's all shot to pieces.

"Brandy?" he asked.

"We'll need it later," Richard said. He was still looking at his watch. Thornley began to guess the kind of time he had been having while he waited for them to arrive. Shouldn't have left him alone, thought Thornley.

"This is the track," Richard said, and the car turned from the Brenner road into a wood. Richard was still looking at his watch. He held up a hand to silence Thornley just as he was about to say something. . . . And then Thornley realized that Richard was timing the distance they had to drive.

"Now," he said, and the car swung off the track.

"I'll turn, while the going's good," van Cortlandt said, and maneuvered the car until it rested on the grass, hidden from the track by a clump of bushes, its bonnet pointed back towards the Brenner road. Van Cortlandt unscrewed his flask, and handed it to Richard.

"Bob's right," he said. "We all need it. I've plenty more."

"Rum ration," suggested Thornley.

"Any of you got a gun?" van Cortlandt asked.

They shook their heads. Thornley produced a strong-looking clasp knife and his souvenir torch. Richard had nothing. It might have been the shadow of a smile on the American's face, but his voice was serious enough.

"Well, I have, so if we get into a tight spot . . ." He didn't finish, but tapped his pocket thoughtfully. "Anything else, before we leave the car?"

They waited in the quietness of the trees, while van Cortlandt locked the car methodically. When he joined them, the
three men looked at each other for some moments. Then
Richard turned, and led the way up the wooded hillside.

It was a short climb. They paused on the crest, sheltered
by the pines. Below them, the hill sloped gently to Dreikirchen. They could just see three spires above the last trees.

Thornley pulled out his knife, and motioned to them to
wait. He disappeared back towards the road they had left,
lopping off a thin branch from every third or fourth pine, as
he passed. Van Cortlandt exchanged glances with Richard.
The idea was good; the cuts on the trees were white and
jagged. When Thornley returned, he seemed pleased. He
must have found his way back in a record time. As they
followed Richard down through the trees, he used his knife
continuously. It slowed up their pace, but now that they were
so near their objective, there was little they could do but
wait, until the clear afternoon light had given way to the
dusk of the evening—except for spying out the lie of the
land. So they went slowly, walking carefully in order to make
no noise, while Thornley worked silently and unhurriedly.
The spires had disappeared as they descended through the
wood. Richard, who led the way, hoped that his sense of
direction was as adequate as Thornley's trail blazing. He
would soon know, for at last they were reaching the edge of
the wood. A steep bank and a garden were all that separated
them from Dreikirchen. Behind the cover of the trees over-
shading the bank they lay and watched.

The Fathers who had built the community had had an eye
for balance and neatness. Into a curve of the wooded hillside,
which had formed both a shelter and a background, they had
built their miniature castle with its large chapel. Two smaller
chapels flanked the main buildings on either side, standing at
a respectful distance, and round these were grouped a few
cottages. The effect was that of a semicircle which paralleled
the curve in the hill, so that the small castle, as the center of
the crescent, dominated everything.

From where they lay they could see the road which came
from the south. Straight, broad and white, it approached the
center of the curve of buildings in a dramatic sweep. That
was something, Richard thought, which the founding Fathers
had never even imagined. He remembered the map on which

this road had been marked only as roughly as the track which they had followed. Anni had been right. Dreikirchen had changed.

In front of them was the garden which lay behind the right-hand chapel. It was the kitchen garden with its rows of neatly planted vegetables protected on one side by a hedge of red-currant bushes, which stretched from the bank almost to the chapel itself. On its other side, the side which adjoined the garden of the castle and the large chapel, there was a row of fruit trees. Pear trees, Richard thought. They were obviously intended as a screen, so that anyone walking in the castle's flower garden wouldn't have his eye offended by the patchwork quilt of vegetables. They served the purpose well enough, for it was difficult for the three men to see the flower garden. It would be better to move behind the castle itself, and from there they would be able to see not only the flower garden but whatever lay behind the third chapel. For the curve of the buildings now hid that completely.

"Mark this spot," whispered Richard. The others nodded, and looked at the shapes of the trees and bushes, at the outcrop of rock behind which they lay. It wasn't easy, but it had to be remembered. If they got safely away from the castle, and were in a hurry, as they probably would be, then they would have to depend on being able to find the blazed trail quickly. Without the trail they might miss the car. It was unpleasant to imagine what it would be like to be searching desperately for the car on an unknown road with pursuers behind them. The best thing to remember, thought Richard grimly, was the outcrop of rock which lay about twenty feet away from the red-currant bushes. If they could reach the red-currant bushes, he added to that thought.

Under the cover of the trees, they worked their way carefully along to the back of the castle. It gave them the view they had hoped for. It was easy to see that an approach would be more difficult through the castle garden, planted with rose trees and small flowering shrubs, than it would be through the kitchen garden. There was much less cover here. As for the ground behind the third chapel, it was quite hopeless. It consisted of tennis courts and a stretch of grass. There was no sign of life from the cottages on this side of the castle, either ... no movement, no sounds of men's voices. If it hadn't been for the curl of smoke which came from the back of the castle, where a low, narrow building had been added as an afterthought, they might have been looking at a picture in a German calendar.

Richard motioned the others to go farther back into the wood. They reached some bushes, and sat down behind them. They talked in whispers.

"I can do the scouting," said Thornley. "I've done some deer-stalking. This should be easy." He drew his diary from a pocket, and began making a rough diagram of the buildings and gardens. Richard and Thornley exchanged glances. Thornley was obviously the best man for the job. Richard remembered the way he had climbed the balcony of the Pertisau house.

"All right," he said. "We'll watch from the top of the bank."

"This is how I'll go," Thornley said. He traced a line on the diagram with his pencil. He would use the red-currant bushes and reach the right-hand chapel. From there he would follow the path in the kitchen garden which seemed to enter a kind of shrubbery as it reached the line of pear trees. That would bring him to the right wing of the castle, to the back of it where the smoke came from. Then he could perhaps find out who was in that part of the building, or a possible back entrance to the place, or whatever was to be seen or heard.

"All right," Richard said again.

Thornley didn't waste any time. He was already moving quietly down through the trees, in a slantwise direction which would bring him out of the wood near the red-currant hedge.

Van Cortlandt abandoned the plans he had been making while they had watched the castle. He would have liked something with more action than this—one of them to have made some kind of distraction, while the other two rushed the place. The trouble was that they had no weapons worth a nickel, not compared with the arsenal they might expect to face. Still, there seemed to be no one there; perhaps just a cook in the kitchen where the smoke came from, and Frances in a locked room upstairs with someone left to guard her, while the others held their jamboree in Innsbruck or searched for Richard. All Thornley's caution would then be a waste of good time. He had the gloomy afterthought that Frances might not be there after all; that had been worrying him ever since they left Innsbruck. In that case, they would have to invite old Barney Finnigan. . . .

They had retraced their steps to the edge of the wood again, and had lain behind a fallen tree which would protect them from being seen. They themselves could see through its skeleton roots. As soon as Thornley reached the pear trees and followed the path towards the shrubbery at the side of the house, they could watch him. If anything went wrong before he reached the trees, then they would have to depend on their hearing. Richard raised himself to listen, but van Cortlandt shook his head. He was right; there was nothing.

They waited in the silence of the wood, and watched the tops of the trees moving gently against the background of the evening sky. The strain was beginning to tell on Richard. Again the fear came back to him that they might be on the wrong trail. Frances might be a hundred miles from here—injured, dead. He began to count the branches above him. Anything, anything to keep him from thinking.

CHAPTER XXII

Viking's Funeral

THORNLEY felt a sudden wave of excitement as he neared the edge of the wood and saw the small chapel and the quiet little houses beside it. It was the kind of feeling he had when he'd stand patiently waiting for the birds to break cover; only this time he was one of the birds. It wasn't the excitement of fear or nervousness. It was the excitement of expectation. He had always lived in the country, and what might have been difficult for Richard or van Cortlandt seemed fairly simple to him.

He moved confidently and quickly, knowing that under cover of this string of bushes he could only be seen from the woods behind him. In that case, he would be seen even if he went slowly and carefully—and time was short: they could hardly wait until complete darkness, for he felt that the castle might not remain deserted so very much longer. This was what Henry called playing a hunch; well, he was going to play it as hard as he could.

He had almost reached the chapel. He flattened himself out under the last clump of bushes and waited. So far so good. He strained to hear any sound from the cottages or the chapel, but they were completely silent. What was more, the doors and windows of the cottages were shut. It would be strange for anyone inside them to sit that way on a warm summer's evening. He measured the short dash to the chapel with his eye, and timed it neatly. He stood flat against the wall, hidden from the main buildings. In two or three moments, he would slip round the corner of the chapel and reach the path. The fruit trees would shelter him from the castle gardens, the large shrubs growing along the path would shelter him from the castle's windows; the only danger lay in being seen from the other end of the path. As he waited, motionless, he became aware that the windows beside him were not the usual high, narrow windows of a church. They were square and broad, with ordinary glass. He edged to one and looked cautiously inside over his shoulder. The interior was very strange for a chapel indeed—it was a very complete gymnasium. He gained confidence; only now would he admit to himself that the responsibility of discovering Dreikirchen's existence had worried him. Now he was pretty sure of its purpose. It would be the natural place for Frances to be taken if von Aschenhausen hadn't turned her over to the regular police, and it wasn't likely that he had done that. This was more a case for secret police, with abduction, not arrest, as their weapon.

He left the security of the east wall of the chapel, and entered the kitchen garden. Fortunately, the path curved to suit the arc which the buildings formed. He was hidden from the end of the path where it probably skirted the castle. If he could reach the pear trees, then at least the path would be safer because of the shrubbery. At this point, it was rather unpleasant. There wasn't much shelter in a row of cabbages, or on the long north side of the chapel.

He had reached the pear trees. As he did so, he sidestepped into the shrubbery. The path itself was now too open. It curved straight to a door in the castle itself, a side door just where the low wing was joined to the main building. The smoke from the wing was curling up steadily. Kitchen, almost certainly, thought Thornley, and regained his breath in the shelter of the bushes. The door had been unexpected. In fact, it had given him a jolt, as he had come round the path and suddenly met it staring at him from the end of the path. It meant he would have to push his way carefully and slowly between the thick shrubs, sometimes almost through them. Not the pleasantest way of travel, he thought savagely. The earth here hadn't the clean wholesomeness of the earth in a wood. It seemed dank and stale, and a fine dust from the branches and leaves blackened his hands.

He had almost reached the castle wall. . . . And then he heard voices; at first distant, and then gradually getting louder. But they were far enough away to be indistinguishable. He must get almost to the end of the bushes before he would be near enough to hear them. The voices were clearer; two men were talking. Only two, he was sure of that. But he still couldn't hear any words. He knelt down on the molder-

ing earth. He pushed down gently the branch in front of
him. It let him see the side of the castle right up to the front
corner. He saw that there was a broad path along this wall of
the castle, which must meet the path from the kitchen garden
in front of the side door.

Thornley moved his head to get a clearer view of the front
corner of the castle. He dared not push the sheltering branch
any more to the side. He judged that the men were walking
in front of the castle, that any moment they would appear at
the corner. The voices were coming nearer, and he could
hear the heavy footsteps of men aware of their own authority. . . . And then there was a laugh, the belly laugh a man
gives when he has just heard an unexpected end to a good
story. The trooper who had laughed was still enjoying the
joke when they reached the corner of the path. They were in
their shirt sleeves, and capless, but they still wore revolvers at
their side and the one who had laughed carried a loaded
cane. He beheaded the large yellow daisies growing at the
side of the path as he listened to his companion. They paused
as they turned in their walk, and both looked up at the same
window as if they had heard something. They were silent for
a moment, listening. Then the one who had laughed said
something to the other which made them both snicker, and
they began their walk back along the front of the castle, and
the corner of the building hid them.

Thornley wondered they had not heard his heartbeats. The
man who had laughed and chopped off the flower heads was
the one who had questioned him last night when he had
returned to Innsbruck with van Cortlandt. Anyway, he had
found out that there were two of them in front of the castle.
They weren't on guard; they had lounged too much for that.
But they were armed. It looked as if no one at the castle
expected any uninvited guests. And why should they? This
was one of their own strongholds, and once their prisoners
disappeared from their homes the shock or the fear which
petrified their friends ended all help for them. It took weeks,
even months, for anyone who was mad enough to ask, to
discover what had happened to those who had disappeared.
So why worry about a foreign agent who had walked into an
alley and had "vanished" at the other end? Her friends
couldn't even make inquiries about her; they couldn't afford
to. Thornley smiled grimly as he moved back towards the

path from the kitchen garden. That was how these blighters worked it. Bribe enough men with a sense of power, reward them with luxury and grandeur, and they'd be loyal terror-izers. It was Faust all over again. Body and soul for sale to the man who could give them the things they had always wanted. And the greater the sale, the greater the rewards.

Thornley had reached the path. There, at the edge of the shrubbery, he could see clearly across the rose beds to the bank of the wooded hill. Would he go back now, or would he try to find out who was in the place he thought was the kitchen? The smoke was rising in greater volume. When he had first seen it, it had only been a trickle. He looked at the door. Could he risk stepping onto the path to reach the wall, and perhaps a window? The two men pacing in front of the castle would have nearly reached the other end of it. Then they would probably turn and come back. Now was the time to move. . . . And then the door opened, and as Thornley automatically drew back into the bushes, he heard a thin voice raised in its anger as high as a woman's.

The voice followed a man out into the path.

"Don't waste any time, either," it screeched. "I've had enough of you. Everyone else does the work while you stuff your belly. Go on, now."

The young man paused, his mouth stuffed with a large piece of cake.

"Shut your gub. If you're late, then get on with your work. What do you think you are anyway?" He came slowly down the path, grumbling to himself. "It's Hermann this and Her-mann that. As if I hadn't my own job to do. As if I were a . . ." He didn't finish, but pitched forward suddenly on his face. Thornley pocketed the torch again, and dragged the man into the bushes. Quite a neat rabbit punch, he thought. Pity if it had broken the torch. He reached for one of the heavy stones which edged the pathway, and cracked the man over the head with it for good measure. He used his own handkerchief as a gag, and the man's belt and necktie to truss him neatly. The only place from which his attack could have been seen was from the woods. He hoped to God that Myles and van Cortlandt had been watching.

They had. They had seen him clearly as he had come out of the kitchen garden, had seen him hesitate as he left the cover of the pear trees, had seen him slip into the shrubbery.

They waited for some minutes, wondering what on earth he had found interesting there. They hadn't heard the voices, but they began to understand when they heard a man's laugh. They strained their eyes, but they could see no one, not until a trooper walked slowly down the path, past the bushes, to drop suddenly like a stone. Then they saw Thornley again as he had pulled the body into the shrubbery. Van Cortlandt grinned: this was more like it. They waited impatiently. . . . But there was no further movement, no signal which they were hoping for.

Thornley waited. He was listening for the voices: the men should have reached this side of the castle again by this time. What was detaining them? Or was he misjudging the length of the minutes in his anxiety? And then he heard them. Almost there; pause; turn. They were walking away again. He relaxed, and looked at the man beside him. He was out cold—for a long, long time. He stepped back onto the path, and waved.

The others had seen him, thank heaven. He watched them scramble down the bank near the pear trees, and then it was difficult to see them. If they hurried, they would manage it. His anxious eyes saw them again for a moment. They were moving quickly and silently. They had reached the end of the trees, and like him they had noticed the door at the end of the path. Like him, they shied from it, and worked their way along towards him by way of the shrubbery.

They found him examining the man's revolver. He gave a satisfied nod, and slipped it into his pocket.

"Complications," Thornley whispered quietly. "Two thugs in front; one overworked cook in the kitchen; and this." He pointed with his foot.

"Cook next on the list?" Richard whispered back. Van Cortlandt was testing the knots; he seemed satisfied.

Thornley nodded. "Thugs due back any minute. Quietly ..." He motioned them to follow him, and led them to the point where he had watched the two men. Their feet made no noise in the moldering soil, and the green branches could bend without breaking. And then they heard the voices, and were motionless. Richard and van Cortlandt looked carefully through the branches as Thornley had done. Van Cortlandt pursed his lips in a silent whistle as he saw one of the men. That was the guy all right, the one who had questioned him last night when they got back from Pertisau. So Thornley might have found the right track after all. He looked at the Englishman thoughtfully. Bob was looking at the watch on his wrist. Pause; turn; walk back—he would soon have this timed to a nicety.

They suddenly stiffened, and looked at each other. They heard a voice, excited, hurried. The heavy measured tread of the Nazis' boots broke into a run. The voice was giving directions; they could hear the tone, but not the exact words. Van Cortlandt looked inquiringly at Richard, who shook his head. No, that wasn't von Aschenhausen. So there was still another on the list. They waited, their bodies tense, their minds alert. The commands had been given. There was a loud "*Zu Befehl!*" That at least they could hear, that and the sound of running feet, clashing on the stones of a courtyard. And then the noise of motor bicycles ripped the silence.

"Two, I think," murmured van Cortlandt. They edged to the front of the bushes, and saw the roadway which approached the entrance of the castle. The two motor bicycles had already passed through the large gates, and were sweeping down the broad road. There was something peculiarly ominous in their speed.

"I don't like it," said van Cortlandt. "It's only a hunch, but I think we should get going."

The failing light helped them. They moved silently, one by one, from the shrubbery over to the castle wall and, keeping close to its shadow, edged towards the kitchen door. They heard a sound of movement inside, as Thornley's nail-studded shoe slipped on a stone at the side of the path. They stretched themselves more closely against the roughness of the wall. Thornley slid the gun out of his pocket and held it by the barrel. The kitchen door opened, and a broad beam of light streamed down the path to the kitchen garden. They could see the edge of a white apron, as the cook halted on the threshold.

"I heard you. You can come in. Where did you find the parsley? In the red-currant bushes, I bet." He stepped out of the doorway, peering towards the darkness of the garden. "Hermann. God in Heaven, I've always to do everything myself." His thin, high voice rose. "Hermann!" He sprawled forward as the revolver butt thudded dully against his square head.

He was a heavy man. It took the three of them to lift him back into the kitchen. Thornley locked the door, and then stood guard at the only other entrance—a door which led into a passage—while van Cortlandt helped Richard to gag the man, and tie his hands and feet. Then they thrust him unceremoniously into his own storeroom, and locked its heavy door. Richard pocketed the key, and nodded; they moved silently into the passage.

Thornley whispered, "There was a room which seemed to be interesting."

Richard looked sharply at him. Had he heard something while he had waited? A cry? His speed increased.

The passage led to the main entrance hall, a large, square, imposing place, with a broad stairway curving up the paneled walls. Richard had stopped, and looked again at Thornley. Where was the room? Thornley pointed above their heads to the first floor.

They mounted the staircase slowly, carefully, because of the nails in Thornley's shoes. Richard was thankful for the second time in two days that his shoes were soled with rubber. At any moment, he expected the door above them to open, and a volley of shots to pin them against the staircase wall ... But the door didn't open. Its double panels remained shut. It was only when they had reached them that they could hear the voices from within. A man's voice, and then another man's voice. Again the first voice. Richard looked at the two men beside him and nodded. This time the voice was von Aschenhausen's.

He was speaking in German, his voice as angry as the other man's had been. They were not arguing with each other. They were talking to a third person; talking savagely. Von Aschenhausen had raised his pitch. Richard closed his eyes: he could see the two scars ridging the cheek. The words reached them in waves.

"... regret your stupidity ... advantage of my humanity. In two hours my young barbarians, as you called them, will return. I shall turn you over ... If that fails ... Gestapo ... murderess and dangerous spy." The voice was clearer now, as if the man's anger were becoming cold and cruelly calculating.

"Your remaining days will not be pleasant. We shall catch Myles just as surely as we caught you. And your stupidity will be quite in vain." The voice altered again. This time it was speaking in English, rapidly, persuasively.

"You know how I have always regarded you. Otherwise I should not have brought you here: you would have been at the official Gestapo headquarters as soon as I had found you. Instead I bring you here, but do not mistake my feelings. I *will* find out. If you accept my offer, you will only remember these days as a bad dream. Otherwise any unpleasantness which you have suffered will be nothing, nothing to what is to come, and I am not being melodramatic." There was a pause. Von Aschenhausen spoke again. "You fool, you stupid little fool. Don't you see I *must*, I *will* find out? My patience is limited. Kurt, try some more of your persuasion. This is really tedious. You have only one . . ."

They had heard enough . . . two men in there. Richard saw the others were watching him, waiting. Van Cortlandt's mouth had an ugly look. Thornley was fingering the revolver thoughtfully, his eyes narrowing. Richard nodded his head towards the door. Van Cortlandt put his hand gently on the handle. He was feeling it; it was unlocked. He shoved both panels violently open. He and Richard entered as one man, with Thornley just behind them.

The surprise was complete.

In the flickering candlelight of the room, they saw von Aschenhausen sitting on the edge of a large desk. His eyes were fixed on the other man standing over the girl roped to a chair, as he himself paused in the lighting of a cigarette. The match was still burning as Richard's full weight knocked him backwards, pinning him against the desk. As he tried to throw Richard off, the grip on his throat tightened. He struggled but the increased pressure warned him. He lay still, choking. It was his only chance.

Frances felt the hand of iron release her aching shoulder. She tried to get her face away from the glare of the powerful lamp in front of her as she heard the rush of feet, but the light still pierced her eyelids with a dull-red burning. She heard the flat sound of a hard fist meeting solid flesh. She heard someone cursing loudly and exultantly with each blow. She knew the voice. . . . Van Cortlandt. Henry. She struggled weakly against the rope which held her. And then there was Bob's voice, too. Beside her. She heard the lamp fall, and the glaring circle of light had gone. The ropes had suddenly stopped cutting into her breast and thigh. Her body was falling forward, but an arm caught it before it slipped off the chair. The arm held her there gently. Bob's voice was telling her to move slowly, to get the blood in circulation again. She was not to worry; everything was all right. Everything was all right. So Richard must be safe too. Richard must be safe.

In front of her she could hear the heavy breathing of the two men as they fought, the half groan, half gasp from the man Kurt as van Cortlandt landed his blows. She forced her eyes half-open. She could see Thornley's face as a white blur, gradually steadying, slowly shaping into lines she could recognize. He was watching the punishment which van Cortlandt was dealing with a look of admiration mixed with pleasure, watching the man as he staggered under the hard punches. The man was trying to gain a moment. A gun, thought Thornley, but before he could yell his warning the man had side-stepped a blow successfully and his hand reached into his hip pocket.

Van Cortlandt had seen the movement in time: his hand gripped the man's wrist and twisted. The bullet dug into the paneled wall, and then the revolver was wrung out of the man's hand. It fell at their feet. Thornley, watching the man's bleeding face, contorted with rage, slipped his free hand into his pocket; that type knew all the tricks, he thought grimly. It came as he expected. As van Cortlandt tried to knock the gun out of reach, the man kicked suddenly, viciously. Van Cortlandt doubled up with a groan, and the man's hand was over the gun. Thornley's revolver flashed first. There was no doubt about that bullet. The man lay as he had fallen.

Frances heard Thornley say something, but his voice was so low that the words eluded her. Then he was speaking to her, his voice once more calm and clear.

"Can you hold on now, Frances? I'll come back."

She nodded, and watched him as he helped van Cortlandt to sit up against the wall where he had fallen. She could see more clearly now; she could see van Cortlandt's face twisted with pain as he doubled over.

"Trusting fellow you are," Thornley said gently, and was glad to see the attempted smile on van Cortlandt's lips.

The American spoke, his words coming in spasms. "How's that son of a bitch over there?"

"Passed out a minute ago." It was Richard's voice. "Frances . . . all right?"

"Richard." She tried to rise from the chair.

"Easy now, Frances," said Thornley, and moved quickly back to her. She was glad of his firm grip. He had picked up the rope which had bound her and, coiling it loosely round his right hand, he threw it towards the desk.

"You'll need this," he said to Richard. "I'll be with you in a minute." He helped Frances back towards the chair. He looked over his shoulder at van Cortlandt. The American was all right. He had slowly and painfully stretched out his legs, and was leaning against the wall with his hands in his jacket pockets.

Richard looked at von Aschenhausen lying limply across the desk. He was unconscious, and his arms, with which he had tried to grip Richard, sprawled inert over the dark wood. One hand fell over the edge of the desk; the other pointed helplessly towards the glimmering candles in their heavy-silver base. Richard picked up the rope with one hand, still keeping a firm grip with the other on von Aschenhausen's throat, but one hand was not enough; he sensed his mistake even as he caught hold of the rope. The split-second warning was too short. Before he could use both hands again, von Aschenhausen had swept the branched candlestick in his face. As he stumbled back under the weight of the blow, rubbing the burning wax from his left eyelid and cheek, he saw von Aschenhausen's hand come up from the drawer with a gun, and he heard the shots.

Frances saw the long barrel point towards Thornley and herself. She was pushed violently aside even as the gun crashed twice. The echo of the shots stabbed her head. Or was it the echo? Von Aschenhausen stiffened and slid grotesquely from the desk. His revolver thudded dully on the thick carpet. Richard had risen from the floor beside the burning candles. Thornley was on his knees where he had dropped as he had thrust her aside. Van Cortlandt alone was smiling, and with a grim satisfaction, as he held his still smoking revolver pointed at the crumpled figure.

For a moment they looked at each other . . . All safe.

Frances heard van Cortlandt's voice saying "I'm a quick learner, Bob," and Thornley's not very successful laugh.

Richard had picked up the fallen gun, and was coming

towards her, his hand to his face. She raised her arms, and
then she felt the burning pain. The men saw the expression
on her face change to one of amazement, like that of a child
who has fallen and only realizes it is hurt when the blood
begins to flow. So Frances looked as the searing pain showed
her a neat groove in her left arm. Unbelievingly she watched
the blood as it welled up and overflowed the wound in a
slow-moving stream. And then she felt the real pain; with
each heartbeat it seemed to throb farther down her arm and
claw her shoulder.

Richard was beside her. She wondered if she looked as
white as he did. He was looking at her arm, but he didn't
speak.

It was Thornley who said, "On the inside, by God." Van
Cortlandt rose slowly, and limped painfully over to them.

"*And* a Lüger," he added quietly. "How close was your
arm to your body?"

Frances remembered how close. That must have been the
hot wind on her left breast just before she had heard the
crash of the gun.

"I'd like a . . ." she began, but the word *drink* evaded her.
The men were going away from her, moving back towards
the desk, down the lengthening room. It was like looking
through the wrong end of binoculars, she thought, and felt
the black darkness smooth round her with its velvet touch.
Then it was light again, and the men were beside her, and
Richard's flask was at her lips, forcing her to drink more
than she could swallow.

Someone said, "She'll be all right. Better look at the arm."

Richard was kneeling beside her, fumbling for his handkerchief. Van Cortlandt produced a very white one, and folded
it methodically into a wad. Thornley went over to a table and
came back with a decanter of whisky. She didn't need that,
she thought; not now. The clammy sickness had gone, leaving
her tired, tired. But she must tell them . . . she must tell
them, now. If only she could remember things in the right
order, the important things first. She gripped Richard's hands
as Thornley poured whisky on the wound. She struggled to
control her voice as she looked at van Cortlandt.

"They stopped your car at Jenbach, and found your friend
in it. They brought him back to Innsbruck. They phoned
about it, and . . . that man—" she looked at Kurt's body—

"was told to go down and order the two troopers into Innsbruck. They were to trace your movements . . ."

Van Cortlandt nodded thoughtfully. "Yes, they knew me well by this time. That means the car we've got is dangerous." He dug his hands into his pockets, and walked slowly across the room to the desk.

"We'll have to find another car, that's all, or travel by train, or if the worst comes to the worst we'll have to climb over the pass together." He stopped suddenly, and ran a hand through his hair.

"Say, Richard, what's the thing these boys use when they want to sneak into a country without having their baggage examined?" He prodded von Aschenhausen's body with his foot contemptuously. Frances tried to remember desperately: there had been something which fitted into all this. Richard was saying that there wasn't much chance for them that way, but van Cortlandt could take a look in the desk and see what was there. Henry was already searching von Aschenhausen's pockets. He had found some keys.

"Do you smell burning, any of you?" van Cortlandt asked as he tried the drawers in the desk. One was locked; it needed two different keys to open it. Inside the drawer lay a folder containing papers, a neatly bound notebook, a seal and a rubber stamp.

Thornley, holding Frances' arm while Richard bandaged it, looked up and said, "Probably the candles on the rug." Van Cortlandt was too engrossed as he examined the documents in the folder. He whistled to himself, and then looked towards Thornley.

"As a newspaperman, I find this all very interesting." He waved a sheet of paper in the air. He was almost excited. He looked at the rug. "Yes," he replied to Thornley, "and a nice little fire is just about to start in the wastebasket. Just like the Reichstag. . . . Such ideas these boys put into your head . . ."

Frances heard the amusement in his voice, and opened her eyes. It was true. The wastepaper basket was smoldering, and even as she looked she saw the first sign of flame. It was fantastic. There was Henry, reading the papers he had found in the desk as calmly as if he had just made a remark about the weather. Then, on the desk, she saw the crumpled envelope, still lying where von Aschenhausen had thrown it contemptuously. Money wouldn't help them, he had said.

Richard was looking at her intently.

"The money," she said, "is on the desk. That's it. They—searched me," she finished lamely. Richard said nothing, but his mouth tightened. Frances thought again of the moment when the money had been discovered. Money wouldn't help them. Oh, if only she could think straight. Money wouldn't help them. What was it he had said then? He had twisted the envelope and thrown it on the desk.

"He said," she began slowly, her eyes closed—he had said so much, but there *was* something which could help van Cortlandt—"he said money wouldn't help, that it was no use trying to hide where you had gone." Her eyes opened, and the words were now faster as she remembered. "Even if you had got over the frontier, any frontier, you would be followed at once and brought back. It wasn't the first time that escapers had been caught in Italy or Switzerland. He had all the powers, and you had none. He held up some papers with one hand and hit them with his other hand, the back of his other hand, and all the time he was looking at me." Her voice altered again. "These were some of his reasons to persuade me to be reasonable. He said that Kronsteiner had been caught, that Henry and Bob had admitted everything in order to save themselves, that our movements had been traced completely."

Thornley wondered what other kinds of persuasion had been used, as he noticed Frances' wrists, the torn blouse showing the ugly marks on her shoulder, her right cheek which was swollen and red, the angry stripes already turning purple on her legs, her eyes. Again he thought of Tony's letter, of Maria. At least Frances was alive and her body would heal, at least they had saved her from becoming a second Maria. Tony's words ate into his heart like vitriol into flesh. He moved to the door. Better begin to leave, he thought.

"I'll scout round, and find the garage," he suggested. "Don't wait too long in here: there's the makings of a good going blaze."

Van Cortlandt looked up as the door closed. "Frances, did you see where he put those papers he was waving at your face?"

"He was at the desk. They must be there." Unless, she thought, they were a lie, like the other things he had said. He had mixed lie with truth so cunningly. She watched van Cortlandt search once more, and then relaxed as he suddenly smiled.

"Well, this might be twisted to suit us," he said. Frances had never heard his voice so optimistic ... And then the telephone rang.

The three of them looked at it as if it were a cobra.

"I might have known," van Cortlandt said, and the optimistic voice was gone.

Richard left Frances, and walked quickly over to the phone. He lifted the receiver. Frances and van Cortlandt, motionless, scarcely breathing, watched him tensely. But the German which he spoke was that of von Aschenhausen. Van Cortlandt caught Frances' eye, and nodded slowly, approvingly, before he went on with his careful writing. The wastepaper basket was flaming nicely; the thick wool carpet smoldered where the fallen candles had burned three round black holes.

Again Frances had the same awareness of unreality which would sometimes grip her for a timeless moment in the middle of a dream, which would drag her back to waking and the hotness of a crumpled pillow. But this was no dream. The high, paneled room was now filled with a stronger light from the leaping flames in the basket beside the desk. The smoldering rug and the guttering candles, the two bodies lying so quietly on the floor, the rich draperies and carefully arranged flowers, were all as real as the burns on her wrists and the blood which had flowed down her arm like a stream of warm red lava. She looked at the American, working at the other end of the desk; at Richard as he spoke in that excellent, rather hard German. So far, he had said little: he was listening to some story.

And then he cut short the long explanation impatiently. He was giving his own instructions. The American was quite useless. The girl had talked, and he knew nothing at all. He was to be released after he had given them a description of his own car. They would be able to trace that to St. Anton, where the other American van Cortlandt and the Englishman Thornley had gone. That was the meeting place; Myles would reach it tomorrow. They then intended to cross into Switzerland. That frontier was to be carefully watched.

The man at the other end of the wire spoke again. Richard

listened impatiently. The flames from the wicker basket lit up his face as he concentrated on the man's words.

"Yes," he said, "I'll allow them to stay longer. I shall remain here with Kurt until the investigation is completed. I shall arrive in St. Anton tomorrow morning. Get all three of them, alive if possible. I rely on you."

Richard replaced the receiver thoughtfully.

"That takes care of your friend, Henry," he said, "and gives us a breathing space. The apprentices have had a successful parade, and are now eating heartily before they attend a meeting. I very generously allowed them to stay for that. They will return here by ten o'clock. It's getting rather warm in here, don't you think?"

Van Cortlandt rose, and handed him the sheet of paper on which he had just finished applying von Aschenhausen's seal.

"Not warm enough, yet, but it should be satisfactory by ten o'clock—with a little help."

He moved to the other end of the desk, and kicked the flaming basket over the smoldering carpet. The desk itself was beginning to glow just where the basket had stood, and a small streak of flame rushed up its side as he heaped the papers from the drawer beside it.

Richard folded the document and put it carefully into his breast pocket.

"Good piece of work, Henry," he said. The American, placing the other branched candlesticks under the long curtains as he opened the windows, only smiled. It had been easy enough: all he had had to do was to alter a very little to suit their purpose. That was the advantage of dealing with a very systematic and thorough enemy. They made the arrangements and you borrowed them. It had been almost as easy as this. He threw the last candle lightly onto the couch with its pile of cushions.

"Keep moving, fellas," he said, and picked up the two caps and the jackets from a chair.

They left the doors wide open. Richard, his arm round Frances, turned for one last look. The current of air between the windows and the wide door was serving its purpose.

"Regular Viking's funeral," van Cortlandt said. "Too damn good for them."

They walked in silence down the cool staircase. Behind them they heard the indrawn breath of the flames.

CHAPTER XXIII

The Brenner Pass

THORNLEY was waiting for them in the darkness beside a large official-looking car.

"There was another in the garage, and some motor bikes. I've taken care of them," he reported.

Richard was putting Frances into the car.

"Darling, we've got to get the other car and the stuff inside it. I'll see you soon." He turned to Thornley. "We'll meet you five miles south of this road. Wait for us there." Thornley nodded, and handed him something. It was the electric torch.

Van Cortlandt threw the caps and jackets into the car. "Better wear those. We'll only keep you about twenty minutes."

The large car moved off, and the two men started towards the gardens. As they passed the kitchen door, they suddenly remembered the cook. Richard cursed and tried to enter the kitchen. But they had locked the door from the inside, and it was too heavy to break open. Richard swore again.

"If you must; but we're God-damned fools," van Cortlandt said, and raced back towards the front entrance of the castle. "God-damned fools," he repeated when he opened the door into the kitchen. Together they carried the unconscious man into the shrubbery.

"Not too near the other blighter," the American said. "Hell and damnation, that's at least five minutes gone."

They broke into a run across the garden and fields. The woods were dark and silent; it was too early for any moonlight. Richard shaded the torch with his hand, as they searched for the path, scrambling along the edge of the trees.

Van Cortlandt said, "Just about here, I think. There was a mound. Rock."

Richard nodded. He tried to measure the distance to the long dark shape which must be the red-currant bushes. . . .

247

And then the torch showed them the outcrop of stone. The path should be here.

They looked at each other with undisguised relief when they found it. The white slashes on the branches were picked out by the light which Richard held. Their feet stumbled and slipped in the darkness of the ground, but they pressed on hurriedly. They had passed over the crest of the small hill, and they were running and sliding down towards the road, following the trail which Thornley had blazed. They reached the cart track, and the bushes. The car was still there.

"Ten minutes late, already," van Cortlandt said, but his voice was good-humored again. He gave a laugh. "And there I was, having a fine joke all to myself about Thornley being the good boy scout."

Richard found himself relaxing calmly as the car jerked dangerously over the rough track and then gathered speed on the smoothness of the Brenner road. What would have seemed suicidal only forty-eight hours ago now only appeared all in the day's work. Van Cortlandt's driving had results; it was only a matter of minutes before they sighted the large dark car tactfully drawn up at the side of the road.

The first stars were beginning to appear over the Brenner. The man lounging at the doorway of the customhouse was watching the other side of the white barrier with interest. He wondered what it was this time. All day, the Germans had been giving themselves double work. They had stopped the cars coming out of Germany as well as those going in. It was a nuisance, waiting here with your eyes on the headlights, not knowing how long they would be before they came up to you. Sometimes it would be only a matter of minutes. Sometimes, a car would be held up for half an hour. Again he wondered what it could be. These Germans never told you much unless it was unimportant. He shifted his weight onto his other leg, and glanced back into the brightly lighted office. The man at the desk looked up.

"Anything happening, Corradi?"

"Two still held over there."

The tall thin Italian at his desk gave a sardonic smile and went back to his writing. The other heaved a loud sigh, and walked slowly towards the barrier. The tension, on a day like this, always unsettled him. He heard the voices of the others as they came out of the café down the street. About time too, he thought moodily. He could do with some coffee himself.

At the doorway of the café, the two officials halted. They stood looking out into the empty village street with its meager lights. Only the doorway of the customhouse was bright. The younger man shivered, and looked bitterly at the scattered houses, the long wind-swept station, the towering dark shapes on either side of them.

"Godforsaken place," he said.

"Wait until you have been here for a winter," advised the other. "You can't grumble at overwork today, at least. Not with our good friends over the way doing all our work for us."

He looked at the younger man's smart uniform, and buttoned his own crumpled jacket. It was just like the young, he thought. They never knew when they were lucky. A few more pretty girls to admire the way he wore his cap, and his young friend would have no doubt found the place tolerable.

"We could have had another coffee," he suggested, but the young man had already stepped into the street and was waiting impatiently for him.

"When you've been here as long as I have," the older man grumbled, "you will know it is hardly worth our while, on a day like this. Our German cousins don't leave much to be confiscated."

The other tilted his hat contemptuously. Here as long as this fat fool, he thought in amusement, who would now be in a comfortable office in a decent town if he had had any brains at all. Even the way he would speak of the Germans, with that sly note in his voice which he thought was funny, showed he had no brains ... But curiosity overcame the young man's contempt.

"Is this usual?" he asked, as they reached the customhouse.

"Whenever someone who shouldn't be leaving the beloved Fatherland is being ungrateful enough to try to leave."

"They are fools to try to pass this way."

"There is only this way, or the mountains, or the railway. The border patrols have been increased, and there is pandemonium on the trains. Have you seen *them* on the trains, today?"

"It is efficient organization," the young man said sharply.

The fat fool had no brains, but he was crafty enough. He always chose his words so carefully that you couldn't even report him. The tall thin Italian, who had come out from the office, exchanged amused looks with the older man and ignored the remark. They were both getting a bit tired of the new broom.

They saw the headlights of the two small cars begin to move at last. Behind them a large car advanced authoritatively in the middle of the road. Corradi seemed excited about something.

"They didn't stop this one. Salutes for this one," he called across to them. "Better not keep this one waiting. They never like it."

The tall thin man nodded, and turned to the young one.

"You deal with it, and see some of the efficient organizers of efficient organization. Probably diplomatic pass. You know."

The young man nodded as casually as he could, and moved over to the large car. He didn't feel as casual inside. Corradi had been right. The Germans didn't like being kept waiting. An officer's sleeve waved a paper peremptorily to him. He heard a request for urgency, which was a command.

The Italian took the document. His German was not so adequate as he pretended, but he knew his salute had been just right. He looked as efficient as possible as he glanced quickly at the paper. The signature on it made him hold his breath. . . . Four people in the car. That was right. He felt the cold impassive stare of the German. Further curiosity would be an impertinence. He folded the paper with a businesslike gesture. Speed and courtesy: that would show them efficiency could be found here, too. He held his salute as the officer acknowledged it, and the large black car swept past the raised barrier.

He turned back to the others. Corradi, he noticed, had saluted too. But the other fools were too busy examining and stamping passports, were even wasting good breath making polite replies to three middle-aged Englishmen.

When the two insignificant cars crawled slowly away through the village street, the others joined him.

"Well, who was it? The Archduke von Ribbentrop himself?"

He ignored their smiles. He made his voice as casual as possible.

"Freiherr von Aschenhausen, and three others, authorized by..."

But the others had lost interest and gone back to the office.

The young man stood outside, and looked at the stars. He forgot the cold wind. There was a warm, comfortable feeling inside him.

CHAPTER XXIV

End of a Journey

THE SWIFT journey down the Brenner road was a nightmare to Frances. She was conscious of a stiffening arm, of the burns on her wrist nipped by the cool air. She was so tired that the muscles of her body refused to relax. Thornley, unexpectedly gentle, tried to protect her from the twists and turns of the mountain road. In front of them were Richard and van Cortlandt, both of them silent and grim under the peaked hats. Van Cortlandt's eyes never left the road. Richard had a map spread over his knees. Although the Brenner was safely passed, there was no relaxing of the strain. Thornley persuaded her to eat something. He was so obviously worried about her that to please him she tried. She was surprised to find that the sick feeling was no worse, that the coldness which had first gripped her as they waited for Richard and van Cortlandt on the Innsbruck-Brenner road began to disappear.

That had been the worst moment for her, she decided. Worse even than the frontier and the silly boy with the exaggerated cap and salute. She remembered again when she had waited tensely with Thornley at the side of the road, when she had begun to think that Richard and Henry had been caught. She remembered the sense of haste which had almost choked her as the suitcases were lifted into the Mercedes and they had waited again while Thornley had set the American car crashing down into a ravine. Each minute, each passing car, were full of danger. Already, behind them, there had been a tell-tale glow of fire. Bob had said simply, "Garage, too, by this time, I'd think." After that they had driven in silence towards the frontier, and she had felt sick and cold. When the Brenner was passed (if it were passed) she had told herself she could sleep. That would heal the throbbing of her eyes. But the Brenner lay behind them, and the sleep which she had resisted refused to return.

It was not until they had driven through Bolzano and all the villages in between that she felt the tension lessen. Bob even made some mild jokes about all these places called Believe Obey Fight, like the English stations called Ladies and Gentlemen. He got her up to sip some more brandy, as she ate the dry biscuits. They tasted wonderfully. The others were eating, too. She watched them drowsily; she was warm at last, and her body relaxed. *Ladies and gentlemen, ladies and gentlemen lend me your ears I come to Dreikirchen with rings on her fingers and bells where who, where who, where . . .*

At first she thought it was von Aschenhausen holding her shoulder, bending over her, but the grip did not tighten and hurt. It was Richard. Richard trying to smile and making a failure of it.

"Fran," he said, and kissed her.

The car had stopped in the shadow of trees. The trees were a different shape, the night air seemed milder, the ink-blue sky was more beautiful. And Richard's arms were round her. She suddenly remembered Bob and Henry.

"Where are they?"

"Freshening up. There's a stream over there. We'll go when they've finished. We can change, too: Henry has brought our things along with him in his case."

Frances looked at the trees again, dark islands in a sea of moonlight.

"We are farther south," she said.

"Almost at Verona, darling. It's one o'clock and all's well."

"All's well," answered an American voice. "Well Frances, how's everything?"

She gave him her right hand.

"That's the ticket," he said. "I'll get your clothes, and Bob will guide you to the stream. Here's your towel." He handed her one of the white shirts. "And your purse." He handed Richard her bag.

They reached the stream, and they bathed their faces in the cool water. The bullet graze had bled a lot; it looked unsafe to disturb the bandage, so Richard hacked a piece off the shirt and bandaged on top of the bloodstained handkerchiefs. The clothes for her consisted of a nondescript belted gray coat, a gray beret, a shapeless dress and shoes and stockings. Richard had an *ersatz* tweed suit, a rough green-felt hat, and a tie of indescribable hideousness. Frances dressed her hair and disguised the bruises on her cheek as well as she could with her one hand. It would be almost impossible to get the dress on without starting more bleeding. Richard helped her into the coat, and even that was difficult enough. The shoes were too big, but fortunately they had straps. Richard and Frances looked at each other, and she actually smiled; and then they went back to the car, carrying the discarded clothes and the rejected dress.

"Go on, laugh," said Richard good-humoredly.

Thornley and van Cortlandt grinned.

"It's not bad, you know," Bob said tactfully. "I've seen hundreds like you traveling in Germany. Have a cigarette? How long is it since we could risk one?"

"One thing I must say for these blasted Nazis," said Henry, and paused to enjoy his effect. "They make you damned well appreciate the simple pleasures of a peaceful life."

Thornley drove them, this time. In the swaying car, they made their last plans. They were brief. They were to travel on their German passports, complete with Italian entry stamps (Schulz had earned his money), towards Grenoble. If the station would accept their marks, they could catch an early morning train. If not, they would have to wait until the banks opened. Van Cortlandt and Thornley, cutting back on their tracks, would drive through Lombardy until daylight made the car too dangerous. They would then get rid of it, and make for the Swiss border, if they hadn't reached it by that time. Van Cortlandt was confident that they would. They divided the marks they had, and van Cortlandt emptied the smaller of his suitcases to carry the dress and two extra shirts and socks for Richard. They could think of no other main points; the details would depend on quick wits and luck. They would meet in Paris. Van Cortlandt gave them the address of a hotel he knew.

"It's run by an American, who stayed over from the last war. You'll feel safe enough there. Just lie low until we get there. And then we'll celebrate. Better catch up on your sleep before we arrive."

His confidence and high spirits were infectious. Frances found herself laughing. And then the tears were running down her cheeks; even the pain they caused in her eyes couldn't check them.

"Well, " said van Cortlandt, "well, now."

Thornley switched on the wireless tactfully. The overture of "Aïda," badly recorded, swelled scratchingly into the car. Thornley tuned it down.

"Goes well with the writing on the wall," he suggested, and nodded towards the house they were passing. The lights from the car pointed the lettering on its wall. "WHO TOUCHES THE DUCE TOUCHES DEATH. Dear me!"

"One up on the Victorians," said Richard. "They only hung banalities round the house. Now we get totalitarian mottoes in two-feet-high letters all over the gable ends."

Van Cortlandt, keeping his eyes away from Frances, tried to think of something to add to that, but he could only think of the silent way in which she wept. He peered out into the darkness.

"Houses are getting closer now," he said at last. "Better waste no time."

Frances had regained her control. She made a pretense of powdering her face.

"I'm ready," she said, "any time. We'll see you in Paris." She managed a smile. "I'm sorry. It was all my fault. I've ruined all your plans."

The American shook his head. "My plans were going to be ruined anyway, although I kept persuading myself that they wouldn't be. We all have our wishful thinking, but it's just as well to come out of it."

Thornley switched off the motor carefully, and turned to face Frances.

"I have no plans either, Frances. Don't worry about that. I had a letter from Tony this morning."

"Tony?"

"Yes. He's on his way home to enlist."

"And the girl in Czechoslovakia?" Frances could have bitten her tongue. Thornley examined the back of his hand.

"Suicide," he said, too coldly.

Frances saw the three men exchange glances. So they

knew. Bob must have told them as she had slept. It must have been something which they thought would have sickened her, unnerved her. As if the man Kurt, when he had tried to break her silence, had not described in detail her possible future. As if she couldn't guess. ... But knowing evil could be worse than guessing. When you guessed, you could always hope that evil things might not be so bad as your worst fears. But when you knew, then there was no hope left. Then you knew this and this, and the evil of it drove away all hope.

She said nothing, only remembering the look on Thornley's face when he had looked down at the man Kurt. He had spoken as if to himself, and the words had made no sense then. Now they took shape. One for Maria ... the first one for Maria. Frances leaned forward and touched Thornley's shoulder with her right hand, and then van Cortlandt's.

Richard helped her to step out of the car. The savageness of his voice did not startle them.

"Yes. I'm all for international understanding: *real* understanding." He looked at the other two men, and voiced their thoughts. "This isn't the end for any of us. It's just the beginning."

They were all silent for some moments, and then Thornley switched on the engine, and the car moved into the night.

Richard picked up the suitcase, and gripped Frances' right arm. They walked softly through dark streets, guided by scattered lights. At last, they saw the station. Frances pressed his hand to her breast, and held it there.